ROUGH AND READY JACK:

HIS ADVENTURES E. W. N. AND S.

BEAUTIFULLY ILLUSTRATED.

COMPLETE.

LONDON:

HARKAWAY HOUSE, WEST HARDING STREET, FETTER LANE,
FLEET STREET, E.C., AND ALL BOOKSELLERS.

ROUGH AND READY JACK:
HIS ADVENTURES E. W. N. AND S.

"'ARE YOU PLAYING, GENTLEMEN?' ASKED THE MILITARY-LOOKING MAN."

No. 1

ROUGH & READY JACK:

HIS ADVENTURES E. W. N. AND S.

CHAPTER I.

ROUGH AND READY JACK—HIS FRIENDS AND HIS FOES.

"HELP! help!"

The cry was in the piercing tones of a woman in distress, and came from the entrance to a well-lighted tavern, in a somewhat crowded thoroughfare of the West-end of London.

The appeal for aid was almost drowned by the loud, gruff voice of a man, ribald laughter, and the rumble of carriage-wheels rolling over the well-stoned road-way.

"Oh, help!—will no one help me?" shrieked the despairing voice, but in fainter accents.

Then came the rush of feet, the sound of two heavy blows struck in rapid succession, a sudden scattering of a little crowd in front of the tavern, and a man, staggering over the pavement, swayed on the kerb and fell into the roadway.

A shout of mingled rage and applause, and then a youth of about eighteen sprang into the road, and, with clenched fists, stood over the prostrate man, who lay in the gutter, bleeding from the mouth and nose.

"You're a rough 'un," said one of the bystanders, addressing the youth.

"Aye, and a ready one, too!" retorted the youth, with flashing eyes. "Get up, you cur, and face *me*, if you have the spirit to stand before anything but a woman or a cripple!"

The speaker was a tall, sturdily-built youth, with handsome features, and dark, curling hair, fashionably yet plainly attired, and whose bearing proclaimed him to have moved in a higher sphere than the generality of those who stood around him.

The man who was struggling to his feet was perhaps five-and-twenty years of age.

He was a few inches taller than his assailant, but his form was neither so symmetrical, nor his limbs so neatly formed as those of his young opponent.

His light hair was straight and limp, his features far from prepossessing.

The expression of his eyes were sly and treacherous, and his thin lips were drawn tightly over his close teeth.

Struggling to his feet, he confronted the youth.

"What right have you to interfere?" he hissed through his clenched teeth. "She's only an orange girl—a street mendicant, and—"

"She's a female—a poor, weak, defenceless girl, and that's enough for me to stand up for her. You are a despicable cur, Baxter Sharp, and if you want somebody to ill-use try it on me, *if you dare.*"

And the speaker closed his hands and threw himself into a position of defence.

But the man called Baxter Sharp lowered his own arms and took a step backwards.

"I don't want to have anything to say to you," he said. "Mind your own business, and don't interfere with other people's quarrels, or perhaps you'll regret it."

"Coward!" hissed the youth, indignantly. "I always thought you a cur, now I *know* you to be one."

"Mind my bite, then," said Baxter Sharp, in a meaning tone.

"You brute!" cried the other, contemptuously. "Bah! You dare not do more than bark, unless it is at a woman."

"Think so," said Sharp. "But you'll feel it yet. I hate you."

And the fellow slunk away towards the door of the tavern.

A jeer of derision from the crowd assembled followed him, which culminated in a perfect yell, even from those who but a moment before had stood calmly by and seen him offer insult, and even violence, to a poor girl, who now leaned weeping against the tavern door-post.

Goaded to fury by the taunts of the crowd, Baxter drove the girl aside by a thrust of his arm, and she would have fallen to the pavement had not the youth, who had proved himself her champion, caught her.

"Coward!" cried the young man. "But don't cry, Polly. I'll teach him to treat you better. He sha'n't go scot-free. I'll thrash him for this, or he shall me."

And with a bound he reached the door through which Baxter had passed.

But on the threshold he was stopped by a burly, dark-browed fellow of about thirty years of age, whose large, coarse features were deeply bronzed by the sun, and to which the hairy cap he wore gave a fierce low cast.

"Avast, there!" he cried, stretching out an arm that was large and muscular, to bar the youth's passage. "Avast, I say. If you run foul of me, you'll go down, youngster."

"Then stand aside, and let me get at that cur, who has lately found your friendship and company so necessary," said the youth. "I want nothing with you; my quarrel is with him."

"You'd better not quarrel with him, Master Jack Tempest," said the fellow, "'cos, you see, Baxter Sharp happens to be a particular friend of mine, and I always take a friend's part, always."

And the man gave him a significant look.

"As he is too great a cur to take his own part, he employs you as his bully, I suppose?" sneered Jack.

"Shut your mouth, or that'll close it for you!" cried the fellow.

As he spoke, he struck at Jack's face.

But the huge fist was stopped neatly, and, to the surprise of the burly fellow, a small but hard hand struck him with the force of a cricket ball between the eyes, and sent him staggering back through the doorway into the bar of the tavern.

Then, with a bound Jack passed him, resolved to punish the assailer of the girl, but was suddenly brought to a stop by a glass of hot brandy and water flung into his face by the cowardly Sharp, who, fearing the assault, snatched it from the bar and hurled it at him.

The hot liquid entered his eyes, and, half blinded, he uttered a cry of pain and clasped his hands over his face.

The fellow with the hairy cap had bounded to his feet, and with an oath was about to launch a heavy blow at the smarting and bewildered Jack, when a young man threw himself before him, and giving vent to a loud, shrill whistle, cried—

"No, you don't, my pippin!"

"What do you mean—who are you?" yelled the fellow. "You long-legged, thin-waisted snip, sheer off, or I'll bung your eyes up for you, and snap those pipe-stem legs of yours in a twinkling."

"Will you, now? Take my advice, don't try. No, you don't. Two to one ain't fair. Ah, would you?—no, you don't."

While the youth with the thin legs was speaking, he kept jumping first on one side and then on the other, which-ever way the man in the hairy cap moved in his endeavours to get at Jack com-pletely baffling him, and finally thrusting one of his long legs between the ruffian's, threw him fairly on his back.

"Hi! hurrah! Here come the boys!" he shouted capering over the bar, and finally seizing Jack by the arm.

"The cowardly villain has half blinded me," said Jack; "but I'll pay him out for this."

And though he could scarcely see what he was about, Jack dashed at Sharp and planted a heavy blow on his throat.

At this moment four young fellows came tearing down the stairs into the bar.

"Hallo!" cried one. "Here's Rough and Ready Jack and Spider Legs in for a mill. Come on, lads. What's the odds as long as you are happy?"

Sharp and Jack were now hammering away at each other, for the former finding the youth partially blinded by the brandy, mustered up courage for the battle.

The man with the hairy cap had quickly raised himself, and catching Spider Legs by the ankle hurled him to the floor.

The long thin legs went up as his body

went down, and his feet swept the counter of its contents of glasses, bringing them to the floor with a crash.

"At him, boys! Stop him, Tom! He's got a knife!" cried the youth who had before spoken, addressing his companions.

As he sprang forward with the words on his lips, the man with the hairy cap made a plunge at him with a large clasp-knife he had drawn from his pocket.

The blade ripped up the sleeve of the youth's coat.

"Has he stabbed you, Hal?" cried one, aghast.

"No, Tom; but he will if you don't take the knife from him. Lay hold of his arm—quick!"

"I—I can't," said Tom, falling back, as the ruffian turned threateningly upon him.

But the others threw themselves upon the villain and wrested the knife from his grasp, and the rascal was held firmly by three of the indignant youths.

At the same moment Sharp measured his length on the bar floor, and the landlord and a couple of waiters flung themselves between the combatants.

"Gentlemen, gentlemen!" cried the landlord, "I cannot permit this. I must insist on better order being kept in my house."

"Then why do you encourage such villainous rascals as these two fellows, Sharp and Sternway?" asked Jack. "Scarce a night has passed lately but they have been accused of cheating or interfering with your customers. There was none of this before they came here."

"I cannot close my doors against them," said the landlord. "They are very good customers if they are only quiet. Come, gentlemen, don't quarrel any more. Take a glass together and shake hands."

"Shake hands with a cheat, a coward, and a would-be assassin?" cried Jack, indignantly. "Not if I know it."

"I'd put them under a pump, or tar and feather them," said Charley.

"Or tickle their ribs till they bu'sted themselves with laughing," said Hal.

"Well, gentlemen, I'm very sorry," said the landlord. "It's a pity you can't be friends."

"Friends," said Jack, with a sneer.

"I'm no friend to a brute who can offer violence to a poor girl, or a coward who is ready to use a knife."

"Unless it is to cut his own wizand," said Charley.

"I'll cut yours if ever I get the chance," said Sternway.

And the look that accompanied the threat told that the fellow meant it.

"It wouldn't pay," retorted Charley.

"Wouldn't it?" hissed Sternway. "Don't be too sure of that."

There was something in the tone and look of the man that made Charley—Comical Charley, as he was always called by his companions—look anxious and ill at ease.

"You're a cold-blooded assassin, and a fit chum for such a despicable cur as this Sharp," said Jack. "Who and what you are I neither know nor care, but I warn you both, don't interfere with us or that poor girl who tries to get an honest crust with her oranges, or you'll find me a rough one and a ready one, too."

"And you'll find me the same, youngster," said Sternway. "I never forget the man who threatens me, mark you that."

"Bah!" cried Hal. "No fear of anyone forgetting you. Such a hang-gallows dog ain't to be forgotten in a little while."

"Confound you, I'll—"

"No, you won't," said Hal, coolly. "You ain't got your knife now, remember."

"Gentlemen, I beg —" began the landlord.

"Shut up," said Charley. "What's the odds as long as you're happy?"

"But I am not happy, gentlemen. It grieves me to see you such bad friends. Be advised. Bury all animosities in a glass of liquor."

"That's one for us and two for yourself," said Charley. "You know your book."

"I only seek to make peace," said the landlord.

"Don't try, there's a good fellow," said Hal. "It's quite a mistake for you to seek to make peace with a fellow who would only be too happy to cut us in pieces."

"Well, gentlemen, if you won't be friends, I can't help it."

"Of course you can't. Who said you could?" asked Hal.

"Let 'em alone," said Sternway. "I'd sooner kill myself than shake hands with either of them. They've declared war, and war be it. They are six, we are two, but I'll warrant you they'll have to knock under yet."

So saying, he moved to where Sharp stood holding his handkerchief to his eye, and, taking him by the shoulder, hissed in his ear—

"We'll bide our time. It only wanted this to warm us to the work. Come."

"Hang them, yes," whispered the other. "You will agree now, won't you?"

"Yes; if not for the coin, I will for revenge," he whispered. "There's my hand on it."

He suffered his huge brown hand to fall from Sharp's shoulder till it clutched his companion's fingers, and gripping them in his horny palm, he drew him towards the door.

The friends fell back to allow them to pass out.

On reaching the door, Sternway threw it open, to discover a poor, but pretty girl standing before it, her eyes red and swollen, her cheeks pale as death.

As her gaze fell upon the two men, she uttered a cry, and drew back quickly.

Sharp fixed his eyes upon her, and through his clenched teeth he hissed—

"Polly, I'll make you more fearful of me yet than you are now. You're the cause of this to-night, and you'll regret it—mark me, you'll suffer for it."

The girl replied not, but, turning quickly, lifted a small basket of oranges from the ground, and fled along the street.

Sharp tore his hand from his companion's hold, and would have started in pursuit, but Sternway drew him back, and whispered—

"Not now. Your time will come soon."

"It shall!" said Sharp, suffering himself to be dragged along in the opposite direction. "I hated them before, but I hate them doubly now. I'll have my revenge—aye, I'll have it, and you shall help me."

"To the death!" said Sternway.

And as their hands again gripped each other's they hurried down a side street, and disappeared in the darkness.

The youth who had taken the girl's part, and who had been called Rough and Ready Jack, followed them to the door of the tavern, and watched them down the street till they turned out of it, then he went in and rejoined his companions.

"They are gone," he said; "but, hark ye, lads, I don't believe we've seen the last of them. They are a bad pair, and they have mischief on hand. I'm not one to be scared by black looks, or blacker threats, but I confess I don't feel so much at ease as I should like. However, let their game be what it may, they'll find they have got a tough customer to tackle in Rough and Ready Jack."

CHAPTER II.

THE THREE VILLAINS—THE COMPACT—THE SUDDEN CRY.

It was in a long, narrow and ill-furnished apartment of an old house in the purlieus of the Seven Dials, that an hour after the event recorded in the previous chapter, Baxter Sharp and Ralph Sternway sat before a rude deal table, on which stood a bottle and two glasses.

The former wore a handkerchief bandaged over his left eye, while the latter was smoking a short black pipe, from which the smoke rose in clouds above his head of red hair, now denuded of its hairy cap.

He was a low-browed, high-cheeked, sunken-eyed, villainous-looking man, his natural repulsiveness made more hideous by the dark scowl on his features.

"A pretty sight I shall be to-morrow," said Baxter. "I've got a swelling under my eye as big as a hen's egg, and my teeth are as loose as dice in a box. I thought I could hit hard, but that Jack Tempest strikes with the force of a cannon ball, confound him."

"Bah! what's a black eye, or a few loosened ivories?" growled Ralph. "Don't take on like that about such a trifle."

"And we expected old Wentworth to-night," said Baxter. "I shouldn't care so much only for his seeing me like this. He's a stiff-starched old fellow, albeit he is a scheming rascal."

"He be hanged," growled Ralph. "He don't expect to get real gentlemen to do his dirty work, does he? Instead of growling, I think you ought to be pleased you got something to show him to prove you ain't taking his money without running a risk and danger for him."

Baxter was silent, but not convinced.

"And now," said Ralph, taking his pipe from his mouth, and leaning over towards his companion, "since I've consented to join in this business, I'd like to know a little more about it. What's the reason this old fellow is so anxious to get the youngster out of the way?"

"To secure for his own what Jack will be entitled to when he comes of age."

"Is it much?"

"Pretty considerable, I believe; but I don't know how much," returned Baxter Sharp.

"And, of course, the old boy will pay well," remarked Ralph.

"He's rather a hard flint to skin."

"Oh, is he! Well, then, we'll have to soften him," said Ralph. "I don't go in for these sort of things without a good reward. Look at the trouble and the risk, especially with such a fire-eater as this John Tempest has proved himself to be."

"The hound!" hissed Baxter, through his clenched teeth, and bringing his hand on the handkerchief bound across his eye. "If old Wentworth wouldn't pay a farthing, I'd help him in his work, if only for revenge on the boy."

"Would you?" sneered Ralph. "Then I wouldn't. No pay, no work, is my motto. And the old buffer will have to shell out pretty stiff, and no mistake about it."

"Hush!" cried Baxter, as a knock at the street-door sounded through the lofty, empty house. "This is he. Do not say anything to annoy him."

"That will depend upon whether he gives me cause," said Ralph. "Let him in, and let's see what sort of a fellow he is."

Baxter rose and went to the door.

A moment after he returned to the room, followed by a man about fifty-five, wrapped in a huge Spanish cloak, and with the air and gait of a gentleman.

As he entered the room he paused, looked round with a glance of contempt, and fixed his eyes upon Ralph Sternway, who sat blowing thick clouds of smoke from his mouth.

"Phew!" he exclaimed. "The place is poisoned with foul smells. Who is this man, Baxter?"

"A friend," replied Sharp. "One who is willing to assist us in getting the youth out of England, and leaving the coast clear for your wishes."

"Provided he's well paid," put in Ralph.

Wentworth looked at the fellow indignantly, then turned his gaze to Sharp.

"Can you trust him?" he asked.

"Yes, of that I am sure."

"How are you sure—is he in your power?"

"No; but he hates your nephew. John Tempest struck him, and Ralph Sternway is not the man to forgive a blow," said Sharp.

"So he has an enmity against the boy himself. So much the better. Has my nephew struck you, too, that you wear that bandage over your brow?"

"Aye!" hissed Sharp, bitterly. "I was seeking to induce that pretty orange girl you have so often admired, to listen to my suit, when he dealt me a blow that cut my cheek. Better he had not though, as it decided me to hunt him to his death, for I had almost resolved not to have anything to do with this business, and no doubt should have backed out of it."

"Then the blow came in time to remind you of the danger you were likely to run by so doing!" said Wentworth, pointedly.

"Danger of what?" asked Sharp.

Wentworth leant his head forward till his lips nearly touched the ear of Baxter Sharp, and in a whisper that sounded like the hiss of a serpent in his ear, said—

"Transportation for forgery !"

Sharp sprang back as if a serpent had stung him, and his face blanched to an ashy paleness, while his gaze wandered nervously from Wentworth's face to the coarse features of Ralph Sternway.

"You understand me?" said Wentworth.

"Yes," stammered Sharp.

"That is well. But now I must know a little more of this fellow here. Confound it, man, put that filthy pipe down awhile. I have no wish to be poisoned with the smoke of that foul tobacco."

"It's as good a pipe of 'bacca as never paid duty," growled Ralph; "and as to your being poisoned, I take it you're a sight more likely to be hanged. However, if you don't like smoking, I'll put the pipe out."

And ramming his little finger fiercely down the bowl, Ralph laid the pipe on the table.

"There ; perhaps that will suit you," he growled.

"Yes, thank you, that will do. You are a seafaring man, I perceive?" said Wentworth.

"Been so all my life nearly—off and on."

"Exactly. By the way you remarked just now that the tobacco you were smoking had not paid duty. How do you know that ?"

"How do I know it? Why, didn't I —"

Ralph Sternway paused abruptly.

"Just so," remarked Wentworth, quietly. "I understand you perfectly. You smuggled it ashore. How long now have you been a smuggler—all your life, eh ?"

"Who said I was a smuggler?"

"Who? Only yourself, man! How should I have known if you hadn't informed me ?" remarked Wentworth, calmly fixing Ralph with his eyes.

"Well, I don't think I did," said Ralph.

"Nonsense; not exactly in so many words perhaps. Now I dare say you have been engaged in a good many acts quite as illegal, and are quite ready to engage in more, or I should not find you so deep in the confidence of Baxter Sharp."

"I ain't particular what I do for money."

"Of course not ; anyone could see that you are not a man to stand upon trifles, Captain—Captain—"

"Sternway," said Ralph.

"Sternway—Captain Sternway, of the—"

Wentworth paused.

Ralph remained silent.

"What vessel shall we say, Captain Sternway ? " asked Wentworth.

"Look here, governor ! " cried Ralph, springing to his feet, and bringing his clenched hand down upon the table with a force that sent the glasses dancing over the board, " if you take me for a fool to be pumped dry by the likes of you, you're mistaken."

"My dear captain," said Wentworth, in the calmest tones, " I have too much discernment to commit such an error. I do not take you for a fool, but I know you to be—"

"What?"

"A rogue."

"A rogue ? " roared Ralph.

"A rogue—rascal—scamp—thief, if you will," said Wentworth.

Ralph's eyes blazed with fury.

"You old—"

"Silence," cried Wentworth, rising.

"You grey-headed old sinner, what should prevent me from breaking your back and flinging you into the street ? " cried Ralph, furiously.

"What should?—your fears," said Wentworth, calmly. "Come, you cannot intimidate me. Sit down, sir, I have not yet done with you."

"You're a cool fellow, and no mistake."

"I am glad to see you have the sense to perceive it."

"I've the mind to knock you on the head, that's what I have," said Ralph.

"Very likely; but I have the power to prevent you, Captain Sternway."

"I'd like to see it."

"It is here," said Wentworth.

And thrusting his hand beneath his cloak, he drew forth a pistol and levelled it at Ralph's head.

The burly ruffian instinctively drew back a pace.

"There it is, you see, captain. Now, pray be seated. I dare say you can scarcely believe it, yet it is nevertheless a fact, my aim is so sure that I can send a ball through any square on the seven of diamonds without injuring any of the other marks, and that at a distance of twelve yards."

Ralph Sternway drew a long breath, and sat down.

"That's right, captain. Why, bless you, man, you and I will soon understand and appreciate each other. But, by the way, you forgot to tell me the name of the barque you command."

"I didn't intend to," said Ralph.

"Oh, but how can we do business together unless I know where to find you—and we are going to do business it seems, since Sharp here has taken you into his confidence."

"Well, perhaps we are. The name of my ship, then, is the 'Poisoned Arrow.'"

"I shall remember her name. There's nothing like confidence, captain; and now that I am sure you are a desperate ruffian, all that remains for us to do is to thoroughly understand each other."

"I'm blest if I can understand you," growled Ralph. "If I'd known you were the sort of fellow you are, Sharp wouldn't have got me to promise to help him carry out your little plot, and if it wasn't that I'd like to smash that young Tempest, I'd have nothing to do with you or your games, I can tell you."

"Nonsense; you are too sensible a man to throw away a good chance of making money so easily. I wished to be certain of the kind of man you were before I consented to accept your services, and I have discovered all I desired to find—a fellow who has already placed himself without the pale of the law, a man with a brutal bearing, and a revengeful nature; indeed, in a few words, a ruffian who would stop at nothing to minister to his passions and greed. Such a man I required, and you are he."

"And suppose I disappointed you, after all?" said Ralph.

"You will never do that, Captain Sternway. I am an unprincipled man, but I am also a cautious one. Before I trust my reputation in the hands of another, I make sure that it would be against his interest to denounce me or play me false."

"How?"

"By having him in my power."

"You ain't got me in your power, though," said Ralph, with a grin.

"Not when I know that you are Ralph Sternway, captain of the smuggler barque 'Poisoned Arrow,' whom the authorities are so anxious to get into their clutches, and whose capture and transportation would be certain were I to go forth and denounce him?"

"Before you could do that I'd batter your skull in," cried Ralph, springing to his feet, to meet the gleam of the pistol-barrel within two feet of his head.

A cold, cynical smile wreathed the lips of Wentworth as he said—

"Captain, what a terrible bad memory you must have. I declare you have quite forgotten what I told you of the pistol and the cards. Come, man, I'll bet you one hundred pounds to one that I shoot away the lobe of your left ear without grazing your cheek."

Ralph sat down sullenly in his chair.

"Don't care to wager? Very well, you would be sure to lose. A truce to all this—we perfectly understand each other now, I think. Sharp!"

"Well?" said Baxter.

"Of course this person knows perfectly well the service for which I am prepared to pay?"

"Yes; I could not get his help without telling him."

"True. So there is no need for me to go over the ground, and the price only remains to be agreed upon."

"That's so," said Sharp.

"Stay; there is one thing more. The youth must not die by either of your hands. If he fall overboard, break his neck by accident, or meet his death by any way or means, it must not be traced to you; do you understand?"

"Why not?" asked Ralph.

"That's my business," Wentworth said. "It does not suit me to murder him or directly cause his death; but should he die, I care not. At present I am only anxious he should leave England and never return to it again, and to ensure this you must concoct some scheme."

"And what do you intend to pay for it?" asked Ralph.

"Five thousand pounds," Wentworth said. "Two thousand pounds when the lad is safe on shipboard, the remainder when proof is furnished me that he can never return to his native land."

"It must be a large sum that you expect to get by his absence," Ralph said.

"What does that concern you?"

"Only that you can afford more."

"Indeed!"

"We ought to have ten thousand. It's risky work, and if brought home to us would ruin us," said Ralph.

"It must not be brought home to you. You must lay your plans too well for that."

"Still, five thousand ain't enough. It's only two thousand five hundred apiece," said Ralph.

"It's all I feel disposed to give," said Wentworth. "But if one of you like to murder the other after the work is done, the survivor will get the whole of the sum for himself."

"That's a neat bit," said Ralph.

"Whatever it be, it would be no business of mine," was the reply. "Now, let me have your answers. Are you agreed to remove this youth from my path for the sum named, or must I seek elsewhere for others to do it?"

"Suppose we refuse?" said Sharp.

"You would be very foolish, seeing as I have the power by the knowledge I possess of sending you across the seas at the Government's expense. Forgery and smuggling are great crimes in England, you know."

"You are a shrewd man, Mr. Wentworth," said Sharp; "but, since I believe you will keep faith with us, I for one am willing to agree to the sum you name."

"And I suppose I must," said Ralph; "though I think you are a stingy hound not to add a couple more thousands to it, for if you weren't going to gain a lot by it you wouldn't want the work done."

"Quite true," said Wentworth, in his calm, cold tone. "I am not the man to work without an object or gain. Now, hark ye: Five thousand is the sum I will agree upon, but if you can one day prove to me that this nephew of mine is so effectually secured in a foreign land that it is impossible he can ever return to his native shores, I will present you with a thousand pounds each for the information, and there is my hand upon it."

And he held out a hand to Ralph and Sharp.

"Then it's as good as done," Ralph said.

"I'll never rest till I have torn him forever from his home and kindred," said Sharp.

"Enough. You, Sharp, know me to be a man of my word, and where to find me when wanted. Set to work at once, but take your time and be cautious. Hurry may spoil all. Patience is sure to triumph. John Tempest is a brave lad—remove him from my path, and your fortunes are made. And now, farewell."

He moved towards the door, and as he did so, a sound like a cry in a woman's voice, caused each to pause in surprise.

But a hurried search through the house revealed no one, and Wentworth took his departure.

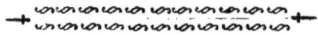

CHAPTER III.

JACK AND THE ORANGE GIRL—EAVESDROPPING—THE MISHAP.

THE fracas at the tavern had the effect of breaking up the party which assembled there some two or three nights every week to play billiards, a party which had till very recently kept themselves aloof from the other frequenters of the house.

This party, which consisted of John Tempest, William Forsyth, Charles Calvert, Samuel Summers, Thomas Evans, and Harry Houghten, all young men of eighteen or twenty years of age, and respectably connected, had been lately broken in upon by Mr. Baxter Sharp and one or two companions of that gentleman.

He had forced his acquaintance upon them, as it were, and had led them on to play for larger stakes, and had induced them to remain longer hours than had been their wont.

But the young friends had soon become tired, suspicious, and disgusted with their new companions, whom they were not long in discovering to be men devoid of all honour, unprincipled, and treacherous rascals, who had desired to ingratiate themselves into the friendship of Jack Tempest, with evidently some ulterior object in view.

What this object was, our hero could not imagine, but that one existed both he and his companions felt assured.

Once or twice Baxter had been detected in cheating, but had laughed the matter off as if it were merely done in a joke.

But the friends, though they appeared willing to look upon the affair in the light in which Baxter represented it, resolved to cut him and his companions, and from that time an ill-feeling sprang up between the two parties.

This became deeper when Baxter offered pointed insult to a poor girl who nightly stood near the tavern with a basket of oranges for sale, and who had appealed to the young men more than once for protection.

But it was not till the night on which our story opens that Baxter Sharp had ever offered personal violence to the poor girl.

Hitherto he had confined himself to words—words which had brought the blush of shame flushing to the pale cheeks of the poor, but pretty orange seller; but now he had descended to violence, and struck her, because, in reply to an insulting question, she had threatened to induce John Tempest to chastise him for his insolence.

The villain's hand, perhaps, had not fallen on the fair shoulders with a force that hurled her to the earth, had he known that close behind him stood one who had before rebuked him for his unmanly conduct—Rough and Ready Jack.

The chastisement the villain received at the hands of the youth for his dastardly conduct was well merited, but even Jack Tempest, brave and impulsive as he was, might have held his hand had he have known that it needed but a blow to induce this fellow to take a leap into a vortex of crime, on the edge of which he had been a long time wavering.

Yes; that blow was like striking the knell of his own doom, and the one aimed at the repulsive face of Ralph Sternway had effectually sealed it.

But Rough and Ready Jack, as his companions called him, knew not this; and, though the squabble at the tavern had broken in upon the night's amusement, he bade his friends good night, and went on his homeward way, resolving in future to have nothing to do with any others than his own immediate acquaintances.

Jack was the only son of a widowed mother, whose social position having been lower than that of his father's, had always been treated with coldness and neglect by his family, and who would have ignored her existence altogether, but from the fact that her husband's wealth had been considerable, and that should her son die, the fortune left to him, when he should become of age, would succeed to them.

Left a widow at an early age, and with the certainty of losing the provision her husband had made for her did she marry again, she had turned all her thoughts and affections upon her son, who grew up a kind-hearted, impetuous youth.

But his training had been lax, and though Rough and Ready Jack was the soul of honour, he was self-willed, and found pleasure in the billiard-room, tavern, and places of public resort, leading, in fact, a rather fast life, which neither was good for his credit nor conducive to his health.

But Jack had resolved to give all that up when he arrived at age and was master of the fortune his father had left him, never thinking that the infatuation such places exercise on thoughtless youths prove often too great for resistance.

It was on his way home this night, perhaps, that he thought for the first time that after all he was not spending his youth worthily.

" I'd cut this game altogether at once," he muttered to himself, " only I don't like the idea of turning round on my friends. We have been chums a good while now, and they are all decent fellows. It would look as if I only wanted to get rid of them because I should soon get my money. No, I won't do that. I'll stick to them, as I have always done, and I know they'd stick to me if I had no expectations. But I won't go so often to billiards and pool. A fellow can't well keep away from others he don't want. However, I don't think Mr. Sharp, or his seafaring friend, will trouble me much more, anyhow."

At this moment Jack felt his arm tugged from behind.

Turning quickly, he stood face to face with the poor orange seller.

"Ah! Polly," said Jack, in a kind tone, "is it you?"

"Yes, sir," replied Polly. "You won't be angry at my stopping you, will you?"

"Angry, Polly? Not I. Why should I be angry?"

"I don't know," said the girl, "for you always speak kindly to me, though I am only a poor girl as sells oranges."

"I hope I shall never suffer a woman's poverty to cause me to forget politeness," said Jack. "What do you require—how can I serve you, Polly?"

"Oh, Mr. Tempest, you have been so kind to me in what you have done, that I want to thank you for taking my part."

"Don't do anything of the kind, Polly. I only did what any other person with a spark of honour or feeling would do, and I am sure no thanks are necessary."

"Oh, you are always kind," said Polly. "But do you know, Mr. Tempest, I can't help feeling that I wish you had not interfered to-night."

"Not interfered to prevent a scoundrel assaulting you, Polly?" cried Jack, in surprise. "Would you have preferred seeing me the equal of those unmanly fellows who stood tamely by while a woman was being subjected to cruelty?"

"No, no, Mr. Tempest. It's not that. But I fear that you will be made to suffer for your kindness to me."

"Don't fear that, my girl," said Jack. "I am able to take my own part; and Mr. Sharp or his sailor friend will find me ready to defend myself if they try any games on with me."

"Yes, if they do so openly—if they strike from the front and not behind. Oh, sir, you may smile at my words, but I'm afraid you have a treacherous foe in the man you punished for insulting me, and that he has a bad and wicked companion in that sailor."

"Your fears are groundless, Polly," said Jack.

"Heaven grant that they may be, Mr. Tempest. But I cannot think so. Oh, beware of them. Do not trust them, even though their words may be fair and their looks and manners kind. They will strike when you least expect it, and are the least prepared for the blow."

"Nonsense, Polly. They are a pair of cowardly fellows, who may bluster loudly, but whose threats are all air. They are irritated now, but when the smart of the blows I gave them is gone, they will think of me no more."

"May you be right and I wrong," said Polly. "But do not dream in fancied security. I have watched them when they knew it not. They mean you harm, and I would warn you, for I owe you this, at least."

"Well, well, Polly, I thank you, I am sure," said Jack. "There is half-a-crown for you, to make up for your losses to-night."

But the girl waved back the proffered coin.

"No, Mr. Tempest," she said. "I thank you, but will not take your gift. I know it is kindly offered, but I will not accept it. I have experienced more kindness at your hands than perhaps I deserved. I came here only to warn you, for that danger is brewing I am sure, though I cannot define it. But you have been a friend to me, and I will watch till I can learn all, for as you protected me, so will I protect you. Heaven bless you, and good night."

And, turning quickly, Polly darted from the spot.

"A strange girl," said Jack to himself, as he dropped the coin into his pocket. "What a pity she is so poor, and has to gain a livelihood as she does. She is pretty, gentle, and kind-hearted, and well fitted for a higher station in life. I wonder if she was always so poor as she evidently is now? She firmly believes me in danger from these men, but she is very silly to do so. Why should I be? Pshaw! it's not worth a passing thought."

Thus soliloquising, Rough and Ready Jack dismissed the subject from his mind, and continued his way home.

The young orange girl no sooner left him, when she ran hurriedly in the direction of the Seven Dials.

Entering the dark passage of a house, she softly closed the door behind her, and gliding along the dark entry dived down a wide staircase and passed out into a narrow paved yard.

Looking up at the back windows of the adjoining house, from one of which a dim light streamed through a dirty, heavy blind, she muttered—

"He is there, and with his villainous companion, no doubt. The lad fondly thinks himself secure. Perhaps it would have been better had I told him all I know and all I suspect. And yet, what do I know for certain?—nothing; all is surmise."

For some moments she remained with her eyes fixed on the dirty blind of the window, and then, looking around and going to the door through which she had come into the yard and listening intently, she said, half aloud—

"I will be satisfied what their game is. The lad has done me a kind turn, and I will do him one if I can. I have heard too much or not enough. There is some plot against him, I am sure, and I'll know what it is, if I die for it."

Again she listened at the passage door.

"There's none of the lodgers in yet, I think, for there's not a sound and no lights in the house; so I can get over without being seen, and if I can climb onto that old water-butt, perhaps I can get a peep into the room through the corner of the blind. Anyhow, there's a corner out of one of the squares, and I may hear."

Without more ado the girl climbed onto the low wall that separated the small paved yards, and dropped down softly into that of the adjoining house.

A couple of steps and her hands rested on the rim of a tall, but somewhat rotten water-butt.

Her hands trembled, and her heart throbbed, and for some few moments she stood grasping the top of the butt, and hesitating whether to return or proceed.

"I may be wrong, but I can't think it," she thought. "Why has Sharp always watched the lad so closely, and been dogging his footsteps like a hound, and why does he come to this house of a night, and only stop a short time? If he slept here I shouldn't think so much of it; but nobody lives here, though a good many meet sometimes. And what does that soldier-looking old gentleman

want that I've seen more than once? If it ain't mischief for John Tempest, it is for somebody, and I'll find it out, that I will."

And nerving herself to the task, she drew herself up with great difficulty on to her knees on the sharp rim of the water-butt, which was, fortunately, full, and so too heavy to be drawn over onto the top of her.

Here she was in great danger of falling headfirst into the butt, but she saved herself by placing her hands against the wall of the house.

Thus steadied, she drew up first one leg and then the other, and finally stood on the narrow rim, and cautiously drawing her feet along, got a good foothold and succeeded in clasping the stone sill of the window.

But the dirty blind so effectually covered the glass and framework as to preclude the possibility of seeing into the apartment, no matter whichever way she turned her gaze.

Her head was on a level with the pane out of which the corner had been broken, and since she could see nothing, she resolved to hear, if possible.

She placed her ear close to the hole in the glass, and in a moment her whole attention became so riveted that she forgot the danger of a false movement, or of discovery.

She could hear the voices of three men, and every word they uttered came distinctly to her ear.

Not a sentence was lost.

She recognised the tones of Sharp and Sternway; the other she knew not, though she suspected the voice to be that of the tall, military-looking man she had seen enter the house on more than one occasion.

But it was the words they spoke that blanched her cheeks, and caused her heart to beat with a force that almost rendered its throbbing audible.

The occupants of that room were plotting ill to the brave lad who had so generously defended her that night— the brave-hearted Rough and Ready Jack.

Her suspicions were confirmed.

The only friend she had ever known was in danger, and she resolved to thwart their base plans.

Yes, she, the poor, friendless orphan,

the despised orange-seller, would denounce their treachery, and shield the brave boy who had so nobly stood between her and insult and outrage.

With this resolve, she turned to spring from her post, but, losing her foothold, uttered a cry of fear and terror, and fell into the icy-cold water beneath.

CHAPTER IV.

THE RESOLVE AND THE AGREEMENT—FOES IN DISGUISE.

To the gratification of Rough and Ready Jack and his companions, neither Baxter Sharp nor Ralph Sternway visited again the " Grand Turk " tavern.

Consequently they played of an evening without interference from these worthies.

But much to the surprise of the young men, and greatly to the wonder of Jack, the pretty orange girl, Polly Peters, had not made her appearance at her usual stand near the door of the tavern since the night of the outrage.

The pretty pale face, the well-shaped, though thinly-clad form, and the modest, retiring manner of the poor girl had won for her the good opinion of the young men who frequented the billiard-room of the " Grand Turk."

Various were the surmises hazarded as to the cause of her absence, but the general opinion was that she had taken up another position for the sale of her fruit, in order to avoid the persecutions of Baxter Sharp.

Jack, who had hitherto been the life and soul of the party, had since the night of the row been considerably subdued in his manner.

This alteration naturally called forth a little surprise from his companions, and considerable chaff at his quiet air and somewhat sombre features.

" Blest if I don't think he is fretting about little Polly, the orange girl," said Spider Legs, as he sent the ball rolling into one of the pockets. " Confess now, Jack, you know you were deeply in love with her."

" A fellow might do worse than fall in love with a pretty girl like Polly, eh, Jack, mightn't he now ? " said Comical Charley, sticking his tongue in his cheek, and digging Happy Hal in the ribs with his thumb.

" What's the odds what she is as long as you're happy," remarked Hal.

" Ah, that's the rub," said Timid Tom. " But anyone can see that Jack's not happy."

" True," said Charley. " Behold his tear-moistened eye, his heaving chest ; hearken unto the throbbing of his beating heart. See the quivering lip, the abstracted gaze—blow it, I've missed that cannon."

And Charley threw down the cue in disgust.

" Serve you right, too, old fellow," said Jack, with a grin. " You're sure to make a mess of it when you go in for the sentimental."

" But I say, Jack, we're all friends, you know," said Hal, with a wink at his companions. " Now tell us the truth, ain't you breaking your heart at the sudden disappearance of pretty Polly ? "

And the happy, hearty fellow gave such a leer around the board, that a peal of laughter broke from the lips of all.

" I'll break your head, Hal, if you don't shut up," said Jack. " What is Polly to me more than any other girl, do you think ? "

" That's just what we want to know all about," said Charley. " But joking apart, old fellow, you are rather sweet on her, ain't you ? "

" Cut your chaff and mind your play, or you'll miss that ball," said Jack.

" You're wrong you see, old man—and a pocket, by Jingo ! By the way, Jack, how would you feel now if I was to make love to the little orange girl ? " said Charley.

" You wouldn't feel very comfortable," said Hal, " if Jack caught you at it. Baxter Sharp tried that game on, you know, so that's a caution to you."

" Make love to her if you like, old

man," said Jack, "only set about it in an honourable way, that's all."

"Should be sorry to cut you out," said Charley.

"Don't try," said Tom; "it would break his heart quite. Poor fellow, he is breaking his heart now."

"Get along," said Spider Legs; "he's only funking in case we find out where he's hidden her. I begin to fancy he's spirited her away. You might be candid with your friends, Jack, and put us up to her place of concealment."

"I don't trouble my head about her, though I should be very sorry if any ill came to the girl," said Jack, seriously.

"Do you think Sharp has laid hold of her?" hazarded Timid Tom.

"I never thought of such a thing," replied Jack.

"Well, it is a rum go," remarked Spider Legs, "what has become of her. She always stood outside of a night, and all of a sudden she disappears. She is nothing to any of us, but still I can't help feeling I should like to know what has become of her."

"So should I," said Hal. "I hope it's no harm, for she was a decent sort of a girl."

"Too good for the life she was following," said Jack. "I've often pitied her, she was so different from those who follow her calling. Bravo, Hal, that stroke puts you out—you've won the game."

"Yes; the game's over. We'll see you another."

"No," said Jack.

"No!" echoed the others. "Won't you play again?"

"No; I've played my last game at billiards," said Jack decisively.

"Why, what's the matter, old man?" said Hal.

"Get out, Jack's only chaffing," said Charley.

"I was never more serious in my life," said Jack.

"Do you mean to say you won't play?"

"I do, indeed."

"Well I'm blowed," said Spider Legs, taking a leap over a chair and looking into the face of Jack. "Why, old man, what's up?"

"Nothing," said Charley, "but something's down, and that's Jack down in his luck—down in the dumps."

"Now look here, my friends," said Jack, seriously; "I've been thinking, and I've come to the determination that it's time to cut the life I'm leading. I don't know what set me at it. I've been thinking that we are all a set of fools to waste time and throw away opportunities as we have been doing for a long time past."

"Touched here," said Hal, tapping his forehead.

"Tile decidedly loose," remarked Charley.

"Chaff away," said Jack, "I shall never get out of temper with fellows I like so well as I do you. But, whatever you may think of me, I tell you I've made up my mind that it's time to cut this sort of game."

"Going in for the Church, Jack?" asked Spider Legs.

"Joined the Mormons?" remarked Hal.

"Going to turn a virtuous young man, and feed on milk and water for the future?" said Charley. "Ah, what a falling off is here, my friends. He's viewed the course he's been pursuing, and thinks he's drifting fast to ruin."

"You are right, Charley, and I think you'll admit it is so."

Then, turning round, he continued—

"We have known each other a long time, most of us have been at school together. There is not one of you I would not help with hand or purse, and I'm sure you would do the same for me."

"That we would," said Charley, "and if you've overrun the constable, Jack, and want a little tin, you shall have half of mine—"

Jack held up his hand.

"No, thank you, Charley, I do not want for ready money, and I only wish all your chances of future supplies were as good as mine."

"Wish they were," cried Hal, "but there, what's it matter as long as you're happy?"

"And are you happy, Hal?" said Jack.

"Rather," said Hal.

"Then I'm afraid you won't always be so if you don't give up the games we have all been playing latterly. Now listen to me, lads. As I said, I've been thinking, and I've come to the conclusion that young fellows in the enjoyment of health and strength are fools to waste it all in their youth in drinking, gambling and late hours."

The others made no remark, so Jack went on.

"We all belong to respectable families, and do we fulfil the wishes of our friends? Are we showing that respect which is due to those who have studied our happiness, by devoting our time to pursuits such as these?—by learning to become gamblers and drunkards; by sowing the seeds of disease in our robust frames; by squandering our money in maddening drinks, and passing hours in the poisoned atmosphere of a public smoking-room? I say we are fools, we are guilty of injustice to ourselves. We were born for better things, and I, for one, shall cut it."

"Oh, cut it! Don't preach, Jack. Here, let's have another game. Give him his cue, Charley," said Spider Legs.

"No," said Jack, "let me give you the cue, lads—the cue to something better, nobler by far, than the pothouse and the billiard-room. If you need excitement, let it be healthy; if you wish for adventure, seek it in the fresh air, and amid the beauties and wonders of Nature; if you desire peril, brave it on the stormy ocean or in the wilderness. Boys, I, for one, feel the necessity of all these to give a charm to life, and I've therefore resolved to go to sea, and strive to be worthy of the name I bear, and prove that there is more real enjoyment in a life of toil and peril, than ever was, or ever will be enjoyed, where the wine-cup flows freely, and the dice-box rattles."

"Do you mean it?" said Hal.

"I do, and, what is more, I mean to go as a common sailor," said Jack. "I have done with this life of laziness, which has of late been growing distasteful to me. I should have been glad if some of you were going with me, but I won't press you to do so. But all I ask of you is to forsake the drink and play, or, rest assured, in time to come, you will regret it."

The lads were silent for a few moments, and then Happy Hal held forth his hand to Jack.

"Jack," he said, "I don't know, old fellow, but what you are right. Instead of ruining our health and emptying our pockets, it's better to try and strengthen the one and fill the other. I don't care for the desk, at which I am compelled to sit day after day, and so, if you are bent on going to sea, I will go with you."

"You will?" said Jack, shaking his hand. "Hurrah! The only regret I should have had would be the loss of all my old friends."

"Well, you don't go without me," said Charley. "If you two are going, I go, too."

"And I," cried Spider Legs.

"And I," said Tom.

"I'm blowed if I'm going to be left all alone," said William Forsyth, a burly young fellow, whom his companions designated Blustering Bill. "No, blow me if I am. So, if you go, I go, and so we will all go together."

"Hurrah!" cried Jack. "That will be jolly."

"But, I say, Jack," said Hal, "what can be your reason for wishing to go as a common sailor? You are so differently situated to us fellows, who are only the sons of poor tradesmen. You can well afford to go as midshipman, even if you do not get help from your mother."

"No, boys, as you will rough it, so will I. What, do you think I'll disgrace the name you have given me? No, no. I'll go as a common sailor, and be in truth what I am in name—Rough and Ready Jack."

Up to the present time there had been no other person in the room but Jack and his immediate friends, but now the door leading onto the stairs opened, and two men entered the apartment, so suddenly as to cause the youths to look round in surprise, and stare almost rudely into their faces.

One was a tall man, with a keen, flashing eye, and gentlemanly bearing.

His hair and whiskers were long, and of a glossy blackness.

Looked at in the face, he appeared to be a man in the full vigour of life, but, when looked at from behind, the slight curve in the broad shoulder would have induced the observer to add twenty years to his age.

The appearance of his companion was quite the reverse.

His frame was that of a young man, but his hair and beard were grey.

"WITH A HOWL OF PAIN STERNWAY STAGGERED BACK."

No. **2**

Over one eye he wore a close black patch, which gave to his features a rather repulsive cast generally, though, examined separately, they were well formed.

The one eye which he fixed upon Jack as he entered seemed to twinkle maliciously, then was turned quickly in another direction.

His companion, meeting his gaze, nodded and simply remarked—

"Are you playing, gentlemen?"

"No, sir," returned Charley. "The board is at liberty."

At the sound of the man's voice Jack stared hard at him.

But the tall stranger's back was turned to him, and he appeared to be intently engaged in examining the tip of a cue.

"Do you know him, Jack?" whispered Charley.

"No; only his voice sounded very like someone's I have heard before."

"Did you ever see such a gill as the other fellow looks with that patch on his eye!" said Hal, *sotto voce*.

Jack merely smiled in reply. Then, in a low voice, he said to his companions—

"Then are you really all decided, lads, in accompanying me to sea?"

"We are," was the reply.

"But some of you have engagements it would not be honourable to break immediately."

"True," said Charley; "but all can be ready in one month, I am sure, and during that time, Jack, as you have no engagements on hand, you could be deciding on the ship, unless you have already got one."

"No; and as I have got the most time, I can be looking after a captain who is willing to take the half-dozen of us."

"Yes, we must all sail together. That's understood."

"Quite," said Jack; "and I believe we shall never regret our decision to-night. We will meet as usual of an evening, and arrange our plans and all that."

"Here, of course?" said Hal.

"No," said Jack. "When we leave this place to-night, let us bid it farewell for ever. Here there is the temptation to drink and play, and where there is temptation it is better to avoid it. From this hour we strike out a new course in our existence. It is yet early, and the night is fine. Let us stroll through one of the squares, and decide on our next move. Come, boys, I am sure you will never regret joining the career of Rough and Ready Jack."

In another moment the boys left the room.

As the door closed behind them the tall man dropped his cue on the table, and, looking at his companion, said—

"Baxter Sharp, our disguises seem very effectual. From what we learned by listening at the door, it seems the youngster is playing into your hands, and will himself take away half the difficulty of his removal from my path."

CHAPTER V.

A COWARDLY BLOW—THE STRUGGLE FOR LIBERTY—IN THE POWER OF A VILLAIN.

THE search through the house having failed to render any explanation of the cry the two villains had heard, they returned to the room and the liquor they had left upon the table.

"That was a rum go," said Sternway. "I should have thought it was all fancy on my part, only you say you heard it yourself."

"So I did; but I suppose it was somebody in the next house," Baxter said.

"Whoever it was, they must have halloed pretty loud, then," said Sternway.

"Yes, and a deuce of a squealing there is there sometimes. It's got about a dozen families in it, and now and then there's such a shindy with one another of them. But there, they are used to it, I suppose, for nobody seems to take much notice."

"That accounts for the squeal, no doubt. The women will hallo, whether they are hurt or not. Here, ain't you going to have a pull at this brandy?"

And he pushed the bottle over towards Sharp.

Sharp poured out some of the liquor, and pushed the bottle back again.

"I say that's a rum sort of a fellow that Wentworth," remarked Sternway, as he tapped the bowl of his pipe on the edge of the table; "a fellow that don't seem inclined to stand much nonsense—pulls the rein pretty tight, and orders you about as if you mustn't dare refuse to do as he likes."

"Yes," said Sharp; "he's all that."

"He'd make a fine skipper. But I was a little bit riled, I can tell you. I ain't used to being talked to in that manner, and if it hadn't been for that barker of his, I'd 'a' let fly at his figure-head and made him take in sail a bit. How came you to have anything to do with him?"

And the sailor's eyes were fixed intently on those of his companion.

"I have known him a long while," replied Sharp. "But, bless my soul! what's that?—hark!"

Both listened.

"Sounds like water splashing against a ship's side," said Ralph.

They both rose to their feet.

The noise continued.

"Thunder! what's it mean?" said Ralph. "It's just outside that window, and it's water sure enough."

Baxter Sharp sprang to the window and drew aside a dirty curtain.

He could not see out into the darkness, but he could distinctly hear sounds as of something splashing in water just beneath him.

In a moment he remembered the water-butt.

"Oh!" he laughed, as he let the curtain fall. "It's some stray cat tumbled into the water-butt, I expect; and it was the row it made that startled us before."

"Cat be hanged," cried Sternway. "No cat ever splashed like that, unless it be a two-legged one."

Baxter Sharp gave a quick start and turned pale.

"You don't think—can anyone have been listening outside the window, and fallen into the butt?"

"That's more likely," said Ralph.

"And heard all that has transpired?" cried Sharp.

"If they have it won't be well for them," hissed Ralph. "Lead the way, for I don't know the hatchways here. Look alive, man!"

Thus admonished, Sharp sprang for the door, seized the light from the table, and led the way down the stairs to the paved yard.

As he drew back the bolt of the yard door the splashing became more furious.

Ralph sprang past him into the yard.

The light of the candle fell upon the butt and the figure of a girl making frantic efforts to draw herself out of it.

Her head and shoulders were drawn over the side, her hands grasping the rim in her desperate endeavour to release herself from her uncomfortable bath.

The brutal Ralph no sooner caught sight of the girl, when he raised his clenched hand and struck the bowed head a heavy blow.

Not a cry escaped poor Polly.

But her hold on the side of the butt relaxed, and she fell back, stunned, into the vessel.

"That's stopped her mouth if she heard anything," said Ralph, brutally.

With a trembling hand Sharp held the light above his head.

There being little or no wind stirring, the light Baxter carried burned brightly.

The reflection fell upon the pale, up-turned face resting against the side of the butt, with the water up to the chin.

A cry escaped his lips.

"Why," he exclaimed, "it's Polly, the orange girl; and you've killed her!"

"So much the better. How did she come there—what has she learned? She must have come spying, and she's got her deserts."

"Lift her out, quick," said Sharp.

"Just douse that glim," whispered Ralph, "or people in some of the houses will see what's up. I'll give her head a push under the water, and she'll be silent enough for ever afterwards."

Quickly blowing out the light held by the trembling hand of Sharp, the villain turned to perform the diabolical deed he contemplated.

But ere he could do so, one hand of Sharp's seized his throat, and the other flourished the heavy candlestick above his head.

"Hold! or I'll brain you," he cried.

"Why, what do you mean?" exclaimed Ralph in utter surprise.

"You shall not kill her. Stand back!"

"You infernal fool, would you have her live to denounce us—to rob us of the five thousand pounds! Are you fool enough to think she hasn't been listening at that window, and knows nothing of our agreement? Besides, didn't she get you that beautiful black eye? And now you want to save her to peach on us. Sheer off, and put her out of the way of doing mischief while we've got the chance."

"No, no!" cried Baxter, "I will not consent to her being murdered. I like the girl, and—"

"And so you'll let her transport or hang you."

"No, I'll take care she don't do either. I'll prevent her doing either of us any mischief, but you shall not kill her."

"Then you are a fool and a cur," growled Ralph. "How will you stop her blabbing if we don't stop her breath?"

"I'll do all that," said Sharp. "Stand aside; if you won't help her out, I'll get her out myself."

Ralph drew back, and Sharp essayed to draw the insensible girl out of the butt.

But her clothing being saturated with water, and herself in a dead swoon, the task was too much for him.

"Help me, Ralph," he said. "You have nothing to fear from her, I tell you. I'll keep her where she will be powerless to harm you or me. Besides, I would have my revenge on her for her scorn. Come, man, don't sulk, but help me."

"You are an infernal fool for your pains," said Ralph. "Mark me, she'll make you sorry yet for your lily-heartedness!"

And, with a terrible bad grace, he aided Sharp to drag the girl out of the water-butt on to the stones of the small yard.

Ralph's eyes wandered up at the windows, but no one appeared to be near them, so he lifted the girl in his strong arms and bore her into the house, followed closely by Sharp, who told him where to step and where to pause.

A light was soon kindled, and flashed over the white face of Polly.

The water dripped from her thin garments and formed a pool at her feet, and Ralph, himself saturated, thrust her into a chair, with an oath.

Sharp set the light down on the table, and strove to restore her to her senses by calling her by name and chafing her hands.

"And when she comes to, what are you going to do with her?" asked Sternway. "Let her run to the first police-station and tell her story and have us arrested?"

"Nothing of the kind," said Sharp. "I mean to keep her prisoner until she consents to become my wife."

"Whew!" whistled Sternway; "any-one would think she was an heiress instead of a little snip of a hawker. Your tastes are not much to be commended, Baxter Sharp—ha, ha, ha!"

Baxter Sharp bit his lip, but was silent. He almost feared the immersion, combined with the shock caused by the blow on the head from the huge fist of Ralph Sternway, had deprived the poor girl of life.

"And where will you keep her safe?" asked Ralph, taking the pipe from between his lips.

"Where? Why, here in this house, as long as I stay in it," returned Sharp. "Hand me some of the brandy. Fury seize you for hitting her like that."

"Didn't know it was the wench you were so sweet on," said Ralph, handing him the brandy. "I think you're a fool for your pains."

"I don't," said Sharp, placing the glass to the girl's lips and forcing some of the liquor between her closed teeth.

In a moment or two Polly began to show signs of returning consciousness.

"She is coming to," said Sharp.

"And when she does a pretty howling there'll be. You'd better stop her, for if you are fool enough to run the risk of bringing the police upon us, I'm not, so if you can't keep her quiet I'll see what I can do."

"Look here, Ralph," said Sharp, turning on him, "it ain't policy for you and I to quarrel; we should lose by it. But this girl is my fancy, and I'll do as I like about keeping her. You have got nothing to fear, for I shall take care she don't get a chance of rounding on either of us."

"You seem mighty tender just now," sneered Ralph. "Why, it ain't two hours ago since you struck her yourself."

"I was mad with rage because of her scorn, but I can laugh at that now she is in my power."

"Mind she don't get out of it, then," said Ralph. "I haven't joined you in that job for Wentworth to have it blown by a girl directly, so just put her where she can't whistle too loud, or it'll be the worse for both of us, you may be sure."

"I shall do that for my own sake," said Sharp. "But, hist! or she'll hear what we are talking about."

Polly opened her eyes and looked around her in a dreamy kind of way.

Then, suddenly, as she seemed to realise who it was that bent over her, she sprang to her feet with a shriek and turned to flee.

But her wet clothes clung to her limbs, and she staggered and fell to the floor.

Sharp bent over her and seized her by the arm.

"Silence!" he hissed. "If you scream I'll kill you."

"Let me go," she cried, struggling to her feet.

"No, you don't," said Sharp. "You have run into my arms, and you don't get away from me in a hurry."

As he spoke he held her tightly by the arm.

"Villain! what would you with me?" she said. "Let me go hence, or my screams shall bring those to my aid who will shield me and prevent your villainous plot on the liberty of Rough and Ready Jack."

"Confound her!" yelled Ralph. "What did I say? She's overheard all. She has learned too much for our safety. She must die!"

As he spoke, the sailor sprang forward and seized the girl by the throat.

His huge hand was raised to deal her a fearful blow on the temple, but Sharp grasped his wrist and held it back.

"Hold!" he cried. "Strike her not."

While they glared into each other's face, and while the girl was becoming suffocated by the terrible pressure on her throat, her starting eyes perceived the rough horn handle of a knife protruding from the waistband of the sailor.

In her despair she clutched at it and drew it forth from its leather sheath.

The long, bright Spanish blade flashed in her upraised hand, and then, with a quick thrust, was plunged into the shoulder of Ralph Sternway.

With a howl of pain, the fellow's fingers relaxed their hold, and he staggered back; and, still grasping the knife, she dashed across the apartment to the door.

But as she tried to open it, Sharp sprang upon her from behind, and seizing her wrist, forced the knife from her hold and flung it across the room.

Sternway had sunk into a chair, and was pressing his hand upon the wound, from which the blood was flowing copiously.

"Kill her, kill her!" he hissed, through his teeth.

Despite her wet, clinging garments, and the pain and sickness from which she was suffering, Polly turned upon Sharp like a tigress, and tried to fling him from her and make her escape.

But her struggles were useless.

Back into the centre of the room he bore her, where, overcome by terror and exhaustion, she sank down insensible.

"She is safe enough now," he said, "and when she rouses up again, she will be where she may howl herself hoarse, for none will hear her."

"Where's that?" growled Ralph, faintly. "If you wasn't such a cowardly fool, she'd be dead now."

"She is quite as harmless as if she were," said Sharp. "That ain't much of a dig she gave you; it'll be all right again soon. I'll bind it up for you as soon as I've made her comfortable."

And taking a large silk handkerchief from his pocket, he twisted it into a rope and bound the girl's wrists together.

Then, throwing open the door, he lifted her in his arms, threw her slender form across his shoulder, took up the candle, and bore her from the room.

"Where are you going to put her?" asked Ralph.

"In the swag-hole under the kitchen," said Sharp, pausing on the threshold. "If she gets out of that she may go, and if anyone finds her there, they'll be more clever than those who have searched the old house many a time, and gone away disappointed."

CHAPTER VI.

AT THE "BLACK BO'SUN"—BOB ACTS SUSPICIOUSLY.

"WHAT cheer, my hearties, what tack are ye on? You seem to have lost your bearings. Shiver my timbers, but Bob the Bo'sun's the boy that will take you in tow and steer you safe into port, if so be as you know to which port you're bound."

As these words, uttered in a gruff tone, fell upon the ears of half-a-dozen youths who stood as if undecided which course to take, they turned and confronted the speaker.

He who had announced himself as Bob the Bo'sun, was a rough-looking seaman of about forty years of age, a powerfully-built man, standing some five feet nine inches, and possessing great breadth of shoulders.

His shirt, open in front, exposed a brown, hairy chest, on which was tattooed a ship in full sail.

His hair was short and crisp, his eyes small and twinkling, his features somewhat coarse in expression.

His left cheek was puffed up, as though he had received a heavy blow on it, but from the movement of his massive jaws and the continuous expectoration of tobacco-juice from his mouth, it was evident that the swelling was caused by an enormous quantity of pigtail held in that side of the mouth.

The party he had addressed was Rough and Ready Jack and his five companions, who, true to the resolve they had made in the tavern, had thrown up their employment, and were now in search of a vessel lying in the docks, to the captain of which Jack was anxious to present a letter of introduction he had in his pocket, and who he expected was prepared to engage himself and friends.

"We are looking for the 'Mountain Flower,'" said Jack; "can you point out the vessel to us?"

"The 'Mountain Flower,'" said the sailor. "You don't mean to say as any of you thinks of shipping aboard that 'ere old tub, and with such a skipper as her captain? Set me adrift on a corkscrew, but darn me if I'd ship a dog aboard such a barque."

"And why not?" asked Jack.

"Why not?" reiterated the sailor. "She's the worst vessel afloat. Why, lor' love you, youngsters, they couldn't get a captain for her as could show a certificate, or a crew if a single one on 'em would be allowed to put his foot on the deck of a decent craft. She's bad —very bad—thundering bad, that's all I've got to say about her."

"Surely there must be some mistake," said Jack. "It must be some other vessel bearing the same name you allude to. The captain I wish to find bears the name of Harry Goodson."

"Same—just the same," said Bowsprit. "I know him and his craft, too. And hark'ee, youngsters, take the advice of an old tar, and give him and his ship a wide berth."

"I was recommended to him as a good-hearted, noble gentleman," said Jack, "who commanded one of the finest vessels afloat."

"Bosh—all bosh!" growled Bob. "Whoever told you so don't know him as I do, or knowing that none but a greenhorn would sail with him, told you so. But, there, if you'll go foundering on a mud-bank when I warn you off, it's your own fault, youngsters, not mine."

And the sailor turned indignantly away.

"Stay," said Jack, catching his arm.

"What for?" said Bob. "To be laughed at for taking the trouble to warn you of danger ahead?"

"No, no," said Jack. "I am sure myself and friends are much beholden to you; but the fact is, I had heard such a good account of the 'Mountain Flower' and her captain, and from what I believed to be a reliable source, that I may be excused for doubting whether the vessel you allude to could be the same as the one we were seeking."

"Well, well, I daresay you was mad at learning how near you was to being shipped aboard the worst craft on the seas. Why, shiver me! you'd been ready to eat your head off with vexation 'fore you'd left the Channel, if you'd been gulled into signing articles by old Goodson."

"What is his vessel, then?" asked Hal.

"Well, here, of course, she's supposed to be a honest trader, and all fair, square, and above-board."

"And is that merely a blind, then?" asked Jack.

"In course it is," said Bob, in a whisper. "She's a—"

"What?" asked Jack and Hal, in a breath.

"Hush!" said Bob, looking mysteriously around. "Look here, lads. I like the cut of your jibs, I do; and I won't see you lost for the want of a little advice, which an old sailor can give a greenhorn. But not here. I've got a few shots in the locker, and if you'll come over to the 'Black Bo'sun,' I'll pay for grog, and put you a-fly to something as you'll thank me for."

Jack looked questioningly at his friends, whose faces had become considerably glum at what they heard.

"Shall we go?" asked Jack.

"Do as you like," said Bob; "I ain't particular as to whether I drink a glass of grog alone and keeps my secret to myself."

And the sailor made a move towards the tavern just opposite the dock, on the sign of which, over the door, was painted a black sailor, with a glass of steaming liquor in one hand and a long clay pipe in the other.

"Let's go," said Hal and Charley.

"We will come with you," said Jack, "for I confess that you have aroused my curiosity to learn what sort of a craft it is we were directed to."

"Just as you like," said Bob. "If you've got any doubts or distrust of me—"

"No, no!" cried Jack; "and I am sorry that anything I have said to you gives you offence or pain."

"You are?"

"On the honour of a gentleman I am," replied Jack.

"Then just put your fist in mine. I see you are a proper sort of chap, and I can understand how mad you must be at being sent to such a ship as the 'Mountain Flower,' and to such a captain as Harry Goodson. But here's the 'Black Bos'un'; 'tain't quite so nice-looking a crib as some of them London taverns, but it's good enough for the fools as works for money at sea, and slings it about ashore."

He led the way through the dirty, sanded passage to a door at the back of the entry, and, lifting a latch, said—

"'Tain't often that any but skippers or their mates comes in here; the sailors and their gals always use the long room in front, where they can swill and dance to old Jones's fiddle."

Bob pushed open the door, and revealed a small room, with plain wooden benches against the wall, and a table running along the centre, which, from the appearance of several brown and sticky rings upon its dirty top, had evidently not been cleaned for days.

"Not a particularly inviting place," said Jack, looking around him.

"I know it ain't," said Bob, "but it's the quietest room in the house, and we can talk here without being overheard."

"What would it matter if we were?" asked Hal.

"Look here, youngster," said Bob, "if I'm willing to serve ye I don't want to bring a shoal of sharks round me. I ain't the only one who knows Goodson and his ship, though I'd take my davy I'm the only one as would save a lot of decent fellows like you from shipping aboard a floating coffin, and under a captain as would make your lives a burden to you if you didn't do all he asked, and I ain't no judge of honest fellows when I see 'em if you'd agree to do it."

Jack and his companions exchanged glances.

"Well, now you are here, sit down, and I'll order the liquor," said Bob. "See here, you lads, it was Providence that brought you afoul of Boatswain Bob, and so you'll say when I've spun you my yarn."

And with this, Bob left the room to order the grog, closing the door behind him.

After giving orders for seven glasses of rum hot, instead of returning to our friends, he made his way to the large room in front of the tavern.

There were but three persons there at the time, and each looked up as Bob pushed open the door and entered.

We have met these three before. They were Hugh Wentworth, Ralph Sternway and Baxter Sharp.

Bob placed his finger to his lip, and softly closed the door.

Wentworth and Sharp wore the same disguises as they did on the evening they entered the billiard-room where Jack had announced his resolve, but Sternway was attired as before.

"Well," said Ralph, "what is it, Bob?"

"Good news," said Bob, turning the huge quid in his mouth.

"Then out with it, man," said Wentworth, "and don't stand grinning there like a monkey. I suppose this fellow is the crimp you spoke of?" he added, turning to Ralph.

"The same. But go on, Bob," said Ralph.

"They have come, and one of them, the best looking of the lot, has got a letter to the captain of the 'Mountain Flower,' and if I hadn't been pretty sharp, him and his mates would have gone aboard her, and you'd have lost your chance of nabbing him."

Ralph struck his thigh a heavy slap, and his small eyes twinkled maliciously.

Bob quickly made the trio acquainted with what had transpired at the docks, and the fact that he had induced the lads to enter the tavern, and of his promise to let them know something that would make them hesitate to sail with Captain Goodson in the "Mountain Flower."

"You are a cute one, Bob," said Ralph.

"I reckon I don't go floundering out of my depth often," said Bob.

"And if you let him escape you, it won't be well for you, Bob," said Baxter Sharp, in a warning tone.

"No fear but I'll steer my course right," said Bob. "I've kept my eyes open, and the lads are here instead of aboard the 'Mountain Flower,' and now it's for you to act."

"But you have got to play your part first," said Ralph, "and then it will be our turn to decide what's to be done to get the fellow aboard the 'Poisoned Arrow.'"

"And I'd better be sharp about it," said Bob, "or they'll suspect there's something in the wind, and haul off."

So saying, Bob went to the bar and asked if the grog was ready.

"I'll bring it in directly," said the landlord, an ill-favoured looking fellow, in his shirt-sleeves. "The missus is just mixing the last glass."

"All right," said Bob. "Just give me the six there, and you can bring the remainder for me yourself."

The landlord looked hard at Bob for a moment, and then leaning forward whispered—

"Mind you don't go too far. There must be no bother in my house."

"Trust me," replied Bob, with a wink.

The landlord put the six already filled glasses on a tray, and turned away to where his wife, a slatternly-looking woman, was engaged with the seventh tumbler.

Whether by accident or design, the landlord stood in such a position as to neither see much nor allow his wife to perceive the strange, hurried actions of Bo'sun Bob.

Casting a hurried glance along the passage towards the door of the room in which Jack and his chums were seated, he thrust his huge brown hand into his shirt-bosom and drew forth a small flask.

Withdrawing the cork, he held the neck of the bottle for a moment over each glass, and then replaced the flask in his bosom.

Then taking up the tray he carried it to the room.

"Here you are, my hearties," he cried, as he pushed open the door and placed the tray on the table; "that landlord takes as long to mix a glass of grog as a ship's cook to swallow a bucketful. I wouldn't wait for the other, but let him bring it in when ready. Now, sling the grog aboard, boys, and I'll tell you what I know, and a good many others for the matter of that, about Goodson and his coffin-ship the 'Mountain Flower.'"

At this moment the landlady of the "Black Bo'sun" appeared with the seventh glass, and Bob took it from her hands after he had placed the other six before the lads.

The fumes of the steaming liquors filled the apartment.

"Come, lads, drink," said Bob, raising his glass to his lips. "Drink to the good little cherub that sent this old hulk steering down full across your bows, to save you from the maw of a ship-skuttling shark."

CHAPTER VII.

BO'SUN BOB PLAYS HIS PART—JACK CONFRONTS BAXTER SHARP—IN THE POWER OF THE ENEMY.

WHILE Bob had been absent from the room Jack and his companions had held a low and hurried conversation, but, deceived by the hearty and truthful manner of the crimp, had come to the conclusion that he was a well-meaning fellow, and that he could be fully relied on.

So now when called upon to drink the toast by the brawny sailor, each raised his glass to his lips.

Ben gulped down half the liquor in his own glass, but seeing that the young men had only sipped theirs, he said—

"Shiver my toplights, if you fellows don't take your grog as a fine miss does her *sal volatile*. When you've been at sea, my lads, and weathered out a hurricane, you'll take more kindly to your grog, and be looking anxiously for the boatswain to pipe all hands to splice the mainbrace."

"What's that?" asked Tom.

"What's what, my lad?" said Bob, taking another swig, and nearly emptying his tumbler.

"Why, what's a brace got to do with rum and water?"

"Ha, ha!" laughed Bob. "That question shows what a greenhorn you are."

"I know," said Hal. "It's when all the men are told to stand on a rope, and each is given a glass of spirits."

"Well, you are nearer than your chum, youngster. Only the men don't stand on a rope."

"But," said Jack, "you have not yet told us what in truth is the character of Captain Goodson, of whom I am sure, the gentlemen, whose introduction to him I have, must be as deceived as we have been."

"Don't let your grog get cold," said Bob, jerking his quid from his mouth and putting in a fresh one. "It won't do to let the skipper or his mates of any ship you may sail on, see you don't like rum as well as the oldest amongst the crew. If you ain't been used to it, get so as quickly as you can, or, hang me!

if we sha'n't be getting teetotal ships, and then the service will go to Davy Jones."

The lads laughed, and again raised their glasses, taking a deeper draught of the drugged liquor than before.

"Now, Mr. Boatswain, if you please, for I'm getting impatient," said Jack.

"Bob Brittle, my hearty," said Bob. "Boatswain is the position I hold aboard one of the safest ships afloat, if she isn't the largest, and the skipper and first mate of which are two of the best seamen afloat. Why, bless you, lad, they're that kind to the men that there ain't one of them, not even the cabin-boy, as wouldn't jump up and stop a cannon-ball with their own bodies if they saw it coming towards him."

"Is he so beloved, then, by his crew?" asked Hal.

"Aye, aye. He treats them like his own sons. I tell you there's as much difference between the skipper I serve and Captain Goodson as there is between a honest man and a thief. Ah! mates, if I hadn't 'a' run foul of you to-day!"

And Bob squirted a stream of tobacco juice from his mouth and shook his head sadly for a few moments.

Then he snatched up his glass.

"Here's to the sweet little cherub that sits up aloft!" he said, "for bringing me to my moorings at the docks, and making me able to prevent you all going to the bottom of the sea in a scuttled ship."

"A scuttled ship?" said Jack.

"Aye. That's what that old villain Goodson is put aboard her for. He'll save himself and perhaps his mate, but none of the rest of the crew. But drink your grog, lads, and then order another jorum."

"No," said Hal. "The liquor seems to have got into my head already."

"And mine," said Tom.

"And mine," said Spider Legs, getting on to his feet. "I can't drink any more."

And Sam Summers placed his hand upon his brow.

"Why that's some of the best ship's rum ever stilled," said Bob.

"There's more good in a thimbleful of gin or whisky than in a pailful of that," said Jack

"It's fancy, lads, because, perhaps, you ain't used to it. There's no headache or doldrums in this stuff, and I mean to have a few more of them before I cry out avast. Have another jorum, mates. I'm pretty flush of rhino, and I'll pay the reckoning," said Bob.

"No," said Jack, in a husky voice. "If I or my friends felt disposed to drink more, I should myself insist upon paying for it, but as you say, we are not used to the spirit, and must decline to consume any more at present."

"I won't press you then, lads," said Bob. "But you'll soon get used to it, and laugh at the idea of it making you groggy. Lor' love you, that wouldn't make a fly tipsy."

"I will drink no more of it," said Jack.

"Then I'll go and order something else," said Bob, rising.

"No, no," said Jack, speaking more thickly; "but tell us why this Captain Goodson is sent on board a ship to scuttle it?"

"Why, to get the insurance, of course," said Bob. "I should have thought a greenhorn would have known that."

"For whom?"

"The owners, of course."

"I don't quite understand," said Jack.

"The owners insure the old tub and its bogus cargo for a big amount, and if the captain bores holes in her sides and bottom, the ship is lost, and he and her owners between them pocket ten times her worth."

"But that would be murder," said Jack, as Hal's head sank heavily onto the table.

Sam's long legs now gave way beneath him, and he fell to the floor.

Jack sprang to his feet.

"What is this?" he gasped out. "Hal—Sam! The place swims round with me. I—I— Ah, villain, you have drugged or poisoned us!"

And he sprang at Bob, and made a clutch at him.

Bob leaped aside, and Jack, grasping at nothing, fell across the form.

His forehead came in contact with the wall, and he slid sideways to the floor.

As he did so, he heard a loud, harsh laugh.

With difficulty he staggered to his feet, and turned to where Bob had stood, but the boatswain had disappeared.

Jack looked dreamily around him.

Tom, Bill and Charley sat with their heads resting on their chests, while Sam and Hal lay upon the sanded floor.

With his hand clasped to his brow, Jack staggered towards the door.

"Treachery!" he gasped. "We have been drugged or poisoned. Help!"

He clutched at the latch, but the door was fast.

He tried to call out, but his voice sank to a whisper.

Darkness seemed to close around him, and he fell back clutching at the table.

Again he essayed to reach the door.

Again he tried to call for assistance.

But in vain. All power seemed to have deserted him.

Suddenly the door opened, and three men entered the apartment.

A gasp of joy came to Jack's throat.

"You have done your part well, Bob," said a voice.

Jack strained his dimmed eyes to see the speaker.

Despite the fellow's disguise he knew him, and with one terrific effort to burst the thrall that bound him, he leaped forward, gasping out—

"Baxter Sharp!"

As his enfeebled hand struck Baxter a blow in the mouth, Ralph Sternway thrust his leg forward, and Jack fell over it, and lay bereft of sense or motion beside his friend Hal.

Bob took a fresh bite at his pigtail, and, twisting it into his left cheek, said—

"There was no bad steering there, mates, eh? Kept the course you marked out, and here they are."

"You have played your part well, Bob," said Ralph; "but it would have been better if this fellow had come alone in search of the 'Mountain Flower.'"

And he touched Jack with his foot.

"Perhaps so," replied Bob; "but you've got the fellow you want, without much trouble, and I've earned the rhino."

Then a loud, triumphant laugh burst from the villains' lips as they looked down upon their victims.

CHAPTER VIII.

POLLY FINDS HERSELF IN A STRANGE PLACE, AND IS STARTLED BY THE APPEARANCE
OF POOR JOE.

WHEN Polly, the orange-seller, recovered her senses, she was shivering in every limb.

She lay upon the damp earth in her saturated garments.

Where she was she could not imagine, and the pain she endured from the egg-like lump on her head, prevented her, for a time, from rising.

At length she got upon her feet.

She was in semi-darkness, for the place was but dimly lighted by a small oil-lamp, secured to an iron box let into the roof of her prison.

Holding her hand to her throbbing brow, and shivering with wet and cold, she tried to make out her surroundings.

Her eyes gradually growing more accustomed to the gloom, she made out a heap of female garments lying on top of a large chest beneath the lamp, a few other boxes of various sizes, and several small kegs.

"Oh, merciful Heaven!" she gasped, at last, "I must have been taken on board some ship, and put into its hold by those villains Baxter Sharp and Ralph Sternway. Now I remember, he told the tall man that he was a smuggler. Oh, Heaven help me, and protect and defend that noble youth, against whom all three have some foul design."

Mechanically she took up from the lid of the large chest a stuff dress and some under-linen, and, holding them up to the light, cried—

"Why, these things are mine. They were safe in my room. How came they here?"

For some moments she pondered, and gazed again and again at the old stuff frock and the many patched articles of clothing, and then she added—

"The villains must have broken into my room and taken them, and brought them here with me while I was insensible. What can it all mean? If they intend to kill me, why not do so in these cold, saturated garments? Ah, Baxter Sharp swore he'd make me his, and, to force me to his unholy arms, has brought

me here, where none can help me and there is no chance of escape from his persecutions. But there is. I loathe the wretch—I defy him, for, if nothing else can, death shall release me."

She came to the conclusion she had been carried insensible aboard Ralph's vessel—that the clothes had been stolen from her humble lodging and placed there for her to attire herself in, and, trembling with cold and discomfort, she looked searchingly around her.

The rays of the oil-lamp did not penetrate more than a few feet on either side of the place, and, listening intently for a moment, she staggered into the darkest corner, and, with trembling fingers, removed her soaked and clinging garments, almost shrieking aloud at every fancied sound lest someone should come upon her.

In a short time she had changed the wet for the dry clothing, and then, feeling more comfortable, and hearing nothing save the squeak of a rat and the pattering of its feet among the kegs and boxes, she sat down on the large chest to think.

She still shivered with cold, and her temples throbbed violently with the pain of the blow inflicted upon her by the villainous smuggler.

Gradually the events recorded dawned upon her mind, and she muttered—

"Ah, perhaps I killed the villain. I saw him fall backwards when I plunged the knife into his body. Ah! what was that?"

She sprang to her feet, and glanced around her.

"Hist! Polly—Polly Peters," said a voice, in a low whisper.

"Oh, heaven, who is it?" gasped the girl.

"Don't you be frightened and go a-squealing out," said the voice. "You knows me, Polly, and you knows, if I am a little 'un, I'm all square to you. Now don't you squeal."

Polly gazed in the direction of the voice, and could hardly suppress a scream when she saw the lid of the chest rise up and a head thrust forth.

"It's Joe, and he won't hurt you, Polly."

"Joe—Joe Jilks!" she gasped.

"Himself, and not nobody else. Joe Jilks, the crossing-sweeper. Look out, Polly, and don't you squeal, mind."

The lid of the chest was pushed full up, and a diminutive boy, habited in ragged garments, with his head and feet bare, sprang over the side of the large chest, and stood before her.

"Didn't expect to see me, Polly, did you now?" he said.

"Heaven knows I did not," she whispered. "Oh, Joe, how came you here, and where am I?" she gasped.

"Blest if I know," replied Joe, "only it's some place under the house."

"Under the house!" cried Polly. "What house? I thought I was in the hold of some ship."

"I never seed a ship in the Dials, Polly," said the boy; "unless you mean the 'Ship' publichouse."

"Oh! then, in what house am I?" she asked, eagerly.

"In the next to the crib you lives in. Now, don't you tremble so hard, Polly," he added, as he took her benumbed and shaking fingers between his own two begrimed hands. "Ain't I here to fight for you, as that fellow does at the penny gaff in Tuttle Street? Don't I like you, Polly, for haven't you often given me threepence for a bed at the lodging-house, or let me doss outside your room when neither of us had got any money? Oh, I'm a rum 'un, I am, but I ain't one of them chaps as forgets his friends."

"But how came I here in this place, and how came you to be where you were?" she asked, eagerly.

"How you came I don't know," the boy replied, "but I knows how I did."

"How?"

"I'll tell you, never fear. I ain't done nothing wrong, so I don't care," said Joe. "It's this way, Polly. I'd only got tuppence, and old Mother Bloggs, the landlady, won't give no trust, and I went to find you, and ask you to lend me a penny, and found you hadn't come in; so as I knowed you wouldn't mind it, I thought I'd wait till you came, so I sat down in the corner of the landing, but I was so tired I fell asleep there."

"Yes—yes," said Polly.

"Now, I'll tell you, and I won't tell you no lies either."

"I am sure you will not, Joe, but, oh, make haste. I am so afraid that brute may come and find you here."

"Don't you mind me, Polly," said the boy, "I ain't worth minding for. Who cares for poor Joe? No one but you."

"Poor orphan," sighed the girl.

"Poor orphan," said Joe; "yes, and more often as I gets kicks nor ha'pence. But I told you, Polly, I fell asleep. Well, I woke up, and heard somebody scratch a light in your room, and I thought it was you, but only a moment, for as the match burnt up, blow me if I didn't see a fellow there instead, and it was that fellow as got such a fine mouse landed him outside the 'Turk's Head' for checking you."

"Yes, Joe, go on; tell me all."

"Well, Polly, I didn't get out of that dark corner then, but I foxed him through the doorway, and saw him take your things off the nails in the wall, fling 'em over his arm, then he blew out the light, shut the door, and crawled like a sneak down the stairs."

Polly understood now how her clothes came to be where she found them.

"I wasn't a-going to see you robbed, so I crawls down after and followed him into the next house, and into this place, without his seeing me, and, big as he is, I'd have tackled him, but some fellow called out to him from overhead, and I was so flabbergasted at seeing you laying wet and white down there that I didn't know what to do for a moment. I couldn't have pitched into him then for a fortune, and I felt, if he saw me, him and the other fellow would have soon settled my goose; but I wouldn't bolt, and I looked where I could hide myself, and while he was a-stooping over you, I ups with the lid of that box, and in I steps, and I'd no sooner pulled down the lid, when flop he sits on it, and I hears him swearing as how he'd make you have him or he'd have your life. I was afraid to touch the lid till I heard you speaking, and then I chanced it."

CHAPTER IX.

WENTWORTH STARTLES BOB AND HIS CONFEDERATES—THE BROKEN FIDDLE—UNDER HIS THUMB.

THE four ruffians—for such indeed were their number if we count, as we certainly can do, the villainous crimp and pretended boatswain, Bob—after laughing immoderately for a time and making sure that not one of their victims was in a position to assail or resist them, left the room, securing the door behind them.

All four returned to the long room, which now had several occupants, among these being an old man with a very bulbous, red nose, who was tuning a dirty fiddle by twisting up the pegs with very dirty fingers.

As the four conspirators ensconced themselves in a corner of the room away from the rest of the company and the old fiddler, Ralph said—

" When you've done twisting at that old box, fiddler, play us something lively, and I'll see if I can't find a sixpence for you. Let it be loud and lively, mind you ; none of your sentimental nonsense for me—keep that for the girls."

The old man nodded and grinned, and Ralph turning to his companions whispered—

" Let the old shark begin his scraping, and then we can talk without fear of being observed or overheard."

The others nodded.

In a few moments the fiddler, anxious to possess the sixpence and the rum it would purchase, struck up a quick jig.

" Now," said Wentworth, " the boy is at your mercy and the others can lend him no assistance. In a short time it will be dark enough for you between you to lead him as if he were drunk to the stairs, hail your boat, and take him in it to the ship. That is all I am interested in. With respect to his friends I have no feeling whatever."

" Ain't you going to take either of them as well ? " asked Bob.

" Not likely," said Ralph. " A pretty hornet's nest I should be putting aboard the ' Poisoned Arrow ' if I took the lot of them."

" Jack Tempest will be quite enough to tackle by himself," said Baxter Sharp.

" He's a rough and a ready one, and will raise squalls enough without the help of his mates."

" Well then, what's to be done with the other five ? " said Bob. It won't do to let them stop here till they recover their senses."

" No," replied Wentworth. " they must be got out of this place for the landlord's sake, if for nothing else, and so, as you brought them here, you'll have to get them away."

" Have to ! " said Bob.

" Exactly," was the reply,

" 'Tain't in the contract, governor," said Bob. " I was only engaged to trap the game, not to dispose of it."

" You will have to do so, whether you arranged for the work or not," said Wentworth, " and no doubt you will be careful how you do so in order to save yourself and your friend the landlord from unpleasant consequences."

" You talk as if I was obliged to do what you want done," said Bob.

" I do."

" Then you may get the boys out of this if you want to yourself, or I'll be paid a thundering big sum for doing the job myself," blustered Bob.

Wentworth looked at him, half amused, half pityingly, and then turning to Sharp, said—

" He does not quite understand me, Baxter, I think."

" No," replied the other ; " but persuasion will do more than threats with him."

" You think so ? "

" Yes."

" We'll see," said Wentworth.

At that moment the fiddler stopped playing, and the song of a half-tipsy sailor was silenced also.

Ralph threw the man sixpence, and bade him rattle off the sailor's hornpipe.

At the first bar of this up sprang the tipsy seaman, and began to execute the double shuffles to the delight of the rest.

Wentworth placed his hand in his

breast pocket, and looked up at the ceiling.

"What is that?" he asked.

Baxter, Ralph and Bob looked.

"There," said Wentworth, pointing, "it moves, I think."

"Why, it's a fly," said Bob, "walking on the ceiling."

"So I thought. It annoys me to see it running there, and when anything offends me I do not hesitate to remove it, as you see."

Quick as lightning, Wentworth threw up his arm. There was a small flash, a not very loud report, and the body of the fly was smashed by the small bullet that embedded itself in the ceiling.

"Avast there, what's that?" cried the sailor, stopping so suddenly in his dancing as to cause him to lose his balance, and fall back heavily onto the fiddle and the fiddler.

"Nothing, my dear fellow," said Wentworth. "I am sorry that by my carelessness I should have interfered with your amusements. Proceed with your dancing, there's no harm done."

"Ain't there; look at that violin," cried the fiddler, holding up his cracked instrument. "That instrument got me my living, and now it's done for, and I'll have to go into the workhouse, unless you subscribes to buy me another."

"There's four times its worth for you," said Wentworth, placing a sovereign on the table.

The musician grabbed at the coin like lightning.

"You're a real brick," said he; "and I'll go to the bar and drink your health in six of rum hot, with lemon and sugar."

Then slapping the muddled sailor on the back, he added—

"Come on, my hearty, and I'll stand a glass to you—if I don't, blow me."

Wentworth's lip curled with contempt as the two men passed out of the room.

"Now," he said, turning to his companions, "there must be no bungling over this job. You, Sharp, and you, captain, will smuggle young Tempest on board the 'Poisoned Arrow,' and so dispose of him that he shall never return to England again, and you, my pretended boatswain, having brought the others here, must get them away again."

"How can I do it?" asked Bob.

"You found little difficulty in inveigling them into the tavern, and a man of such wonderful resources as yourself can have no trouble in getting them out of it, and leaving them while yet the effects of the drug you administered is still upon them. By the way, the punishment for hocussing and drugging is very severe—seven years at the least, and perhaps fourteen, when committed by a crimp and an impostor."

"Look here," hissed Bob, starting to his feet—

"No; look here, my dear fellow," said Wentworth, producing another pistol. "But don't put your eyeball too close to the muzzle, for if my finger should happen to slip, it would be driven out of the back of your head."

Bob sank back in his seat all of a heap.

Ralph and Sharp gave him a warning look.

Bob's red face grew deathly pale.

His lips parted wide, and his huge quid fell from his mouth with a flop upon the sanded floor.

"You—you," began Bob, "are a—"

"Just so," interrupted Wentworth. "I am a strange man, a determined, and when opposed, a revengeful and unpitying one. I have always had my own way in the past, and I intend to have it in the future. It is my desire that the lads should be removed from here before they recover from the effects of the narcotic you administered to them, and since their removal may cause you some little labour, and labour ought to be paid for—"

"If I'm paid for the job," interrupted Bob, "of course I don't mind. I was only paid to bring them here and keep them here, not to take any of them away again."

"Exactly," said Wentworth. "As I said, labour should be rewarded, and I have not the slightest doubt you can find a very large reward upon their own persons, for it is not likely that the lads started from their homes without money."

Bob's eyes glistened, and the colour stole back to his face.

"I didn't think of that," he said.

"You didn't?"

"No, shiver my timbers if I did," said Bob.

"That is strange, and you a professional thief," said Wentworth, with a sneer, that caused Bob to clench his hand till the dirty nails cut into his palm.

A long, low laugh greeted this action of Bob's.

"My dear boatswain, it would not be safe for you to ride rusty with me," said Wentworth; "you will gain more by making me your friend than your foe. One word of mine would consign you to a prison cell, as it would also these men, did I care to speak it."

And he waved his hand towards Sharp and Sternway.

Baxter Sharp went white to the very lips, and Ralph set his teeth viciously together, and muttered to himself—

"My time will come yet, and when it does, beware."

Wentworth rose, and drew his coat closer over his bosom.

"It is getting dark, and it will be a black night, for there will be no moon till midnight; by that time you will have your passenger on board, and the anchor weighed. You know where to find me, Baxter Sharp, when you can bring me the proof that Jack Tempest can never again return to England, and your reward is certain, for you know me to be a man of my word."

So saying, he strode from the room.

CHAPTER X.

JOE PROVES HIMSELF A MATCH FOR BAXTER SHARP—THE ESCAPE—JOE AND THE POLICE—THE DOCTOR'S VERDICT.

POLLY, who had listened eagerly to Joe's story, now began to shiver and tremble again with cold and apprehension.

Not only for herself did she fear now, but also for the poor orphan crossing-sweeper.

He had run, as it were, into the lions' den, and would be rent to pieces by the cruel paws of those monster fiends in human shape, Baxter Sharp and Ralph Sternway.

Eager as she was herself to escape, yet her anxiety was greater for the poor, but kind-hearted boy.

"Oh, Joe," she said, "what can we do? We are in the power of villains. I have learned a terrible plot to-night for the destruction of that good young man who has been so kind to me, and, to prevent me exposing their villainy, they have made me a prisoner here, after brutally beating and nearly drowning me. Oh, Joe, is there no means of getting out of this terrible place and communicating with the police? I could suffer all for myself, but John Tempest must be saved."

Quickly she told the boy all she could remember, and he, in turn, listened to her with wide-open eyes.

"Don't you give up yet, Polly," he said. "I'm up to a dodge or two, if I am a little 'un, and I'll try if I can't get you out of this place."

"How?"

"Can't tell yet, Polly. But don't let them teeth of your'n chatter so awfully, or you'll be taking all the edge off 'em."

"Oh, I am so cold, Joe," she said, "and my head aches so bad."

"I ain't cold, though I hasn't got much clothes on me," replied Joe, "and 'tain't my head as aches, but my heart, it such a poor hunted boy can have a heart."

"We all have hearts, Joe."

"Perhaps we have. I sometimes thinks as how some can't have 'em—'specially the police. They kicks, cuffs, and hounds you from place to place. If you sleeps in a doorway, they chuck yer out of it; if you tries to earn threepence for a bed, they moves you on; if you asks a fellow for a ha'penny, they gives you a cuff on the head; and if you checks 'em, they shakes the life out of you. No, the police ain't got no hearts. They've only got buttons and bounce, and won't let a poor fellow be honest if he tries to."

NOTICE.—With this Number is Given Away a splendid Coloured Picture. Another with No. 3.

"'DON'T ASK QUESTIONS. COME, DOWN YOU GO!' CRIED THE SAILOR."

No. 3.

"Don't say that, Joe," Polly remonstrated. "The police are obliged to act as they do. They know as we do, Joe, that poverty is closely allied to crime."

"Don't let us talk like that now," said Joe. "Let's talk about how to get you out of this."

"Where is the door, Joe?"

"Over there in that dark corner. That's where he comed in at, and I slipped in arter him."

"Let us see if it is fast," she said, tremblingly and faintly.

They went to the door of rough planking and pushed and pulled at it.

It was fast.

"Thought I heard a bolt scrape ag'in it," said Joe, "but wasn't certain."

"Ah, Joe, there is no hope of escape for me. Would to heaven that you, too, had not placed yourself in the power of these monsters."

"Don't you mind me, Polly. What's the use of me? If they kills me, it won't be no loss, I reckon. But they sha'n't hurt you if I can help it—s'elp me never, they sha'n't."

"How are you to prevent them, Joe?" she asked, faintly.

"Don't know yet, but I'm going to find out," replied the boy.

Polly felt a strange giddiness coming over her, and sat down on the box.

The light of the lamp seemed to dance before her eyes.

Her temples throbbed violently, and her breath came in short gasps.

She leaned her head back against the wall and closed her eyes.

Joe looked around him.

"Nuffin here to break down that blooming door," he said. "If I'd only got a knife now, I could cut a hole in it and get at the bolt. Wish I was bigger and stronger, oh, wouldn't I let that fellow Sharp have it, as Mr. Tempest did. I'd give him another mouse on his 'tother eye, and a couple more on his nose, I would, s'elp me tater. And that other chap as hit poor Polly, I'd smash him, I would."

In his excitement, Joe struck his clenched hand, with all his force, on the head of a keg, splitting in its top staves and sending a cloud of dust around him.

As he drew back out of the cloud, he heard the bolt of the door being withdrawn.

"Polly," he whispered, springing to her side, and shaking her, "he's coming. Run, the moment the door opens, and I'll prevent him stopping you."

She sprang to her feet, as Joe bounded away from her side and stroked up handfuls of dust on the tops of the kegs.

Another moment and the door softly swung back, and the figure of a man was outlined dimly in the opening.

One step only did he take into the cellar, and then he recoiled with a loud cry.

"I am blinded!" he cried, putting his hands to his eyes.

Joe had flung the dust he had gathered up full into his eyes, and Sharp, after rubbing them for a moment, groped for the door.

As he found it Joe ran at him, and with all his force, and butted Sharp in the stomach with his head.

With a gasp, Baxter Sharp clutched at the door, missed it, lost his balance, and fell all of a heap on the floor of the cellar.

Joe seized the arm of the startled and shivering Polly, and, without a word, drew her through the doorway.

Then he shut the door, slipped the bolt into its socket, and whispered—

"Don't speak; there's another of 'em here, and he will hear you. Come on. I know the way out of this house."

Silently he led her up a kind of ladder and through a trap, now open, into the kitchen of the house.

Here he paused and listened, pressing Polly's hand, cautiously.

Hearing nothing he drew her into the passage, and as they reached the broad stairs they could hear the loud snoring of Ralph in his drunken slumber above.

He drew her along the passage to the door, which was locked, but the key was in it, and, turning this, and feeling for the bolt, he softly opened the door, and drew Polly out into the dark street.

"Hooray!" cried Joe. "Polly, we've done 'em, we've—Polly, Polly!"

With a moan, Polly staggered a few steps and then sank heavily to the earth, bringing Joe down onto his knees.

"Polly, you are safe—you are at home. Oh! she has fainted; what shall I do?"

"Why, clear out of this pretty sharp,

youngster, or I'll clear you," said a gruff voice above him. "Don't try any of your games on while I am about. I ain't a young 'un in the force, to be deceived by your pretended sympathy for a drunken woman while you pick her pocket. Now you slope, or I'll just hoist you off a yard or two with the toe of my boot."

"It ain't a drunken woman. It's—"

"Hook it!" interrupted the policeman, giving the boy a cuff that sent him floundering from his knees onto his face. "Go on, or I'll put my strap about you to some tune, that will make you dance, I'll wager. Now then, up you get, and off you sheer."

Poor Joe struggled to his feet.

"You're a brute," he said, "a beastly brute; and if I was big enough I'd smash you."

A slap on the side of his head from the officer's open palm sent him reeling up against the wall of the house.

This goaded Joe to fury, and jumping well out of reach of the policeman's arm or foot, he placed his thumb to his nose, extended his fingers, and shouted out—

"Yah! Who stole the goose?"

"I'll goose you, my boy!" cried the policeman, as he made a dash for him, but slipping under the arm extended to grasp him, Joe bounded off some distance.

"You come here, and I'll warm you, my beauty!" cried the policeman. "If I get hold of you I'll pull those ears out of your head. I know you, and I'll mark you."

"Big words off a weak stomach!" yelled back the boy. "Yes, and I know you; you're the slop as stole a penny out of the blind man's hat while his dog was asleep. Oh, you're a beauty, ain't you? You know them clothes wasn't made for you. They was made for your grandmother, who pawned 'em for a shilling, and you sneaked the ticket, and got a berth through 'em at the police station."

"Pay him!" cried the policeman, as he lifted his head after flashing his lantern over the insensible form of Polly. "Pull his young ear out for him."

Joe turned, to see another policeman making for him.

"Ah! two to one!" cried Joe. "It's scarper."

And he doubled and fled as fast as his limbs would carry him.

"What is it?" asked the second policeman, joining the first.

"Drunk," was the reply.

"Can she walk?"

"No, she's too far gone for that," was the reply. "She'll have to go on the stretcher."

"All right. Stay with her, and I'll fetch it."

Half-an-hour later Polly lay, white and cold, in the police station, with a white-haired old gentleman bending over her.

"The girl is not the worse for liquor," he said. "She has had some terrible shock. She is evidently suffering from brain fever. She must be taken at once to the hospital."

CHAPTER XI.

JACK FINDS HIMSELF ON BOARD THE SMUGGLER—RALPH'S ASSERTION GETS THE LIE DIRECT.

WHEN Rough and Ready Jack awoke to consciousness, he found himself lying upon a hard mattress in a small confined space, reeking with the odour of tar.

There was a burning sensation in his eyes and throat, and his legs were knotted with cramp.

For some time he could not make out his surroundings, or imagine why he was there or how he had come.

As he grew more sensible, he experienced a rocking motion, as though someone was under the pallet on which he lay, moving it up and down.

Jack sat up, with his hand to his brow.

"Am I dreaming," he said, "or have

I had a fall and hurt my head? Heavens, how it does ache; but what place is this, and why am I here? Ah!"

As a light seemed to flash upon his brain, Jack threw himself off the straw mattress on to the floor.

With lightning-like rapidity he remembered all that had transpired.

"I am on board a ship," he said; "have been brought here by those who drugged me at the tavern near the docks; but where are the others?"

He looked round the cupboard-like place, but could see nothing but smoke-begrimed timbers, the rude bunk from which he had sprung, a coil of tarred rope in one corner, and several tin utensils in the other.

Through a hole in the wall came the rays of a horn lantern, which evidently served the purpose of lighting some other place, and as he listened beneath it, he could hear the creaking of cordage as it strained through the blocks at each rise and pitch of the vessel.

"I must be at sea," said Jack. "There is no other motion like this that I know of but that caused by the waves, but how I came here and on what ship I am, I cannot imagine."

Jack staggered back to the bunk, sat down upon it, and tried to think.

Gradually every incident dawned upon him, from the time that he and his friends had encountered Boatswain Bob at the docks, till he fell insensible in the room of the "Black Bo'sun," his last remembrance being the sight of the triumphant features of Baxter Sharp.

"That was all a plant to get me into his power and that of Ralph Sternway," he muttered. "Bo'sun Bob was one of their clique, and sent to prevent me and my chums shipping on board the 'Mountain Flower,' and the story of the captain and the coffin-ship was all a lie."

Again he pressed his hand to his throbbing temples.

"I can read it all now, as plainly as in a book. Sharp and his sailor friend swore to be revenged upon me for the licking I gave them at the tavern that night, and they have kept their vow so far, but Rough and Ready Jack ain't one to knock under easily, as they will learn to their cost ere long. But where are the others—where's Hal and Sam and the rest of them—are they on board

I wonder, or have I been brought here alone?"

Jack's eye caught sight of a small porthole just over the bunk, and kneeling upon the mattress he unhooked the catch and threw the window back.

As he did so, a shower of spray fell upon his face, and the wash of the water upon the ship's bows and sides came plainly to his ears.

"I am at sea," he muttered, "but how long have I been here? It's still dark. Have I been here only a few hours or days? I seem as if I had been consumed by a burning fever. There is no sound but the washing waters and the creaking of the ropes. Oh, heavens, can I have been sent afloat on the wild ocean alone?"

Jack could not thrust his aching head through the small round hole in the ship's side, but he knelt on his bunk and let the cool wind and spray play upon his fevered brow for some time, and then he once more looked around the confined space in which it was evident he was a prisoner.

He could not judge where he was, for the white spray and the black night would have prevented him seeing more than a few feet from the ship.

Once he caught sight of a light, but it was a long distance off, and he would not have seen it at all, but that the vessel gave a downward plunge, and shivered from stem to stern.

Jack examined the walls of his cupboard-like cabin.

They were bare, but he found that the means of ingress and egress to and from it, were through a small door just beneath the lantern.

He tried it, and found it fast.

"That proves I am a prisoner," he thought. "Were I not so, the door would not be secured so firmly. However, I can do nothing, think of nothing till my head is better, and I'll try sleep till daylight."

He closed the window as the spray dashed in through it, and then laid himself down in the bunk.

"What is the time, I wonder?" he said.

And as he spoke, he placed his hand to his fob.

Then he sat up quickly.

"My watch is gone!" he said.

Quickly he dived his hands into his pockets.

"Money—all gone!" he said. "I have not only been drugged and kidnapped, but robbed of everything into the bargain, even to the miniature of my poor beloved mother. Oh, Baxter Sharp, this is your work, and I swear it shall be a day of reckoning for you when next you cross my path."

With a sigh, Jack turned his head on his hard pillow and tried to sleep—to forget, for a time at least, his anxiety and his misery.

The plash of the waves soon lulled him off, and his slumber was both long and refreshing.

When he again awoke it was daylight, and, though he was parched with thirst, his temples no longer throbbed.

He sat up.

He heard the trampling of feet above, and now and then a gruff voice giving utterance to a coarse oath or a coarser laugh.

He opened the little window and looked out.

Nothing met his gaze but white-crested waves.

Neither land nor sail could be seen, and he closed the port-hole, and sprang from his pallet.

Then he saw what he had not observed before, and what he was sure was not there when he looked around previously.

On the coil of rope in the corner was a wooden tray, on which was a piece of salt beef, a couple of ship's biscuits, and a pannikin of water.

As Jack's thirst was all consuming, he seized the pannikin, and drained it nearly of its contents.

Then he felt the pangs of hunger assail him, and he set to work on the beef and biscuits.

"It's what they call hard tack, I believe," said Jack; "but it's better than no tack at all."

As Jack took up the last biscuit, and drained the pannikin, the narrow door was opened, and a man stood on its threshold.

He wore a pilot jacket and a hairy cap, in his right hand he carried a huge pistol, and at his side was a cutlass, devoid of sheath.

At the first glance Jack, as he sprang to his feet, recognised the intruder.

"Ralph Sternway!" he cried.

"Captain Sternway afloat," said the ruffian; "and look here, Mr. Jack Tempest, you'll have to give me my title while you're aboard my vessel."

"Yours?" said Jack. "Then this is—"

"The 'Poisoned Arrow,'" interrupted Ralph, "and I'm her skipper; and don't stand no nonsense from any man or boy aboard her. And, since you've elected to sail with me, I give you warning you'll have to do as you are told, and no murmurings, or you'll find that though I'm one of the best captains afloat, yet I can be one of the worst if I'm thwarted."

"How dare you kidnap me on board your ship?" cried Jack.

"Avast there!" said Ralph. "You know I found you drunk, with your pockets cleaned out, lying close to the docks, and that you begged of me to give you a berth, and I promised to do so, though you had attacked me in a cowardly manner when we met at a tavern in London."

"I agree to sail in your ship, and with such a villain as you are?" said Jack. "I say it's a lie!"

"Oh, that's your gratitude, is it," said Ralph, "for saving you from being murdered as well as robbed by Bob Brittle and his mates. You were glad enough to ask my protection and my help then; and now, you ungrateful cur, when you feel you are safe, you turn upon the man who saved you."

Jack looked at the speaker as if he could not believe the evidence of his senses.

"How long have I been here?" he asked.

"Since the night afore last," replied Ralph.

"Where are my friends?"

"What friends? Ain't you got over your drunk yet?" said Ralph.

"I've been drugged, and brought here against my will," cried Jack. "This is the work of you and that villainous scoundrel, Baxter Sharp, and by heavens, you shall both suffer for your villainy, or I'm not worthy of the name I bear of Rough and Ready Jack!"

HIS ADVENTURES E. W. N. AND S.

CHAPTER XII.

JACK STRIKES OUT AND STRIKES HARD—PLACED IN IRONS—ALONE IN THE DARKNESS.

As Jack spoke, he dropped the biscuit, and sprang forward.

Sternway took a step back, and pulled the trigger of his pistol.

Something at that moment jerked his arm, and the bullet buried itself in the planking of the deck above.

Before he could recover himself, Jack was upon him.

Three blows struck in rapid succession upon the eyes, nose and mouth of Ralph Sternway sent him floundering into the narrow passage beyond the cabin door.

With a yell he flung his discharged pistol at Jack, and seized the hilt of his cutlass.

The pistol flew wide of its mark, and, before the ruffian could draw his steel, a terrific blow beneath the chin from the small hard fist of Jack, dropped him, as if shot, to the floor.

As he fell, something like a bundle of dirty rags bounded over him, and past Jack.

Jack cast a quick look round to see what it was, but it had disappeared.

Had he desired to do so, he could not then have satisfied his curiosity, for through a doorway, at the end of the narrow passage, sprang Baxter Sharp.

"Ah! villain," cried Jack, "you, too, are here."

Jack leaped forward, but Baxter, with a cry of fear, sprang back and closed the door quickly, locking it on the inside.

"You cur," cried Jack, "come out, and I'll serve you as I've served your villainous companion."

And Jack struck fiercely at the door.

The reply to this was the loud ringing of a bell from within.

At the farther end of the passage was the companion-way, and as the sounds of the bell pealed through it, half-a-dozen villainous-looking men came thundering down the stairs.

Ralph Sternway had raised himself on to his elbow.

The blood streamed from his nose and lips and one of his eyes had begun to swell and close.

"Help!" he gasped. "Seize him—he has tried to murder me."

Jack turned to confront the new-comers.

"Keep back," he cried; "the first who assails me I will serve as I have done that lying cur there."

For a moment the rough-bearded fellows hesitated.

There was something in the gleam of Jack's eyes that terrified them.

With an oath, Ralph repeated his order, and two of the men sprang upon Jack together.

Thud—thud!

Jack had planted a well-aimed blow on the face of each, but the next moment he was hurled to the floor and pinioned there.

The others now threw themselves upon him, and he was powerless to move hand or foot.

The door of the end cabin opened, and Baxter Sharp came out into the passage.

He saw that he had nothing to fear now.

Jack's head was towards him.

The cowardly villain raised his foot, and dealt the brave youth a kick upon it that broke the skin and caused the blood to flow.

Thus partially stunned, the men had little difficulty in lifting Jack to his feet and holding him thus.

Ralph, by the aid of one of his crew, stood up.

"Kill him—throw him overboard!" cried Sharp.

"Hold!" said Ralph, wiping the blood from his face with the back of his hand. "That might earn the money, but it would be a poor revenge for this."

And he held up his ensanguined hand.

"He will cause more trouble if you don't," whispered Baxter, as he stepped close up to the ruffian captain. "Wentworth would rather know that he was dead, and he could trouble us no more."

"I say he shall not die," hissed Sternway through his clenched teeth, "but he shall live a life a thousand times worse than death."

"If he lives he may—"

"Shut up your mouth," cried Ralph. "Death is a momentary pang. Slavery—the torture of years—a long, lasting, living death. Would you counsel mercy for him? Out on you, Baxter Sharp, for a fool and a craven cur."

"I am not one of your crew, Ralph, to be talked to like that," said Sharp, blusteringly.

"It is well for you that you are not," was the reply. "But there, we won't quarrel, but I tell you this, I'll have my way on board my ship."

"And that?" asked Sharp.

"He shall become a slave."

"But—"

"Hold your row; it will be a few hundreds more in our pockets than if we sling him overboard, and it will be a greater and more glorious revenge for what he has made us feel. Now go in, for the men are listening to us."

With a growl, Baxter Sharp turned away and entered the cabin.

"Put him in the hold and into irons," said Ralph, "his blood is too hot, and wants cooling, and by the time I let him up again, I'll wager he'll have some of the pluck taken out of him, and not be quite so rough and ready."

"You cur, if you think to break my spirit or escape me, you are mistaken," said Jack. "I'll drag you and your villainous comrade to justice yet."

"Bah!" said Ralph, "take him away, and let him have the rats to talk and boast to."

"I am no boaster, you mongrel, as your face shows," cried Jack.

"You took me unawares," cried Ralph.

"You despicable, lying hound," roared Jack, as he was forced up the stairs, "and I'll prove you the cur you are again, as I've proved it before."

Jack made two or three ineffectual efforts to break from his captors, and then, feeling the uselessness of the attempt, he suffered himself to be led onto the deck.

The sea was comparatively calm, the breeze just sufficient to belly the canvas and drive the vessel on her way.

On either side, nothing but water.

Not a sail in sight, and the hot sun streaming down upon her decks.

Jack could not repress a sigh.

He felt that he was indeed alone, for what were those around him but enemies, and what was the vessel to him but a coffin ship!

"Come on, youngster," said one of those who held him. "It's no use cutting up rough. Captain Ralph ain't the one to favour a foe. If you wanted to keep all right you shouldn't have cheeked him. He's all right when you know how to manage him, but war hawks to them as defy him. Here, down you go."

A hatchway had been lifted, and the fellow pointed to a ladder leaning against its side.

"Tell me," said Jack, "for what port is this ship bound?"

"Don't know," was the reply.

"Has anyone else been brought aboard as I have been?"

"We never knows nothing, mate, aboard this yer craft," was the reply.

"What is she?" asked Jack.

"Don't know."

"Nonsense," said Jack, "you do know."

"Don't ask questions, and you won't get told no lies, mate. Come, down you go."

Jack saw it was useless to question further.

He cast one more look around upon the sea, another upon the sunlit sky, and then went down the ladder.

The moment he touched the bottom, two men, who had preceded him, seized him, and held him till the others had descended.

Then he was carried a few feet aft, and bade sit on the floor.

Jack did so, for he felt he could do nothing else.

An iron bar was placed over his legs and shot into a socket, a padlock put through a hole in its end, and the key turned in the lock.

"If you get out of that, youngster, you'll be the first as ever did, and it's held a good many down, I can tell you."

"The last blackbird as was caged there broke his heart and died," said one. "That was a clean fifty pounds lost through a fool's obstinacy."

"Heavens, this ship is a slaver!" cried Jack.

"She's anything and nothing, mate," was the reply.

"What is the fate intended for me?" asked Jack.

"Just what you make it, I reckon," replied the fellow, with a grin, "and seeing as how you made it hot for the captain, he'll be bound to make it hot for you. But, there, we've made you nice and comfortable, and so we'll say, as the Frenchmen say, ' *bong sour.'* "

With a laugh the men went up the ladder to the deck, the hatchway was closed, and Jack was left in darkness and alone.

CHAPTER XIII.

THE STOWAWAY—JOE RELATES HIS STORY.

JACK did not give way to despair.

He was indignant and disgusted, but not at all despairing.

"I've been prettily trapped," he muttered, "but I ain't done for yet. What's that? Rats, I reckon; ships' holds generally swarm with those vermin."

"Hist!"

Jack's eyes opened wide.

"Surely someone spoke," he said. "Is anybody here?"

"Only a very little 'un, Mr. Tempest," was the reply.

"Who are you?"

"Myself, sir. I'll take my davy I ain't nobody else, sir," said a thin voice.

"But who are you—a prisoner like myself?" asked Jack.

"I'm an orphan, sir. You knows me. I'm Joe, as swept the crossing; the boy you used to give a penny to, and what was better, always a kind word."

"How came you here?"

"Sneaked on, sir. Nobody but you knows I'm here. It was me, sir, as hit up the arm of that fellow when he tried to shoot you."

"Then you saved my life," said Jack, "Can you give me your hand?"

"When I can find you."

"I am here."

"I know where you are," was the reply; "but I've got to get out of this empty cask. I dodged into it when I heard those fellows coming."

"Why did you do so?" said Jack.

"'Cos, if I hadn't, they would have seen and collared me," replied Joe.

"Why should they?"

"I've no right here, that's why," replied Joe.

"Are you a stowaway?" asked Jack.

"I don't know what you mean; but I reckon I've stowed myself away a good many times, but the slops always hauled me out and cuffed me away. Blowed if I ain't took the skin off my shin with that iron hoop. Here I is, Master Tempest."

"I can scarcely see you, for it is so dark down here," said Jack.

"'Tain't darker nor the Dark Arches. Did you ever doss in them, Master Jack?" asked Joe.

"Thank heaven, I never had occasion to do so," replied Jack.

"No, you've been one of the fort'nite ones in this world. Hallo! what's this I'm tumbling over?"

"My foot," said Jack.

"Oh, that's all right. Hope I didn't hurt you?" said Joe.

"Not in the least."

"I'm sorry as they've put you down here, sir," said Joe.

"It is not a position to be envied," replied Jack.

"Well perhaps not, but I'm glad you are here for all that."

"Why should you be?"

"Don't you see I get company."

"Oh, that's it."

"Just so, Master Jack. I ain't good enough company, I know, for you, but I want to feel that there's something near me besides rats."

The boy's hand touched Jack's shoulder, and our hero took it in his own.

"I am very glad to have you with me, Joe. But tell me how you came to be on board this ship?" said Jack.

"Do you think anybody will hear us?" asked Joe.

"I do not think so."

"Well, sir, I'll tell you, and I'll tell you straight."

"Go on then, my lad."

"It was this way. You know Polly?" said Joe.

"Polly—what Polly?"

"The gal as sold oranges."

"Oh, yes," replied Jack, "and have been surprised that I have not seen her since that unfortunate affair at the tavern."

"Oh, you don't know then?"

"I know nothing, Joe."

"Didn't you know she was in the horsepital?" asked Joe.

"Certainly not. Is she ill, then?" said Jack.

"She's a lot iller than ill, sir. She's worse nor a corpse."

"Pray explain yourself, Joe. I do not understand you," said Jack.

"You know when you give Baxter Sharp that mouse, don't you?"

"If you mean when I knocked him down for assaulting Polly, of course I do," said Jack.

"That's it," replied Joe. "S'elp me 'tater, you never see such a blooming eye in your life. It was a pictur, fit to present to a dukess on her wedding day."

"Joe."

"Sir to you, sir."

"Stop there," said Jack. "I struck Mr. Baxter Sharp because he insulted a poor and defenceless girl. I take no pride in inflicting pain on an enemy, or hearing the results of what I may have been forced to do, either in self-protection or in aid of others."

"You're a rum 'un, Mr. Tempest. S'elp me 'tater you are. Oh, Jerusalem, if I could land a slop one so as to make his eye go into mourning, I'd fox him round every corner, and—"

"Stop, Joe, stop," said Jack, "and tell me how it is I find you here."

"Do you think any of the fellows will come down?" asked Joe.

"I can't say, Joe, but I should think certainly not for a little while."

"All right, then, Master John, if I may take the liberty of calling you so," said Joe.

"Call me Jack, I'm not a bit proud, Joe."

"You always was a brick, Master Jack, and that's what Spiffin, the baked 'tater man as stands outside the 'Turk,' always said on you."

"Never mind that, Joe, but gratify my curiosity by explaining how it is I find you on board this vessel."

Joe related all he had seen, heard, and taken a part in in the house in the Dials, and when he came to relate how he was chivied by the police, and poor Polly carried away on a stretcher to the station, he gave half-a-dozen imaginary blows at the air, and cried—

"Oh, if I had only been as big and as strong as you, I'd 'a' let 'em had it. Said she was tight, as if poor little Polly ever got tipsy—why, she couldn't make enough for bread and lodging."

"And what happened then, Joe?" asked Jack, eagerly.

"Ah, sir, that's where I'm coming. I saw Bill Simmons—you know, the cove as takes his pitch with his coffee-stall every night at the end of the mews. He'd always let me have a warm at his fire, you know. Well, sir, when the slops chivied me, and I had to run for it, I told him all about it, and he says, 'I'll be bail for two pounds for her, I will.'"

"And was he?"

"No, Master Jack, for when he went to Bow Street, the sergeant told him as how the doctor had said she wasn't tight, and they'd took her to the horsepital."

"What was the matter with her, then?" asked Jack.

"She'd gone off her nut, Master Jack," replied Joe. "They said as how she'd got a fever on her brain, and nobody must see her."

"And did you not communicate what you had heard and seen to the police?"

"I told Bill Simmons, and he said, 'Joe, shut up; don't you go and say nuffin, or you'll get yourself into trouble. There's lots of queer things a-going on in the Dials, that's sartin, but it's not for you or I to blab about 'em. Just keep what yer knows to yerself, 'cos the bobby will take all the credit, and you'll get all the kicks.' So you see, Master Jack, I never blowed the gaff."

"Poor Polly," said Jack; "and haven't you seen her since? I know now how it was we all missed her at the 'Grand Turk.'"

"No, Master Jack, I ain't seen her," said Joe. "Just afore I come to the docks and sneaked onto this ship, I tried to, but a fellow in a little coat and big buttons says, ' She ain't here, she's gone to a convulsionist home.' "

"Convalescent home, you mean, Joe, somewhere in the country," said Jack; "but, after all, you have not told me how it is that I meet you on board this ship."

"I know I ain't good at telling things, Master Jack, but I came because my mother told me."

"Your mother?" cried Jack. "I always thought you were an orphan."

"So did I till that night."

"What night, Joe?"

"The night when she died."

"Your mother?"

"Yes. I never knowed she was my mother till then—s'elp me, I never did."

"I will not ask you anything about her if it would pain you, Joe."

"Oh, I don't mind telling you, Master Jack; 'sides, lots knows it now."

"You have excited my curiosity, my lad."

"Then I'll tell you all about it, Master Jack," said Joe.

He paused a moment, and then he went on.

"You knows I swept a crossing, don't you?"

"Of course I do, Joe."

"Well, arter I'd cheeked the bobbies when they said that Polly was tipsy, they wouldn't let me stand with my broom. I got a kick from one, and a clout from another, and they was always a-telling me to move off or they'd run me in, and if they seed me ask for a copper they was down on me like a cartload of bricks."

"Perhaps they had orders to be."

"Perhaps they had and perhaps they hadn't. I only know as how they was."

"And what did you do then, Joe?" asked Jack.

"What could I do? Old mother Bloggs wouldn't trust me a night's lodging, and if I went to the coffee-stall the police drove me away, and so I had to sleep in the Dark Arches."

"Of the Adelphi?"

"Yes; underneath the big swells as lived a-top on 'em."

"A rather uncomfortable lodging, Joe, was it not?" asked Jack.

"'Tain't the worst I have had to put up with. There was always one there as was kind to me, and if she'd got a crust she'd share it with me."

"Who was that, Joe?"

"Let me catch hold of your hand, Master Jack, and I'll tell you. I didn't know who she was till she was dying. It was my mother."

"Yes, you mentioned her before," said Jack.

"I seldom seed her face, because it was so dark down there, but I knew her voice and she knew mine. She'd let me sleep alongside of her, and I have woke up with my head on her bosom."

"And you knew not that she was your mother?" said Jack.

"Not then, Master Jack."

"When did you learn it?"

"I'll tell you. It was a spanking fine night, and I'd been trying to get a few coppers by running for cabs for the swells a-coming out of the theatres, but the policemen chivied me off, and I had not got enough for a shakedown, so I went to the Dark Arches. There I saw the woman who had been kind to me, but I did not know she was my mother then. She'd got some cold 'taters and some bread, and we eat 'em between us, and then we went to sleep side by side."

"Go on, Joe. Why, you are crying," said Jack, pressing the boy's hand.

"Can't help it, Master Jack. I ain't much of a sniveller, but there's a big lump in my throat, and I can't get it down. Yes, we went to sleep, her poor thin arm round my neck, when three bobbies flashed their lanterns on us, and we woke.

" ' Get out of this,' said the sergeant, ' or we'll soon put you out of it. Now, then, off you go.'

" ' Where,' asked my mother— ' where can we go?'

" ' I don't care where you go, but you'll go out of this,' was the reply.

" She took my hand and led me down the arches till we stood on the bank of the river.

"The moon was bigger and more beautiful than I'd ever seen it. The lion on the top of the brewery on t'other side of the river looked as if he was made of silver, and the water, as it washed up and down, looked like tiny waves of gold.

"She stood there with me by her side under the dark arch, and then she put her arms round me and kissed me.

"'There,' she said, 'is rest and peace.'

"And then she sprang away and leapt into the river. I saw the light moon-beams on her face as she went down, and I shivered in horror.

"Then I was knocked over by the sergeant, who had been following us up.

"'Stand aside!' he thundered.

"The two slops caught hold of him and pulled him back.

"Lor, Master Jack, you should have seen how he chucked one off that way and then t'other the other.

"Away went his lantern, his hat, and his coat, and then the others were on him again.

"'Back with you!' he roared. 'I have driven the poor wretch to this, and I'll save her, by Heaven!'

"Lor', how he did fling them two slops aside, and then he went in with a big splash, and when we saw him coming back with her in his arms, I tell you, Master Jack, that a peeler never had such a hurraying before."

"He saved her, then?" said Jack.

"Yes, from keeping at the bottom of the river," said Joe, speaking thickly. "He swam with her to the shore, and the other two bobbies pulled them out."

"'Quick—quick,' says the sergeant, as he lays her down on the stones, 'fetch some brandy some of you.' He might as well have said, go and fetch the moon, for there wasn't the price of a brandy-ball among the whole lot as was looking on.

"However, she comed to, and she said 'Where's my boy?'

"I knelt beside her, and she put her arms round my neck.

"'Is this your child?' said the sergeant. 'Who is he, and who are you?'

"'He is the offspring of sin; I, the victim of man's crime and villainy. What care I now who knows my shame! The world is slipping from me. It has been a cruel and a bitter one to me, and I leave it with joy; but my boy—'

"Then she paused, and the sergeant, though he was trembling with cold, lifted her up till the big moon, that seemed to stand on the back of the lion on the brewery across the river, lit up her face like an angel's.

"'Boy,' she said, taking my hand, 'if ever you meet your father, avenge your mother.'

"'Who is his father?' asked the sergeant.

"'Hugh Wentworth,' she gasped out, and then her head fell back on the sergeant's arm, and her hands dropped from my neck to her side.

"There was no need for the other two slops to flash their bull's-eyes into her white face, for the moon showed it plainly.

"'Gone,' said one.

"'All over,' said the other.

"The sergeant laid her poor head tenderly back upon the stones, and then he got up till he looked twice as big as he was.

"'Ah, these laws,' he cried 'that make poverty a crime and force us to hunt these miserable wretches through the world.'

"And then they all drew back, and left me with my mother.

"I don't know, Master Jack, whether she did smile at me, or whether it was only the moonbeams that played on her cold white face. Yes, it was cold, oh, so cold, when I kissed it. And I can't tell you any more now, Master Jack. I ain't a blooming sniveller, but I can't help it, s'elp me 'tater, I can't—I can't!"

CHAPTER XIV.

THE STOWAWAY CONTINUES HIS STORY—BAXTER SHARP VISITS HIS PRISONER—THE THREAT.

IT was some little while before poor Joe could continue his story.

At length, when his grief became less violent, he said—

"You won't make game on me, Master Jack, will you now, because it was hard only to know as how she was my mother just as she died!"

"Heaven forbid, Joe, that I should laugh at your sorrows. I love my own mother dearly, and should grieve deeply if anything befell her."

"I needn't have asked you, for don't everybody know you've got a soft, kind heart, even if you have got a fist of iron, and a arm of steel."

"Now, tell me, Joe, how it came about that I find you here?" said Jack.

"Well, sir, it was this way. The police was always driving me about, they'd got their knife into me they had, and now Polly Peters was gone away, I hadn't a friend in the world, so I gets so miserable I makes up my mind to try and go to sea. I come to the docks and tried to find a berth in one of the ships, but directly I gets on to one, somebody orders me off it. I got more and more wretched, sir, and I began to feel I wasn't worth anything, and I'd better jump into the water, as my poor mother did."

"Oh, that was wrong, Joe," said Jack.

"Perhaps it was, sir, but I was cold and hungry and miserable, and I seemed to see my mother's face in the black water, near where I stood. I don't know whether I should have done it or not, if I hadn't heard somebody speaking, and knowed I'd heard that voice before."

"Go on, Joe."

"I just looked round and listened, and then I knew it was that Baxter Sharp as you give that lovely mouse to for interfering with Polly."

"Yes, Joe, yes," said Jack, eagerly.

"Then I see he'd got two more with him. He and a fellow with a hairy cap, was leading between them another man who was that tight that he'd 'a' fallen down if they didn't hold him up. It was so dark that I couldn't see his face.

"'Get him into the boat, quick!' said Sharp.

"'Bob must have given him a strong dose,' said the other fellow. 'He's like a lump of lead.'

"'Yes,' said Baxter Sharp, 'but he'll wake up by-and-by, and then, I tell you, Rough and Ready Jack won't be quite so quiet as he is now, not by a long shot.'"

"It was they who brought me here, then. I'll be even with them yet," said Jack.

"Lor', Master Jack, when I heard 'em say your name, you could have knocked me down with a poleaxe."

"Rather a potent weapon for such a purpose," said Jack, with a short laugh.

"I was so tumbled all of a heap that I couldn't say nothing. I wanted to halloa out to you that you were in the hands of villains, but somehow the words wouldn't come, and before I'd pulled myself up a bit they'd tossed you into a boat, and got in after you. Then the cove with the hairy cap shoves an oar out of one end of the boat, and Sharp flings a rope off a piece of wooden post, just at the edge of the water, and away goes the boat over to where a lot of big ships were laying in rows."

"Well?"

"I ain't a fool if I am a poor unfortunate," said Joe. "I knowed in a minute that it wasn't out of kindness to you them men was taking care of you, and preventing you getting into the hands of the bobbies. I see plain enough they intended you harm; you had been kind to Polly, and I didn't care what happened so as I could warn you and help you if I could, though 'tain't much a boy like me can do for a strong chap like yourself."

"You had the desire if not the power," said Jack, "and I am thankful to you, Joe."

"Yes; I'd go anywhere and do anything for you, Master Jack. I was a-wondering what I could do, when back comes the boat, and as soon as it was close to the edge of the ground, the chap who I know now is Captain Sternway says to Sharp—

" ' Climb ashore and get it. I'll keep her nose into the wharf. There's my pistol and papers in the breast-pocket. Lucky no one's about, or I might have whistled for that coat.'

" Well, he drives the boat, and holds her end close to the wood that runs along the edge by keeping a-waggling that oar about, and Sharp he jumps up and runs a little way, and picks up something off the ground."

" The coat, of course ? " said Jack.

" Yes ; and I'd never seen him lay it there and go away without it, or I might have sneaked it as easy as nothing."

" Ah, Joe, I hope you would never think of doing such a thing," said Jack.

" I never did, Master Jack, but when the police won't let you earn a penny and you ain't got not no bed nor had any grub, I tell you, I've often wondered how I've kept from doing many things. But I didn't know it was there."

" Never give way to temptation, Joe," said Jack.

" I won't if I can help it. Well, sir," continued Joe, " the captain stood at the other end of the boat with his back towards me, and while Sharp was a-stooping down, I saw my chance, and dropped into the boat without making a sound. They had covered you over with a lump of dirty cloth, and under this I slips in a whisking of a dead lamb's tail, and lay quiet beside you."

" And you were neither seen nor heard ? "

" No. Sharp he jumps back again.

" ' All right,' he says, ' I've got the coat.'

" ' Throw it down, then,' says the captain, ' and let's get alongside as quickly as we can. I don't want to be overhauled by the river police, they might smell a rat.'

" Sharp threw the coat down beside where I lay, and that pistol he had spoken of hit me such a clip on the head that I nearly hollered out loud, but I didn't, and I thought that if they found me in the boat they might shoot me with it, so I manages to get my hand on it and slip it out of the pocket into my own."

" You did ! What did you do with it ? " asked Jack.

" Stick to it."

" Why ? "

" I thought I might want it to defend you, sir," replied Joe.

" And have you got it still ? " asked Jack.

" Safe in these here rags."

" What followed then, Joe ? "

" The boat was wriggled up to the ship, and Sharp clambered up the side by a rope. The captain dropped the oar and took hold of a chain, and then, picking up the rope at the other end, he ties it to the chain, and whispers loud—

" ' Tell them to send it down quick.'

" I couldn't see what they was doing, but I know you was lifted up, and I could hear ropes being pulled, and the sound of the wheel of a pulley. Then I heard the captain speaking higher up.

" ' Now, then, a couple of you fellows, bear a hand here, and get him to his berth and lay him on his bunk ; the rest of you get the boat aboard. We weigh anchor directly, and the tide serves.'

" I soon knew that the boat was being lifted up. The captain says, ' Just hand out that jacket.' Lor', how I did tremble then, for I made sure he'd miss his pistol. I was afraid to look up, and I laid as quiet as a mouse, and listened to the men a-pulling at ropes and chains, calling out all the while, ' Hoi—hoi ! ' and then I felt the ship a-moving and a-pitching, and went bang off to sleep."

" What, in the boat ? " asked Jack.

" Yes, Master Jack. And when I woke up the sun was a-shining and the ship was a-swaying, and I felt awful queer, and hungry and thirsty. I looked over and see that there was nobody near me, though there were a few fellows at one end, and seeing a hole with a ladder in it close under me, I drops out, and down the ladder I slips like winking into this very place, and here, Master Jack, I've been hiding ever since, except when I've sneaked out in the dark and gone into the little rooms to seek for wittles ; and it was while I was on that lay that I saw where you was, and hit up that chap's elbow when he tried to murder you. There, sir, now you knows the whole of it, and I shall be glad when we gets a chance to hook it."

Jack was about to make some remark when he held up his hand warningly, and listened.

"Hush," he whispered. "There's someone at the grating—somebody, I expect, is about to come down."

"Then they mustn't catch me here," said Joe. "I'll hide in my kennel till they've gone again."

Joe caught hold of the tub, and pulling himself up over the edge, dropped down into it.

His bare feet made scarcely any noise, and he crouched well down as a stream of light came through the hatchway, and the legs of a man were seen descending the ladder.

When he reached the bottom he flashed a horn lantern in Jack's face.

"All right; we've got you tight enough, Jack Tempest, and there you'll stay till we are in port, 1 can tell you."

Jack looked up at the speaker with contempt.

"My time will come, Baxter Sharp," he said, "and when it does, I won't let you off so easily as I did before, for I'll smash your cowardly carcase to a pulp."

"But, first, I'll begin on you!" hissed Sharp, as he put down the lantern and took a piece of knotted rope from his jacket-pocket.

"Coward! Would you dare strike me, powerless as I am to defend myself?" cried Jack.

"Remember the eye you gave me. I ain't one to forget or forgive a blow. You are at my mercy now, Jack Tempest, and I'll show none to you, I swear."

CHAPTER XV.

A COWARD'S ACT AND A BRAVE BOY'S PROTECTION—DISCOVERED—AN UNLOOKED FOR RESULT.

JACK set his teeth together, and clenched his hands till the nails of his fingers cut into his palms.

The demoniacal look on the face of Baxter Sharp maddened him.

He made a desperate effort to draw his legs from under the bolt, but in vain.

His hands and arms were free, but of what avail were they in the position in which he was placed?

Baxter Sharp raised the lantern and held it so that its light fell upon the face of Rough and Ready Jack.

"You made me look a beauty for a time," he said, "and you've played the same game with Ralph Sternway and one or two of his crew, and if you think you are going to have all the sport to yourself and keep that head of yours clean, you're mistaken. Take that!"

He swung the knotted rope up, and brought it down upon the side of Jack's head.

The cruel and cowardly blow cut open Jack's ear, and the blood poured from the wound over his face and neck.

"You cur, you beast!" cried Jack. "Ah, that my hands were free."

"But they ain't, you see, and you are not likely to get them free either."

"Oh, if I could!" cried Jack,

"If you could; but then, you see, you can't. How do you like that, and that, Jack Tempest?"

He cut a cruel blow at Jack's face.

Jack put up his hands instinctively, and the knotted cord fell across them.

So great was the pain inflicted, that Jack could not repress the cry of agony.

Again the cord descended, but this time upon Jack's shoulders.

"If ever I can meet you on equal terms, Baxter Sharp, may heaven refuse to spare me if I spare you."

"But you'll never get the chance," said Sharp, "and as you'll soon be even beyond my vengeance, I'll have it all now."

He cut furiously at Jack's face, head, and shoulders till the hands that warded the blows from his features were so benumbed that he was forced, with a groan, to drop them to his side.

"Monster!" cried Jack, "would you kill me?"

"No, for you are worth more alive than dead; but I'll spoil that handsome face of yours, Jack Tempest, for if you are as ugly as sin you'll fetch quite as much for a slave as you would before."

He raised the rope again.

"No, you don't," cried a thin voice behind him. "I'll spoil you, you blooming cur."

Crash came a terrific blow on the back of Baxter Sharp's head, and, staggering back with a shriek, the rope and lantern fell from his hands, and he dropped like a log, striking his head against the butt, over the top of which the head and shoulders of Joe were now visible.

The boy grasped by its barrel the pistol that he had secured, and it was with the butt of the weapon that he had struck down the cowardly Baxter.

"S'elp me tater, Master Jack, I never got a fairer smack at a fellow in my life. I wasn't a-going to let him hit you again. Lor', didn't I land him! I could hear his bonce crack, couldn't you, Master Jack?"

Jack was suffering so much pain in his hands, shoulders, and ear that for a moment he could not answer, but at length he said—

"Joe, you have saved me from further torture at the hands of this cowardly villain, and I will never forget you. If I am deprived of the power to reward you, Joe, may heaven bless you for what you have done; but, oh, my poor boy, I fear you will be made to suffer for your kindness to me, for even now those are coming who will find you here. Hide, boy, hide, and I'll die rather than betray you!"

A huge foot was placed on the top step of the ladder.

"What's the row down there?" bawled a gruff voice.

Jack did not answer, and Baxter Sharp could not.

Joe disappeared quickly by crouching down in the butt.

"Who was that gave such a yell just now?" cried the man, taking another step down.

Receiving no answer, he began to descend till his head was below the opening, and then he bent his body forward and looked down.

"Are you deaf down there?" he shouted. "What's the row? Why don't you answer?"

Still no reply.

"There's something up down here," said the man, drawing himself erect and speaking to those on the upper deck.

"The fellow can't have slipped out of his irons," said another, whose voice Jack recognised as that of Ralph Sternway. "If he has, I pity Sharp. Go down, some of you, and see."

"No fear of that, captain," said the man. "No one ever got out of them yet."

"Go and see, I say. Something has happened to Sharp, or he'd answer."

And Ralph Sternway, with a bandage over his face, looked down the opening into the hold.

"The fellow's there right enough, seemingly," he said. "Sharp, d'ye hear, what's up?"

The man who stood on the steps began to descend again, and was followed by two others of the crew.

One side of Jack's face was covered with blood, and his right hand clasped his left shoulder.

"He's tight enough," said the foremost of the men. "But where's the other one?"

As he spoke he stepped back, and trod upon Sharp's leg.

"Thunder—he's here!"

"Where?" cried the other two, looking down.

Baxter Sharp lay with his arms extended and with his head close to the barrel.

The lantern lay on its side, and the candle, still alight, was burning into the horn, and causing anything but a pleasant odour.

"How came he there?" asked one. "The youngster couldn't have laid him out like that."

"Strange," said another.

"Why, mates, he's bleeding like a pig," said the third, who had stooped over Sharp. "He's fell down and cracked his sconce agin this butt."

"More fool he," was the reply.

"Look here, youngster," said one, addressing Jack, "how did he do it?"

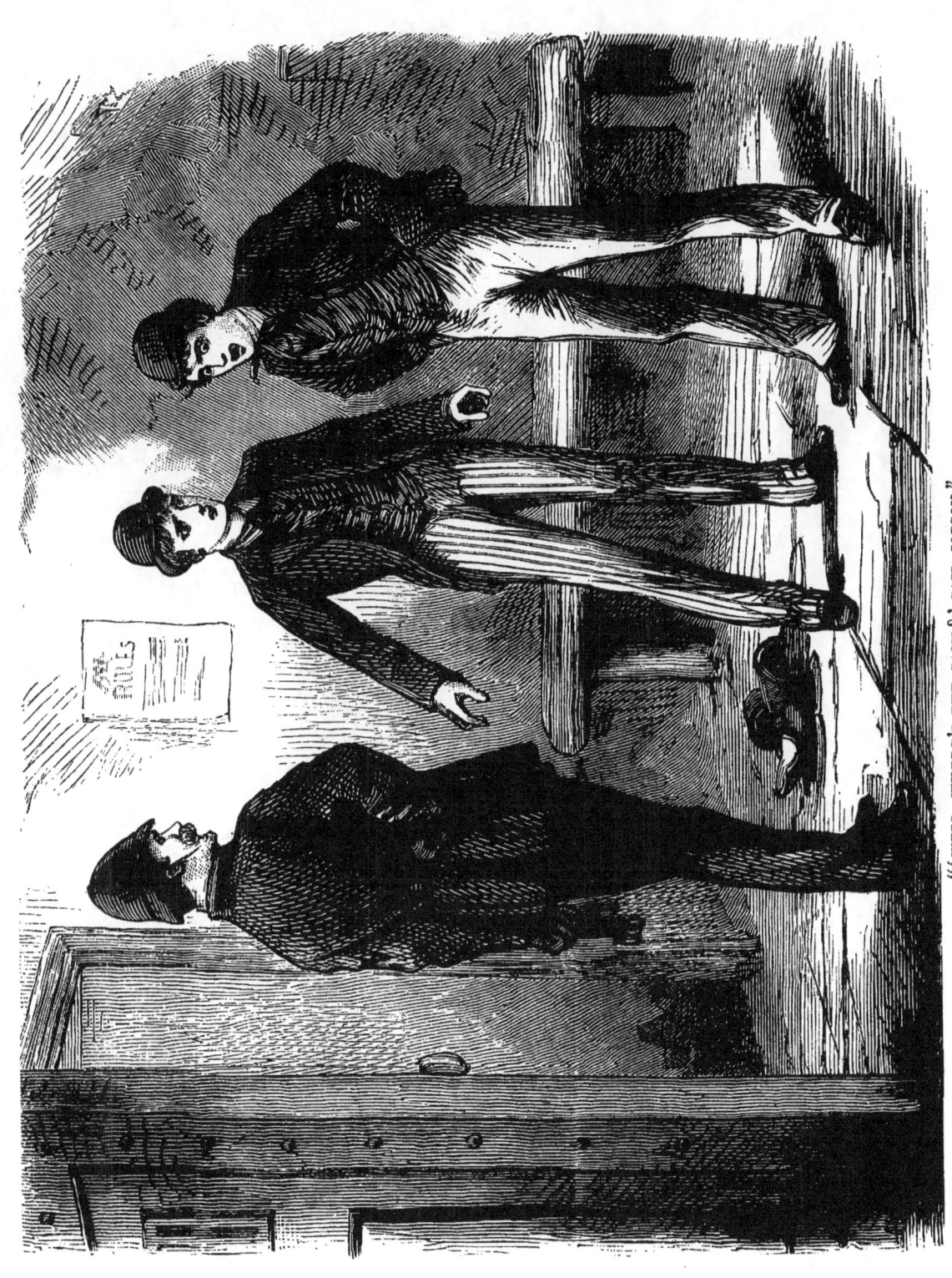

"WELL, WHERE'S THE CASH?" SAID JOBSON.

No. 4

"The cur!" was Jack's reply. "I wish I had put him there with my fist. Do you call yourselves men and British sailors, and allow a wretch like that to beat and torture a fellow who cannot defend himself? Out upon you, you dirty loathsome hounds; you are a disgrace to humanity!"

"Hold on, my young cockerel," said the man who had first descended the ladder. "Just keep your cheek to yourself. We ain't fellows as will put up with it, I can tell you!"

"Like him, you miserable whelp, you'd strike a man when you knew he could not return the blow!" cried Jack. "Take the hound out of my sight. I'd rather be a rat than such a cur!"

"We know nothing of what he is," said the man. "Perhaps he's all you say of him. But don't you go calling Bob Burton names, or I'll forget perhaps that you can't hit back and slap you across the mouth."

"You are cur enough to do it, no doubt," said Jack. "But there is not one of you who are aiding and abetting that villain who shall escape me if ever my hands and feet are at liberty. I am only a boy in years, but I'll prove myself a better man than any member of such a disreputable crew!"

"Shut up!" cried Burton. "And you, Will Burt, go up and tell the captain to come down here."

The man addressed as Will Burt ascended the ladder, while Bob Burton and his mate lifted Sharp onto his feet and stood him up beneath the hatchway.

"His head's cut open," said Bob.

"So it is," replied the other. "Shouldn't have thought a fall ag'in' that barrel would have done it."

"What else could?" asked Bob.

"Looks as if someone had given him one for his nob."

"Who could? Not this cheeky kiddy," said Bob; "'tain't possible. Look here, youngster, say how his head come like this."

"You had better ask him," said Jack, "and perhaps he'll tell you how mine did as well. But I swear he'd never again been able to utter another word if I could have got at him, for I'd have smashed him to a jelly."

"Big words, youngster," said Bob's mate. "You think a lot of yourself, don't you?"

"More than I think of such as you," replied Jack, in tones of contempt.

"Perhaps you'll think more of me now," said the man, giving Jack a kick in the chest that laid him flat on his back on the floor of the hold.

Then, turning to Bob, he said—

"Look here, mate, 'tain't a slip as did this here for Sharp. He's been hit, and thundering hard, too."

"Who hit him? You fool, that boy couldn't, and there was no one down here but these two," cried Bob.

"Perhaps," said the other; "but I smell a rat. Here comes the captain."

Sternway came down the steps, followed by Will Burt.

"This is a rum go," he said, looking at the still insensible Baxter Sharp, as he was held in an upright position by Bob and his mate.

"Very," said Bob. "Don't believe he did it himself, and how the other one could do it I can't see, blow me if I can."

"But I can see it!" thundered Will Burt. "Here's a fellow hiding in this here butt. Out you come, you swab, or I'll pull the head off you!"

As he spoke, he dived his own head and arms into the butt. Then he leaped back with a shriek as a loud report filled the hold, and a volume of smoke poured from the head of the barrel.

CHAPTER XVI.

JOE PRESENTS HIS CARD AND ESCAPES—JACK AND JOE TRIUMPHANT FOR A TIME.

THE sailor made an ineffectual attempt to grasp the barrel for support, and then fell heavily at the feet of his captain.

So surprised were the others, that for some moments not one of them could move.

Even Ralph Sternway himself seemed to have become powerless.

He glanced around him questioningly.

"What boy is that?" he asked at last. "How came he here?"

Then, further recovering himself, he sprang forward and seized Joe by the hair.

"Who are you?" he yelled. "Speak, or I'll tear your heart out! What's your name? Why are you here?"

"You wants a lot of telling for nothing, doesn't you?" replied Joe, shrinking under the merciless hand of Ralph Sternway.

"Tell me who and what you are, or I'll kill you."

"I don't know who I am," replied Joe, as he writhed under the grasp of his long unkempt hair. "But if you wants to know who I am, I ain't no swell, but I'se got my card, and blow you, take it."

And, raising his discharged pistol, the poor stowaway struck Ralph so fierce a blow on the mouth with the weapon, that he cut his lip and knocked out two of his teeth.

"Seize him—kill him!" Sternway yelled, with his hand to his mouth.

Bob and his mate placed Sharp against the steps and made a dash for Joe, but down he went into the butt.

"Come out," cried Bob.

"Drag the young viper out of it," yelled the other.

As they spoke, both leaped up and threw their bodies on to the barrel so as to reach Joe.

The result was that the huge vessel was overturned, and the two sailors were flung to the floor.

Quick as lightning Joe was out of the overturned cask.

Sternway made a grab at him.

"Not for this child," cried Joe, as he dodged under his arm.

Then he turned, and lowering his head, ran full butt at the bottom of Ralph's back.

Ralph's half-blinded eyes did not tell him quickly enough where he was going to prevent a concussion.

His own head struck the body of the half-recovered Sharp.

Down went Sharp with a faint groan, and over him fell Sternway, striking the top of his head a severe blow on one of the steps of the ladder.

Together with the others he rose to his feet, to see the legs of the boy disappearing through the hatchway above.

"Stop him! Fling him into the sea! Roast him alive!" yelled Ralph, dashing at the ladder.

He came near enough to Rough and Ready Jack for our hero to touch him.

Quick as lightning Jack's fist shot out.

The blow struck him on the knee, and caused him to stop short.

"You infernal—"

Ralph Sternway got no further than that, for Jack, having paralysed for a time the leg of the ruffian, seized him by the calf, and jerking his leg from under him, brought him down with a thud at his side.

Then Jack seized him by the throat with his swollen hand, and pinned him to the boards.

"Back!" he cried. "Attempt to help him, and I'll strangle the life out of his vile carcase."

The sailors hesitated.

They saw their captain's danger, and they had had good proof of Jacks determination.

"Help, help!" gasped Ralph. "He is choking me."

"And I will, as there is a sea beneath and clouds above," said Jack, "if you do not at once release me from this vile iron."

"I can't," gasped Sternway. "I have not the key."

"Send for it," said Jack, "or, by all my hopes of salvation, you shall die the death of a mangy dog."

"I don't know who has got it."

"Liar!" cried Jack; "and look here, men, if this bar is not unlocked and I not suffered to go free, I will keep my word, and if you imagine I will not, you don't know Rough and Ready Jack."

Jack's hands momentarily became less painful, stiff, and swollen, and his fingers pressed like iron bolts into the neck of Ralph.

"Get the key," he said, "or he'll kill me."

"And with less compunction than I would a slug," said Jack, "you detestable viper!"

Bob produced the key.

"Shall I release him, captain?"

"Yes."

The sailor stooped, with the key in his hand, when Sharp, who had been gradually recovering his senses, struggled up, crying—

"Don't. Kill him rather!"

He staggered forward a pace, with a bared knife in his hand, when a small keg of tar, out of which some had been taken, crashed down on his head, laying him prone on the floor and covering him from head to heel in the black and sticky liquid.

It was Joe, the stowaway, who had hurled it down upon him.

He saw it near the grating, which had been removed for Baxter Sharp to descend, and he had pushed it through the hatchway just as a couple of sailors made a dash at him.

Joe was not to be easily caught.

He dived under the arm of the first, and, catching hold of the leg of the second, flung him forward, so that he lost his balance and pitched head-first down the hatchway on to the tar-besmeared body of Baxter Sharp.

The fall was not less than ten feet, and diving down as he did without turning, his head struck Baxter so fairly in the pit of the stomach, that he gave a gasp and gurgle, and once more sank into insensibility.

The other sailor above made a clutch at Joe.

He might as well have tried to catch an eel.

Joe flung himself flat on the deck and the sailor fell over him.

Before he could rise, Joe was up and away.

"Done it to a slop many a time," he said, as he dived down the companion-way that led to the cabins, and reaching that belonging to Ralph Sternway, he lifted up the wool mattress of the bunk, and slid beneath it.

Meanwhile, Jack's fingers pressed with terrible force into Ralph's neck.

The bandage around his face, had slipped, and, by the faint light that came through the hatchway, his features showed, swollen, bruised, and repulsive.

"Shall I unlock the bar, captain?" asked Bob, again, hesitatingly.

"Yes—yes. Quick!" was the reply.

Bob placed the key in the lock.

"Let go the captain," he said.

"When I am free—not before," said Jack, fiercely.

"Quick!" gasped Ralph.

The key was turned and the bolt shot out of the socket.

Jack sprang to his feet, pulling Ralph up with him.

"You hound!" he said, holding him for a moment and then flinging him from him, "if I could break my word I would kill you before you could leave this place."

Then, stooping, he grasped the long iron bar which had held his legs so firmly to the deck, and taking a step back, and swinging it round his head, he cried—

"I'll brain the first man who dares approach me!"

So fierce was his manner, and so determined his tones, that those who could do so fell back before him.

He sprang for the steps, despite the pain he was suffering, then, turning again, and holding the bar ready, he mounted them backwards and reached the top of the ladder.

There, close to the opening, sat the sailor who had fallen over Joe.

He was rubbing his nose and forehead, and looking as if he could not understand where he was or what had happened.

Jack sprang towards him with the bar upraised.

"Close that hatchway, put on the grating, and batten all down," he thundered.

"Eh? Thunder and lightning, what's this?" gasped the fellow.

"Obey me," cried Jack. "Close the hatchway, put on the grating, and batten all down, or, by the sea around us, and the sky above, you are a dead man."

The fellow gave one despairing look round, to find himself alone with Jack on the deck, the others having gone in search of Joe.

"Another moment's hesitation and I cleave your skull in twain, fling you into the hold, and leave your filthy carcase to rot there like the rat that you are," cried Jack.

CHAPTER XVII.

THE RECOVERY—IN A STATION CELL—A TRUE STORY, AND A KIND-HEARTED POLICEMAN.

"Now then, you fellows, tumble up, and here's a cup of coffee each for you. Haven't you got over your spree yet? Tumble up, I say, the court sits at ten."

And the speaker laid a rude hand on the shoulder of Harry Houghten, and shook him violently.

"Wake up, d'ye hear," he went on; "and you, too, youngster," he added, turning to a young man who lay like a log on an opposite bench. "A precious fine headache I guess you'll have, the pair of you."

The man who stood just inside the doorway, holding a steaming cup of coffee in each hand, now advanced towards the speaker.

"They are pretty sound, sergeant. They must have had a skinful," he said.

"Yes, there's no mistake about that. I never saw fellows more senseless drunk in my life, and I've seen a lot of 'em. And so young, too; I don't believe either of them is more than twenty years old."

"It's bad for such lads to indulge so heavily," replied the man with the coffee. "If they go on like this now, what will they be when they get as old as you and me?"

"Teetotallers, I hope, Jobson," replied the sergeant. "Dear, dear, I can't get any sense into them. Wake up here, will you."

"Jack, we've been drugged," stammered one of the two occupants of that police-station cell, "and that villain has done it; I see it all now."

"What's he say?" asked the sergeant. "Can you make it out, Jobson."

"Something about drugs," Jobson replied. "He ain't awake enough to know what he says I don't believe. I'd rub his ears, sergeant, that will liven him up."

The sergeant shifted his hand from the youth's shoulder, and commenced rubbing vigorously at his ears.

"Now then, rouse yourself," he cried. "It's eight o'clock, and you've got to go before the magistrate at ten, and pay for your little spree, my joker."

Harry sat up, and looked at the speaker in a dazed sort of way.

The man drew Harry to his feet and held him upright.

"Now then, pull yourself together," said the sergeant. "Here's a cup of coffee for you, and then after a wash you'll be all right."

"Why, where am I—where's Jack?" asked Hal.

"Jack who?"

"Jack Tempest—Rough and Ready, and the other boys?" cried Hal, looking dreamingly round.

"Perhaps this is him?" said the sergeant, as he pulled Charley Calvert up into a sitting position, and began rubbing at that youth's ears as if he intended to rub them off his head.

"Here, whose tickling my ear? Stop it, you fellows," cried Charley. "Stop it now, or I shall—eh?—what the dickens—"

And Charley, partially roused, sprang to his feet.

"What—what's this mean?" he gasped.

"A fine of five bob, if you behave yourself before the beak, or forty shillings or a fortnight if you don't. That's what it means, my cherub."

"But who are you, and what place is this?"

"I'm a policeman, and this is the cell of a police-station."

"The cell of a police-station?" gasped Charley; "and that's Hal Houghten. I don't understand it at all. Why we are here, Hal?"

"Because the pair of you were brought here speechless drunk by the police, who found you in one of the lowest parts of the town. I'm ashamed of you, two such respectable-looking young men to go boozing yourselves into the state you were, and in the company of such characters as you had evidently been, from the place where you were found wallowing in the gutter. But there, there, drink your coffee, then have a good sluice, for you'll have to start in an hour. Your case may be called on first."

"What case?" asked Charley.

"Being found drunk and incapable," replied the sergeant. "Lucky for you the charge ain't drunk and disorderly, or you'd get a month certain, for old Simpson is down on those who resist us like a load of bricks."

Charley and Hal, who had gradually recovered their senses and their memory, looked at each other aghast, and before they could find words to reply, the two officers left the cell and closed the door behind them.

For a moment Charley held the mug of steaming coffee in his fingers, and then he dropped it with a crash upon the stone floor.

"Scissors!" he exclaimed, and then he dropped down on to the stone bench from which he had risen, and covered his face with his hands.

Hal walked over to him.

"Old man," he said, huskily, "this is a rum go. Do you know anything about it?"

"I know nothing," replied Charley. "I know I felt sleepy and queer after drinking that rum at the 'Black Bo'sun,' and I don't know anything more."

"I know that we were drugged there by that sailor fellow. But how in the name of all that is wonderful we came here, and what became of Jack, Tom, and the others, I can't tell. But, here, take a sip of this, Charley. You've lost yours, and I feel a little better for what I've drunk, though my head feels as if a hundred hammers were pounding at it."

The young fellow took the proffered mug, and took a draught out of it.

"It's a rum go," said Charley, handing back the mug. "I can't help thinking I am only dreaming it all now."

"Wish you was, old chum," said Hal. "We've been run in and locked up, but by whom, or for what, I can't think. But where's Jack and the others, and where's that cowardly villain, the boatswain? Hang it, I'll know if they are here as well."

He crossed to the door and gave it a kick.

In an instant it was thrown open by the officer who had brought in the coffee.

"Ready for your douse?" he said.

"All right; come with me into the yard. Hallo! what did you break that mug for—you don't think that will do you any good, do you? That will be added to the charge of drunk and incapable—wilfully destroying property at the station."

"It was an accident," said Charley. "I let it fall unintentionally, and I am quite willing to pay ten times its value."

"Are you?" sneered Jobson.

"Yes, and here's the money!" cried Charley.

He thrust his hand into his pocket.

A look of blank dismay came into his eyes, and he started back.

"Well," said Jobson, "where's the tin?"

"I—I—" stammered Charley; then his face lighted up. "Oh, I have been searched here, and you have my money and watch in your keeping."

"Yes," said Hal, "for mine has gone as well."

"Look here, my lads," said Jobson, "when you were brought in you hadn't got a stiver between you. If you had any money, you never brought it here, nor anything else. You spent it in guzzle, or got picked up by those who you got amongst, and I hope it will be a lesson to you to keep away from drink and bad company. I see enough of the misery that both cause, and take a tee-totaller's advice, my lads, bid good-bye at once and forever to both."

In a fatherly fashion he placed a hand on each of their shoulders, and, looking at them kindly, continued—

"I'm not altogether a bad judge of character, or what a man might be if he liked. There's good in you, I know, and don't drown that good in bad liquor. I am sorry for you, and I'd like to see you go away from here to your own homes and friends without your being hauled up before the magistrate, and charged before a set of dissipated thieves and scoundrels; but the charge has been taken, and you'll have to go. Keep a civil tongue in your heads, and express your regret for giving way to temptation, and you'll perhaps get off with a warning. Now come this way, lads. There's a tub of water waiting for you in the yard."

He led the way into the station yard, and the two lads followed him.

"There you are," said Jobson, pointing to a tub. "Give yourselves a good sluice, and you will both look and feel better after it."

"But, first," said Hal, "will you look me fairly in the eyes and tell me whether you believe I can speak the truth."

Jobson looked at him.

"I said I was a pretty good judge of character, and I think it would put you a little bit out to tell a lie."

"Then you will believe what I wish to say?" said Hal.

"Yes; but you have very little time to talk," replied the officer.

"I will be brief, you may depend upon that, and I will also be truthful."

He then told of himself and his five friends having resolved to go to sea, of Jack having got a strong recommendation for himself and chums to the captain of the "Mountain Flower," their meeting with Bob Brittle, his story of the coffin ship, the sudden and overpowering effect of the spirit they had drunk, and having no remembrance of anything that had occurred since insensibility stole over them in the back room of the "Black Bo'sun."

Jobson listened intently, and when Hal had finished, he said—

"That's a strange story, but I don't see why it should not be a true one. You get washed, and I'll go and talk to Sergeant Sims, who will see the inspector. It's a strange story, but if it is a true one, there's more in it than in an ordinary piece of villainy, and a lot more, my lads."

CHAPTER XVIII.

AT THE "BLACK BO'SUN"—THE CAPTURE OF BOB BRITTLE.

"A strange and, as far as I can see, Mr. Inspector, an improbable story. But, sitting as I have done on this bench for so many years, I have known many an improbable story turn out to be true. I will hold these two young men to bail for a week, in their own recognisances. In the meantime, let every inquiry be made as to their story, and seek out those who, they assert, had left their homes and accompanied them to the docks. You can go, young men; but I advise you to be here at ten o'clock on this day week."

"No pains shall be spared, your worship, to either falsify or substantiate their assertion," said the inspector, bowing, and following Hal and Charley from the court.

During the afternoon a rough-looking, tipsy sailor rolled into the long room of the 'Black Bo'sun.'

"What cheer, messmates," he hiccoughed, as he lurched heavily against one of the tables and sent a tumbler of hot spirits rolling to the floor. "Blue blazes! what's that?"

"My glass of hot rum," said a thin, quivering voice, at the end of the table.

The sailor steadied himself up by the edge of the table, and looked at the speaker.

He was an old man, with a red face and bibulous nose, and habited in a threadbare suit of black.

"Say, are you a parson?" asked the sailor, swaying backwards and forwards, and saving himself from falling by grasping at the table.

"No; I'm a musician," replied the old man.

"Avast there, messmate, avast! That yarn won't do. Think I don't know a parson from any other fish? I tell you, mate, you're a parson."

"I know something," said Jones.

"What's that?" hiccoughed the sailor.

"Why, that you ain't ordered another glass for the one you upset. That was six-pen'orth, and I hadn't had a sip out of it."

"All right; call for what you want. Just paid off. Got the rhino safe here. But where's Bob Brittle?—come to meet him. Don't see him here."

"Don't know him," replied Jones. "Never heard on him."

"What, not Bob the Boatswain—don't know my old friend Bob?" roared the sailor, as the landlord entered the room in answer to the heavy pull of the bell, which the bibulous musician had rung to order the replenishment of the overturned glass.

"Six of rum hot, with lemon and sugar," said Jones.

"Good evening," said the landlord, addressing the swaying sailor.

"Ah, messmate, is it you? Bring me in a glass of grog as well. I've put a few aboard this hulk since I was paid off this morning, but you may take your davy there's room enough in the hold for a dozen more."

"Just come ashore, sir?" asked the landlord.

"Been ashore nearly a week," was the reply; "but didn't get the rhino till to-day, or would have paid Bob the ten shiners I owed him. Couldn't do it yesterday when I clapped my toplights on his jolly figure-head—promised I'd meet him here to-day. He said he'd sure and be here."

"Bob who?"

"Bob Who!" roared the sailor. "Who's Bob Who? It's Bob Brittle I'm looking for—Boatswain Bob, you know. Why, he told me he was a friend of yourn."

The landlord looked up under his heavy brows, and then cast a quick, meaning glance towards the fiddler.

"I may possibly know your friend," he said, "but not by that name. You see, such lots of people come in and out that I haven't got time to notice them all. I'll bring the grog in a moment, sir. Won't you sit down? Jones, make room for him beside you."

"I don't want to sit down till I've paid the shiners to Bob. He did something for me afore I started on the last voyage to China, and I swore I'd give him ten quid when I come back, and I ain't one of them as breaks his word, not me."

"And you saw him yesterday, you said?" remarked Jones, as the landlord left the room.

"Saw him—yes, in the docks, and would have shelled out the dollars then if I'd got 'em, so promised to meet him here to-day. But some of you must know Bob Brittle—him with the ship in full sail tattooed on his chest? Why, I was the very one as helped to do it."

"A ship in full sail on his chest," said a girl, who sat with her arm around a sailor's neck. "He don't mean Bob Brittle—he means Phil Jaggers."

"I remember he called himself Phil Jaggers once when he sloped his ship, but his name is Brittle. Don't I know! But I daresay that's him. Where does he hang out ashore? for I must find him and pay him those shiners, or I'll be melting them and going to sea without squaring up."

"Why, he lives with— Now, then, you fool, why don't you mind where you are coming?"

"So sorry," said the landlord, putting a couple of steaming glasses on the table, and shaking his hands over which the hot liquid had spilled by his slip against the girl. "You know, Jenny, it was an accident. Somebody chucked the lemon out of his grog onto the floor and my foot slipped on it. Here you are, sir. One shilling. Thank you."

The sailor put his hand in his pocket and pulled out a handful of gold and silver.

"If I'd only had half that much yesterday," said the man, swaying backwards and forwards, "my old friend Bob should have had his coin."

"Keep your money in your pocket," said the landlord, "you might lose it."

"No fear of that," replied the other. "I ain't such a fool, if I am half seas over. Don't I know a honest man from a thieving shark? Rather!"

"They are not all honest who look so," said Jenny. "Put your money back, man, or you'll soon be having a perfect shoal of sharks round you."

"Let 'em come on," hiccoughed the sailor, making a grab at his glass, putting it to his lips and setting it down again without tasting its contents. "I'll defy 'em to rob me of my rhino, or Bob either. Good old Bob; jolly—jolly old Bob!"

As he muttered this, maudlingly, he laid his head back in the corner, and went off to sleep.

For some moments the old fiddler watched him intently, then, as the man began to snore audibly, he said—

"Rum sort of fellow, eh?"

"A drunken fool," said Jenny. "If

he wasn't as drunk as a pig and as stupid as a jackass, he'd have held his tongue about his money, and kept it out of sight, too."

The landlord had disappeared after giving Jenny a peculiar look.

"I'll put this out of sight for him," said Jones. "He's had too much already, and it's only doing him a kindness, you know."

And the trembling fingers of the fiddler carried the sailor's glass to his own lips.

When the glass left them the vessel was as empty as his own.

"Jones," said the girl, sharply.

"Yes?"

"You know me," said the girl, pointedly. "Keep a watch over him, I'll be back directly."

"No fear of that, Jenny, I'll keep my eye on him," said Jones.

"Yes, and your hands off, or I'll make it hot for you."

Then, turning to the sailor with whom she had been drinking and conversing for some time, she said—

"Jack, don't go away; I'll be back in five minutes."

"All right," was the reply.

Jenny cast another warning glance at the fiddler, and stepped out of the room and into the street.

A minute after the landlord entered.

"Hallo, mate," he said, "where's your lass?"

"Gone out. Coming back directly," was the reply.

"Gone!" cried the landlord, in surprise. "Where?"

And a look of consternation came over his face and eyes.

He turned upon his heel and hurried from the room.

"That girl, I do believe, has gone to fetch Bob here. That fellow who says he wants him is no more a sailor and no more drunk than I am. I believe he is a detective and wants Bob on account of them boys. Slip on your bonnet, missus, and warn Bob not to come."

The landlady turned pale, but complied with her husband's order.

She grew every moment more agitated, dropped her shawl, picked it up, put it on wrong, then had to take it off and properly adjust it, and by the time she was ready to start, Bob Brittle and Jenny entered the passage.

"Lawks," cried the landlady, "there is Bob going into the room."

"The deuce!" gasped the landlord, springing forward. "Hist, hist!"

If Bob heard him he did not turn back out of the doorway, for his arm was seized in a grip of iron and he was pulled into the room by the sailor who had been caressed and fondled by Jenny.

"What's this mean?" asked Bob.

"That a friend of yours wants to see you," was the reply.

The apparently sleeping man sprang to his feet.

"What, Bob, my old friend Bob!" he cried, coming forward. "I've brought the metal for you old man, and here it is."

There was a sharp click, and before Bob Brittle could realize what had happened, his wrists were secured together by a pair of handcuffs.

"You are our prisoner," said the wonderfully recovered sailor, and then, turning to the landlord who stood, pale, at the doorway, added, "Have a care how you conduct your house, or you'll certainly share *his* fate."

CHAPTER XIX.

THE PARTING WITH FRIENDS—ON BOARD THE "MOUNTAIN FLOWER"—THE COMMENCEMENT OF THE VOYAGE.

"This is a strange story you have told me, my lads, and I confess that I should have had doubts as to its truth, but that I have here in my desk a letter from one of the part-owners of the 'Mountain Flower,' informing me that I might, in the course of a few days, expect a visit from a young man named John Tempest, and possibly one or more of his friends, and begging me to find berths for them in this ship."

And the speaker, a tall, handsome gentleman, of fifty years of age, and who was attired in a semi-nautical dress and peaked cap, laid his hand on the small desk that stood on the table in the centre of his state-room.

Then turning to Samuel Summers, who had been spokesman for William Forsyth and Tom Evans, he added—

"And you say that, in spite of all your endeavours, yourself and mates can learn nothing of John Tempest?"

"Nothing whatever, sir. We had hoped that perhaps, after all, we might find him here on board your ship."

"Strange, very strange," said Captain Goodson; "but there is one thing I am glad to hear, and that is that the police have secured the piratical rascal who played you such a scurvy trick, and as you say that he is known to be the companion of crimps and thieves, he'll no doubt get his deserts. And now, since Tempest has disappeared, and your other friends will be detained in London for the trial of the scamp, what is your desire regarding yourselves? Do you still wish to ship as common sailors?"

"We do, sir," replied Summers.

"Better have kept to your different employments on shore," said the captain. "A seaman's life is a hard one, and at times a very dangerous one, I can tell you. There is not that romance in it that so many lads imagine, and it is not long before the reality drives all of it out of their heads."

"We have all looked forward to its being a hard life, sir," said Tom.

"Well, then, I'll do what I can for you. We sail now in about two days, and to-morrow I'll send my steward with you, to help you in selecting your outfits, and who will see that you are not swindled by the dealer. But, hark you, lads, before you go, take my advice and do not enter a tavern."

"We promise you that, sir," Forsyth said. "We will not give anyone else a chance to drug and rob us."

"Take care you don't. And now, good morning, for I have many things to see to."

The lads bowed, and with a nod the captain dismissed them.

That day Tom, Will, and Sam took leave of Harry and Charley.

"Wish we could go with you, dear boys," said Charley, "but this beastly trial will keep us here long after you have gone. Why couldn't the magistrate have sentenced Bob Brittle instead of committing him for trial."

"Because there are other cases against him," said Harry; "and he has been wanted for some time, Jobson tells me. I only wish he'd say if he knows anything about Jack, but he sticks to it that he left him lying on a doorstep fast asleep, and that it was not he who robbed any of us."

"There's those to prove he was seen with Jack and us, and he'll get it hot, I expect," said Charley; "leastways Jobson and the sergeant say he will, and perhaps others as well, if they can trap them."

"By being compelled to remain here, you may succeed in finding Jack," said Tom.

"I hope so," said Harry; "but I'm afraid he's done for."

"What! you don't mean that he has been murdered? Oh, don't think that," cried Sam.

"I don't know what else to think," said Harry, "though heaven forbid he should have been."

"Oh, let's hope for the best," said Charley, "and that he may suddenly turn up, and we may be able to ship together."

"I wish we could all have sailed in the same one," said Tom.

"So do I; and so do we all, I know," replied Harry; "but Fate seems to have been against that. However, we'll write to each other as often as we can, and perhaps, after a voyage, we may meet and be able to join our forces."

"I hope we may," said Sam. "It's a beastly shame we must separate now. I'll write you home, Harry, as soon as I can get to learn where the 'Mountain Flower' is going, and I know, dear boys, you won't fail to write to us and tell us all you can; and now, as we have all three promised to be with our fathers and mothers to-night, we must say that painful word, 'Good-bye.'"

The lads shook hands all round, and there was something suspiciously like a tear trembling on the lash of one of

Timid Tom's eyes, and the long legs of Sam trembled slightly.

The adieus were spoken, and the lads separated.

Would they ever meet again?

Time will show.

The next morning when Captain Goodson came on board the vessel he commanded, he was saluted respectfully by the three lads.

"Ah! good morning, lads," he said, cheerily. "Have you received any news of your missing friend?"

"I regret to say we have not, sir."

"I met Mr. Welfare this morning, the gentleman who gave him that letter of introduction to me, and he seems quite concerned about him. The lad's father was an old friend, and he is resolved to see if something cannot be done to trace him out."

"I hope he may succeed where others have failed, sir," said Will.

"So do I. But now you want your outfits. Is the steward on board, Mr. Gordon?"

"Yes, sir," said a gentlemanly-looking man, of about forty years of age, as he touched the peak of his cap with the hand he took from his jacket pocket.

"Please send him here."

"Certainly, sir."

"That is my chief mate," said the captain. "I hope you and he will get on together. He allows no skulking, mind you."

"We hope, sir, that we shall never give him cause to be dissatisfied with us," said Sam.

"I hope so, too, my lad. Ah! here's Cantwell—an honest fellow, though a short-tempered one at times. You may trust him, lads, and he will see justice done you."

The lads bowed, and Cantwell, the steward, touched his cap.

"Steward, you will look after these young men."

"The lads you spoke to me about last evening?" said the steward.

"Yes. See that they get everything requisite for the new life they have elected to enter upon, and bring them back as soon as possible."

"Certainly sir," replied Cantwell.

The captain turned to descend to his state-room.

The steward looked hard and long at the chums, as if he was trying to read the character of each, and then he said, half aloud—

"Three young fools! Will wish themselves back before we're out of the Channel. Bah! Wonder the captain agreed to take them. More fit for driving quills than tarring ropes and swabbing decks."

Then, raising his tone, he added—

"Now then, youngsters, when you are ready I am."

"We are quite ready, sir," said Tom. "We only await your pleasure."

"Pleasure, eh? Well, he seems to know how to speak decently. Come on, then, and I'll take you to old Moses Martins, and if you give him more than half he asks you're fools."

"We leave it to you, as Captain Goodson desired us to do," said Sam, "and we are only too pleased to do so."

"Good! Yes, best to leave it to me. I ain't one to be taken in easily."

With this he went over the side onto the wharf, and the boys followed him.

When about an hour later they returned to the ship, the steward and the three lads carried between them a couple of large chests, while two men brought up a third in their rear.

The captain was on deck, conversing with the chief mate when they arrived.

"You will see to the stowing of these young fellows," he said. "Make them as comfortable as you can before the crew comes on board to-morrow."

"Yes, sir."

"Then come to me in my cabin, and we will go over the items together."

The mate bowed, and, turning to the friends, who stood perspiring beside their chests, he said—

"Just come with me, and I'll show you your berths."

They went with him, and, having the places and positions of their hammocks pointed out to them, returned to fetch their chests below.

The next day the rest of the crew came on board.

Half of them were intoxicated; but by the time the vessel was ready to leave her moorings they had become sober.

At five o'clock in the morning she was hauled out of dock, and Sam, Tom, and Will were commencing their first voyage.

CHAPTER XX.

RECAPTURED—JOE CONCEALS HIMSELF IN THE LAZARETTE—IN DOUBLE IRONS—
RALPH'S OATH.

THE man, after looking at Jack for a moment, and evidently seeing that he meant what he threatened, seized the grating, as if he feared to disobey the order.

Jack, seeing this, lowered the bar.

As he did so, something fell over his head and shoulders.

In a moment his arms were pinioned to his sides.

He was jerked violently backwards and flung to the deck.

The man drew back the grating and looked round.

"A good throw, mate, eh?"

"Bravo Ned!" cried the other, as he sprang to his feet. "Hold tight, and we've got him safe."

"He won't get out of that noose, never fear," said the swarthy sailor, whom Jack had not observed at the wheel, and who, letting go the spokes, had seized a rope with a running noose, and by a dexterous throw, had lassoed Jack and brought him down.

Jack still grasped the iron bar, but he was powerless to use it.

The man whom he had threatened stooped and tore it from the youth's grasp.

"I'm a tarnal mind to lay your skull open with it, youngster," he said, "as you meant to lay mine, and I would, too, only the captain don't want you killed."

Jack made no reply.

He knew that he was again at the mercy of his foes, and was silent.

"Here, mates," cried the man who held the rope, as three or four of the crew came trooping up to the deck, "bear a hand here. The ship's drifting out of her course, with no one at the wheel. We've got one of them safe enough."

The men soon realised that Jack had got on deck and been made prisoner.

Into their hands the rope was surrendered, and the steersman sprang to the wheel.

"Where's the captain?" asked one.

"Below here," replied the man with the bar.

"Don't he know that the youngster's on deck? Call to him."

The fellow leant over the hatchway.

"Ahoy! below there," he cried. "We've got him."

Two of those who had gone down came bustling up.

"Got them both?"

"We've got that Rough and Ready Jack," was the reply.

"And not the stowaway?"

"What, the kid we saw run across the deck and dive down the companion?"

"Yes; and we can't find the beggar. But what's to be done with this one?" asked one at the rope.

"I'd like to fling him overboard," said Bob. "He's played thunder and fury with the captain and Sharp, and the youngster has shot Will Burt."

"Shot him?"

"Yes."

"The deuce! But see what's to be done with this one, and we'll hunt out the other."

Bob went below and in a minute he returned.

"Keep him tight," he cried. "I'll be back in a jiffy."

And he ran along the deck, dived down the companion-way, and dashed into the captain's cabin.

"Thunder and fury!" he yelled, and made a grab at Joe, who had emerged from his place of concealment beneath the mattress as soon as he heard the searchers retreating.

But swift as lightning Joe slipped under his arm, and, seizing the door, sprang into the passage, pulling the door close after him and turning the key in the lock, which was on the outside.

"Yah! Copped you," cried Joe. "Did it slick; and you thought you'd copped me."

And then he ran along the passage, dashed into Sharp's cabin, and shut the door behind him.

For a moment, surprise held Bob dumb.

Then he gave utterance to an oath and seized the handle of the lock.

"The whelp," he cried, "I'll flay him alive!"

The door would not open.

"Hang it, I'm trapped," said Bob. "And I may holloa for a blue moon before they'll hear me on deck. I'll have to force the door; but, first, where's the handcuffs?"

He looked around the walls of the cabin, and then he opened a box at the end of the bunk.

"Ah, here they are," he cried, as he dived his hand into the box and brought out a pair of manacles. "Now to get out of this. With these irons on his wrists, and his legs again under the bolt, I don't think Rough and Ready Jack will be able to use his fists so easily."

He looked round for some weapon with which to force the door, but saw nothing.

"I'll have to kick it open," he muttered, and raised his foot, but lowered it as he suddenly remembered that with his knife he might force back the lock.

Unclasping the stout blade, he inserted it behind the bolt of the lock, and, after several ineffectual attempts, he succeeded in prising back the bolt.

Flinging open the door, he sprang into the passage-way, and glared around in search of Joe, but failed to see him.

So great was his rage at that moment, that could he have seen the stowaway, it is more than probable that he would have plunged his knife into his body.

Muttering a terrible oath, he turned and went up to the deck.

Meantime, Joe, who had again been so nearly captured, looked about him for some place to hide, or means of escape.

He did not think it advisable to again try the mattress.

"They'll guess how I did 'em afore," he said, "and they'll cop me for sartin."

Looking down as he spoke, Joe saw there was what appeared to be a trap in the floor.

He stooped down, and seeing a small iron ring let into the trap near the edge, he gave it a pull.

Up came the trap with a jerk.

Beneath it was a small ladder.

Joe rushed to the door and listened.

He could hear no one.

Returning to the trap, he got onto the ladder, and descended its few steps.

The light through the trap enabled him to make out what sort of a place he was in.

It was not very large—in fact, not larger than a couple of the cabins put together, and the open barrels and boxes it contained showed him for what purpose it was used.

"It's the cupboard they keeps their grub in," said Joe. "S'elp me 'tater! what a blooming fine place to hide."

He rushed up the steps and pulled down the trap, lowering it to its former position with his head as he descended again.

The place was now as dark as a dungeon.

The boy had got into the lazarette, but whether he would ever get out again he did not know.

When Bob reached the deck the others had lifted Jack to his feet.

"Pull his arms behind him," said Bob, "and I'll soon make them no use to him."

The fellow closed his knife and opened the manacles.

Jack saw that resistance was useless.

Any attempt at such a thing would only add to the violence already offered him.

Slackening the noose a little, but so keeping it that one jerk would pull it tight again, they seized his arms and forced them behind his back.

Then Bob slipped the manacles on his wrists and snapped them.

"Now, lads, take him below and finish him. Give me the bolt. I'll bet a month's grog he don't get from under it again."

"Don't make too sure of that," replied Jack, as he was forced onto the steps and down the hatchway. "My time will come yet, and then look out."

"Shut your mouth," said Bob, "or I'll shut it for you."

"You can be brave now you're in no danger," replied Jack. "Bah! I despise and defy the lot of you."

They forced him down the steps and onto the floor of the hold.

Bob slipped the bar over Jack's legs and into its socket, then, taking the key, locked it.

"There, captain, he's tight enough now," he said.

Sternway, whose expression was that of a fiend, took a step forward as the others drew back.

For some few moments he looked at Jack in silence, then he thundered out—

"Jack Tempest, I hated you before, but I *hate* you a thousand times worse now. Did they offer a thousand times more to me to spare you as they did to blight your life, I swear I would not accept it. I swore to have vengeance before, but I'll have a double, aye, a treble vengeance now. Mark my words, and remember them well, Rough and Ready Jack."

CHAPTER XXI.

JACK AND BOB—THE ROUGH SAILOR COMES TO GRIEF—JOE APPEARS ON THE SCENE—CHANGING PLACES—IN THE BOAT.

ROUGH AND READY JACK smiled contemptuously.

His danger he knew was great, but his heart never failed him for one moment.

He believed his time would come sooner or later.

Ralph glared at him for a moment, and then, feeling as if he could not trust himself longer in the lad's presence without plunging a knife in his heart or shooting him through the head with a pistol, he ordered his men to help Sharp to his cabin, and carry the wounded Will Burt to his bunk in the forecastle.

But first of all he scrambled up the ladder, his face swollen, and his whole body aching.

Bob and his companions half led and half carried Baxter Sharp up to the deck, and in a short time returned for Will Burt.

He being taken up, the hatch was closed, and Jack was once more alone and in darkness.

He had borne himself bravely up to now.

But now there were none to gaze on him, and his heart sank within him.

"What hope for escape is there for me now?" he thought. "None, none!"

He began to feel his temples throbbing, the smarts of his wounded ear and shoulders, and with a groan he lay back on the deck upon his manacled hands.

"They will keep their word," he muttered; "they will carry me to some place where they can sell me into slavery—into a living death. Oh, my poor mother, heaven grant that you may never know the fate of your loving son."

He closed his eyes for a time, and tried to think.

"Ah!" he muttered, "there is someone in this villainy besides Baxter Sharp and Ralph Sternway, or what did this scoundrel sailor mean by being paid for taking me away from England. But who can he be? I have made no enemies but these two men, and then only through defending a poor honest girl from their insults and violence. Yes, there must be someone else who has had a hand in this vile business; but who is he, what is he, and what can be his motive?"

Jack Tempest asked himself this question but pondered long and deeply to discover an answer to it.

But all in vain, and worn out at length with pain and anxiety, he fell into a deep slumber.

When he awoke a lantern was held over his face, and the voice of Bob Burton was in his ears.

"If you want grub, here's some for you," he said. "But if I had my way on board this craft, may I be slung up at the yard-arm if I wouldn't let you starve to death!"

Jack tried to raise his body, but his arm on which he had lain was so benumbed that he was unable to do so.

"If you are going to have these rations, get up!" cried Bob kicking Jack in the side. "I ain't going to wait down here long, I tell you."

"Beast!" said Jack.

"Get up, I say!" cried Bob, giving him another kick.

Jack made a struggle to do so, and fell back with a groan.

"I cannot," he said. "My arms are paralysed."

"And so would your heart be, my beauty, if you'd only got me to deal with," said Bob, brutally, "for I'd crush out what life in it you have got, may I never break a biscuit again if I wouldn't."

"You are bad enough for anything," said Jack, as he tried again to rise.

Bob seized Jack by the hair and pulled him up into a sitting position.

"You mongrel cur!" said Jack. "And you call yourself a British sailor!"

"Shut up your mouth, or I'll dab something in it you won't like," said Bob. "Here's your grub; are you going to have it, or ain't you?"

And he kicked the tin pannikin that contained a kind of thick soup, on the top of which some pieces of broken ships'-biscuits were floating.

"How can I partake of anything with my arms manacled behind me?" asked Jack.

"I'll undo them while you feed, if you'll only keep a civil tongue in your jaws," said Bob, putting the lantern down on the floor, "and promise that you won't cut up rough. If you don't, then I'll pour it down your throat, if I scald it; for the captain says he won't let you die, you'd fetch too much as a slave, and he wants you to live to make his revenge on you the more bitter and terrible."

"I promise," said Jack.

"You do?"

"Honour," replied Jack. "But there, what does such a thing as you know of honour?"

"If I don't know much about it, I care less," growled Bob.

"For the first time in your life I should imagine you had spoken the truth," sneered Jack.

"Stow your gab, will you?"

"When I please," replied Jack. "Don't like to hear an honest man's opinion of a blackguard, and perhaps a thief, do you?"

"You'll go too far if you don't mind," growled Bob.

"Not so far as I shall go someday," replied Jack.

"What do you mean?"

"That I will yet hang you like the dog you are."

"Hang me?"

"Aye, you."

"You are mad!" cried Burton. "You'll only be too glad to get the chance to hang yourself soon."

"We shall see. Time will show," cried Jack, calmly, and pointedly.

There was something in Jack Tempest's words and manner that caused Bob Burton anything but a pleasant feeling, and, with an oath, he unlocked the handcuffs and then whipped a pistol from his pocket.

"You don't get another chance," he said, "so while you swallow your wittles I'll keep your head well covered with this pop-gun."

Jack's hands and arms were terribly benumbed, and it was some few moments before he could grasp the pannikin and convey it to his lips.

Burton took a step back so as to be out of reach of Jack's hands.

"Just look alive," he said, "I ain't going to stop here long, I can tell you."

"You can go now," said Jack, "I don't want you. Your room is better than your company."

"I ain't going till I've put the irons on again. Once bit, twice shy."

"Then keep your talk to yourself, and let me finish this miserable meal in peace and quietness. I'm not in the habit of conversing with curs, thieves, and vermin."

The soup was very hot, and it was only in short sips that Jack could take it.

"You howling hound," yelled Bob, "who are you calling vermin?"

"You, if you like, and your captain and associates into the bargain."

"You'd better not do it again."

"Why?" asked Jack, coolly.

"Because if you do I'll cut your other ear open with the butt of this pistol."

"Dog, thief, vermin!" said Jack, boldly.

With a yell the fellow turned the long pistol in his hand, and sprang forward.

"Halt!" thundered Jack.

"SHE HALF AROSE FROM THE COUCH AS JACK ENTERED."

No. 5.

With a yell of agony the man recoiled with one hand pressed over his eyes as he received Jack's order to halt, and the nearly scalding contents of the prisoner's pannikin was thrown fairly into his face.

Smarting and blinded with the hot liquid, Bob was unable to see, think, or act, and in the agony he endured he let the pistol fall to the floor, and danced and swore frantically.

At that moment Jack felt he had another chance of escape, but he could not take advantage of it.

He tried to reach the pistol, but it was too far off.

Bob tried to grope his way to the stairs and summon help, but as he reached them his leg was jerked violently from off the lowest step, his forehead came in contact with a crash upon an upper one, and he rolled back into the hold, stunned, blinded, and bleeding.

"It's only me, Master Jack. Don't be frightened."

"Joe!" gasped Jack.

"Yes, Master Jack, it's poor Joe; I've been a-foxing him. He's the cove as had the key of that bar, and if I don't get it from him, may I never sweep another crossing. S'elp me 'tater, here it is! Now I'll have you out of it, Master Jack, and we'll put this fellow in it. Oh, what a blooming spree when they find you've changed places, and that we've got clear off!"

"But, Joe, how can we escape?" asked Jack, as Joe lifted up the lantern to see how to unlock the bar.

"They had a boat lowered to do something to the stern of the ship, and it's left there, held by a rope. I foxed 'em out of a room there, where they keeps their grub. There's a window big enough to get out and drop into the boat, and it's so dark they couldn't see us. There you are, sir. Now help me put him here."

Jack, released, rose, and he and Joe dragged Bob under the iron, secured it over his legs, and then, aided by the lantern, went to the lazarette.

In another minute Jack and Joe were through the window and into the boat.

"Rather," said Jack, "the mercy of wind and wave than that of Ralph Sternway and Baxter Sharp!"

CHAPTER XXII.

AT THE MERCY OF THE WIND AND WAVES—RALPH STERNWAY MAKES AN UNPLEASANT DISCOVERY.

THE line that held the boat was cast off without attracting the notice of the steersman or any of those on deck, and the little vessel fell behind the ship which, under full sail, ploughed her way onwards through the gloom.

The darkness was only lit up by the phosphorescent glow on the waves, and the little vessel pitched, and tossed, and shivered, while its two occupants were ever and anon covered with spray.

But neither spoke for some time.

They were only too glad to remain silent, lest the wind should carry the sound of their voices to the ears of their foes.

There was a sail in the boat, but Jack had little knowledge of how to handle it, whilst Joe had less.

There was also a pair of oars and a boat-hook, but Jack resolved that while the darkness remained, he would trust the boat entirely to the will of the waves and the wind.

They strained their eyes through the blackness in search of the ship, but her white sails had disappeared.

The castaways knew not where they were, or in which direction they were being driven.

"We must leave all to chance and Providence, Joe," said Jack.

"I suppose we must, Master Jack; though it does seem as if it meant to pitch us out into the sea every minute. Oh! there's a mouthful I got, and don't it make your eyes smart?"

"Yes, Joe; and that last lot is running down my back and the legs of my trousers. It won't be long before we'll have to bale her out, Joe."

"What's that?" asked Joe. "Did you say bail her out?"

"Yes; empty the water out of her, Joe," replied Jack.

"Lor'! I thought you meant bailing somebody out of a police-court."

"There are no police-courts hereabouts, Joe."

"Pity there ain't."

"Why, Joe?"

"'Cos we might have landed them fellows in one."

"They'll get their deserts some day, Joe, whether we live to know it or not," said Jack.

"Hope they'll get 'em hot, then, Master Jack," said the boy. "Oh, s'elp me 'tater, what a lark it will be when they find out we've sloped, and left that Bob Burton in your place. Oh, I know I'd die a busting when I seed the captain and Sharp a looking as if they couldn't believe their own eyes, and a swearing and a raving like mad. Oh, won't they swear, Master Jack, rather!"

"You may depend they will, Joe," said Jack. "I only hope that we may not have the misfortune to fall in with the ship again."

"Perhaps we may with another, sir."

"I hope so, Joe, and that before long, for we have nothing to eat and drink, and have no knowledge of how to handle the boat."

"I never thought about the grub," said Joe, "but now I'll be sure to do it, and feel hungry."

"We will trust in Providence, Joe. Day will soon be breaking, and we do not know what the light will reveal to us."

"Wish it was here now, Master Jack," said Joe, holding on tight to the gunwale as the boat was lifted high on the crest of a wave, and then went plunging down into a perfect chasm between the waves.

"Don't be frightened, Joe."

"I ain't frightened, I'm only a little bit afeared," replied Joe. "Oh, ain't the water jolly salt and bitter!"

"Yes, it is not pleasant to the taste, Joe."

"Nor yet to the feel," said Joe. "My face and hands seem hard with it."

"It's anything but a comfortable position to be in, but it's preferable to being a prisoner on board the 'Poisoned Arrow,'" said Jack.

"With such bullies as Ralph Sternway."

"And his cowardly friend and companion in crime, Baxter Sharp."

"I hope you'll be able to let him have it, someday, Master Jack."

"I shall not fail to punish him severely if ever I do get the opportunity," said Jack.

Then they both lapsed into silence, and gave themselves up to thought.

Slowly and wearily the hours dragged on.

The wind grew cold, and they shivered in their wet garments.

But neither Jack nor Joe uttered any complaint.

They knew it was useless to do so.

The black clouds turned to iron-grey —dawn had come.

Jack watched the clouds as they grew lighter, and then turned his gaze over the ocean.

No land, no sail in sight.

Before, behind, and around them, a grey, heaving sea.

They were indeed alone.

"Anything but a cheerful lookout, this," thought Jack, but he said no word.

Joe had curled himself up on the wet sail, and had sunk off to sleep.

"Poor fellow," muttered Jack. "if something does not come to our aid soon, he'll only wake to hunger and misery."

It was just before dawn that the watch changed on board the "Poisoned Arrow."

Ralph Sternway came on deck, with his face partially enveloped in bandages.

His temper was none of the best, and seeing that one of the men was absent from his post, he thundered out—

"Where's Bob Burton?"

The others looked round, to also miss their messmate.

"Skulking, I'll swear," growled Ralph; "go and cut the lashings of his hammock, and that will teach him to turn out another time."

One of the men proceeded below to obey the captain's order.

He was an ill-looking, ill-tempered brute, ever ready to play some trick upon his fellows, and as he went down into the forecastle, he opened his jack-knife.

"I'll let Bob down by the head," he said.

Stealing along softly, he reached the hammock in which Bob usually slept.

In the darkness he did not see it was untenanted, and, drawing his sharp knife across the lashings, he made for the steps.

Down came the hammock to the deck, but the sound the grinning scoundrel waited for came not.

In a moment he realised there had been nothing in the hammock but its blankets.

"He must be on deck," he muttered, and ran up the steps.

"Bob's not in his berth, sir," he said to Ralph.

"Where in thunder is he, then?" roared the captain.

"On deck, I should fancy."

"Then where's he skulking?"

And Ralph set off to search over the deck.

No one had seen Bob, and now more than one remembered he had not been seen since he went below on the night before.

Ralph gave utterance to a terrible oath.

"Search the hold," he cried. "Take a lantern and search the hold."

A lantern was soon procured, and Ralph, with two men, descended into it.

"Thunder and fury! what is this?" roared Ralph, as he held up the light.

"Why, its Bob himself," was the surprised reply.

The three men gazed upon Bob, whose mouth and nose were terribly swollen, and whose hands were manacled.

"What's it mean?" roared Ralph. "Where's that cub, Jack Tempest?

Who put you there? Speak, or I'll dash your brains out with this lantern!"

"I don't know," said Bob. "Something knocked me down on the steps, and that's all I know till I found myself here like this."

"And Rough and Ready Jack, where is he?"

"I can't tell, for I don't know," replied Bob.

"Search the hold, while I get this fool, or traitor, out of this," said Ralph. "Fetch him out of his hiding, and don't spare him. Knock him down, kick his brains in if he resists. He's hiding somewhere, so keep your eyes peeled or he'll land you before you are aware of him."

So fierce was his rage that, having unlocked the handcuffs from Bob's wrists, he hit him across the head with them.

"You hound, I believe you have been playing me false!" he cried.

"It's a lie," roared Bob, smarting under the blow.

"Call me a liar," thundered Ralph.

"If you say I've been playing you false, I say you are one."

In his anger he was about to strike Bob again with the irons, when a cry from the other two men caused him to turn.

"Have you got him?" he cried.

"No, the fellow's clean gone," was the reply.

"Gone! What do you mean?"

"Come here and see, captain. He's got into the lazarette and out of the window into the boat left astern last night, and the boat's gone, too."

Ralph shrieked in his rage and fury, as he saw how Rough and Ready Jack had escaped from the ship and his and Baxter Sharp's power.

CHAPTER XXIII.

THE STRANGE SAIL—THE SIGNAL—JOE'S FEARS—THE COMING BOAT.

THE sun came up out of the sea like a huge red ball, and soon afterwards Joe awoke.

He sat up and looked round him in a dazed sort of way for a few moments, and then he fixed his gaze on Jack.

"Oh, Master Jack, and I was having such a pleasing dream."

"Were you, Joe?" replied Jack. "I am sorry, then, that you woke out of it."

"I was dreaming I was going to have a jolly good supper off bake 'taters and faggot, and just as I took a long sniff at the faggot blowed if I didn't wake up."

"Well, I'm sorry that I have not got such a luxury to offer you for breakfast."

"I feel mortal hungry; the sniff of that faggot made me feel peckish," said Joe.

"And we haven't even a biscuit, Joe," said Jack sadly.

"If we could catch a fish we might eat it," said Joe.

"But we have no means of catching anything but a cold, my boy. I wish to Heaven we could see land or discover a ship in sight, so long as it wasn't the 'Poisoned Arrow.'"

"What's that over there, Master Jack? Oh, it's only a black cloud."

Jack looked.

"Yes," he said, "that's all, I fancy. If I knew which way to go I would put out the oars, Joe, and we'd try to pull the boat to where we might get help."

Jack sighed.

He felt more for poor Joe than he did for himself.

The sun rose higher and higher and grew brighter and more yellow, till at last it seemed to hang like a ball of burnished gold in the sky.

"Ah! look, Master Jack! What is that?" cried Joe, excitedly.

And he pointed over the side of the boat.

Jack shaded his eyes and gazed long and earnestly.

"By Heaven, I believe it is a ship!" he cried.

"Hooray!" shouted Joe.

"Whether it is or not we shall soon know, for I've stood on the beach and watched them rise, as it were, out of the sea; but, even if it be one, it may be the very one to which we wish to give a wide berth, Joe."

"Ralph Sternway's ship?"

"Yes."

Joe's countenance fell, the hopeful look died out of his eyes, and he sank back with a sigh.

"Don't get down-hearted, Joe. Let's both trust in the kindness of Providence to send us friends instead of enemies."

"I don't want to say nuffin agin Providence, Master Jack; but I don't think it cares much for such as we. Polly used to say, you trust in Providence, Joe, and it will help you; but I nearly always found what help I got was from a slop's hand or foot."

"Joe!" said Jack, deprecatingly.

"Well, Master Jack, I ain't telling no story. I never was much account like other people, and perhaps that's how it is that I always got more kicks than ha'pence."

Jack's gaze was fixed on the the masts and sails of a vessel that seemed to be running in parellel lines with the boat.

Every minute her rigging seemed to rise higher and higher out of the water, till at last her dark hull was visible.

Joe, too, had been intently watching the vessel.

"That ain't the 'Poisoned Arrow,' for a penny," he said.

"How can you tell, Joe?"

"She'd got a big white band on her side, underneath her deck," replied Joe.

"Are you sure?"

"Yes, I am, Master Jack, for I see it myself when I peeped from under the sheet in the boat when they was taking you aboard."

"I am glad you noticed that, Joe, for now I will not hesitate in trying to make them see us."

Jack stood up on the thwart of the boat, and taking off his silk neckerchief, waved it over his head.

He would have shouted, only he knew his voice could not be heard at so long a distance.

But the minutes flew by, and no responsive signal came from the ship.

"They do not see us, Joe."

"Perhaps they don't want to," said Joe. "They're all right themselves, and what do they care for such as us!"

"Don't be uncharitable, Joe," said Jack. "They may possess the kindness of heart, and yet not know of our distress and position."

"You wouldn't think that, Master Jack, if you'd run after one and another, telling them as how you'd not any grub for a long while, and seen they pretended not to see or hear you, and kept their eyes staring straight before them all the while. No, sir, because you have got a good heart yourself, you think other people are like you, but I knows they ain't, though I am but a kid to you. You may twist your arm off a-waving that han'kercher, but they'll look t'other way, see if they don't."

Suddenly Jack saw what appeared to be a child going up the ratlines, and two or three figures clustering together at the side of the ship.

Higher and higher went the figure up the ladders, pausing every now and then to look in their direction, while he held on to the shrouds.

After a time the figure descended, and joined those at the side.

Jack still continued to wave the kerchief.

"You may as well save yourself the trouble, Master Jack," said Joe.

"Not so, Joe, for I can see the vessel is changing its course," replied Jack.

"How can you see that?" asked Joe.

"Because her masts and sails gradually get closer together. Don't you notice it, Joe?"

"Well they do seem to be doing so," replied Joe, watching the ship intently. "Well it's a rum go, Master Jack, for now they've all gone into one."

"No, they are still as far apart as before, Joe. The ship has been brought round, either because they have seen us, or have found it necessary to alter her course, and she is heading directly towards us."

"Ah," said Joe, "when they do see us, they'll turn round and go the other way."

"No, no, Joe. They would be less than human if they did that," said Jack.

"I hopes as how you won't see I'm right, but I knows what a lot of unkindness there is in the human heart, for I've seen it too often."

"It would be considered a crime, Joe, for them to refuse us aid if they see us."

"Then there's a lot of 'em as gives way to it," said Joe.

"Poor fellow," muttered Jack beneath his breath. "The world has treated him harshly, and he can scarcely believe there is any good in it."

But there could be no mistake now that they had been seen.

There was a flash, a puff of smoke rising up to the rigging, and the report of a gun came to their ears.

"Lay down, Master Jack," cried Joe, pulling at Jack's trousers. "The beasts are trying to shoot you."

Jack burst out into a loud laugh.

Jack, when his laughter had ceased, said to Joe—

"You silly boy."

"But I tell you they are, Master Jack," cried Joe, excitedly.

"Not so, Joe; they fired that gun to let us know that we had been seen."

Joe could not believe it.

Finding Jack would not sit down, he burst into tears.

"Oh, Master Jack, they'll kill you, and then—"

Jack sank down beside him, and put his arm round Joe's neck.

"You silly little fellow," he said. "What they did was out of mercy to us. They knew how anxious we must be to learn if they had seen us, and fired the gun to inform us that they had, and were coming to our aid. If they had intended not to succour us, they would have kept on their way, and by now we should have been out of sight."

Joe seemed but half convinced.

"I hopes as how you won't find out you're wrong, Master Jack," he said, as he wiped his eyes on his wet and ragged sleeve.

"There, look, Joe; they are laying back the sails!"

"What's that for?"

"To stop the ship as far as possible," replied Jack.

"Then how are they going to save us?"

"Watch and see," said Jack. "They are lowering a boat."

"What for?"

"To pick us up and carry us to the ship, to be sure. Come, Joe, dismiss all your fears now; we shall be rescued and given food. There, look! there comes the boat. Hurrah!"

But Joe could not echo this cry, for he could not wholly dismiss his fears.

As the boat came nearer, it became apparent that it was manned with Oriental sailors, for the sun shone full down on their swarthy faces as they bent to their oars.

"They're blackymores," said Joe.

"They are our friends and saviours, be their colour what it may," said Jack; "and, heaven be praised, we shall not be doomed to a lingering death from starvation on the wide and open sea."

These he placed on one of the boxes and made signs for Jack and Joe to drink it. Then he again left them.

In a few moments he returned, bringing with him some biscuits, meat, rice, and dates, which he placed before them.

Jack and Joe were well set, and fell to with a will.

After they had eaten their fill, Jack was taken up to the deck alone, led aft, and down the companion to a cabin, the door of which was partly opened.

Jack was ushered into this, and a cry of surprise almost burst from his lips as he found himself in the presence of the captain and a vision of female loveliness such as he had never before seen.

CHAPTER XXV.

THE BEAUTIFUL INTERPRETER—JACK'S DELIGHT AND JOE'S FEARS—THE SHIP ON FIRE.

HALF sitting, half reclining on a couch was a young girl in a Moorish costume —a silk tunic, gold-braided muslin trousers, and a pearl-embroidered, silk brimless hat.

She wore no veil, and her features would have been a model for a sculptor.

A smile played in her bright black eyes and round her exquisitely chiselled lips as she half rose from the couch on Jack entering the cabin, and then sank back into her former attitude.

Jack bowed lowly to her and then to the captain, but he felt terribly embarrassed as to what he should say.

But to his surprise the girl spoke to him in English.

"I pray you be perfectly at ease, sir. My father who speaks no other language but his own, has requested his daughter, myself, to act as interpreter."

"I am delighted, lady, to learn that I have now the means of making myself understood to this gentleman and those on board this ship, who so kindly rescued me and my unfortunate companion from a watery grave, or a lingering death from starvation."

"And I am glad that I shall be able to do so. I have spent several years in Paris and in London, and have thus been able to acquire the language of each country. And now, tell me, so that I may repeat to my father, how it came about that you were found tossing on the waves in a small open boat?"

Her manner and tones invited confidence, and Jack resolved to tell all.

While he related his story he kept his eyes fixed respectfully upon her face.

He observed the look of surprise, the expression of amazement as she listened to the recital of the adventures through which he had passed, and when he told how he and Joe had forced his jailer to take his place in the hold, she clapped her hands and laughed aloud.

Deliah, for such was the maiden called, then turned to her father, and in his own language, intrepeted what Jack had said.

When she had finished he stepped up close to Jack and took him by the hand.

Then ensued the following speech, interpreted by Deliah—

"Young Englishman, I am happy to be of service to you. I have received many kindnesses at the hands of your countrymen, both on sea and land. My ship is bound for the port of Mogadore in Morocco, where I shall leave my child, now returning to her home after years of absence. There we may perhaps find an English ship in which you can return."

"I thank you," said Jack, "but, meanwhile, I should be glad to perform any duty that might enable myself and companion to requite at least some of that kindness you have shown and are so willing to extend to us."

"The difficulty in the way of that is that there is none here save myself who can understand you. Besides, the voyage is by no means a long one," said Deliah.

Then after addressing her father, who smiled as what she said to him, she again spoke to Jack;

"What is your name?" she asked.

"John Tempest," was the reply.

"And that of your felllow voyager?"

"Joseph Jilks."

"Well, Monsieur John, would you be willing to wait upon myself and father, and render us any little services we may require till we come to anchor at Mogadore?"

Jack's handsome eyes lighted up.

"I should be delighted," he said.

"Then, Monsieur John, since you have the pride and independence with which your countrymen are so richly endowed, you shall work for your food and passage."

This she said with a look and a smile that caused Jack's heart to give a sharp throb, and he felt at that moment that he could have laid down his life for her sake.

"Your services shall commence after the morning meal to-morrow. Now you require rest." Then she added to her father, in Moorish, "Will you summon Muley, and bid him make these English-men as comfortable as possible?"

The captain went to the door, called to someone without, and, turning, was followed by the sailor who had brought Jack into the cabin.

"Muley will attend to your wants," said Deliah. "To-morrow I will find you something to do."

"There is nothing you can ask of me, if I be able to do it, but what I will gladly perform."

And, with a low bow to the fair girl and her father, he followed Muley from the cabin.

"S'elp me 'tater, Master Jack, I was getting orfully worrited about you when you was down there for such a long while."

Jack smiled.

"I began to be afeard they was making up their minds to chuck us both into the sea."

"Why, whatever could lead you to imagine such a thing, Joe? I have received nothing but kindness at the hands of the Moorish captain, and his lovely daughter."

"What!" said Joe, opening his eyes wide, "you don't mean to say as how there's a blooming girl on this ship, do you?"

"Yes, and she is one of the loveliest creatures I have ever gazed upon!" said Jack, enthusiastically.

"As pretty as Polly Peters?" said Joe.

"A thousand times more beautiful, Joe," replied Jack. "I have never seen her equal in my life."

Joe looked quizzically up at him for a moment, and then he jerked out—

"Well, I'm blowed! A gal—and prettier than Polly, and Polly is pretty enough for a duchess, that she is."

"There are different kinds of beauty, Joe," replied Jack. "Poor Polly's features were pretty and fair, but the lady I have seen is a lovely brunette."

"Brew what, Master Jack?" asked Joe.

"A brunette—her eyes and hair are dark as midnight."

"And her face?"

"Why, dark in complexion, of course, Joe," said Jack.

Joe blew a long, low whistle.

"Well, I'm jiggered," he said, "I never could have believed such a nice young gentleman as you are would go and fall in love with a nigger gal."

"She is not a negress," cried Jack, angrily, "and if you can get a chance peep at her, Joe, you will say she is even more beautiful than I have described."

"Oh!" said Joe, heaving a sigh, "it is all up with poor Polly now."

"What do you mean, you foolish boy?" asked Jack.

"Ah, Master Jack, you know as everybody knowed, you was sweet on Polly. Didn't you give that Baxter Sharp that lovely mouse for talking to her?"

"I struck the rascal for offering insult to a defenceless girl, Joe. Polly was nothing more to me than any other woman."

"Well, people said as how you was sweet on her, sir."

"What people?"

"Some of those who see you give Sharp and Sternway that licking."

Jack felt vexed, but still he could not help laughing.

"Joe, hold your tongue, and don't be foolish. Now tell me, what have you been doing while I have been with the captain?"

"Nearly making myself sick a-eating of them dates," replied Joe, "but they do taste spiffin, don't they? But I say,

Master Jack, do you know what they're going to do with us, and where they're going to take us to?"

"To Morocco the ship is bound, and there we may find an English vessel, on board of which we may be able to obtain a berth or return to England."

"Then you don't think these nigger-looking chaps mean to do us any harm?" asked Joe.

"I am sure they do not. Though they do not know what we say, or we they, yet they have shown us nothing but kindness hitherto."

"That's it, Master Jack. If they'd swored at us for coming here a-eating their grub, I'd been a little less afeard of their little game. You knows how a fellow soft soaps you over when he wants to borrow some money that he never means to pay you back, and how nice and innocent he tries to look when he pinches your ticker. I'm a-fly to some of the dodges, though I am but a poor iggerant kid what's lived in the Dials."

"Poor fellow, you have as yet only seen the worst side of human nature."

"And the biggest side, too," Master Jack.

"I hope that now, Joe, brighter days are in store for you, and that you will see more of the other side. There are thousands of good people in the world, though you may not have met them. Now there's Polly, you know, Joe."

"Ah, but, Master Jack, she ain't a human gal," said Joe.

"Not human?" said Jack.

"No, sir, that gal's a angel in disguise, and don't I know it? Who but Polly would let me doss on the landing outside her door, when I hadn't got threepence for a bed?"

At this moment a voice above them hailed the deck, and the chief officer, who had been pacing up and down, sprang into the rigging.

Following his gaze, Jack saw a sight that blanched his cheek, and caused him to utter a cry.

"Oh, what is it, Master Jack?"

"A ship on fire, Joe. May heaven help all on board of her!"

CHAPTER XXVI.

A GIRL'S APPEAL RESPONDED TO—THE RAFT—THE RECOGNITION.

A SHIP on fire is a thing that strikes terror to the heart of sailors at sea.

The Moors pointed, gesticulated, and chattered in quivering tones and with trembling lips.

As yet the unfortunate vessel was so far away that her hull was scarcely visible.

But the smoke that rose in huge clouds here and there, penetrated by tongues of leaping flame, showed what a hold the fire had got upon her.

The commotion brought the captain upon deck.

He did not come alone, for with him was Deliah, her figure wrapped in a long cloak.

A dozen hands pointed out the ship to the captain.

"Can nothing be done for them?" the girl asked.

The captain shook his head sadly.

Joe stood by Jack's side in speechless admiration for some few moments, and then he said, as the sinking sunlight lit up the girl's face—

"Oh! what a stunner."

Jack looked round at him.

"Is that her?" asked Joe.

"The lady I spoke of? Yes, Joe, that is she," was the reply.

"She's all you said she was, Master Jack. She's spiffin, and no mistake."

"Hush, Joe, she may hear you!" cried Jack, clutching his arm.

"If she does, what's it matter? She won't know what I say."

"But she will. She understands English. It was only by her aid I was able to converse with her father."

"Then I'll shut up," said Joe. "But ain't they a-going to do something to help the poor fellows on that ship?"

"As they were so willing to aid us,

you may be sure they would if they saw any probability of doing so," replied our hero.

"And why can't they?"

"That vessel is a long way off, Joe, and before we could reach her she will be burnt to the water's edge."

"Yes, but won't they get away from her in the boats?"

"They will try, you may be sure, whoever they are, and of course we might pick them up; but no aid that I could see can save the ship from destruction."

"Don't you pity them?"

"Of course I do. For I can well understand the agony they must endure."

"But if it was the 'Poisoned Arrow,' Master Jack?" asked Joe.

Jack did not reply.

The girl had been all this while talking excitedly to her father, receiving in reply only ominous shakings of the head.

Jack could see the tears welling to her eyes.

Evidently she was trying to induce her father to send to the rescue of those on board the flaming barque, and was pained to hear that he felt powerless to render any assistance.

Night was coming on, and the flames grew brighter and more numerous.

Jack, in his excitement, gradually got nearer and nearer to her.

"Can nothing be done to aid them, lady?" he asked, at length.

"My father says it is impossible, and so it must be, for he would not deny my prayer if he dared to comply with it," was the reply, in pained tones.

"Might I presume to ask what the prayer is?" said Jack.

"That he would have every available boat lowered and sent toward the doomed ship, so that if he could not save her, he might, perhaps, save human lives. But Captain Hamed, I fear, allows himself to be overruled by Seyd, who tells him the men would never go on an errand of which nothing but disappointment would come."

"I am no judge of distances at sea, or how long a ship or boat would take to reach yonder burning vessel," said Jack, "but she really seems near enough to be able to offer assistance."

"She is full twenty English miles away, and in this wind and on this course we do not sail more than six miles an hour," said the girl.

"And the boats, lady?" he inquired.

"Would depend upon the vigour of those who went in them."

"I am sorry, then, that nothing can be done. But surely, lady, something might be attempted?"

"I will speak to my father again," she said.

"One word, lady, before you do so," said Jack.

"Yes—but be quick."

"If whatever services I and my fellow Englishman can give might prove of any avail, you may tell him that he can command them, and we will be only too happy to obey his orders."

Deliah gave the handsome youth a grateful smile, and said—

"I will tell him."

For some few moments she remained in excited discourse with the captain and his chief officer, Seyd, then she turned to Jack.

"My father and Seyd both protest that nothing can be done, but if I can induce some of the crew to set out for the burning ship, and that you are willing to go with them, a boat shall be lowered."

"Would I had the power to induce them," said Jack; "but, alas! I know not one word of their language."

"Then I will appeal to them," she said, quickly.

And she turned to the men who were watching the burning vessel.

What she said Jack did not know, but her impassioned tones assured him that she was appealing to their feelings and their manhood to help those who were sure to be in such dire distress.

At last Muley stepped in front of his companions.

A moment after, five of his messmates advanced to his side.

Then the captain, who had been watching and listening, gave an order, and the men flew to lower a boat.

Soon she was in the water, and the men descending over the side into her.

"May I go?" asked Jack.

"Yes."

"And my companion?"

"Yes; and may you succeed in cheering those who, I know, have little heart for the work—not that they are bad or indifferent, but that they consider the attempt is useless."

"If we save but one life, lady, we shall have earned a glorious reward," said Jack.

"Go, and Mahomet be with you," cried the girl.

Jack lowered himself into the boat, and Joe was quickly by his side.

Then the boat was pushed off, the mast was steeped, and away she went, scudding in the direction of the burning ship.

But the sun had gone down into the waters now, and darkness was above and around them.

The vessel, however, continued to burn, and they made for that terrible beacon.

The men put out their long sweeps, and bent desperately to their oars, but their progress was slow, though the Moorish ship was soon left behind.

In about an hour the flames had burned themselves out—the tar and canvas no longer fed them. The rigging had been consumed, and only the hull, seen as the boat rose upon the waves, remained a seething furnace of fire.

"Oh, Master Jack, isn't it grand, but isn't it awful!" said Joe.

"It is, indeed, and I fear we shall be able to do no good."

"Oh, what is that? I can see something out there, sir, can't you?" cried Joe, rising and pointing.

Jack strained his eyes into the gloom.

"Look—look!" he cried; "there—there!"

The Moors ceased to row, and looked in the direction indicated.

Then they began to talk all at once, and brought the boat round with the aid of their sweeps and rudder, the excitable Joe being prostrated across the knees of Jack as the wind caught the sail round and knocked him down.

"Are you hurt, Joe?" asked Jack, in excited tones.

"I reckon I'll have a bump on my head as big as a cow cabbage," replied Joe; "but what's it matter, Master Jack? I'm only a poor orphan."

And Joe sat up and rubbed his head with both his hands.

"You'll know better when we get more used to boats and ships, Joe," said Jack.

"I thought I knowed something about 'em."

"Why, where could you learn, Joe?"

"In the puddles, when the broad beans was in," replied Joe. "I used to get hold of the shucks, and stick 'em open with a bit of wood, and set 'em afloat when the slops wasn't looking."

Jack burst out laughing.

"Oh, Joe, you are a caution," he said.

"And so would you be if you'd been cautioned to move on and hook it as often as I've been; but, so help me 'tater, Master Jack, that 'ere's something with a lot of people on it."

It was evident the Moors thought so, too, for they set up a loud shout, and encouraged each other to renewed exertion.

The shout was replied to, and the two parties gradually drew nearer together.

As they approached, a lantern was flashed, and those in the boat could see that a number of persons were on a raft.

"They must have escaped from the burning ship," said Jack; "but who and what can they be?"

"That's what I was a-going to ask you, Master Jack, who and what are they," said Joe.

An answer to this question came in a few minutes, when the raft and boat touched, and Jack's heart gave a wild bound as he heard the harsh voices of Ralph Sternway and Baxter Sharp.

CHAPTER XXVII.

DESTRUCTION OF THE " POISONED ARROW "—AN UNEXPECTED MEETING—A
VILLAIN'S THREAT.

IT was the " Poisoned Arrow " which had been burned at sea.

Enraged at the escape of Jack and the probable loss of the five thousand pounds which Hugh Wentworth had promised for the certainty of Rough and Ready Jack never being permitted again to set his foot on British soil, the men gave themselves up to drinking.

Nor did they stop at this.

They accused Bob Burton of having aided Jack to escape, and that worthy, smarting from the blows he had received and maddened by the liquor he had managed to possess himself of, knocked Sharp down, a no very difficult matter, considering the punishment he had undergone during the last few days.

This led to Ralph Sternway striking the sailor with a belaying-pin, when some of the crew took sides with Bob, and in a short time there was a scene of riot on board.

Some of the crew broke into the liquor store, and helped themselves to the rum and brandy which it contained.

Drunkenness soon reigned from one end of the ship to the other, and, at length, one of the men, maddened with drink, said that he would set the vessel on fire, and burn all on board.

This threat was treated with derision by the rest, but whether by accident or design, in a short time the ship was found to be in flames.

The discovery sobered the men as if by magic, and all set to work to keep down the flames, which were leaping and roaring in the hold.

Ralph Sternway and even Baxter Sharp did all in their power to extinguish the fire, but, in spite of all their efforts, the flames gained upon them, burst through the hatchways, and swept over the deck.

Now it was evident that the ship was doomed to destruction.

The fury of drunken madness gave place to despair, and loud cries were raised to seize the man who had threatened to destroy the vessel and roast him alive in the flames.

But he could not be found above, and none dared now venture below.

Soon the flames had seized upon the rigging, and the fiery tongues went leaping up the sails and cordage, till the men, driven again to desperation and despair, were willing to listen to the orders of Captain Ralph, for his had now become the coolest head amongst them.

The flames had seized upon the boats, and escape by them was therefore now impossible.

Ralph ordered that everything that could be saved from the devouring element and which would float should be lashed together, and that a raft should be constructed that might assist them in saving their lives.

The men set to work with the energy of despair, and just as darkness closed over the ship, a roughly-constructed raft was launched from the burning and smoking side, and with but a few kegs of water, a barrel of biscuits, a lantern and a compass, the men went on board of it.

They pushed off, for their position was becoming extremely dangerous.

Masts cracking, and spars snapping, fell crashing on the deck, or went hissing into the sea.

The smoke, too, at times was blinding, while sparks fell around them in myriads.

" This is a pretty go," said Ralph, as he watched the burning ship from a safe distance. " I believe it's a punishment on me for listening to your suggestions, Baxter Sharp, and having anything to do with that whelp, Rough and Ready Jack."

" You were only too glad to listen to them and engage in the dirty work," retorted Sharp.

" Silence ! " cried Ralph, fiercely.

Baxter Sharp knew that he was no match in strength for the man who had aided him in his villainy, so he wisely held his tongue.

The flames went slowly down, and the raft floated away in the darkness.

The men who had drunk and fought but a short time before, stood, sat, and lay in silence upon the frail work of their hands, which, if a gale arose, would part into a dozen sections, and hurl them all to eternity.

But help was nearer than they imagined.

They had not sighted the Moorish ship.

Indeed, they had had no time to look around them.

Every thought, every energy had been necessary to subdue the flames, in which one, if not two, had lost their lives, whilst all had lost their belongings.

Will Burt, lying wounded in his bunk, had perished, but whether Black Peter, the fellow who had threatened to fire the vessel, had perished or escaped, none could tell.

Certainly he was not on the raft.

Suddenly a cry came floating to their ears, and everyone sprang to his feet. Ralph, with a little difficulty, lighted the lantern, and flashed it over the waves.

Again came the shout of many voices, and louder than before.

"Saved, saved!" cried Sharp. "Hurrah! we shall be saved."

"Shout, men," said Ralph. "There is a boat near us."

The men did shout, and with all the power of their lungs, for a gleam of hope, almost of thankfulness, had come with those shouts to their hearts, while Ralph waved the lantern round his head to show the position of the raft.

Soon they discerned the boat, and urged the raft as well as they could towards it.

When they touched, Baxter Sharp, with a cry of joy, clutched at the boat's gunwale.

"Saved, saved!" he cried, and sprang from the raft into the boat.

As others attempted to do so, the rowers repulsed them, and, by the aid of the light he held, Ralph, though he could make nothing out of what they said, saw by their motions that they were willing to take the raft in tow, but its occupants must still remain on board of it.

Ralph could see that they were Orientals, and that they could not understand each other, but suddenly catching a glimpse of a figure in European habiliments, whose face was turned away from him, he cried—

"Can you, there, speak English?"

"Yes, Ralph Sternway." cried Jack, turning quickly, "and so you will find to your cost."

Baxter Sharp uttered a cry as Jack's voice fell on his ears.

"Rough and Ready Jack!"

"And the man who will hunt you, Baxter Sharp, to a felon's doom."

"And here's one as will have a hand in that little game," said Joe. "When we gets you on board our vessel you'll find there's a dozen police a waiting for you."

"Look here, youngster, what vessel is it?" said Sharp.

"Oh, you'll find out when you gets to it," replied Joe.

"Retribution has soon overtaken you," said Jack. "Though had I imagined for a moment that it was the 'Poisoned Arrow' in flames I would not have implored its captain to come to the rescue of such a shameless pair of cowardly villains?"

By this time the raft had been made fast by a rope to the stern of the boat, which, by the manipulation of the sail and tiller, now headed for where they believed the ship would be found.

"Had I a pistol I'd send a bullet through you!" hissed Sharp.

"Don't threaten," said Jack, "or you may feel my fist again. You are soon played out, Baxter Sharp. I did not expect my turn would come so soon."

Ralph Sternway was so surprised at this unexpected meeting that for a time speech appeared to have been denied him.

He felt a cold sensation pervade his frame, and he seemed half inclined to sever the rope that held the raft and float away in the darkness.

Then he shook off his fears and laughed hoarsely.

"Jack Tempest," he called out, "you think it is your turn now, don't you? But you'll find yourself mistaken. For firing a ship at sea there is not a sailor, English or foreign, who would not strike at your life or liberty. We all here can swear that, when you stole our boat, you set fire to the 'Poisoned Arrow.'"

"SAVE ME! I AM THE DAUGHTER OF MUBAL HAMED," CRIED DELIAH."

No 6,

CHAPTER XXVIII.

ENEMIES ON BOARD—JACK ENTERS UPON HIS DUTIES; HIS SURPRISE AND DISGUST.

JACK felt a cold chill pervade his frame, and his heart sank.

Would the villain Sternway denounce him as the cause of the destruction of the 'Poisoned Arrow,' and would Baxter Sharp and the crew swear to this lying accusation?

"It is true!" cried Ralph, "as every man here will swear. You set fire to my ship, and then escaped in a stolen boat."

"You villain!" said Jack.

"Ha, ha!" said Ralph, "you thought you had got me, but it strikes me I have got you."

And Ralph laughed triumphantly.

"I only wish you could reach him, Master Jack," said Joe, "so as to knock him off that raft."

"Let the villain do his worst," said Jack. "I defy him and all his scoundrelly crew."

Then, turning upon Baxter Sharp, he said—

"And that is your game, is it, you dirty mongrel? You will back him up in his villainy, will you?"

"I didn't say so," said Sharp.

"No, you cur; for you know that I would knock you out of the boat, if you did."

"I want nothing to say to you," said Sharp.

"Of course not, because here we are equal. I've half a mind to hurl you into the sea and cut the raft adrift."

"You are not captain of the boat," said Sharp.

"A good thing for you and your villainous companions I am not," replied Jack, "or I would leave you to the mercy of the wind and waves."

A blue flame was now seen, and the Moors, giving a cheer, steered towards it.

They were burning a blue light on the ship so as to show its position.

By the aid of oar and sail the boat soon came up with the ship.

Lieutenant Seyd hailed those in the boat, and soon learned how matters stood.

The raft was secured alongside, and the occupants clambered from it to the deck of the vessel.

Then Baxter Sharp was motioned to ascend.

As he rose to do so Jack laid his hand on the villain's arm.

"Now I give you fair warning," he said. "If you attempt to play any of your dirty tricks upon me or this poor boy, it will be the worse for you. You know me, Baxter Sharp, and you had better be careful, so be warned—and beware."

Baxter answered not; but, seizing a rope, hauled himself on deck.

Joe followed, and then Jack.

The captain and his officer received them in silence, and when the boat's crew had come on board, and the boat hoisted up, the raft was cut adrift.

The men were taken below, berths provided for them, and food placed before them.

Deliah had retired, and so no questions could be asked till the morning.

Jack and Joe were forced to share the forecastle with their enemies, as there was no help for it.

They did not fear personal violence at the hands of their foes, and so went off to sleep, and slept soundly.

The ship still ploughed on her way, and, after breakfast, Jack attended the cabin to commence his duties.

The captain received him with a haughty bend, and Deliah with a bewitching smile.

"And so, Monsieur John," she said, "you are prepared to perform your new duties?"

"I am at your command, fair lady," he said, as the captain left to go on deck. "What is your will?"

"That you sit down and tell all about those poor fellows you rescued last night, and also about the destruction of their vessel, for, of course, you have learned all about it."

Jack sat down as she requested.

"Lady," he said, "I have a surprise, doubtless, for you. The vessel which you saw burning last night was the very one from which I and poor Joe escaped, but the cause of the destruction of the ship I am unable to inform you."

"The same vessel from which you escaped?" she said.

"It was none other; and the only enemies I have in the world, as far as I know, are now on board this ship."

"Then I am sorry I pleaded so hard with my father to send a boat to their relief."

Then she added quickly—

"And yet it would have been inhuman not to have done so. But they will be powerless to harm you here."

"I hope so, lady."

"My father is not one to allow it," she said, "and I will speak to him when he comes down from his duties. And now, Monsieur John, fetch me my slippers."

And she pointed to the far end of the cabin where they reposed.

Jack sprang up, brought them to her, and placed them in her hands.

"Monsieur John, I do not wear slippers on my hands," she said.

Jack did not reply.

"I thought you— But there, I see that I must teach you your duties."

And she gave him a tap on the head with one of the embroidered slippers, and then flung them to the floor.

Jack looked at her half surprisedly, half questioningly.

"Pardon me, lady, if I do not perform my duties as you wish."

She held up her small foot a couple of inches from the floor, and said—

"Place them, sir, where they should be worn."

Jack eagerly seized the slippers and placed them on her feet, and then, with his face flushing, he rose and stood before her.

Sitting down upon the couch, she pointed to a guitar that hung upon the wall of the cabin.

"You shall sing and play to me one of your English airs," she said.

"Lady, I cannot play," replied Jack.

"Not play?"

"Indeed, no, for I never learned to do so," he answered.

"But you can sing?" she asked.

"Only in such a manner that you would be pained to hear me," Jack replied.

She looked at him quizzically for a few moments, and then asked—

"I suppose you have learned to read?"

"Oh, yes, I have had a fair education," he replied.

"I brought with me a few French and English books to amuse me on the voyage, but had scarcely looked at one of them; you shall read one to me."

"I shall be delighted to do so," said Jack.

She opened a desk and drew forth a book, which she handed to Jack.

Jack took it with a bow and opened it.

Our hero started and looked quickly up.

"Lady, do you know this is a Bible?"

"Of course I do."

"I thought—I imagined—that—that you—" he stammered.

"You thought that I was an Infidel, I suppose?" she said, with a smile.

"I thought, lady, that you were a Mahometan."

"And so I am," she said, "but is that any reason why I should not hear the Bible of the Christians read?"

"Not if you wish to," replied Jack.

"Then I do wish, so sit down and begin," she said.

"At what part shall I commence?" asked Jack.

"Not at the end, but at the beginning," she said. "I was not aware that Christians read their books backwards."

And she pointed to the book, which Jack had unconsciously turned upside down in his hand.

Jack blushed red and turned the book.

"Now take your seat and begin. But first make me a cigarette, so that I may smoke while I listen. You will find the tobacco in that box."

"Smoke?" said Jack, looking at her in surprise.

"I presume you have no objection to my doing as I please?" she asked.

"Pardon me, certainly not," cried Jack, laying down the book and going to the small inlaid box she had pointed out to him.

Jack opened the box and found paper and tobacco within.

He rolled a cigarette and procured a light for her to ignite it, and, as she blew the smoke through her lips, Jack muttered to himself—

"She is loveliness itself, but, ugh! that destroys half her charms."

CHAPTER XXIX.

A NIGHT OF HORROR AND BLOODSHED—A BASE REWARD FOR NOBLE SUCCOUR.

JACK was about to commence reading, when the captain entered the cabin.

He looked at Deliah.

"Monsieur John, I will release you for awhile. Return when you hear the sound of this gong," and she pointed to a small gong that hung on the wall.

Jack rose, bowed, and left the cabin.

Deliah then informed her father who those were he had taken on board his ship.

Captain Hamed's smile died out as she informed him of what Jack had told her.

"This is bad," he said. "I believe they have set their vessel on fire."

"For what reason?" she asked.

"To get the insurance," he replied. "It is often done, my child. I will have a close watch kept upon them, for I like not the looks of them. I noticed how they signalled to each other with their eyes; two or three of them whispered together as though they feared their words would be heard and understood."

"Do you think they will try to injure John? You have heard it was those who carried him away on their ship."

"I think so, but I will bid my men keep a watch on them, for I have taken a great liking to the young Englishman. His face is open, and I believe his heart is true, and since there is nothing like work to keep men from plotting mischief, they shall labour on the ship, and John shall tell them what to do."

"But John is no sailor," she said.

"True, my child, but I will give my orders through you to him. We shall soon now enter the Straits, and we will put them ashore as soon as we reach Mogadore."

"I think that, were I you, I should make prisoners of them till we reached port," said Deliah.

"That I could not do."

"Not under suspicion of having wilfully fired their vessel?"

He shook his head.

"We have no proof that they did so, and I dare not act on suspicion," he replied.

"I fear they will but sadly hamper your crew," she said, "for as neither can understand the other, confusion, and perhaps danger, will arise from setting them to work with your men, but I would have a strict watch kept upon them."

"You are perhaps right, my child. The Prophet be praised, we shall not have them long on board."

Jack waited a long while for the gong to sound, but it did not do so till some minutes after the captain had gone on deck to consult with his chief officer.

"Keep a good watch on these strangers, Seyd," he said, "I like not their looks. They may be better than I think they are, but it is always best to be careful whom we trust."

Seyd promised to do so, and also gave the crew a hint to watch them narrowly.

Jack fulfilled the duties assigned him by his young mistress greatly to her satisfaction.

He rolled her cigarettes, put her slippers on her feet, read to her, and performed every order cheerfully and respectfully.

Neither the captain, Seyd, nor any of the crew saw anything to lead them to adopt severe measures with Ralph, Baxter, or the crew of the "Poisoned Arrow," but could they have understood their whispered words they might not have been so much at their ease.

Ralph and his crew had been on board some days, and Joe, by his antics, standing on his head, throwing handsprings, and capering about the deck, had become a general favourite with the Moorish crew, though not one could understand him, or he them.

It was just as they entered the Straits that Ralph and Baxter for the first time caught a glimpse of Deliah.

She had come on deck with her father, and broke upon their gaze like a vision of loveliness.

Ralph plucked at Baxter's sleeve.

"Thunder! what a beauty," he whispered.

"The loveliest I ever saw in my life,"

replied Sharp. " I'd give all I hope to get from Wentworth to secure her for my own."

"And so would I," said Ralph ; " so I tell you that you will have to be content with Polly, if you can ever get the orange girl again in your power, and leave this Moorish maiden to me. Ah, you may frown, Baxter Sharp, but I tell you that, if we succeed to-night, that girl is mine."

" Perhaps," he said, meaningly, and turned away.

" You dog, beware," hissed Ralph.

Baxter only replied by a scowl.

" Now I can guess why that Jack Tempest is everlastingly down with the captain in his cabin. He has somehow or other wormed himself into her good graces, and perhaps, like me, has fallen head over ears in love with her, so my revenge on him will be all the greater. Oh, how I hate the whelp ! "

And he ground his heel on the deck.

Deliah had heard from her father and Seyd of the antics of poor Joe, and she bade Jack request him to perform his tricks for her amusement.

Jack sought out Joe.

" Joe," he said, " the beautiful lady wishes you to stand on your head, and throw wheels and dance for her amusement. You'll do it to oblige her, won't you ? "

" Would a cat collar a bird ? " said Joe. " Rather. Tell her I feel proud."

"Then now, as she is looking this way, begin."

" Just give us room, Master Jack, and I am on," said Joe.

To the delight of Deliah Joe went over and over on his hands along the deck.

Then he stood on his head and clapped his bare feet together, and finished up his performance with a double shuffle in the most approved London Arab fashion.

By this time Joe was perspiring from head to heel.

" Blow it, but I am jolly hot," he said. " But didn't she seem to like it ! "

Deliah laughed heartily, as, indeed, did all else save Ralph Sternway and Baxter Sharp.

They knew what they owed to the poor waif, and they ground their teeth as they inwardly vowed to pay the debt.

" He'll laugh the other side of his mouth before long, I reckon," muttered Ralph, " aye, and you, too, Jack Tempest. Both of you little guess how soon your joys will be turned to misery and and your smiles to tears."

Night came—a dark night, with every indication of a storm coming on.

The wind whistled ominously through the cordage, but otherwise all was silent.

Seyd had command of the deck, but in a short time the watch would be changed and the captain take his place.

He stood leaning against the rail, looking down at the waves as they rolled by, when suddenly his legs were seized, and he was jerked over the rail, and fell with a cry into the sea.

The man at the wheel heard the cry, and peered eagerly into the darkness.

As he did so a knife was buried in the back of his neck and he fell forward across the spokes.

In a moment, he, too, was seized and hurled over the stern into the sea.

Then dark figures crept forward, and one by one the watch were stabbed in the back and their bodies dropped over the sides.

Then, with naked feet, three men strode aft.

" Now for the captain," hissed one, " and the ship is ours."

It was Ralph Sternway who spoke, and his companions were Baxter Sharp and Bob Burton.

" But those below ? " asked Baxter, in tremulous tones.

" I have made sure of them," Ralph said.

" They cannot get up on to the deck ? " whispered Sharp.

" No fear of that till I let them come," was the reply. " But close your mouth now ; at the slightest alarm the captain will be prepared with scimitar and pistols, and it would be better for him, and perhaps for us, too, if he were put out of his misery in his sleep."

They reached the companion and stole softly down it.

Just as they reached the bottom a door opened and a stream of light was thrown across the darkness, and into this stream of light issued the figure of Captain Hamed.

For a moment he stood there, and then, as he caught sight of Ralph, he uttered a cry and sprang back.

His hand reached out for his scimitar that hung upon the wall, but, with a terrible oath, Ralph rushed forward, and his knife was buried to the hilt between the captain's shoulders.

One loud shriek he gave utterance to, and then fell, weltering in his blood.

Scarcely had that cry died away, when an opposite door opened, and Deliah, pistol in hand, sprang forward.

As she beheld her father lying, with Ralph standing over him, she uttered a piercing shriek and fired.

The bullet missed Ralph, but buried itself in the brain of Bob Burton, who fell like a log—dead !

Another shriek, and she hurled Ralph aside, and, flinging herself upon her knees, clasped her father in her arms.

"Murderers !" she shouted, " you have killed him ! but may I never find mercy on earth or in Paradise if I do not hound you to a murderer's doom !"

CHAPTER XXX.

THE STARTLING CRY—JACK'S FEARS—THE FORCED HATCH—THE DEADLY RECEPTION.

JACK, who lay half sleeping, half waking in his bunk, suddenly started up into a sitting position.

"What was that cry ? " he muttered. "Pshaw ! the scream of some sea-bird as it passed over the ship, nothing else, for all is silent now, and it does not appear to have awakened any of the slumbering men."

In the next bunk to him Joe was snoring audibly.

"I'm getting sleepless," said Jack. "now that Baxter Sharp and his villainous confederate are on board this vessel. But here they can do no harm to me, whatever they may seek to do when we get into port, which I believe will be but a short time now."

Jack grew more and more wakeful, and a sort of undefined dread stole into his heart.

"Hang it !" he said at last. " I'll dress myself and go on deck. I'm getting as nervous as a cat."

He got out of his bunk and quickly slipped on his clothes.

"Wish they would let me take a turn with the watch," he said, " and then I should sleep sound enough when we turned in, I'll warrant."

Putting on his shoes, he tip-toed through the bunks till he reached the foot of the ladder.

"If I cannot sleep myself that's no reason I should prevent others getting their well-earned rest. I'll just take a turn or two on deck and then come below when the watch is changed."

He went softly up the ladder.

"What a dark night," he said ; "why the gloom is Stygian. Hallo ! why, what does this mean ? "

Jack recoiled, for instead of stepping out on to the deck he struck his head a hard blow.

He put up his hand, to find that the hatchway was closed and fastened from without.

Our hero might well ask, " What does this mean ? "

Again and again he tried to force it, but in vain.

A cold perspiration broke over Jack's face and body, and he held on to the ladder to think.

Then he gave a start as a thought flashed through his mind.

"Perhaps it is a precaution taken against Ralph and his men by the captain and his officers, and the hatch will be opened when the watch is changed. It may have been secured every night for all I know, for I never wanted to pass through it before at this hour."

A lantern threw a dim light over the forecastle, as it swung to and fro on its chain attached to the upper deck, and he perceived that the bunk Bob Burton had occupied was empty.

This caused Jack to tip-toe to the others which had been given to the Englishmen.

One after the other he examined, but

all were unoccupied, though the bed-clothes had been so rolled up as to present to a casual observer the appearance of a body in repose.

Again that cold feeling came over Jack, and great beads of perspiration stood on his brow as he put that cry which had aroused him beside the fact that Ralph Sternway, his crew, and Baxter Sharp were absent.

Oh, how Jack wished then that he could make himself understood to the seven or eight Moors around him, how he could explain to them his suspicions of foul play, and get them to aid him to force a way on deck.

He touched Joe lightly on the shoulder with a trembling hand.

Joe gave a turn, and muttered in his sleep—

"Who are you a-shoving on? Sha'n't move on for you."

"Joe!" whispered Jack.

"Can't you let a fellow sleep without always moving him on? Got a feather bed yourself, bobby, and won't let me sleep on a doorstep."

"Joe! Joe!"

And Jack shook him more roughly.

"Eh?" said Joe, looking up.

"It is I, Joe."

"Master Jack?"

"Yes; but speak low, Joe."

"What's up?" asked Joe, opening his eyes with wonder, and clutching at his friend's arm.

"Joe, I have a terrible fear that something worse has happened on board."

"What, Master Jack?"

"I do not know. But I was awoke by a shriek, and when I went up to the deck to find out what it meant, I found that the hatch was fastened down, and, on coming back, that neither Baxter Sharp nor Ralph Sternway and his crew were here."

"Not here?"

"No, for all their bunks are empty," said Jack.

Joe sprang from his bunk and began hurriedly to put on his rags.

"What will we do, Master Jack?" he asked, excitedly.

"If I could but make these Moors understand my fears, I'd arouse them and force our way to the deck."

"Look here. You wake 'em up, and if they can't tumble to what you say,

I'll show 'em what you mean. But who did the cry come from?"

"I was but half awake, Joe, and for a time I thought it was the cry of a sea-bird as it flew over the ship."

"Couldn't been her as did it, could it?" said Joe.

Jack knew that he meant Deliah, and his heart sank within him.

"Heaven only knows!" he gasped.

"Well, rouse 'em up, sir," said Joe. "I'm 'bliged to be very careful how I put on these here togs, in case I spoils 'em; but I'll have 'em on as quick as possible."

Jack's fears were now joined with those of Joe's.

They had both had proof of the desperate natures of Sharp and Ralph, and felt that neither of them would stand at anything which might serve their purpose.

Joe aroused the Moors, who, thinking the watch had been called, sprang from their bunks with alacrity, and began hurrying on their clothes.

Then Jack, by gestures, tried to make them understand that the hatch was closed, and the men they had picked up from the burning ship were perhaps doing murder above.

Joe tried to inform them that he feared some ill had befallen their mates; but it was not till Jack had seized two of them and led them to the bunks which Sternway and his crew had occupied that the Moors could realise his meaning.

Then they grew wild with excitement.

They seized upon their long knives, thrust them into their girdles, and, with loud words and furious gestures, made for the ladder.

Up this they went, each thrusting Jack aside.

Jack and Joe followed them closely, though having no weapons but those with which Nature had adorned them.

The Moors brought all their force to bear upon the closed hatchway, and burst it open with a loud crash.

Then, with a yell, they drew their knives, and prepared to leap on deck.

As they dashed forward, there was a belch of fire, a stunning report, and five of the Moors pitched headlong over their companions into the forecastle.

The little carronade which stood on

deck, and which had never been intended for any other use than signalling, had been loaded with shot and pieces of iron, and its execution had been fearful.

Then the voice of Ralph Sternway rang out loud and triumphantly.

"Bravo, lads! Finish the rest with your pistols, but don't shoot Jack Tempest. The ship is ours, and that girl is mine!"

Jack sprang forward.

"Villain!" he shouted.

But, as his head appeared above the hatch, he received a blow upon it from a belaying-pin held by one of the sailors, and he fell, stunned and bleeding, down the ladder onto those who lay below.

The other three Moors hesitated a moment, and then dashed up the ladder, brandishing their knives; but, one by one, they were shot down, and only Joe remained unscathed.

What could a boy like him do against a dozen strong men?

He drew Jack farther into the forecastle out of reach of a shot from those above, and then he sank down beside him and wept aloud.

"I'm only a little 'un, and a poor orphan, Master Jack," he sobbed; "but you are the only fellow as has been kind to poor Joe, and if they've killed you, and they let me live, I'll be the death of that Ralph Sternway and Baxter Sharp."

Ralph turned to those around him.

"We want no carrion here," he said. "Go below, fetch up the dead and wounded, and fling them overboard, but spare Jack Tempest and that cub of a stowaway. We have got a better ship than the one we have lost, and, what's more gratifying, we've got once again in our power Rough and Ready Jack."

CHAPTER XXXI.

RALPH PERSECUTES DELIAH—HER INDIGNATION—IN DANGER—THE RESCUE—
JUST IN TIME.

RALPH STERNWAY's orders were quickly obeyed by his men.

The Moors were brought upon deck, and the wounded and dead were consigned to the waves with a brutality and inhumanity that was truly appalling.

Jack's head was bound up, and he was laid in his bunk, from which they knew he would be powerless to rise for some days, for the blow he had received was a severe one.

The captain's body had shared the same fate as those of his men.

Deliah had been made a prisoner in her cabin.

The ship was overhauled from stem to stern, and was now worked by English instead of Moorish seamen.

A considerable amount of booty was discovered on board, and Ralph found himself a richer man than he had ever been before by many thousands of pounds.

Yet his sordid heart craved for more.

He would sail for Morocco, and sell Jack and Joe for slaves.

Then he would return to England and demand his reward of Hugh Wentworth.

In his pride he almost ignored Baxter Sharp, and had he not thought that his presence would be necessary to obtain from Wentworth the thousands offered for the disposal of Jack Tempest, he would have hurled him overboard.

But even Baxter Sharp was too valuable to sacrifice.

He snubbed him, though, on every occasion that he could, till at last that amiable young man began to regret the hour that he had ever leagued himself with such a villain.

Means were found of disguising the vessel, which was re-christened the "Victory," and, worked by English sailors and flying the English flag, she sailed into the Mediterranean.

Then it was that Ralph Sternway found time to think of love.

Up till now he had not persecuted Deliah, but he determined either to woo or force the beautiful Moorish girl to his arms.

He tried to alter his usual rough appearance as much as possible, and unceremoniously entered her cabin.

Deliah, who was sitting weeping on a couch, sprang up at his entrance and confronted him with a look of mingled horror and aversion.

"What, you are still crying for your father," he said, brutally. "Here, just wipe them eyes of yours and listen to what I've got to say to you. It's no use pretending as you can't understand me, because I know you speak our lingo."

She turned from him with disgust and loathing.

"Murderer!" she said.

"No hard words," said Ralph. "Remember I am the captain here, and that this ship is mine."

"Obtained by blood and villainy," she said.

"Never you mind that. I tell you I'm master here now, and that you, like all the rest, have got to obey me."

"Obey you, vile assassin!" cried Deliah, her eyes flashing with indignant fire; "I'd sooner obey the veriest slave that ever worked in chains than such a monster."

"I can take a lot of cross words from a woman," said Ralph, "but don't go too far with me."

"You dog—you mean—" she said, boldly.

He sprang forward and seized her wrist.

"Dog, am I?" he hissed; "then beware my bite."

"I defy, despise and loathe you," she exclaimed. "And now, you English cur, let go my arm."

"When I please, my dainty miss, and not before," he said. "You've got to listen to me, and you'd better do it quietly."

He gave her such a look that her heart quailed in her bosom.

"Yes, you've got to listen to me," he added.

"There is nothing such a wretch as you can say to me but what would fall like poison on my ears, you contemptible Englishman."

"Nevertheless, you'll have to listen," said Ralph.

"Release me, you hurt my arm," she cried, giving it a sudden twist and wrenching it from his grasp.

"Well, my beauty, if you don't like my hand on your arm, I'll put it round your waist while we talk."

"Stand back!" she cried, fiercely.

"I shall have to cool your hot blood, it seems. You have a strange way of receiving a lover."

She looked him up and down for a moment, with such a gaze of contempt and disgust, that any other man than Ralph Sternway must have stood abashed.

"A lover—a murderer!" she gasped.

"Never mind the past," said Ralph. "We'll only talk of the future now."

"If you have one spark of mercy still left in your callous heart, you will take your hateful presence from me and leave me alone in my sorrow."

"Can't do it, my girl," replied Ralph. "Haven't I come here to comfort you?"

"Comfort me!" she cried. "Callous-hearted villain."

"I ain't so bad as you think me," said Ralph; "if I had been, I'd have had you thrown overboard with the rest of them."

"Would you had," she replied, "for then I should have been out of my misery."

"I've come here to put you out of it," said Ralph, "for what's the loss to a girl of a father when she can get a husband, eh? and that's what I have come here to offer you. Will you accept me?"

She fell back in horror and disgust.

"Yes, for I tell you, Miss Deliah, I love you, and mean to make you my wife."

"Your wife?" she cried.

"Yes, mine."

"Coward!" she gasped. "I'd sooner be the wife of the most loathsome reptile than of such a heartless monster."

"Ah, that's what you say now, while you're out of temper, but lor', we shall be like two little turtle-doves after we've been married a week."

And he approached to throw his arms around her.

"Oh, heaven, can this thing be human!" she gasped.

"That I am," said Ralph. "I don't suppose I can palaver love to you like Jack Tempest would, but I can love you as much, if not more than he. Besides, he will never have the chance to get you.

So you had better make up your mind to be mine without delay."

"Never, villain."

"Never?" he sneered.

"By the beard of the Prophet, I swear it—never!" she replied.

"You may hang on to the Prophet's beard as long as you like, but I mean to have you in spite of his beard or himself either," cried Ralph. "If you won't give your consent, I'll have you without it. I've set my mind on having you, and I will, if I have to use force."

He sprang upon her and flung his arms around her, and before she could recover from the shock his lips were pressed to hers.

"Help, John, help!" she cried.

"He can never help you. Will you be mine?"

"Never—death rather," she shrieked.

"Then, by heaven, I will force you to my will, and then I'll sell you for a slave."

His hot breath fanned her cheeks, his strong arms held her powerless.

She was at the villain's mercy.

Her eyes swam with tears, her brain grew dizzy, and her heart seemed bursting.

"Ah, you have not thought of me!"

As Ralph looked up to see from whence the words had come, a blow fell upon his temples, a thousand stars flashed before his eyes, and his arms fell from around the form of the horrified maiden.

"That's one for your nob, you villain, and there's two for your heels."

And the iron bar that had already rendered him nearly insensible, fell with all the force of poor Joe's strength across the shins of the ruffian, and he fell to the floor with a howl of agony.

"I ain't got no beard, miss, like the Prophet, or I'd tell you to hold on to it, for you look as if you was going to fall," said Joe. "Lor', didn't I spoil his courting! Bless your life, miss, I never had such a fair smack at a fellow in my life—not even a policeman."

Deliah struggled hard to prevent herself from going off into a faint.

"Oh, don't you mind him now," said Joe; "he won't get up unless you help him, for I knows I won't; so you no need to think he can collar hold of you again unless you jest stoops down beside him."

"Boy," she said, with trembling lips, and holding onto the head of the couch, "how came you here?"

"Sneaked down, miss, and been a-foxing through the key-hole. I knowed as how he was up to summat, and I thought I'd spoil his little game, as Master Jack's too bad to get on deck."

"You have saved me from—"

"That 'ere willin; yes, miss. And ain't I proud of it!" said Joe. "But look out—quick!"

Joe seized Deliah by the arm and drew her down, just in time to save her from the bullet which the now half-recumbent Ralph fired at her.

CHAPTER XXXII.

BAXTER SHARP COMES TO GRIEF—THE ATTACK—THE CRY FOR HELP—DESPERATION.

THE sound of that shot, the only one that Ralph could fire, had scarcely died away, when another and louder one came bounding over the sea.

The next instant Baxter Sharp came tearing into the cabin.

"Ralph, Ralph—ah, what's this?" he cried.

"That!" said Joe, diving between his legs, and sending him flat onto his back.

Deliah clutched fearfully at the boy's arm.

"Ah, what is that?" she asked.

"A clean floorer, miss. Laid him on his back."

"You fiend!" cried Baxter, rising and clenching his hand.

"Get out. I don't fear you. I'm ready," said Joe.

"I'll kill you!" shouted Baxter.

Before Baxter could attack Joe, he lowered his head and made a stooping run.

His head hit Baxter fair in the stomach, and that worthy's heels flew up in the air, and the back of his head came with a thud on the floor of the cabin.

"Ugh!" he gasped out. "You young villain."

"Yes, it's me, and no mistake," said Joe.

"Kill him!" cried Ralph, "the wretch has crippled me."

"Sorry I can't buy you a pair of crutches," said Joe.

"I'll be the death of you!" growled Ralph.

"That's what the doctor said to the fellow as wouldn't pay for his medicine," said Joe.

Baxter Sharp sprang to his feet, and made a grab at Joe.

"You infernal whelp," he yelled, "I'll punish you!"

"Punish away!" said Joe, diving under the arm that was thrust forth to seize him.

But Joe, escaping Sharp, fell foul of Ralph.

"Now I've got you!" yelled Ralph, as he seized the boy's leg fiercely.

"Hold tight!" said Joe.

And as he spoke, he sat down quickly on Ralph's face.

A yell of pain burst from the smuggler captain's lips, and Joe, turning a sort of catherine-wheel, was up again.

Baxter made a grab at him.

But Joe was like an eel, and slipped away from him.

He then seized Deliah's arm and drew her towards the door of the cabin.

"Run!" he said.

"Captain, captain!" cried a voice, and one of the sailors came tearing down the stairs. "Halloa, what the dev— oh!"

"Beg pardon," said Joe, "didn't see you coming. Captain Ralph is in there, and wants to see you very bad indeed."

And with this he pushed past the sailor against whom he had run.

"Quick," he said—"I've got the wretched lot of 'em."

He pushed Deliah before him, then quick as lightning, Joe pulled the cabin door to and turned the key, which Ralph had taken care should be on the outside.

"Got 'em fast," said Joe.

Bang, bang!

Joe paused on the stairs.

"What's it mean, miss?" he asked.

"I cannot tell," replied Deliah, "but the firing must be from some vessel, or a fort we are approaching."

Joe crawled up, keeping hold of her hand.

Just as they were about to emerge upon the deck, there came a terrific crash, and huge splinters of wood went whirling into the air and fell upon the deck.

"Oh, heaven, we are attacked!" cried Deliah.

Joe drew her back a pace.

"Captain, captain!" cried a half-dozen voices. "Quick, quick! we are attacked by a strange vessel, and she's firing shot into us."

"Oh, lor'!" said Joe, what shall we do, miss?"

"What can we do?" said Deliah. "Oh, heaven! this is fearful."

Crash—and another shot sent the splinters flying in all directions.

"I wish I could take you to Jack, miss; but just you stay here, and I'll do a bit of secret service."

Deliah did not know what the boy meant, nor did she ask an explanation.

She did not attempt to detain him, and he bounded on to the deck.

As Joe went whirling over the deck, a ball cut the mainmast away and brought down spars, sails and cordage in wreck upon the deck and bulwarks.

Fortunately Joe escaped injury from the falling spars.

Not so others, for two of the men were hurled, stunned and bleeding, to the deck, and one man was carried over the rail with the falling mast.

Joe looked around.

A ship was bearing down upon them, the smoke of her gun rising in clouds over her deck.

As Joe gazed towards her a stream of fire poured from her side.

"Oh!" he yelled.

He was lifted high in the air and then he came down like a shot.

Not onto the deck, but through a huge opening in it and headlong into the hold.

Fortunately he fell upon something that gave way beneath him, or poor Joe would have no longer formed a character in this story.

Dazed, bewildered and shaken, Joe rolled off the object on which he had fallen.

The deck above him was torn away for the space of six or seven feet, and a flood of light streamed through the orifice into the hold of the vessel.

Joe was startled by hearing a voice near him.

"Oh, Joe, what does this mean?"

"Master Jack, are you there?"

"Yes. What does the firing mean? Is the ship attacked?"

"'Tacked," said Joe, turning to where Jack lay prostrate. "It's untacked she is being, for they're knocking every blessed nail out of her and sending the wood a-flying like winking."

"Is she a man-of-war, Joe?" asked Jack.

"I guess she ain't a man of peace," replied Joe.

"Is it an English ship?"

"Don't know, Master Jack, but it means fighting."

Bang—crash!

Again the timbers were sent flying in all directions, and, with the thunder of an avalanche, the spars came crashing on the deck above.

"Did you hear it, Master Jack?" said Joe.

"Heaven! yes," replied Jack. "Oh, that I could get up."

"You're safer here," said Joe.

"But Deliah?" gasped Jack.

Joe sprang to the opening, saying, "I'll find her."

Then he recoiled.

The steps had fallen and he could not reach the deck.

"Oh, Master Jack, and I saved her from that Ralph, and the coward Baxter Sharp."

"They have not dared to molest her?" cried Jack.

"Captain Ralph did, and I crippled him for it."

"You, Joe?"

"Yes."

"Heaven bless you, but—"

A loud shout caused him to pause.

Then came a trampling of feet, the report of pistols and the clash of steel, oaths and cries of agony, and the fall of bodies on the deck.

"Deliah," cried Jack, "oh, heaven! that I could shield or save her."

Soon a shout of triumph went up, loud and clear.

After this there was a momentary pause.

Then came a shriek in a woman's voice.

"Help, help! John, save, oh, save me! Oh, pirate, kill me, in mercy, kill me!"

As those words fell upon his ear, Jack made one tremendous effort, and sprang to his feet.

CHAPTER XXXIII.

THE ALGERINE PIRATES—BAXTER'S ACCUSATION—JACK'S DANGER—A SUDDEN APPEAL.

JACK and Joe managed to scramble on deck, where a sight fell upon their gaze that filled their hearts with horror and dismay.

Some fifty Algerines stood guard over the British sailors, whom they had disarmed, while in their centre was the tall, superbly attired captain of the pirate crew.

At his feet knelt Deliah, crouching in terror, while he held her wrist in his left hand, his right grasping his bared and gleaming curved sword.

In his silken sash were a dagger and two pistols, showing plainly against the crimson vest, around which the blue silken sash was tied.

He was about as fine a picture of manly form as could be met with.

His white teeth showed gleamingly under his long black moustache, and his black hair hung in short natural curls beneath his spotless turban.

Boots with silk embroidered tops reached to the knee.

His crew were all well attired, and a group of colour was the effect as they stood with their gleaming swords about the centre figures.

Ralph lay upon the deck, and Baxter Sharp seemed as though he was only being held up from falling by the two powerful Algerines who grasped his shoulders.

But a few fathoms off lay the pirate vessel while three of her boats rode closer, containing each a dozen oarsmen.

Jack took all this in at a glance, and then, dashing forward, he confronted the captain.

Jack's fist was upraised to deal the pirate captain a blow, when he was seized from behind, hurled to the deck, and a couple of curved swords held to his throat and bosom.

Joe also found himself in the grasp of a couple of the pirates.

"Let go, you beast!" he yelled.

While he spoke he struggled and kicked, and one of the pirates gave him a blow on the side of the head that set his face and ear tingling.

"Yah, you cur, why don't you hit one your own size?" yelled Joe.

"Silence, boy!" cried the captain, in good English.

Then looking down upon Deliah, he bade her rise and fear not.

The girl, with eyes streaming with tears, obeyed, and stood trembling before him.

She saw that Jack was a prisoner, and all hope of succour from him cut off.

She also saw that her persecutor, Ralph, the murderer of her father, was powerless to offer her further insult or harm.

But she stood sobbing and trembling before the pirate captain.

"Assuage your grief, maiden," said the pirate. "We war not with women, but with men. We love not blood for the sake of shedding it, though we will pour it out in rivers if necessity compels."

Then, pointing to Jack, he said—

"Let him rise."

The Algerines suffered Jack to regain his feet.

"Hark you, sir," said the captain, addressing Jack, "you seem the most likely to answer me truthfully. How comes it, then, that I find this, a Moorish ship, manned by Europeans? It is what your countrymen calls dog bite dog? Are you English pirates?"

"Oh, answer him truly," sobbed Deliah, "we are in his power, and dare not anger him."

"True, maiden, but that power shall be gentle if you and these men so will it, but if not there is a rope and a plank, without soiling our bright blades with the blood of fools. But as I said before, we war not with women. Suffer me to conduct you to your cabin, where away from the gaze of my men, you may compose yourself. Nay, fear not, for no violence shall be offered to you, I swear it. I swear it by the honour of Sidi Ashouri, the pirate, and the beard of the Prophet."

She looked up at him doubtingly for a few moments, and then placed her hand in his.

"I will trust you," she said, "and as you do with me, so may the Prophet do with you."

"I am content," he said.

And with all the grace of a cavalier he led her below.

"Maiden," he said, as he led her to the couch, "when you are more composed I will see you again."

And with a bow he left her and returned on deck.

He motioned Jack to be brought forward. This was done, and then, leaning gracefully upon his sword, he said—

"You are English?"

"I am proud to say that I am," replied Jack.

"Ah! well, all men should be proud of the land of their birth," said Sidi Ashouri.

"I do not think so," Jack said. "I should not be proud to belong to a nation of pirates and assassins."

For a moment the pirate's eyes flashed, and he half raised his sword.

But the fire died out of his eyes and the point of his weapon again rested on the deck.

"How is it I find a Moorish ship manned by Europeans, and a Moorish maiden on board?" he asked.

"Because her Moorish crew were murdered by these Englishmen, and only that poor girl's life saved that she might be tortured by a villain."

"And you tell me this—you, one of her vile crew?"

"I, a prisoner like that poor girl," replied Jack, boldly. "A prisoner of these men who have sworn to sell me and my young friend here into slavery."

The captain looked at him for a moment or two as if he would read his very soul.

The pirate captain pointed round at the prisoners and asked—

"Are you not one of these men?"

"No, I am not," answered Jack, "neither is this poor boy. We are captives, persecuted for a vile purpose of gain or revenge."

"It is false!" cried Ralph Sternway. "He is the man who induced us to rise against the captain and crew of this ship, that he might secure the person of Deliah, the captain's daughter, and embark upon an expedition of slavery and plunder."

"You villain!" thundered Jack.

And springing forward before he could be stopped, he struck Ralph so fierce a blow on the face that he fell like a log to the deck.

In a moment he was seized and dragged back.

Seeing him secure and powerless once more, Baxter spoke.

"It is not false," he cried. "We took you on board the 'Poisoned Arrow' from motives of pity and generosity, and how did you repay our kindness? By firing our ship and flying in a stolen boat, you and that boy there. Fortunately we were rescued by the captain of this vessel, who had previously taken you on board. But you told us that he had saved us only that he might eventually sell us into slavery. Keeping before us the horror of such a life, we listened to your proposals, and when you had struck the Captain Hamed down by a cowardly blow in the back, we, to save being murdered by her crew, fought and conquered, and thus the ship became ours."

Jack and Joe listened thunderstruck to this audacious story.

The pirate captain took their wonderment to be a proof of Baxter's assertion.

"The English," he said, "have a saying that 'Many a dog bites the hand that feeds him,' and now I believe it to be true. We cannot claim to be men of honour or of honesty, but we are not dogs to turn upon our benefactors. Run out a plank there. I thought him a brave youth, but I find he is one who stabs in the back."

"It's false!" shrieked Joe. "Jack Tempest is a gentleman, captain. Don't you go for to murder him."

The plank was run out over the damaged side of the ship, and as the captain turned upon Jack, Deliah hurried on to the deck and flung herself at the pirate's feet, crying—

"Mercy, mercy! Oh! have mercy on an innocent man!"

CHAPTER XXXIV.

THE APPEAL GRANTED—THE FINAL DECISION—NEMESIS CONFRONTS RALPH
STERNWAY AND BAXTER SHARP.

THE pirate captain looked down upon her for a moment, and then raised her gently to her feet.

"Would you ask mercy," he said, "for your father's murderer?"

"It is false!" she cried. "My father's murderer lies there."

And she pointed to Ralph.

Then turning to the pirate captain, she said—

"It is you who will commit murder now, if you hurl this young Englishman to death. Oh, captain, pirate though you are, you will not deny my prayer. Hear me, I beseech you. These eyes saw my father struck down, this hand levelled a pistol at the assassin's heart, but the shot went wide, and one of his base companions fell with a bullet in his brain."

The captain hesitated.

"Oh, you will believe me. Monsieur Jack is guiltless of either mutiny or murder. He was a prisoner in the forecastle, both he and this boy here. The others are the mutineers and the assassins, the murderers of my father and his crew, and yonder wretch the persecutor of myself. Oh, do not stain your hands with innocent blood, or hurl an innocent soul to perdition, lest the houris hide their heads in shame and the gates of Paradise be closed for ever against you."

Her clasped hands, her supplicating eyes, her pleading tones, had their effect, and the captain gruffly ordered the plank to be withdrawn.

When this was done, he said—

"The youth shall not die, nor shall any of the others, but the fate this young man said was intended for him and that boy shall be meted out to one and all. Nay, I have said, and will not be persuaded. I save their lives, but sell them all into slavery."

"Oh, mer—"

"Not a word," he cried, almost fiercely.

"And my fate?" she gasped.

"Is in your own hands," he replied.

"What mean you?" she asked.

"Of that we will speak when on our way to Algiers," he replied.

Then addressing his men, he cried—

"Convey your prisoners on board our ship, and see that they be well secured below. After which let all that is of use or value to us be taken out of this vessel and carried on board our own."

"And this ship?" asked one.

"Will be fired and burned to the water's edge. So set about your work at once."

"And you will make me a prisoner?" asked Deliah.

"Nay, maiden, you shall be my guest," he replied, "and, perhaps, something more, an you will."

She looked up at him through her tears.

"Ah, what mean you?" she gasped.

He bent his head down and whispered—

"My wife!"

She recoiled as if a serpent had stung her.

"It shall be as you will," he said. "I will not force you. If you come willingly, the life of a pirate's bride shall be yours, but if you refuse—"

He paused and looked hard at her.

"If—if I refuse?" she gasped.

"I will sell you for a slave, though your beauty will secure you a life of ease and luxury, I doubt not, in the harem of some wealthy Moor. But there is time enough before we anchor in the bay of Algiers for you to decide which life you will accept."

Deliah tottered and reeled for a moment, then clasping her hands over her eyes, she plunged down the companion-way and was lost to sight.

The captain smiled grimly and twisted his long black moustache as his gaze followed the retreating form of the Moorish maiden.

He little doubted which her choice would be.

He turned to issue orders to his men with a smile upon his face—orders which were at once obeyed.

Jack was led to the side and ordered into one of the boats.

Joe followed him.

As he placed himself beside Jack, he whispered—

"Oh! Master Jack, that gal's a brick. If it hadn't been for her we'd 'a' been at the bottom of the sea by this time."

"Don't talk now, Joe, my brain is in a whirl. Cruel fate seems to pursue us at every step."

"Perhaps we'll get a chance to bolt, Master Jack."

"From whom? From where? There are no back doors to a ship, my boy, and they'll keep too close a watch upon us to let us get away from them in a boat."

"Oh! I mean when they have sold us for slaves with that villain Ralph and Baxter," said Joe.

"Ah!" said Jack, "how the curs' faces blanched white with horror when they heard that threat of the pirate captain's; but think, Joe, of the terrible fate we will have to share with them."

But Joe, who could not realise the horrors of slavery, was not so cast down at the idea of such a life as his older and and better educated companion.

These men had made him tremble with fear, and, if they could have done so, would probably have thrown him overboard to perish in the waves, and now that they were powerless to harm him, he took a delight in tormenting them.

"I say, you fellows," he cried, "you won't look so white about the gills soon. I hopes as how they'll give me the job to paint you black afore they sells you for slaves."

Ralph turned to aim a blow at the boy, but Jack stopped it with his arm, and the ruffian hissed through his teeth—

"Oh, that I could kill you both!"

"BAXTER SPRANG FORWARD TO DEAL ARABI HIS DEATH BLOW."

No. 7.

The sailors thrust Ralph and Baxter into the bottom of the boat and, at an order from above, pushed the vessel away from the side.

Then one of the others drew up.

Into this the rest of the Englishmen were ordered.

When all had descended, together with several of the armed pirates, this, too, was pushed off and the third boat was brought to the ship's side.

Jack's heart gave a great throb as, looking up, he saw the pirate captain aiding Deliah to descend the side of the vessel.

Strong arms received her and placed her tenderly in the stern of the boat, and after some hurried orders to those left on board, Sidi Ashouri descended to her side.

"Give way!" he said. "We will first secure our prisoners, and then attend to our booty. Give way with a will, my brave comrades!"

CHAPTER XXXV.

ALGIERS—THE PIRATE'S LAST APPEAL—THE BEY'S SECRETARY AND THE MERCHANT'S DAUGHTER.

THE sun had risen and its rays lit up the towers and minarets, the mosques, houses, and forts of Algiers.

The bay looked like a sheet of molten gold, and reflected the ships and towers in its depths as in a looking-glass.

The city, white and still, lay beyond it, but here and there might be seen the fisherfolk on its banks.

Few would have fancied that this city and bay were the hotbeds of piracy and slavery.

Yet many Christians toiled in the city and surrounding country, who had been sold into slavery by those who had made them captive, and many a fine ship lying in the bay was a pirate of the most merciless nature.

The muezzin was calling the people to prayers.

"Come to prayers," was his cry. "It is better to pray than to sleep."

And by those who reside in the city of Algiers this invitation is generally accepted.

After their devotions the business of the day commences. The merchants to the bazaars, the fisherman to his net, and the labourer to his fields.

A vessel lying just opposite the fort now became alive with men.

Boats were lowered, a party of Algerines descended into them, followed by a number of Europeans, while a group of men on the deck kept them covered with guns.

The last to descend into one of the boats was a tall, handsome Moor and a veiled lady, and when these had taken their seats in the stern of the boat, the little vessels were rowed with long sweeps towards the shore.

In the foremost boats were Jack and Joe, besides Baxter Sharp, Ralph Sternway, and two English sailors.

As they had descended into the boats the pirates seized them and secured them together by the arms with cords, so as to prevent them throwing themselves into the bay, or in any way attempting to escape by sea or shore.

The centre boat contained the remainder of Ralph's crew, and the last only the rowers, the pirate captain, Sidi Ashouri, and the weeping Deliah.

"There is yet time, maiden," said the pirate captain, bending over the poor girl. "Will you consign yourself to a life of seclusion, when you may roam the seas with me, free as the sea bird that skims the blue ether and shrieks at his shadow in the waves."

A sob was the only reply she gave.

"Look," he said, pointing to the city, "once secluded in one of those flat-roofed houses of the wealthy Moors, you resign yourself to a prison, the bars of which you can never break, and be forced to profess to love some man, whose very presence may be repulsive to you, for remember you have travelled in lands where women are free and considered the equals of men. Again I say there is time to prevent this sacrifice. I love you—"

She held up her hand.

"Forbear!" she said. "I have chosen. A living tomb rather than a pirate murderer's wife."

"And this is your final resolve?"

"As unalterable as the law of the Medes and Persians," she replied.

"Then blame me not," he said. "Your fate now be on your own head."

"You have told me you love me," she sighed.

"And I have spoken truly."

"And yet you persecute me and keep prisoner the only man I have learned to love."

He ground his heel on the bottom of the boat.

"But for him," he hissed, "your resolve would have been different. But for him, I could woo you to my heart."

"Think it not, Sidi Ashouri," she said; "for a Christian weds not one whom he calls Infidel. A woman may love a star, but can she possess it? Oh, no, for did he know my feeling towards him, the young Englishman would turn from me, even as I feel compelled to turn from you."

"The Christian can adore beauty as well as a Mussulman," said Sidi.

"True," she replied. "I can admire your stalwart frame and handsome face, but do I not know that beneath the one and hidden by the other from mortal ken lies a heart as black as Hades, and as merciless as a fiend's!"

"Have I not been kind and gentle to you?" he asked huskily.

"Aye, but for what?" she replied. "Why has the tiger's claws been drawn in, and his fangs covered, with a smiling lip? Sidi Ashouri, I would rather be the veriest slave than the bride of such a man."

And she spurned the hand he had placed on her arm.

"I will ask no more," he said.

"I pray you do not," she replied. "I cannot love, I cannot respect a pirate and an assassin."

"Say no more," he said. "You have elected between love and slavery, and chosen the latter. But in the days to come, when a lover has turned to a tyrant, when caresses have changed to blows, blame not me."

"I shall only blame you for ever crossing my path," she said, "and I hope that fate will destine that we never meet again."

She buried her veiled face in her hands and sobbed aloud.

The pirate chief played nervously with his dagger.

More than once he felt inclined to call upon the men to cease rowing and plunge his blade into Jack's heart, for to him he attributed the determination of the girl, though they had spoken no word together since the capture of her father's ship by the pirates.

Then, as if annoyed at the thought, he plunged the half-drawn blade back into its sheath, and called upon his men to hurry. Soon the boats touched a landing-place.

A group of Berbers, Moors and negroes met them and stood looking on when the pirates led their prisoners ashore.

Here they were left, surrounded by an armed band, Sidi simply asking a question of one of the onlookers, and then going off at a rapid pace.

Jack tried to force his way towards Deliah.

But he was prevented by the guard, and also by Ralph, who drew him back.

"You cur," hissed Jack; "if I could bring myself to do so un-English a deed, wounded as you are, I would strike."

"You have led me into this, Jack Tempest," hissed Ralph, "and I will yet find time for revenge. I dare say we shall be sold together, and have to work in chains together. That will be some gratification to me, knowing how we hate each other, Jack Tempest. If I am forced to share your slavery, you will be compelled to share my company, and put up with my taunts, and my hatred."

"Oh, heaven, that my arm was free but for one moment," cried Jack.

"You'd be Rough and Ready, then, I know," sneered Ralph; "but your arms are bound, my young bantam, and your words can't hurt me."

"But my fist can, Master Jack, though I'm only a little 'un."

And Joe, whose one arm was free as well as Ralph's, swung round, and gave the ruffian a blow on his sneering lips.

With a yell of fury, Ralph raised his arm.

But as the furious blow descended, the hand of the half-maddened man was stopped by the butt of one of the pirates' muskets, and fell numbed to his side.

"Hooray!" cried Joe.

The pirate pushed Joe back with the butt of his musket.

"Hush, Joe," whispered Jack.

"I'll be mum, Master Jack," said Joe. "But, I say, what's they keeping us here for?"

"I do not know. But we shall soon learn, Joe."

"Ain't that pretty girl a-pumping the tears up!" said Joe.

"My heart aches for her."

"You don't think that pirate will make a slave of her, do you?"

"I am afraid such is his intention," was the sad reply.

"Then it's a shame," said Joe. "She's pretty enough for an angel."

"But that she could not be, unless——"

"Unless what, Master Jack?"

"She was dead."

"Perhaps she'd like to be," said Joe, thoughtfully.

"It were better, perhaps, that she were," said Jack; "would to heaven I had the power to aid her."

The wondering throng, which had momentarily been increasing in numbers, now opened to allow a couple of horsemen, half-a-dozen slaves, and Sidi Ashouri to advance.

Then, as they recognised the newcomers, they bowed low and fell back murmuring—

"'Tis the Bey's secretary, and Aza Murad, the slave-dealer."

Deliah caught the words, and throwing herself before the foremost horseman, she raised her hands and cried—

"Save me, save me! I am the daughter of Mural Hamed, your faithful but murdered friend."

CHAPTER XXXVI.

HAL AND CHARLEY AT THE DOCKS—A STRANGE COUPLE.

WE must take a hurried trip from Algiers to London, to see how our old friends Harry Houghten and Charley Calvert, are faring.

Boatswain Bob, as that disreputable scamp called himself, was brought to trial and transported, despite the fact that he was defended by most eminent counsel.

Now Harry and Charley were free to act, and after the trial they met in the park to arrange their future course.

They had, as we know, resigned their situations, and, being too independent to become a burden to their friends, they decided to follow the career which they had before chosen, and which was so suddenly interrupted by Bob Brittle and his employers.

Day after day they wandered about the docks, but avoided all conversation with sailors lounging about. A week passed, and they were beginning to believe there was no chance of their going to sea, when a rough voice exclaimed—

"If you two young swells ain't got anything better to do, just run over to old Bill Smithers, the ship's chandler, and tell him to be sure and have the rope aboard the 'Betsy' early to-morrow, and there's a shilling for you for the job."

Hal and Charley looked round at the speaker.

He was short and stout, with a face as red as a boiled lobster.

"Well, didn't you ever see beauty before," said the man, as he still held the shilling towards them, grasped between thick brown fingers with very short nails.

"Sir," said Hal, "we are not above doing you or anyone else a favour, but we do not know the ship's chandler or where to find him."

"What!" cried the other, diving his hands into the pockets of his rough pea-jacket, "don't know old Bill Smithers? Why, how many hours have you been born? Why, everybody knows old Bill, the cantankerous old curmudgeon."

"I assure you, sir, that we do not, but if you will inform us where to find him, we shall be happy to give him your message."

"Go out of that gate yonder, steer to the left, and you'll bear down on to his place. If you don't find him there, just put your helm over, and you're into the 'Midshipman.' You'll find him there, sure enough, behind a pipe, in the corner."

"A public-house, sir?"

"What, the 'Midshipman'?—of course it is. And when old Bill ain't in his warehouse he's bound to be there, for he never sailed farther than one house to the other all the time I've known him, and that's nigh on thirty years."

"Your message, sir, shall be conveyed to him," said Hal. "Come on, Charley."

And he turned to go.

"Avast, there, you lubber!" shouted the man in the pea-jacket.

Hal turned.

"Didn't I tell you I'd give you a shilling?" said the red-faced man.

"Yes, sir; but we are willing to perform so slight a service without any reward," said Hal, flushing, and drawing back from the hand that again proffered the shilling. "And besides, if we desired to be paid, we have no right to accept payment before the work has been done; for all you know, we might take the money and fail to earn it."

The man's red face appeared to grow more red, and a look of half surprise, half amusement twinkled in his small, dark eyes.

"Oh, if it ain't the first time I ever fell foul, 'specially about the docks, of two such swabs. But there, there, come back and tell me what old Bill says, and you shall have the shilling and a glass of grog, too. I shall be aboard the 'Betsy.' That's her with the Blue Peter flying from her maintop."

"We see, sir; but how shall we get on board? She lies some distance out," said Hal.

"Aye, aye, she's been hauled out because she's loaded in her cargo. But just you sing out, ''Betsy,' ahoy!' and a boat will come for you."

Hal turned, and the two lads went on their way.

"'Betsy,' ahoy!" roared a voice, that caused them to turn.

The skipper in the pea-jacket stood on the edge of the dock, with his chubby brown hands up to his mouth.

"'Betsy,' ahoy!" he yelled again. "Send a boat off!"

"Come on," said Charley. "He seems a good sort. Wonder what he is?"

"A sailor."

"Yes, there's no mistake about that; but he don't appear as if he held a position that would enable him to assist us into a berth."

"No, he don't look like a captain or mate. Perhaps he's a genuine boatswain," said Charley. "But, I say, Hal, shall you go aboard?"

"Rather."

"And have the grog?"

"No."

"Well, I don't mean to. No more rum for me, after what we have gone through."

"Still, we'll go aboard, since he told us to do so," said Hal.

"As you please."

They waited just long enough to see a man come down a rope hanging over the side of the vessel, and drop into a boat moored to its chains, and then they went on their errand.

Hal and Charley found the ship's chandler; old Bill was in his warehouse, and they delivered the message to him.

"In course the hemp will be aboard in the morning," he said. "When did Captain Briggs know me fail to send everything in time?"

"Captain Briggs; was that the name of the gentleman who sent us here?" asked Hal.

"Who else would it be but the skipper of the 'Betsy'?" growled Smithers. "Just you tell him that I'll be wild if he don't have a glass with me at the 'Midshipman' afore he sails."

"I will tell him, sir," said Hal.

"You can come with me."

"Where, sir?" asked Charley.

"'Cross to the 'Midshipman.'"

"If you mean drink, sir, certainly not," said Hal.

"Well, I'm—"

And he paused and looked at the lads in surprise. Then he sat down on a huge coil of rope and laughed loudly.

"Rum sort of chap," whispered Hal to Charley.

"Not drink !" laughed Smithers. "Oh, what would Dick Shields think of the 'Midshipman' if there was a lot more of 'em like these ?—why, the house would be ruined in a month. But there, if you won't take a drink, youngsters, here's somebody as will."

He jumped up and strode to the door.

"Hi, Sam Slops, ahoy !" he yelled.

Hal and Charley followed the ship's chandler to the door and looked out.

Standing on the pavement opposite were a short, stout man and a tall, thin woman, both loaded with parcels wrapped in brown paper.

The man's face was pale and flabby, the woman's was thin to attenuation, and the skin, which alone seemed to cover the bones, was seared as if by fire.

"A funny looking couple that," Hal whispered.

"She has got a wooden leg," said Charley.

"So she has. I see the stump of it now."

"We will say good day and be off," said Charley. "They are coming over here."

Then raising his voice, he said—

"We will wish you good day, and assure Captain Briggs that you will not disappoint him with the rope."

"Well, lads, if you won't have a glass at the 'Midshipman' with me, Sam and his Angel will, so good day to you, and a pleasant voyage."

"We are not sailors, sir," said Hal.

"Any fool could see that," growled Smithers ; "but ain't you going as passengers with Captain Briggs on board the 'Betsy' ?"

"No, sir."

"Well, I thought you were, that's all, and would have Sam and his Angel to wait on you. Oh, don't she throw that stump of hers about ! There it goes, slap onto Sam's toes, and there goes his parcels in the mud. Now they'll go at it like hammer and tongs. If I was old Jim Briggs, I'd hang up one at the fore and t'other at the mizzen."

Hal and Charley bid him good day once more, and hurried away.

But their steps were arrested by a shrill voice, and, turning, they saw the little stout man engaged in picking his fallen parcels from the muddy ground, and the long, thin lady prodding him savagely in the ribs with her wooden leg.

"Did ever a poor, defenceless woman have to put up with such a man ?" she cried ; "and the fifth husband, too."

CHAPTER XXXVII.

THE ANGEL BRINGS MORE THAN ONE TO GRIEF—ENGAGED—THE START ON THE FIRST VOYAGE.

LAUGHING loudly, Hal and Charley hurried back to the docks.

"Ain't she a caution !" said Hal, as they passed through the gates and went along the wharves. "I can guess now why the captain and the chandler called her the Angel."

"Because it is very evident that she is just the reverse of one," said Charley.

"Let us hail the 'Betsy' from here. This is about the best place, I think, and Captain Briggs can see us if he is on deck," remarked Hal.

"You can holloa loudest, Hal, and if they can't hear you by yourself, I'll join in, too."

Hal placed his hands to his mouth, and, in the loudest voice he could, shouted—

" 'Betsy,' ahoy !"

"Ahoy !—ahoy !" came back over the water.

"Thought you could fetch them, Hal," said his friend.

"Send a ship ashore to take us to the boat !" called Hal.

Charley burst out laughing.

"What's the matter now ?" asked Hal, in surprise.

"Do you know what you shouted just now?" said Charley.

"Told them to send a boat ashore, of course," replied Hal.

"No, you didn't. You told them to send a ship ashore to take us to the boat."

"Did I?" said Hal.

"You did."

"Well, that is funny. I did not notice it. But they understood what I meant, all the same, for there comes the boat."

And Harry pointed to where a man was casting off the painter preparatory to rowing the little vessel to shore.

"Shall you ask the captain if he will find us berths, Hal?"

"I just shall."

"I hope he will, for I do not admire this lazy life we have been forced to lead for so many weeks."

"Nor I."

The boat gradually approached the wharf, the man in it propelling the vessel forward by working a single oar at its stern.

Except that he was a trifle taller, he bore a strong resemblance to Captain Briggs.

He had a good-humoured expression of face, and a happy-go-lucky, don't-care-for-nobody sort of style about him.

"Ahoy!" he called out. "Are you the two youngsters as wants to go aboard the 'Betsy'?"

"We are, sir," replied Hal.

"All right, my lads. You can jump in directly; but I see I'll have more company than you two."

Hal and Charley followed the man's gaze, and perceived the tall woman and short man making their way over the wharf.

"The chandler did not keep them long at the 'Midshipman,'" said Hal.

"Perhaps he changed his mind when he saw what a temper she was in," replied Charley.

"Most likely."

"The Angel and Sam Slops are coming to go aboard, and one journey may as well do," said the man in the boat.

"That tall woman, there?" said Hal.

"That's the Angel, my lads."

"Why is she called the Angel?"

"Ah, that's a long yarn," was the reply. "But generally from her temper, because it is so angelic and so gentle."

The boys smiled, and entered the boat.

"Sit down there, my lads," said the man. "I can see that the Angel is flapping her wings like a seagull. Something's put her out with Sam; but, lor'! that's nothing unusual."

The two lads burst into a loud fit of laughter.

When the lads had ceased laughing, Hal said—

"We saw her showing a little temper in the road yonder."

"Did you? Then don't say anything about it, my lad, or she'll hoist you out of the boat into the water with that wooden leg of hers. The way she can swing it round is a caution," said the sailor.

"Oh, if here ain't the boat waiting for us."

"Yes, I see there is," said Slops.

"You see?" cried the Angel. "You know you are as blind as a bat, and never saw it at all till I pointed it out to you!"

"Why, my dear, how could you point it out with your arms full?" said Slops, meekly. "Besides, you know that you are taller than me, and would naturally see an object first."

"An object! I wish I'd never seen such an object as you, Sam Slops."

"I'm sure I always try to be kind to you, Liz."

"Kind to me?" cried the woman, raising her leg off the ground.

Sam drew closer to the edge of the wharf.

"Yes, you'd like to go away and leave me behind, wouldn't you?" cried the Angel.

"My dear, I'm sure I—"

"Here's my arms a-breaking with the load I'm carrying in them, and my heart a-breaking with the miseries with which you—you, Sam Slops, have filled it. Why don't you take them from me, you unfeeling monster?"

"Pitch them into the boat. Ain't I loaded as well?"

"Yes, and you wanted to go and have more with Bill Smithers. But, no, I put my foot down on that, I did."

And down came the wooden leg with a thud on Sam's foot that made him utter a yell and drop the parcels into the boat and onto the boys.

"Ah!" cried Sam, "if you ain't smashed my foot this time. Why don't you keep that stump behind instead of throwing it out sideways, or else come ashore without it. That's the third time it's come down on my foot within an hour."

"Here, Mrs. Slops," said the sailor, "pitch those parcels down, and these lads will catch them from you, and then hurry into the boat, for the captain's aboard, and has been calling out for the steward. Get into the boat; these youngsters will help you."

"With pleasure," said Hal, as he and Charley put forth their hands to assist her.

The Angel managed to grasp them, and swung herself forward.

"Look out!" cried Sam and the oarsman, in a breath.

But the warning came too late.

The stump caught Hal so forcible a blow on the ribs that he was hurled sideways onto the heap of ropes packed between the thwarts, and then the stump came down upon his foot with force.

Sam slid into the boat.

"Ah, Liz, I'm afraid you have hurt the boy," he said.

"Whose fault was it? Why didn't he get out of the way? I'm always being blamed."

And the Angel sat herself vengefully down on one of the thwarts, her wooden leg shooting out like a piston-rod against her husband's shin, and making him drop down as if he had been shot.

Charley picked Hal up.

"Are you hurt, old man?" he asked.

"Not much," said Hal. "It will be all right soon."

"Let it be a lesson to you, young man, to keep your eyes about you," said the Angel. "My leg couldn't see, but your eyes could, and, if by your carelessness you ran against it, don't blame me."

"Well, if that ain't cool, tell me what is," said the sailor, as he plied away at the oar and sent the boat once more towards the ship. "If I was you, Mrs. Slops, when I got aboard I'd get Chips to saw about six inches off that pin, it's always a-getting in the way and doing some mischief."

"Cut off a part of my leg?" asked the lady. "You brute!"

And not another word was spoken till the boat reached the "Betsy."

"Now, up you go, lads. You'll find Captain Briggs in his cabin."

Hal and Charley, by the aid of the rope, were soon on board.

The skipper came forward with a smile.

"So you are here to your promise, lads," he said.

"Yes, sir. Mr. Smithers will have the rope on board, and would like to drink a glass with you at the 'Midshipman' before you set sail."

"Aye, aye; but come with me into the cabin, for I'm free to confess that I've taken a liking to you both."

They followed him into the cabin, and when, after about an hour, they came out, they had both got berths; Hal as captain's clerk, and Charley to assist the steward.

The next morning the Blue Peter was hauled down and the "Betsy" set sail, and as the lads start on their first voyage, we will back to Algiers and follow the fortunes of Rough and Ready Jack.

CHAPTER XXXVIII.

JACK AND JOE SEPARATED FROM THE MUTINEERS—IN SLAVERY—DELIAH'S VAIN APPEAL.

THE foremost horseman looked down upon Deliah as her appeal fell upon his ears.

"The daughter of Mural Hamed, the Moor?" he said, half doubtingly.

"I am!" cried the girl. "My father was foully murdered at sea by those two Englishmen, whose lives he saved."

And she pointed to Baxter Sharp and Ralph Sternway.

"Is this true?" he asked of Ashouri.

"I have no means of denying," he replied. "I and my crew had no hand in the destruction of the Moors, not one of whom remained on board when we attacked her."

"And the ship?" he asked.

"Was rifled and burned, as is usual with us."

His mounted companion whispered something,

"Be it so," said the other.

Then he turned to Ashouri.

"Captain," he said, "the Bey demands a share of your captives."

"And always obtains it from us," replied the pirate.

"And well for you it is so," said the other, meaningly. "For his share I take these three captives, the rest you may dispose of to Kula Arabi, who will doubtless give you a fair price for them; but these I claim for the Bey."

And he pointed to Deliah, Jack, and Joe.

"I am powerless to do aught but accept," said Ashouri. "Be it as my lord commands."

"Cast off their bonds."

Jack and Joe were instantly released from their villainous companion.

"So," said Jack, "there is one comfort in this great misery—I shall not be chained to such a hound as you."

The other gave him a look that sent a shudder to Jack's heart, so full of fiendish vengeance was it.

So delighted was Joe that he turned a handspring, stood on his head, and clapped his bare feet together.

Those present, save the English and Deliah, had never before seen such a feat as this, and looked on in wonder. But Jack called him sharply to his side.

"For Heaven's sake, Joe, be careful what you do now."

"Lor, Master Jack, I could dance a horn-pipe on my head. I'm so happy to know we won't have to be with them villains."

"Heaven only knows with whom we shall be placed. Keep quiet, Joe. We must do nothing to give these people offence or suspicion. So, for my sake and poor Deliah's, be careful what you do or say."

Sidi Ashouri and the slave dealer drew aside.

Then Arabi gave a command to his slaves, and Jack's late companion was fastened to the others and they were ordered to march.

"Good riddance to bad rubbish!" cried Joe.

Baxter Sharp and Ralph threw both Joe and Jack a meaning glance.

"We shall meet again," said Jack; "and when we do I will keep my vow."

"With my lord's permission, I will follow my slaves," said Arabi.

"Be it so," was the reply; "but send my guard hither."

"Peace be with you."

"The Prophet have you in his keeping," was the reply.

They saluted, and Arabi turned his horse's head and rode after his slaves, but paused when a short distance away to speak with the officer of a small body of soldiers.

Again he dashed forward, and the officer, giving a command, the little squad marched down to the beach.

Ashouri came to the side of Deliah, and whispered huskily—

"There is yet time, maiden. Swear to become mine, and in spite of all resistance, I will bear you to my ship."

"Leave me," she said. "I am now in safer and more honourable hands than yours."

"You w... regret this," he hissed.

"That, time will alone show," she said. "Persecute me no more, or I will appeal—"

"Fool!" he hissed, and turned away.

The little band of soldiers had now arrived.

"To the palace," said the mounted man. "See that you bring them safely there."

"On my head be it," replied the officer, saluting. "But the maiden?"

"Goes with them. See she speaks not with her companions. For, by the beard of the Prophet, I think she feels more love for them than for us."

"Your wishes shall be obeyed," said the officer, with another salute.

Then he ordered his men to separate and surround the captives, himself taking up a position by Deliah's side.

Then, with a haughty salutation to the pirates, the secretary gave his horse the rein and dashed away.

It was a sad disappointment to Deliah

not to be allowed the chance to speak to Jack, and Jack felt equally sorrowful that he could not bid her be of good cheer, for he had determined that if ever he could escape he would seek to rescue her.

But no chance was given them of conversing even for a moment, in fact, the compact body of soldiers prevented them even seeing the forms of each other.

Soon the forts were left behind, and the city, glowing in the sunlight, presented a quaint, but not uncheerful appearance.

The flat-roofed houses were relieved by the towers and minarets that rose above them on all sides, and the palace of the Bey rose proudly and majestically above the neighbouring buildings.

An up-hill march brought them to the palace.

The great gate of the courtyard stood wide open, guarded by negro troops.

Through the gates could be seen the three sides of the buildings, whilst in the centre, surrounded by beautiful flowers, and shrubs, a marble fountain threw up its waters into the sunlight, and fell in showers of gold back into its basin.

On one side were the apartments of the Bey and the harem, on the other those of his officers and guards, while the third presented the offices of the servants and slaves, beyond which were the stables and other outbuildings.

Up till now the poor girl had borne up bravely, but when she saw her companions in misfortune borne away, and found herself standing before the grand entrance of that majestic pile, she broke down and burst into tears.

Breaking from the guard, she flung herself upon her knees on the marble steps.

"Oh, have mercy!" she cried, holding out her hands. "My sojourn in England and France makes me look with horror upon the life upon which I fear you would consign me. You have power, you were my murdered father's friend—then oh, be merciful, and send me not to a doom, worse to me, a thousand times, than death."

"Girl," said the man on the steps, "your pleadings must be addressed to one higher and mightier than myself. You treat me as your foe, while I am indeed your friend; you are fatherless and almost a stranger in the land, and yet to you is offered a share in a monarch's harem."

"And a broken heart," she cried, "a life of horror, and a wretched doom."

"Peace, girl, you know not what you say; you have suffered much, and your heart is sad. But grief will wear away, and joy once more fill your bosom. Then will the smile come back to your lips, and the lustre to your eyes."

"Never!" she sobbed.

"Think it not," he replied, as he helped her to her feet. "It will come, and none will have earned more fully your deepest gratitude than your father's friend and his daughter's saviour."

CHAPTER XXXIX.

THE SLAVE BARRACK AND THE SLAVE DRIVER—JONATHAN SLICKEM COMES TO GRIEF—A VICTIM OF THE LASH.

JACK and Joe were taken into a large garden where nearly every kind of fruit was planted, and where the walls of the buildings were covered with vines, their huge bunches of fruit hanging in hundreds from their stems.

Across this they were conducted to a low range of buildings having the appearance of a number of Berbers' huts joined together.

This building was also covered with vines, save where the low doorways were made and holes without glass that served for windows.

Into this building they were led, through one of the narrow doorways, and when they had entered the soldiers retired, pulling to and fastening the door behind them.

Then the captives could hear the tramp of their footsteps as they recrossed the garden to the courtyard of the palace.

Jack and Joe, who had seen that resistance would be useless, and imagined that silence would prevent them receiving hurt at the hands of their guards, now looked about them in the gloom in which they found themselves.

"A queer-looking place this, Joe. It don't look like a stable inside, though it did out."

"And yet there's a lot of straw and leaves lying heaped about," said Joe.

They walked along from one end to the other, and found only rude benches and the heaps before mentioned.

"Joe," said Jack, laying his hand on the boy's arm, "I think I can guess for what this building is used."

"Do you think it's where they keep all their slaves?" asked Joe.

"No; but where they keep them when they are not toiling in the gardens and fields," replied Jack. "Those heaps of leaves and straw are the beds of those poor wretches, and it is with them, and in such a place, that we will be forced to rest after our weary labours."

And Jack sat down on a bench and covered his face with his hands.

"A slave!" he muttered, at last; "but, no, I will die first. I was born free, and I'll live free."

"Perhaps we can manage to bolt, Master Jack. They haven't shut the windows."

Jack looked up at the openings. Then he got upon a bench and looked out.

"Joe, they are too narrow for a child to squeeze out of. They are only air-holes."

"It's as bad as the Dark Arches, Jack," said the boy. "But you don't know how bad they are, and I'm afraid you'll feel it worser nor me."

"I seem suffocating already, Joe. Even now the stench of this place is horrible."

"Master Jack, have you got a knife?"

"No. Why?"

"You might, perhaps, scrape that hole bigger, and I could slip out and unfasten the door, and we could make a bolt afore anyone comes."

"We've nothing with which to aid us, Joe. They took care of that."

"Well, that's a jolly shame, for I do believe the stone's soft enough to cut. But, I say, do you think they're a-going to give us any wittles?"

"I suppose the slaves are fed here when they come in from their work, and we shall have some then."

"I hopes it will be a good tuck out of roast pork and 'taters, don't you?"

"Yes; but I am afraid, Joe, we sha'n't get anything so substantial. Some peas, perhaps, and a bit of bread, or a little rice."

"Pease-pudding ain't bad with plenty of gravy on it, Master Jack, especially if they only puts a faggot in with it."

"I am afraid our fare will be nothing like that either, Joe. As there is plenty of fruit, we may get some dates, or grapes, or perhaps a water melon, but meat and vegetables, I fear, is out of all question."

"Then we will have to fill up with that. But can't you put your hand through the hole and pull a few bunches off?"

"I'll try, Joe."

And Jack stretched his arm to its utmost, and the points of his fingers just touched the vine, when he drew them back with a cry of pain.

"What is it?" cried Joe.

"Something has bitten my fingers, I'm afraid. Oh, how they do tingle, and the tips of them are bleeding."

He got down from the bench and examined them.

"I hope it ain't a wenermouse reptile as did it, Master Jack," said Joe, wiping the blood from Jack's fingers with his sleeve.

"It seemed like the cut of a sabre, but I saw no weapon," said Jack, "nor can I hear anyone outside."

At this there was a harsh laugh, and Jack sprang to his feet.

"There is someone," he cried. "Did you hear that, Joe?"

"Rather," said Joe, "and I'd like to spifflicate him, whoever he is."

"Let's listen, Joe, for it's someone put on guard."

"Can he understand us, d'ye think?"

"I can't say; but I have heard there are English slaves in Algiers, and sometimes they become the worst of slave-drivers themselves."

"The brutes!" said Joe.

"Harsh treatment will make some men brutes," said Jack. "Heaven grant it may never make one of me. Hush, Joe!"

And Jack held up his hand warningly.

Softly a bolt was shot on the outside, and the door flung open.

They looked, to see a man, carrying a sword at his side and a long thin whip in his hand, step over the threshold.

As he gazed, the light from outside fell upon his face and figure.

He was not a Moor, that was certain. He might have been a Spaniard, but his face looked more like that of a bronzed Englishman or American.

Jack was in some litte doubt as to his nationality till he opened his mouth, and said in a nasal twang—

" Guess you didn't know I was looking, did you, younker? "

" It was you, then, who cut my fingers with that whip? "

" I reckon you're about right thar. I can flick a fly off a flower stem without hurting the flower, so I never miss my aim."

" Who are you? " asked Jack.

" I calculate I ain't forgot my name," said the fellow with a leer. " I'm Jonathan Slickem, and I am boss of the Bey's slaves, and so, you see, I'm your boss."

" You think so," said Jack, his face flushing and his fingers closing ominously.

" I never think—I know," said the fellow, " and when any of the slaves on this plantation shows only the shadow of resistance to me, I puts this little joker round his arms and legs, and gets a piece of flesh out at every cut. Oh, yes! Now you know me, and how you've got to behave."

" You scoundrel! "

" I guess I've heard that kind of talk before, and I've always put it down slick; so now unlock that fist of yours, or I'll cut it open with my howl-forcer."

And the fellow swung the whip in the air.

Jack recoiled when he saw the long, thin circling thong, for too well he guessed its hitting and stinging power.

" I guess you think better of looking ugly at me," said the man, as he suffered the thong to fall to his side.

" I am at your mercy," said Jack.

" And that's what I mean you never to forget," said the fellow. " I never lets a slave be troubled with a bad memory on that score. If he forgets who I am, he don't forget what this is."

And taking a step nearer Jack, he again raised the whip.

In his desire to use his whip on Jack, the ruffian passed the spot on which Joe stood, trembling for his friend.

Joe saw his chance to help Jack.

Quick as lightning he seized one of the benches, and drove its end with all the force he could in the small of the back of the slave-driver.

Thrown off his balance, the ruffian could not regain it, and pitched forward against another bench, bringing it to the ground, and striking his head heavily against the wall.

Throwing the bench down, Joe seized the thong, and tore the whip from his hand.

" Jack, Jack, take his sword! "

Our hero needed no second bidding.

In an instant he drew the sword from its leathern scabbard, and gave the Yankee a fierce blow on the head with its flat.

" It's cowardly to hit a man when he is down, Joe," cried Jack, as he sprang to the boy's side and drew him to the open door, " but liberty, perhaps life itself, depends upon his silence."

As he spoke, he cast a quick glance around, and then drew Joe through the doorway, closed the door, and shot home the heavy bolt.

Then he stood panting and hesitating what to do, or how to act.

" Let's make a bolt for the big gates, Master Jack," said Joe.

" No, no! We should be captured directly. You forget the guard."

" So I did. But couldn't we get past them with that sword and this whip? "

" It would be madness to try."

" What shall we do, then? "

" Get into concealment as quickly as possible. We know not from what point we may be seen," said Jack.

" How's that place over there? " said Joe, pointing.

" Let's try it, Joe; the trees are densest there."

And giving one more searching glance around, they sped across the garden and dived into the shadows of a clump of dark-leaved, close-growing trees.

" I hope we have not been detected," whispered Jack, " and if not discovered before darkness sets in, we may manage to escape while it lasts."

"Ah! here's something to eat," said Joe.

"What is it?"

"Don't know," said Joe; "but I do believe they are figs. They're jolly nice, Master Jack, whatever they are. Oh, ain't there a lot of 'em!"

And Joe, with the whip, cut the fruit from its branches, and Jack gathered them up as they fell.

"Don't talk, Joe; we know not who may hear us, and while daylight lasts, I must try to discover some way of getting out of this place."

"And going where, Master Jack?"

"Where Providence may guide us, Joe," replied Jack, sadly; "and would to heaven we could bear Deliah with us, though that is impossible. But if fortune favour us, I will return to save or perish with her."

"You do think she loves you, Master Jack?"

"Yes."

Jack, having partaken sparingly of the fruit, proceeded to look about him as well as the trees and shrubs would allow him to do.

He could see that the garden was very extensive.

"I'll climb the highest of these trees, and look round," he said to himself. "The foliage will conceal me."

Having made up his mind to do this he bade Joe not move from where he stood, and, leaving the sword at the foot of the tree, he commenced the ascent.

It was not till he had reached the highest boughs that he could see over the tops of the other trees.

Now he could discover a high wall which stretched away to the right and joined the palace on the left.

In this wall was a low door, beside which stood a man grasping a whip.

As Jack looked, the door opened, and a female figure was seized roughly by the man, who instantly began to ply his whip upon the arms and shoulders of his captive.

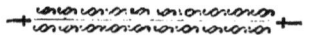

CHAPTER XL.

JOE PROVES HIMSELF A HERO—THE ODALISQUE AND THE EUNUCH—JACK TO THE RESCUE—DISCOVERED.

JACK had some difficulty in suppressing the cry of indignation that rose to his lips.

To see a girl lashed by a big powerful man was repulsive to his nature.

What could he do to protect her and punish her assailant? Nothing!

To make his presence known would be perhaps to secure his recapture.

He set his teeth hard, and gripped the swaying branch with a grasp of iron.

"If I could—oh, if I dared!" he gasped, "I'd smash him, the cowardly hound!"

The cries of the poor girl as she writhed under the brutal lash of the Algerine came plainly to Jack's ears, and worked him up into such a fury of disgust that he was about to descend the tree, seize the sword, and fly to her rescue, when he saw something that made him pause.

That was Joe, who, whip in hand, bounded from the sheltering trees and confronted the startled ruffian.

Joe did not give the fellow a moment to recover from his surprise at seeing a ragged white boy there.

With a yell, Joe sent the long, thin, wiry lash round his head, and cut a deep wale across the fellow's face that caused him to release his slackened hold of the girl and recoil back several paces.

"Don't you be frightened," cried Joe, as he sent the whip singing again through the air. "Just you stop there and see the licking I'm going to give him for hitting of you."

Again the long, cruel thong curled round the man's head, and proved the words of Slickem that it would cut out a piece of flesh at every blow.

The end of the lash laid the fellow's face open to the bone, and his cheeks and neck were instantly deluged in blood.

Again and again did Joe send the curling thong singing through the air, and again and again did the Algerine writhe beneath the stinging lash.

Not once did he seem to have the power of retaliation, surprise or pain, or both mingled, evidently rendering him powerless to do so.

The girl leaned against the wall in a half fainting condition, watching the scene with dazed eyes and throbbing heart.

"Dance, you coward, dance!" cried Joe. "Hit a woman, will you? Not when Joe Jilks is about. Oh, you're a brave 'un, ain't you? I'm only a little 'un, but you're afraid of me. I'd buy a dozen fellows better nor you for a half-penny any day. Oh, you are a cur!"

But the man, now goaded to fury by the pain he suffered, flung down his whip, and drew a long, broad bladed knife from his belt, and made a stab at Joe.

Jack, up in his tree, closed his eyes with a gasp of horror.

He thought Joe's last hour had come, and his heart sank within him.

But when he opened his eyes again, he breathed a sigh of relief.

Joe was dancing round the man like a harlequin, keeping him at bay with the whip, and lacerating the dusky hand that held the knife with that deeply cutting thong, and yelling out the while—

"No, you don't, my brown-skinned beauty! Just keep your distance, or you'll get hurt. Drop it, d'ye hear!"

And with a swish of the whip, he cut the knife from the fellow's hand.

"That's a good boy, always obey your superiors," said Joe, as he kicked the knife out of the fellow's reach and over to where the girl stood leaning and trembling against the wall.

Possibly, without knowing why, the girl stooped and secured the weapon.

With a shriek of agony, the man dashed upon his tormentor, but Joe was like an eel, and as the lacerated hand of the maddened Algerine was thrust forth to seize him, Joe slipped under the upraised arm, with a—

"Don't you wish you may get him?"

This movement so surprised the man that he stood clutching at the empty air.

Joe's lash came down upon his shoulders, and with still extended arms he leapt at least two feet into the air.

"Wake up!" said Joe. "What are you stopping there catching flies for? Oh, ain't you getting to look a beauty!"

The maddened man again sprang at Joe, and could he have clutched him, no doubt would have strangled him on the spot, but Joe was too nimble for his heavily built and somewhat obesive opponent.

Quick as a flash, Joe dropped on the earth, and the Algerine, unable to check the impetus of his rush, fell over him and lay sprawling at the feet of the terrified girl.

"Why didn't you hold him tight?" cried Joe springing up like a cork. "That's how we serve the bobbies in the Dials. Oh, Jumbo and Jerusalem!"

It was Joe's turn now to start and recoil, for as the bewildered and smarting man rose to his knees the girl seized him by his turban and raised the knife above him.

"Better death than this continual beating," she said. "But you shall not fit the bowstring to my neck, nor witness the deed done by others. This for the blows you have given me so often, and this!"

As she spoke she plunged the knife twice into the man's bosom.

Had all the wealth of Algiers been offered to Joe, he could not have moved at that moment, all he could do was to look on like one in a dream.

With a deep groan the man sank back, but she still held him by his turban.

"Cruel unmerciful monster, server of a base and wretched tyrant, this at last is your punishment and my revenge."

Again she plunged the weapon into his chest, and let go the hold of his turban.

The man fell back—a corpse.

A moment she gazed at his lifeless body, then she raised the knife, crying—

"This now to release a suffering soul from a lacerated and cruelly tortured body!"

"Hold, stop! Woman, what would you do?"

These words were uttered by Jack, as he sprang from the shelter of the trees and seized her upraised hand.

The girl glared at Jack in surprise and terror.

So sudden was his appearance, so sharp his tones, so firm his grasp.

"Hurray!" cried Joe, now coming forward. "Oh, Master Jack, I couldn't have stopped her, I was so flabbergasted."

"I have seen all, Joe, and I fear that we also have been seen, and that our hopes of escape are annihilated. Take the knife out of her hand, Joe. She must not commit self-murder."

Joe took the knife from the girl's now palsied hand and slipped it into the waistband of his ragged trousers.

Jack, still holding the girl's wrist with one hand, while his other grasped the sword he had brought with him, said, hurriedly—

"I have saved you from one great crime. Can you, in return, point out to me the way to escape from this prison?"

"Who are you?" she gasped, in a tremulous voice.

"An Englishman who has been consigned to slavery, but who would escape even at the hazard of his life. And you?" he asked.

"A slave, like yourself—a wretch who is tired of a life of torture and blows. But if you would escape, fly, before the palace or the guards are aroused."

"Whither can we fly?"

"Go, or it will be too late," replied she, quickly.

"But where? Point us out the way that may lead to freedom," cried Jack, excitedly.

"There is but one way by which you may escape," she said, hurriedly. "But, oh, if you are seen and captured, not the whole power of your country could save you."

"And which is that?"

"Through the women's bathing garden," she replied, "where none but the Bey himself dare tread, and to enter which to any other man is death."

"Was it from thence you came when you passed through yonder door to find yourself in the clutches of this inhuman wretch?" asked Jack, pointing to the door in the wall, and then to the dead man at his feet.

"Yes."

"Is there anyone there now?"

"I know not. If so, it would only be one of the ladies of the Bey's harem."

"Are you one?" asked Jack.

"I am an odalisque—a slave."

"And why did this man attack you with his whip?"

"The eunuch had his master's orders to punish me," she replied. "But oh, if you would escape, fly. From the garden yonder you may escape over its wall into the open country, and flee for the bay, where I hear an American ship rides at anchor. But if you do escape, which I doubt and fear, trust no Algerine, for they are all pirates and villains, and would sell you back to slavery again."

"If the life you lead is hateful to you, flee with us and we will protect you with our lives," said Jack.

"You may bet your last penny on that, miss, and stand ten to one to win," said Joe.

"Ah! too late—too late! Fly—fly!" she shrieked, tearing her hand from his grasp and pointing towards the palace; "you are discovered. Oh, fly ere it is too late."

Two men in white tunics and turbans, and armed with scimitars, appeared in the path in which they stood.

"The key—quick, fly!" cried the girl, pointing down at the body of the eunuch and then at the door in the wall.

Joe guessed what she meant, and stooped and quickly tore a key from the dead eunuch's girdle.

"I cannot flee, and leave you to perish alone," said Jack, as the two Algerines, having caught sight of the group, drew theirs scimitars and dashed forward with a yell.

"Too late! Leave me to my fate, and fly," she shrieked, wildly.

"Never!" cried Jack. "We will save or fall with you. Look out, Joe, for we've got our work to do now."

And Jack, sword in hand, sprang before the trembling girl.

"I'm with you, Master Jack," cried Joe, drawing his knife, and leaping to Jack's side.

Just in time; with the spring of a couple of tigers the Algerines were upon them.

"THE CAPTAIN RAISED HIS HAND AND POINTED TO THE FLAG."

CHAPTER XLI.

VICTORY FOR THE ENGLISHMEN—IN THE PRIVATE GARDEN—THE BEY'S SUDDEN
APPEARANCE AND DISAPPEARANCE.

JACK received the cut of one of the men's scimitars on the blade of his sword, but Joe made a leap backwards and brought the thong of his whip across the forehead of the other, who aimed simply at the air.

The girl, fearful of violence, and having got over her desire to die, fled towards the gate.

She knew what her fate would be should the Algerines prove victorious in the struggle.

Not a word was spoken by either for some moments.

The gleaming scimitars swept through the air, but the one clashed on the steel of Jack and the other met no obstruction, for Joe was like a parched pea in a frying-pan and always out of reach of the descending blade.

And all the while his whip went singing and cracking first on one side and then on the other.

"Go it, you cripples," cried Joe. "Crutches are cheap, and so are second-hand coffins. You never tried a horn-pipe on a cellar-door, or you'd foot it better than that. Oh, what a shame!"

This exclamation was called forth from Joe as the downward cut of the whip was parried by the sharp and glittering scimitar and the thong severed close to the handle.

Joe seemed now at the mercy of his antagonist, who, with a shout of triumph, rushed towards him.

He thought he had an easy conquest, but Joe thought differently.

Lowering his head, he charged his opponent like a bull, striking him fairly in the pit of the stomach.

"Ugh!" gasped the Algerine, as he sat suddenly down on the ground.

"Yes, it's me," said Joe. "There's no mistake about that, I'm all here when I'm wanted."

The fellow made a slash at Joe's legs with the scimitar he still retained in his grasp.

"Much obliged," said Joe, springing back, "but not being troubled with corns, I can do without your cheeseparer."

With an exclamation of rage the Algerine sprang to his feet.

"I'll have your life," he cried.

"I want it myself," said Joe.

"Die, you Infidel dog!" yelled the man, as he made a cutting blow at Joe, who threw a handspring that took him clean out of reach of the furious man.

The force with which the Algerine brought his scimitar down was its ruin, for meeting with no obstruction till it struck the path, it was shivered from from point to hilt.

"Who broke the window?" cried Joe, pointing to the pieces of glittering steel.

The fellow drew back. He had no other weapon, and Joe was armed with a knife.

He saw his companion engaged with Jack and sorely pressed by the young Englishman.

"Step it, missus," shouted Joe, throwing the girl the key of the garden door. "Me and Master Jack is going to hannahhiherlate these wicked willings, and we'll be after you in two twos."

The girl sprang for the door and flung it open.

"Fly!" she cried. "I can hear the tramp of the guards. The whole palace is aroused."

Joe was still keeping his gaze fixed on his adversary, occasionally throwing a quick glance towards Jack, who was holding his own with his opponent.

"Master Jack, they're coming," he shouted, as he heard the tramp of feet.

The two Algerines heard also the tramping of their friends, and set up a loud, triumphant shout.

"Quick, quick!" said the girl, holding open the door.

"Here, here! this way!" yelled Joe's opponent, turning and fleeing towards the advancing men, whom as yet the bend in the path and the dense vegetation hid from sight.

"We are lost!" cried the girl, wringing her hands. "If you would escape, fly at once."

"Ain't got no wings," said Joe. "But that fellow got my sting."

The yell that pealed out on the gradually darkening air was fairly blood curdling as Joe, with as true an aim as ever was taken, flung his knife so that it went quivering up to its hilt in the bottom of the Algerine's back.

Down the fellow went with a cry of pain, clutching wildly behind him.

Jack had heard the advancing men, and cold drops of perspiration oozed out on his forehead.

"Get away, Joe," he cried, "and leave me to fate and Providence. Take the girl with you and go, and may heaven protect you!"

"I ain't a boy of that sort," said Joe, springing forward and dealing Jack's antagonist a heavy blow with the handle of Slickem's whip.

The blow staggered the man, and Jack, taking advantage of his confusion, thrust his sword into the Algerine's side.

Throwing up his arms, the fellow fell heavily to the earth.

"Secure his weapon, Joe; we may need it," said Jack, "and follow me."

He sprang to the door.

"Come," he said, seizing the girl's arm.

"I should hinder your flight," she said. "Go, and the Prophet guard you."

"Without you—never!"

And handing his sword to Joe, who had secured the scimitar, Jack caught the girl up in his arms and sprang with her through the gateway.

Joe paused just long enough to pull the key out of the lock, and then bounding through, pushed the door close behind them.

"Go it," said Joe; "I'm after you, in the twinkling of a dead lamb's tail."

As Jack bore the half-resisting girl away, Joe sank down close to the gate.

He could hear that a number of men had entered the path and discovered the Algerines for there arose quite a commotion on the other side of the gate.

"They dare not come this side of the wall," said Joe, remembering the words of the girl.

But looking up at a scraping sound, he saw a copper-coloured face peering down upon him from the top of the wall.

"Oh, scissors to grind!" said Joe. "The fellow's foxed me."

An exclamation burst from the man's lips, and he half withdrew his head.

"Sorry I ain't got a baked 'tater to stop that mouth of yours," said Joe, picking up a stone, "but this will do as well."

And with a fair aim he hit the man on the lips with the missile.

"Run, Jack; the police are after you," cried Joe, bounding to his feet and dashing after Jack and the maiden.

Joe had no time to look about him, or he would have imagined himself in fairyland.

Enclosed in trees was an artificial lake, and on either side were arbours, covered with beautiful flowering vines.

Under the trees, Joe could see the forms of Jack and the girl as they hurried along the border of the lake, ever and anon casting an anxious glance behind them in search of the poor waif.

"I'm arter you, as the policeman said to the thief," cried Joe. "Never mind me. Hallo! Oh, what a swell!"

From one of the arbours came a short, corpulent man of about forty years of age, attired in the most gorgeous raiment that Joe had ever seen.

In the front of the spotless white turban he wore round his head, were several diamonds and other precious stones.

His loose gown was embroidered with gold thread, diamonds and rubies marking every seam, and flinging out glints of fire at every turn.

His shoes were also sprinkled with precious stones, while the hilt of the scimitar he wore at his side was encrusted with diamonds.

With an exclamation of surprise he turned to glare upon Joe, and then he shouted something with all the force of his lungs, while his jewelled fingers twined themselves round the hilt of his studded weapon.

"How do, sir?" said Joe, not knowing what to say. "Are you the man what plays in the pantomime at Christmas?"

"A slave—and here," gasped the other. "Here, where no other presence but mine is tolerated. He shall die by the bowstring at once."

And drawing his scimitar, he waddled towards the gate in the wall, shouting lustily.

Joe saw half-a-dozen faces, most of them black, now looking over the wall.

"Jack, Jack," cried the boy.

Jack turned, and the girl shrieked—

"The Bey, the Bey; we are undone!"

"That man?" asked Jack.

"It is the Bey; he is calling to his guards. Oh, we are lost!"

"Not so," cried Jack; "we may yet get time to escape."

"No, no," she cried; "he will suffer his guards to enter here, and then farewell to hope—to life."

"Hang me if he shall," cried Jack, "if I can prevent him."

"Oh, what would you do?" she cried, clasping her hands.

But Jack did not answer her. With a bound he sped away from her side.

"Stop him, Joe, before he can reach the gate," he shouted. "Stop him, or we are lost."

At the sound of Jack's voice, Joe turned and sprang after the puffing and excited Bey.

"Hold on," he yelled. "None of your tricks with Englishmen, whoever you are."

The Bey turned, his glittering scimitar half raised.

Then he saw Jack bounding towards him, and with a cry he sped towards the gate in the wall.

But as his hand seized the lock to open it, Jack was upon him.

He knew that all depended upon keeping out the guard.

With a leap he seized the Bey by the right arm and the collar of his embroidered gown, and hurled him back from the gate.

"Attempt to open that gate and I'll stretch you at my feet," cried Jack, clenching his fists.

The Bey, despite that he still grasped his bared scimitar, recoiled before the fierce glance of the young man.

Jack was desperate. He knew that life and death hung in the balance, and he strode forward again till they faced each other on the edge of the artificial lake.

"Got him to rights," cried Joe, springing behind the Bey, and with a quick thrust hurling him headfirst into the water.

"Quick, Joe," cried Jack, "follow me, the guards are forcing the gate. It is now a battle for us 'twixt life and death."

CHAPTER XLII.

THE SECRET PASSAGE—HUSBAND AND WIFE—CN THE EDGE OF THE BAY.

THE terror of the girl was something painful to behold.

"Oh, what have you done?" she cried when Jack and Joe joined her; "you have consigned yourselves to certain death. See the Bey is struggling on to the land, and will order pursuit, and if captured, you must die."

"We'll think about death after our capture," said Jack. "Lead the way."

"I will point it out to you," she said; "your chances will be greater if you leave me where I am."

"I shall do nothing of the kind," said Jack, decisively. "We will live or perish together."

By their backward glances they saw the Bey struggle out of the water and make for the gate in the wall.

They hurried on in the direction she pointed out.

Night was deepening, and objects began to grow dim, but they saw several forms enter the ladies' garden.

"This way," cried the girl.

She drew Jack into a clump of flowering trees.

"We shall be trapped like rats here," he said. "We must get out into the open country if we would save our lives."

"Come, and trust me," she said, taking his hand. "I would not betray a friend and protector."

"Trust her, Master Jack," said Joe.

"I will," replied Jack, "though she intimated that our only chance of escaping a life of slavery was by reaching the bay and seeking refuge on board an American ship."

"It cannot be done now," she said, "our foes are too near us. Look!"

She placed her arms around the trunk of a huge dead tree, and swerved aside.

To the surprise of Jack and Joe, the tree moved, and an opening appeared where it had stood.

"Quick," she said, "go down. Trust me, and fear not."

"What, down that hole?" said Joe.

"Yes; there are steps on the side of the hole. Go, I hear our pursuers approaching."

"And you?"

"I will follow."

"Down here?"

"Yes; down there the opening is wider than it appears. There is not a moment to lose, for if they come hither before the hole is closed, our secret is discovered, and—"

She paused, for Jack, feeling steps cut on the side of the opening, unhesitatingly descended.

"Is this where they shoots the coals for the palace?" asked Joe, as he prepared to follow Jack. "How many does they have in at a time?"

"Joe, Joe," whispered Jack, "make haste; it's not far to the bottom."

The boy plunged down the opening.

The girl followed them rapidly, and the faint light that had been admitted was shut out as the tree was by some strange agency restored to its former position.

The girl grasped an arm of each.

"Hush!" she whispered; "do not speak, do not breathe till I tell you. Hark!"

They could hear the trampling of feet above them. After a time they died away, and all was silent as the grave.

"Come," she whispered, and drew them along.

They could feel the moist walls of the passage through which they were taken, but the darkness was of such density that they could perceive nothing.

On, on they went, Joe and Jack side by side, with the girl in advance, their wrists grasped in her hands.

"Wait," she whispered, at last, and let go her hold.

"It is worser nor the Dark Arches, Master Jack," whispered Joe.

Jack did not reply.

They waited for about a minute, and then a hand touched them.

"Come; all is safe."

The hand that touched them drew them onwards, and they saw a faint streak of light before them.

Jack breathed a sigh of relief.

"Hush!" said the girl. "Precaution is necessary, since your discovery in the private garden will put the Bey's guards on the alert. Had they not seen us, this secret would never have been divulged to you."

"This passage, you mean?" whispered Jack.

"Yes; it is known but to myself and one other."

"Does the Bey know of it?"

"No, nor any other person save him who made it."

"And he?" whispered Jack.

"My lover. But hush! Another moment and we shall be in the grove of dates, and who knows what those trees may shelter?"

She led them on and upwards, and soon they stood beneath a sky in which here and there a star was faintly gleaming.

Jack looked back at the opening through which they had come, but it had disappeared.

A black and blighted branchless trunk only met his gaze.

She led them on a few steps to where they could see through the vista of trees, and then, pointing, she said—

"There lies the city of Algiers, and beyond it the bay. The Prophet have you both in his keeping. Farewell."

"Farewell!" said Jack. "Are you not coming with us? Will you not escape from a place where you are treated more unkindly than the lowest slave?"

"I would escape from my thraldom there, and the hateful life my parents doomed me to lead."

And she pointed towards the palace.

"Then come with us," said Jack. "I believe that Providence will assist us to leave this land, and in happier climes you may find a happier home."

Jack took her hands in his as he spoke.

"Englishman," she said, "my place is here."

"Where misery is?" asked Jack. "What you have suffered has turned your head. We would be your friends, even as you have been ours."

"Listen!" she said. "Never to mortal other than my own family have the words been uttered that I will speak to you. I was forced by the Bey's will and a father's greed to become an inmate of the Bey's harem when I had already a husband."

"A husband! and forced to become another's?" cried Jack. "Impossible!"

"You forget I am an Algerine," she said.

"But laws of man—of—"

"Englishman," she interrupted, "pity while you condemn, and thank Him who rules the universe that you are not a native of Barbary."

"I thank heaven I am not," said Jack.

"That passage through which I led you hither was made by him I love, that we might meet and commune without the knowledge of the Bey and his spies. It was my prolonged absence from the palace that brought upon me the ill-usage you witnessed, not for the first time, for had it ever been suspected I had gone beyond the palace walls the bowstring would have been placed round my neck, but I and my beloved Musjid meet in secret and mingle our tears together at the risk of our lives. Oh, may the day come when—"

At that moment a strong hand hurled her roughly back, and a fierce voice cried—

"When an outraged husband's blade shall find the heart of his wife's adorer."

"Musjid!" she cried.

"Away!" he cried, fiercely. "Is it not enough to know that my heart is broken by one all powerful here, but I find you in the arms of a stranger? This to his heart."

"Musjid—husband!" she cried, springing before him. "Oh, mercy, I—"

"Wretch, you have killed her!" cried Jack, springing upon him.

"The knife was for your heart, vile Frank!" shrieked Musjid, "and by the soul of the Prophet there shall it find its sheath."

He drew the ensanguined blade from his wife's bosom, and Joe caught her falling form in his arms.

With the fury of madness, Musjid grappled with Jack.

"She is mine—my wife," he cried, "and I will kill all who approach her."

The descending arm was caught in Jack's iron grip.

"Man," he cried, "you are mad. What would you do?"

The Algerine gnashed his teeth and struggled to free his arm.

"You have struck the woman who loved you," said Jack; "would you slay the man who has saved her?"

"For who—for himself!" shrieked the madman, for it was evident that reason had deserted him. "But you shall not have her—she shall not fly with you, for I will kill you both."

By a desperate effort he wrenched his hand free.

"Die!" he yelled.

"Heaven forgive me," gasped Rough and Ready Jack, "but it must be done."

As the madman sprang towards him again with the upraised knife, Jack shot out his arm, and his iron hand fell with the weight of a sledge-hammer between Musjid's eyes.

The man staggered back several paces, and then fell to the earth.

Jack tore the knife from his hand, and flung it amongst the trees.

Then he turned to where the poor woman lay gasping in the arms of Joe.

"Oh, this is terrible," he said. "Oh, say you are not hurt to death."

He seized her hand and pressed it to his bosom.

"Better his hand," she gasped, "than that of the executioner of the Bey."

"But you will live!" cried Jack.

"The Prophet wills it otherwise," she muttered. "My time is come."

"Now, don't you go for to talk like that," said Joe, "or you'll set me blubbering like a bull calf what's lost his natural wittles."

"Hush!" said Jack.

"What's she saying on?" asked Joe.

"She is calling on her husband, I think," said Jack.

The mutterings of the poor woman were so weak that Jack could not be certain what she said.

"Oh, Master Jack, you knocked him down," said Joe. "Can't you knock him up again, and make him come to her?"

Jack drew the half-stunned man to his feet.

"See to your wife," he said; "I fear she is dying."

Like a drunken man Musjid staggered to her side, and sank down on his knees beside her.

"Leave us!" he cried, fiercely, "or I shall shed more blood to-night!"

And placing one arm round his wife's head, he thrust Joe aside.

"Who are you a-hitting on?" cried Joe.

Jack's hand fell upon the boy's shoulder.

"Joe," he said, "respect his sufferings and his grief. Silence, if you would not make me angry."

"You let him have one when he wanted to hit you."

"I did so to save my life. Poor wretch, he is harmless now."

"Ah, Musjid, I have suffered for you. Had I betrayed our secret, you—you—"

Her head fell heavily back upon his arm.

Wildly the Algerine peered into her face, then he sprang to his feet.

"Dead—dead!" he shrieked, "and I have killed her. The houris bear her soul to the foot of Mahomet; but it shall not go alone, for parted in life, I join her in death."

"Hold, madman!" cried Jack, springing forward.

But too late!

Musjid had drawn forth another knife, and before Jack's hand could stay him, he had plunged it to its haft in his breast.

A moment he swayed backwards and forwards, muttering—

"Parted in life—united in death!"

And then he fell heavily to the earth.

Jack and Joe stood gazing down upon the two unfortunate beings who had been the victims of so cruel a fate, and a tyrannical ruler.

"Master Jack, you knows I ain't a soft 'un," said Joe; "but these here eyes of mine are a-perspiring awful."

"Joe, I know my own are moist, and I am not ashamed to say so. But we can do no good here now, while to remain longer may be unfortunate for us. We will try and reach the bay. Come."

"You've got the sword, Master Jack?"

"Yes; I've secured it to my side as best I can."

And with another glance at the woman who had befriended them, they turned away.

They passed through the city unmolested, and finally reached the bay.

The fisher folks had gone home to rest after their daily toil, and the shore was deserted by all but a few half-tipsy sailors.

The tramp of the soldiers on the forts, and the washing of the waters, were nearly all the sounds that broke the stillness.

"Where's the American ship she spoke of?" asked Joe.

Jack shaded his eyes with his hands.

"That's her, I think, lying over there."

"Wonder if they'll take us aboard, Master Jack?" asked Joe.

"Common humanity will induce them to do so, if we can explain to her captain and officers our position."

"But how will we do that?"

"I'm trying to think," said Jack.

"What noise is that?" suddenly cried Joe.

Jack listened.

"It is somebody singing."

"Yes; but do you hear what they are singing?" asked Joe, excitedly.

Jack listened, and a cry of joy burst from his lips as he heard the lines of the old song trolled out by at least a dozen voices—

"Our duty keeps us from all terrors;
    And where the gale blows we must go."

"Hurrah, Joe!" cried our hero; "they are either English or American sailors, and either will bear us from this land of tyranny and oppression."

"Oh, I feel as if I'd had a good supper of fried fish and 'taters," said Joe. "I'm so full of joy to think as we'll soon be out of this miserable country."

"Don't make too sure of that!" cried a harsh voice behind them.

Jack and Joe sprang round and stood face to face with Ralph Sternway and Baxter Sharp.

This was indeed an unexpected, and unlooked-for meeting.

For a moment Jack could scarcely believe the evidence of his eyes or ears.

Joe was so taken aback that he started

violently and dropped his scimitar into the bay.

"You don't seem particularly pleased to meet us, Rough and Ready Jack," said Ralph, sneeringly.

"He fancied he had got rid of us for good and all," said Baxter Sharp; "but he ain't the first who has made a great mistake."

"So he'll find to his cost," said Ralph.

"You escaped, and here?" gasped Jack.

"Oh, dear, no," replied Ralph, with a sneer. "They believe here, as we do in England, that you should send a thief to catch a thief, and a slave to catch a slave; and so you see you are our prisoner, Rough and Ready Jack!"

"You lie, you hound!" cried Jack. "No man shall drag me to slavery!"

So saying, he struck Baxter Sharp to the earth, and turned upon Ralph, who warded off the blow.

Then they grappled together, rolled over and over on the shore, and, locked in a deathly grip, fell, with a splash and a cry, into the waters of the bay.

CHAPTER XLIII.

THE STRUGGLE IN THE BAY—RECAPTURE OF SHARP AND ESCAPE OF JOE—IN THE AMERICAN BOAT AND UNDER THE STARS AND STRIPES.

Joe uttered a cry of dismay as he saw the two men sink beneath the surface of the bay.

Up till now the boy had been so thunderstruck at the appearance of their two foes, that he had been unable to utter a word.

But now that he saw Jack and Ralph sink together he found his tongue and pealed forth a loud agonised cry.

That cry was answered in two directions and in different languages.

"Give way, my lads, give way!" was shouted in English.

"Seize them! there they are!" was the shout of a body of negroes, as they sprang towards Joe and Baxter Sharp.

The villain had just risen to his feet as the hands of a couple of stalwart blacks grasped his shoulders.

Joe, also, would have been a prisoner, but, ducking under the arm of his would-be captor, he sprang from the shore into the water and sank as Jack and Ralph rose to the surface, grasping madly at each other's throat.

"Let go your hold," cried Jack, "or I'll smash your face to a pulp."

But Ralph's grasp only tightened.

"I'll kill you now!" he hissed. "Do your worst, and though you slay me, I'll have your life."

Treading the water so as to keep himself from sinking, Jack released his right hand, and sent it crashing between Ralph's eyes.

Still the ruffian held on to Jack's neck.

Again and again Jack sent his fist into the fellow's face, and then they once more sank together.

"Give way, lads, give way with a will!" cried a stentorian voice, and as Joe sank for the second time he saw a boat being rowed rapidly towards him.

When he again shot up, like a cork, above the surface, a huge brown hand seized him by the hair of his head, and he was lifted into a boat in which sat a dozen men, resting on their oars, while a young man in the uniform of the United States navy was leaning forward in the stern, scanning the water beneath and around him eagerly.

"Oh, save Master Jack—save him!" cried Joe, as he sank down between the rowers. "If he gets drowned, I'll drown myself, too, I will."

"There, there!" cried the officer, pointing. "Catch hold of him, boys. Quick!"

Joe sprang up.

"Oh, it's Jack; no, it ain't—it's the willain Sternway, and he's been and gone and murdered— There's Jack! there, there!"

In the second descent the two had released each other, and Jack, rising some yards away, was now striking out for the boat.

Both he and Ralph were seen, and in a few moments were hauled over the gunwale by the ready sailors.

"Oh, Jack!" cried Joe, and burst into tears.

Jack took the poor fellow's hand and pressed it fervently.

"Poor Joe," he said; "and you, too, are safe."

"They'd have got me as well as Baxter Sharp if I hadn't jumped into the water."

"Who, Joe?"

"The niggers."

Ralph had sunk down in the bottom of the boat.

The blows that Jack had struck him were heavy ones, and extremely painful, while the flesh around the eyes was swelling up, and fast closing them.

The negroes on shore, who had succeeded in securing Sharp, now shouted to the boat.

"What are they calling to us for?" asked the young officer. "Give way, there, and let's see what they want."

The sailors sent the boat skimming over the waters of the bay, till within about four yards of the shore.

"Hallo, there!" cried the officer. "Why do you hail us? What do you want?"

"Our prisoners," replied one, in very fair English. "They are slaves who have escaped, and we have been sent to take them back to their masters."

"Slaves!" cried the officer.

"Yes, runaway slaves; and we demand that you give them into our hands."

"Eh, did you say demand?"

"I did."

"Then, look here, my black friend, we ain't the men to be frightened at a nigger's demand."

"In the name of the Bey, I demand them," was the reply.

"And even then you won't get them," said the officer.

"Dare you defy the Bey?" asked the man, aghast.

"Defy him? Yes, and all his forces. Look over there. Do you see the Stars and Stripes floating from her masthead? It's under the protection of that flag that I am going to place these poor fellows, and tell your master to come and take them from under it if he dare."

"If he dare!" cried the sailors in chorus.

"Why, if they were niggers you shouldn't have them, let alone white men," cried the officer.

"Call the guard," cried one of the blacks who held Sharp.

"You may call your grandmother if you like," cried the young officer, "for we should fear her quite as much as the guard. If you want these poor wretches, come and take them, but I warn you it won't be healthy for you to try it."

"Oh, take me with you—take me, too," cried Sharp.

"Jump into the bay, and we'll fish you out."

"Aye, aye," cried the sailors. "Come on."

Baxter made an ineffectual struggle to release himself from his captors.

"I cannot," he cried. "Help—oh, help!"

The negroes bore him back some paces, and the sailors impulsively sent their boat towards the shore.

"Lay on your oars!" cried the young officer, sternly.

The men obeyed.

"What would you do?" he asked, addressing his men. "We dare not land and take him from them. A pretty kettle of fish we should be in, and I should be court-martialled and broken. No, no, lads. If the poor fellow could break away from them and leap into the bay, we would aid him to obtain his liberty, as we have done with these others, but to take him from his captors would bring about a pretty to do."

Evidently fearful that the boat's crew would land and rescue their captive, the negroes bore Baxter Sharp farther and farther away from the edge of the bay.

"They don't mean to let us have him, at all events," said the young officer. "So give way, men, for I see the signal for the boat to return."

The men bent to their oars, and the boat went skimming over the bay, and soon ran alongside an American man-of-war.

"Now, then, you fellows, get aboard as quickly as you can, and some of the men will hunt you up a change of toggery."

Jack and Joe felt only too eager to find a footing on the deck of the ship, which meant certain freedom for them, and clambered on board with eagerness.

"Now then, up you go," said the officer, touching Ralph with his foot. "Hang me if I don't think the fellow has gone to sleep."

Two of the sailors pulled Ralph to his feet.

"Now then, get aboard," said one.

"I—I can't see," moaned Ralph.

"Can't see, why—hallo! Poor fellow, you have hurt yourself. Here, bear a hand and get him aboard. Got this I suppose in his struggles to escape," said the officer.

Ralph only moaned.

He did not care then to explain that Jack's fist had closed his swollen eyes, for this might cause an explanation of the whole affair, and he knew that if the truth were known, his rescuers would only feel for him the greatest abhorrence and contempt. Aided by the men, he was got on to the deck, where, by the light of the ship's lantern, his swollen and bruised face was plainly revealed.

"Come on board, sir," said the young officer, saluting the officer of the deck.

"And the men?"

"All here and sober," was the reply.

"But who are these you have brought with you, Mr. Purseglove?"

"Men whom we found struggling in the bay, sir. As far as I can make out they had been sold into slavery by some of those Barbary pirates, and having escaped, to prevent recapture they leapt into this bay, only one of them being secured, and, of course, I dared not land to take him from his captors. That would never have done, sir."

"One of them at least seems to have received rough treatment."

"Yes, sir. But when or how, I am unable to say."

"I thought, when I saw yonder youngster, that you had carried off a scarecrow from some field," said the superior, nodding towards Joe. "Ask the purser to find him something more decent to wear. I shall not disturb the captain with my report to-night, but have them up before him to-morrow morning."

"I hope he will not be prevailed upon to return them to slavery."

"I should not think he would; in fact, I believe that slavery is becoming abhorrent to us Americans. The English boast that their flag floats not over a slave, and I am no prophet if the Stars and Stripes will not soon be able to echo that boast."

"It is a cruel institution, unworthy of Christian people," said Purseglove. "But having reported myself, sir, with your permission, I will go below."

"Go, sir. The men will see to these poor fellows."

The young officer saluted and turned away.

Jack, Joe, and Ralph were taken below by the men.

Chests were overhauled for garments in which to attire the shivering and drenched unfortunates.

But as nothing could just then be found to suit Joe, he was stripped and tumbled into a hammock, a blanket being tucked well around him.

"Oh, Master Jack," he said, holding out his hand to his friend, "I feels as happy as if somebody had given me a sovereign and put me into a cook-shop to eat all the wittles that was there."

"Ah, Joe, we have, indeed, reason to be grateful for our liberty, and I would to heaven that poor Deliah shared it with us!"

CHAPTER XLIV.

THE MARCH OF THE SLAVES—THE CAMP IN THE SANDS—THE MASSACRE—BAXTER SHARP'S REVENGE.

RALPH STERNWAY spoke falsely when he said that he and Sharp had been sent to recapture Rough and Ready Jack.

Never for one moment had either of the villainous pair expected to find Jack and Joe where they did.

They believed them to be in durance, and therefore it was with the utmost surprise that, in trying to escape themselves, they encountered our hero and his friend on the edge of the bay.

The men by whom they were led away were themselves slaves, and did not keep that guard over them and their companions which the soldiers did over Jack and Joe, consequently upon entering a forest outside the town on their way to the slave barracks of Kula Arabi they broke for the timber, and their guards, unable for the time being to follow them, lest the others should also attempt to get away, were unable to pursue them.

When, however, they had secured the rest, they set out in search of the fugitives.

With what result we have seen.

Bitterly did Baxter Sharp condemn the foolishness of Ralph in desiring to force Jack and Joe back into slavery.

The villain thought that while he could hand Jack over to the mercies of the Algerines, he could make sure of the assistance of the American man-of-war's men.

But Ralph made a mistake. Jack was too quick for them. Baxter was knocked down, and Jack grappled and fell with his companion, as we have seen, and Sharp was recaptured.

Wild at the loss of his friend, his captors did not show him much mercy, for they knew that the slave-dealer would punish them severely for not securing both.

They dragged him along, kicking and cuffing him at every pause, till at last he was thrust into the horrible den to which his companions had been consigned.

No food was supplied to either Sharp or his companions in captivity that night.

On the following morning, however, a meal was placed before them, and they were told that they would shortly have to leave their present quarters and take a long march.

Whither, they could not learn.

After the muezzin had summoned the faithful to prayers, they were brought out and secured in pairs by ropes, then about a dozen negroes, armed with whips and muskets, surrounded them.

Kula Arabi, mounted on his horse, with a scimitar at his side and a musket at his saddle-bow, came forth and gave the order to march.

The slaves cracked their whips, and the newly-made captives set forth, with their faces turned to the mountains of the Atlas.

All that day were they urged forward with whip and voice, and as night approached a camp was made on a wide, sandy plain.

A tent was erected for the slave-dealer, fires were lit, and food prepared at them.

When this was partaken of, Kula Arabi went round the camp to see that all was right, and then retired to his tent.

The slave guards were fairly worn out, and threw themselves on the earth beside their charges, each placing his whip and musket at his side.

When the whole camp seemed to be wrapped in slumber, Baxter nudged his companion.

"Hist!" he whispered.

"Well?" was the half-sleepy reply of the man to whom he was secured.

"Now is our time," whispered Sharp.

"What do you mean?"

"I have been working the rope, so that I believe I can slip it over my hand," said Baxter.

"You can?" cried the other.

"Hush, or you will ruin all."

And he pulled the man, who had half sprung up, down again to the earth.

The fellow lay quiet.

"There," said Baxter, as he worked

his hand out of the cords. "Have you got a knife?"

"No," replied the other.

"Nor I. How can we release the rest?"

"And if we could, what would be the good?" said the man. "They would pour a volley into us before we could move. Their guns are all at their hands."

"Yes; but we might secure them," said Sharp, speaking in the man's ear.

"Ah!"

"Be careful; let them hear no sound."

Baxter, having got his arm free, wriggled himself along the sand till he could reach the nearest guard.

The man from his breathing evidently slept soundly.

Advancing his hand cautiously, Baxter drew the musket towards him and out of reach of the negro.

Then he again advanced.

"If he wears a knife, and I can obtain it, we are free," he thought.

As he stretched forth his hand to feel at the negro's girdle, the man awoke and raised his head.

By the aid of the stars he could see Baxter Sharp.

A cry rose to his lips, and his arm shot forth for his musket.

But the cry was stifled in his throat.

Baxter's hands were upon his neck, and his knees pressed into the man's chest.

Never did Sharp feel more powerful than at that moment.

Tighter and tighter his fingers twined themselves, and fiercer and fiercer was the pressure of his knees on the negro's body.

Not a word did he utter, and not a sound could the other articulate.

The eyes of the negro bulged out from his head, and his tongue protruded from his mouth.

The blood gushed from his eyes and ears and he ceased to struggle.

Still Baxter Sharp's fingers pressed his throat, and his knees his chest.

Nor did the villain release his hold or remove his knees till he was certain the negro was dead.

Then he felt about his body, and at last found a knife. With this he returned to his late companion.

"You are free," he whispered, severing the cord that still bound his limbs.

And then, putting the musket in his hand, he added—

"Take this; but lie still till I have released the others."

The man grasped the gun but obeyed the injunction.

Cautiously, like a snake, Baxter crawled around the captives, placing one hand on their lips and with the other severing their bonds.

"Hush!" he whispered to each. "Lay still till you hear my order, then leap for the guns at the guards' side and send their contents into the niggers' bodies."

In less than five minutes every man was released from his companion.

Then Baxter crawled over to the nearest guard, and, seizing his gun, plunged his knife into the man's breast.

The wretch uttered a piercing cry.

"Up!" shouted Baxter. "Secure their guns!"

Before the startled negroes could seize their muskets, they were in the hands of the white men.

"Strike, and spare not!" shouted Baxter, as he brought the butt of a musket down upon the head of one of the blacks, crushing it like an egg-shell. "Death to them all!"

Not a moment was given the guard to recover themselves.

With a yell and a bound the white men were amongst them, firing and striking on all sides.

The startled and demoralised negroes were mown down like corn before the sickle.

Shouts and cries arose on all sides as the work of slaughter went on.

"Spare none!" shouted Baxter. "'Tis for liberty you strike! Let not one escape to bring succour."

And with his musket he dealt blow after blow.

Aroused by the tumult, Kula Arabi sprang from his tent, scimitar in hand.

"What's this!" he cried. "Ah!"

As he saw the white men on their feet dealing blows as the blacks, he recoiled.

Baxter turned the musket he held, took aim and fired.

The Arab uttered a cry, let fall his gleaming blade, and clutched frantically at the canvas of his tent.

Baxter sprang forward to deal him his death blow, but paused suddenly.

"No, he shall hang like a dog," he cried.

Soon not one of the guard but lay powerless on the sand, which greedily drank up the blood that flowed from their wounds.

Baxter Sharp's glance told him the true state of affairs, and he pealed forth a shout of triumph which was echoed and re-echoed by the liberated men.

Still frantically clutching at the canvas wall of his tent, Kula Arabi, the slave-dealer, fell to the earth.

Baxter went up to him and bent over him, planting his foot upon the scimitar, to prevent the other seizing it.

Arabi, believing that his hour had indeed come, pleaded piteously for mercy.

"What mercy would you have shown me?" asked Sharp; "whither were you taking us?"

"To Morocco."

"To sell us for slaves?"

The other pressed his hand to his shoulder, but did not answer.

"Speak, or die!" thundered Sharp, raising his musket.

"I am wounded—have mercy," pleaded the slave dealer.

"You would have sold us to a life of slavery," said Baxter.

"Yes, yes!"

"And you, who would consign free Englishmen to a living death, confess this?" cried Baxter Sharp.

Then he turned to the men who had gathered near him.

"There is enough rope left of your late bonds to hang him," he said. "Go, bring it hither, and he shall hang like a dog."

The men hurried to get the ropes that had so lately bound them, and brought them to Sharp.

"Tie the pieces together," he said, "and we will teach these slave-dealing hounds to beware how they would make slaves of white men."

The ropes were soon fastened together as few but sailors can fasten them.

"But where shall he hang? There is no tree here," said one.

"True," said Baxter; "I had forgotten that."

"If any of the muskets are still loaded, better let him die with a bullet," said the previous speaker.

At that moment the horse of the slave-dealer uttered a whinny.

"No, no," said Baxter Sharp, "he shall have a more deserving death than that. We will tie him to his horse's tail, and let the beast drag him to death."

The suggestion was agreed to with delight. The horse was caught, and, despite his prayers for mercy, the wounded slave-dealer was secured to the tail of his horse.

Then Baxter Sharp struck the animal a sharp blow with the butt end of his musket, and it tore madly away, dragging Arabi at its heels.

A few minutes later and an unrecognisable mass lay dead at the heels of a kicking and plunging horse.

CHAPTER XLV.

THE AMERICAN CAPTAIN—VISIT OF THE BEY—THE DEMAND AND THE DEFIANCE.

On the following morning Jack, Joe, and Ralph were informed that the captain desired their presence on the quarter-deck of the "Pennsylvania," the name of the American man-of-war still lying in the Bay of Algiers.

Ralph was as blind as a bat, and anything but presentable, so excuses were made for him, and Jack and Joe went aft alone.

The captain, a grey-headed old veteran, stared at the lads through a pair of horn-rimmed spectacles.

"Well," he said, at length, "how is it that my officer and a portion of my crew find you young Englishmen in the bay?"

Jack took a step forward, and, saluting his questioner respectfully, told him all.

"Humph! if I catch sight of one of

those rascals out of native waters, I'll give him a shot 'twixt wind and water, and blow him to smithereens, despite Uncle Sam. This piracy, long since stamped out in civilised nations, must be put down here. But what is this you tell me of the man brought on board with you?"

"Simply the truth, sir, as my companion here will vouch for," said Jack.

"I'd swear it a hundred times over," said Joe. "He's the biggest, willenest willain as ever you seed. He'd take a halfpenny out of a blind man's hat and holler 'stop thief' if a policeman see him. Oh, he's a right-down bad 'un, as the publican said to the smasher when he bit his shilling in half."

"A strange lad," said the captain, looking up at his first officer.

"Lor', that's where you makes a mistake, sir," said Joe; "I ain't strange at all."

"What were you before you left England?" asked the captain.

"Everything and nothing, sir. I was a poor orphan as had a mother."

"No flippancy on board my ship," cried the captain, severely.

The captain glared through his spectacles at Joe.

"Pardon me, sir," said Jack, "but this poor boy has never been taught the respect due to his superiors. He has been a poor, homeless wretch, cast upon the mercy of the world—his food often what he could pick from the kennels, his bed the hard stones. No father's or mother's care has he ever known—a waif, a stray, a castabout upon the tide of humanity, but, despite his hardships, his heart is good and true, and I implore for him a Christian's pity and forbearance."

The old gentleman took off his spectacles and glared for some moments at Jack.

"Youngster," he said, "it's the first time any man except the parson has ever preached to me on my quarter-deck."

"Sir, I trust that nothing I have said has given you offence?" cried Jack.

"Don't know so much about that," was the reply.

Then, as he saw a pained anxious look on Jack's face, he placed his hand on our hero's shoulder.

"There—there," he said, "you have not given me offence, my lad. You have pleaded for your young friend, as far as I am concerned, not in vain. The boy will grow wiser as he grows older."

"I am sure he will, sir," said Jack, "for though his speech is rough, his heart is true."

"Well, make yourselves useful on board my ship," said the captain. "We do not remain long here, and I shall send you on board the first vessel that flies the Union Jack."

"I thank you, sir," said Jack, saluting again.

The captain waved his hand as an indication that the audience was ended.

Jack took the hint and drew Joe away.

"I say, Jack, ain't they give me a spiffin suit of togs," said Joe. "There's not a hole in 'em from collar to boots."

"Joe, be discreet and respectful."

"I try to be, Master Jack."

"You must remember that you are now with gentlemen."

"He was a funny looking one, though, when he was a quizzing of us through them specs. of his."

"But still he is a gentleman, Joe."

"Is he?" said Joe. "I don't know much about 'em. I wasn't dragged up in their company, you know."

"Will you do as I tell you, Joe?"

"Oh, won't I just. You try me, Master Jack," said Joe.

"Very well," said Jack. "If you do you won't go far astray."

"I'll do anything for you, sir."

"I know that, Joe. Now here comes an officer. Put your hand to your head, as I do, and salute him."

"I'll do it, Master Jack."

It was the young lieutenant, Purse-glove.

Jack placed his hand to his forehead. The salute was at once returned.

Joe put his hand up as Jack did, but the poor waif did not stop there.

"Hopes I see you well, sir," he cried.

The young officer stopped short, and then burst out laughing.

"Yes, my lad," he said; "I am quite well."

"You look it," said Joe.

Jack gripped his arm.

"Hush!" he whispered.

"I ain't a telling any lie, Master Jack," cried Joe; "you look at his phiz, and if it ain't the picture of health I never seed a countryman come into Covent Garden Market with a face like his'n."

"But Joe, you forget," cried Jack, pulling him back, and pointing up to the flag floating in the breeze; "you are not in Covent Garden Market, but on the deck of an American man-of-war."

For a moment there was silence, and then Jack said, seriously—

"My boy, I must teach you how to act."

"Lor' bless you, Master Jack, I couldn't act," said Joe. "Why, if I had been cut out for a hacter—"

"Joe," interrupted Jack; "look! Do you recognise the man in the stern of the first boat?"

"Why, that's the fellow I knocked into the water," said Joe.

"And the one at his side. Can you call him to mind, Joe?"

"That's him as claimed us from the pirate captain."

"The very same. Their boats are heading this way."

At this moment loud cries were raised on board the ship, and the boatswain's whistle rang shrilly on the air.

The captain, who had left the deck, came hurrying up from his cabin, and his officers surrounded him on the quarter-deck.

The roll of drums were now heard, and the marines formed in line at midships.

"What's it all mean, Master Jack?" asked Joe.

"The Bey, I think, is coming aboard," was the reply.

"What, arter us?"

"Heaven only knows," said Jack. "Let's slip below."

"Attention—every man to his place," cried the first officer. "Dip the flag and fire a salute."

The flag was lowered three times, and the cannon boomed over the bay.

Then as the boats came alongside, the officers bared their swords and the

marines presented arms, and up the gangway, which had been lowered, the corpulent form of the Bey reached the deck, followed closely by his secretary.

The captain, with his sword still at the salute, advanced to meet him.

"Your highness honours my vessel with this visit," said the captain, bowing.

The Bey returned the bow, and pointed to his secretary.

"Sir Americano," said the secretary, "we hear that you have on board your ship two slaves who belong to his highness, the Bey, and it is to claim them from you, as well as pay a friendly visit, that we are here to-day."

"Slaves!" said the captain.

"Yes; two white slaves. Ah! there they stand."

And catching sight of Jack and Joe, he pointed towards them.

"No slave treads the deck of my ship," said the captain.

"But they are there," cried the secretary. "They have broken out of captivity and left behind them the dead bodies of those whose duty it was to secure them; therefore, Sir Americano, in the name of his highness, the Bey of Algiers, I demand they be given into our hands."

Jack's and Joe's hearts sank within them.

The American captain raised his hand and pointed to the flag.

"Under that flag," he cried, "the veriest wretch, unless he be a thief or an assassin, finds shelter, and woe to him, be he prince or peasant, who would dare to drag him from beneath its folds."

"Madman!" cried the secretary; "do you know whom you defy?"

"I know whom I protect," cried the American, "the persecuted and the oppressed. Though your forts open fire on me, and your legends swarm round my ship, I will not surrender them. There flies the Stars and Stripes, insult it who dare; and hark you, that flag and the Union Jack of Old England can bid defiance to the world!"

"'I'LL TEACH YOU—TAKE THAT!' CRIED MRS. SLOPS."

CHAPTER XLVI.

THE BEY IS MADE RIDICULOUS, AND THE SECRETARY COMES TO GRIEF—SAVED BY A SACRIFICE.

THE Bey shrugged his shoulders.

"He will not surrender unto us that which is ours," he said.

"So it seems, your highness. Shall we take them from him? A signal will bid the forts open fire, and send a number of armed men here."

"Send all you can and all you dare!" cried the American captain. "Every man there to his quarters. Double shot the guns, and—"

The Bey laid his hand upon his arm.

"I come here in friendship," he said, "but you treat me as an enemy."

"If you come in friendship, here shall you find it, but you shall find no slaves."

"You refuse, then, to restore these men to his highness?" asked the secretary.

"These men are free," replied the captain. "If they choose themselves to go with you, I will not prevent them; but if they prefer to press the planks of this deck till they can meet a vessel of their own nation, then I say, take them if you dare."

The secretary seemed inclined to threaten that the Bey would do so, but the corpulent little potentate bade him say no more.

"Now, can I offer you the hospitality of my ship?" asked the captain.

The Bey looked at the secretary for his advice.

The look he received seemed to say, don't accept it.

"Since my first demand is refused, I will shake the dust of your vessel from my feet."

"Be it as you will it," replied the captain, with a bow.

The Bey turned and descended the companion.

As his head passed below the upper deck, at a signal from the captain, the marines, who had all the while stood presenting arms, dropped the butts of their muskets to the deck.

Striking the deck all at once as they did, the sound and shake caused the Bey to start so violently that he lost his footing on the companion, and pitched headfirst into the boat that awaited him at the bottom.

A cry of consternation arose from the secretary and those in the boat, as they saw the rotund figure of their lord and master stand on its head for a moment, and then roll over sideways across the legs of the rowers.

It was with the utmost difficulty the marines and sailors hushed their laughter at the captain's stern order—

"Silence there, men!"

The secretary now hesitated whether to follow his lord or not.

The Bey was anything but merciful when something put him out of temper.

The monarch might take it into his head to blame him for the mishap, and order him to lose his head.

But feeling also that if he did not hurry to his master's assistance, he might still be condemned to the same fate, he ran down the companion at a rate that caused him to step upon his robe, and struggling to save himself, he fell flat on top of the Bey.

No use now was the stern order—"Silence, men!"—for even the captain and his officers could hardly issue it for laughing.

The Bey, rendered desperate, brought his jewelled hand with a heavy slap on the bald uncovered head of his confidential servant.

"Allah!" he cried, "am I to be made the laughing-stock of the Christians by you? Look to it! But for listening to your advice, you dust of the earth, I had now been smoking my chibouk to the sound of the waters of the fountain, or toying with the tresses of the ladies of my harem."

"Most magnificent," began the trembling secretary.

"Silence, dog!" interrupted the Bey. "Bid my slaves take me quickly from the sight of these laughing Christians. Oh, by the soul of the Prophet, I'd like to kill them all!"

The secretary took up a stick and struck at the rowers, shouting—

"Quicker, quicker!"

But the men were already using every endeavour they could to reach the shore.

The Bey looked sulky and dangerous, for ever and anon he bared his white teeth and suffered them to gleam through his black beard.

At length the boat was out of the reach of the sound of the man-of-war, and a sigh of relief broke from the Bey and his secretary.

The servant feared to meet his master's eyes, and pretending to cover his bald head, he drew his white robes across his face.

"Allah, be merciful!" he muttered more than once beneath his breath.

"I'll punish him for advising me to demand my slaves from the Christian pigs," thought the Bey. "By the Prophet, his flesh shall smart and his feet be made sore. Oh, that I have lived to be defied and degraded!"

Shortly the boat touched the shore, and the secretary sprang up to assist his master to rise.

"Away, dog!" cried the Bey, pushing him. "Touch not my hand."

The secretary bent almost to the thwarts of the boat.

"Oh! pardon, all powerful," he cried.

The Bey gave him another slap on the top of the head, and then got on shore unaided, for none of the others dared offer the assistance of a slave to one so powerful.

Some few hours later a crushed and broken man sat in one apartment of the palace, and an enraged one strode from side to side of a magnificent chamber opening out into the courtyard, in which several black slaves and their white overseer stood like statues beside the marble fountain.

The angry Bey presently paused in his agitated walk.

He turned to the window and struck his hands sharply together three times.

At this signal the overseer advanced a few paces beyond the others, and salaamed deeply.

"I have decided," said the Bey. "Let him be led into the courtyard, and there, where I may see it done, give him one hundred strokes on the soles of his feet.

The overseer salaamed again, and then turning to the negroes, bade them follow him. With the slaves at his heels, the Yankee overseer went through the entrance to the palace, and trod with soft steps the matted floors, till he paused before the entrance to the apartment in which the trembling secretary sat moaning and muttering.

As the Yankee and his fellows went off, the Bey turned to a gorgeously attired youthful slave—

"Light my chibouk," he said.

The young slave salaamed to the floor, and then proceeded to obey the order, after which he drew a long silken tube up to the window, and sinking on his knee, presented it to his master.

"Hand me the coffee."

A beautiful cup containing the refreshing beverage was presented in the same way, and then he rose, and with clasped hands awaited any further orders.

"Back to your place," said the Bey, removing the amber mouthpiece of his pipe from between his lips, and sending forth a cloud of fragrance that curled fantastically about his bejewelled turban.

The pipe and the coffee seemed to somewhat compose the wretched feelings of the Bey, for the frown passed away, and his bronzed features were wreathed with a smile.

But those who had studied him most, knew that his smile was more to be feared than his frown.

In a few minutes the secretary, looking more dead than alive, was led into the courtyard.

As the negroes dragged him towards the fountain, and opposite the opening where the Bey sat blowing thick wreaths of smoke from his lips, the disgraced man cried out in pleading tones—

"Oh, most mighty and magnificent, whom Allah preserve and the Prophet ever favour with his blessing, be merciful to your servant—pity your abject slave."

But the Bey only continued to smoke and sip his coffee.

At a signal from the overseer, the negroes forced the secretary down onto the edge of the marble fountain, and removed the slippers from his feet.

This done the Yankee seized a long thin bamboo cane, and gave another signal, which caused a cry to peal from the poor wretch.

With the rapidity of lightning the slaves turned him round and stood him on his head, one holding him round the body, and one each keeping his feet erect by grasping an ankle.

"Strike!" cried the Bey, in a loud voice.

"Hold!" cried a shrieking voice, and Deliah, springing before the Bey, fell on her knees at his feet. The potentate gazed at her in surprise.

"You here?" he exclaimed.

"Yes," she cried. "Swear by the Prophet to spare that man, and I will consent to become yours."

"I swear," cried the Bey, clasping the girl in his arms. "Do him no harm on your lives. Deliah, you have made me happy."

"Aye," she said, bursting into tears; "but at what a sacrifice! Alas, alas! poor dear Jack!"

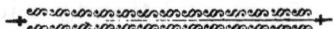

CHAPTER XLVII.

WESTWARD HO!—THE TRADER'S VISIT TO THE MAN-OF-WAR—FAREWELL—MEETING OF LONG-PARTED FRIENDS.

FAREWELL now to Jack's hopes of ever again seeing Deliah.

She had, to save her late father's friend, consented to enter through those portals which would be to her a living death.

*   *   *   *   *

The discomfiture of the Bey and his secretary was the cause of much talk and a great deal of laughter both in the officers' cabins and the men's quarters.

Joe kept the sailors and marines in a roar by the capers he cut and the manner in which he imitated the looks, words, and actions of the Algerines.

Jack, however, could not join in the mirth.

His heart felt for poor Deliah.

Oh, how he hated Ralph Sternway and Baxter Sharp!

To them he owed all the anxiety and sufferings which he had undergone.

There was only one pleasure he felt now.

Baxter Sharp had been dragged back into slavery, and Ralph Sternway would be handed over to justice.

The guns on board the American ship were kept shotted, and a good watch kept.

The Algerines might open fire from the forts upon the ships, or an attempt might be made to board her and secure the runaways.

But there was no need for these precautions.

The Bey thought it best to submit to their loss, and the fact of his not having his demands complied with had brought about the consent of Deliah to become an inmate of his harem.

So, with band playing and flags flying, the anchors were weighed, and the 'Pennsylvania' sailed proudly out of the Bay of Algiers, and pointed her prow westward.

Days, weeks passed, and vessels were only sighted in the distance, and the coast of America was almost looming into view before one was seen sufficiently near to communicate with.

She dipped her flag to the man-of-war, and signals were sent aloft, which caused the stranger to haul over her yards and sail in nearer.

Then a boat was put off and rowed towards the war vessel.

In the stern-sheets sat a short, stout, happy-looking man, but there was something in the appearance of two of those at the oars that attracted and fixed Jack's attention.

"She's a Britisher, youngster," said a gruff, but not unpleasant voice at his side.

Jack looked up to see one of the men leaning over the rail watching the ship and boat.

"Do you think that's her captain in the boat?"

"Maybe. You see, there's nothing to distinguish the skipper of a trader. He wears what he likes and how he likes; but you can tell every man's position on board a man-of-war. He carries his rank in his toggery."

"I wish I could get a sight of the features of those rowing," said Jack.

"She'll swing round in a minute, and then you'll get a look at their jibs."

"How like in many ways," thought Jack.

"Like who, Master Jack," asked Joe, coming to his side.

"Why, Charley Calvert and Harry Houghten."

"Your chums as was?"

"Yes, Joe."

The captain and his officers grouped themselves in haste as a rope was flung to those in the boat, and the short, stout man came up the side of the ship.

He approached the group, and, in true nautical fashion, saluted the captain and his officers.

His salutation was returned.

"Gentlemen," he said, "if I read your signals aright, you requested my presence on board your ship?"

"I did, sir," replied the officer.

"I am here, sir, and have brought with me my papers for your inspection."

"Have I the honour of addressing her captain?"

"I am skipper of the 'Betsy,' hailing from the port of London, and my name is Briggs."

"Well, Captain Briggs, I have certainly no intention of demanding to see your papers, for I have no suspicion as to the character of your vessel; but having three of your countrymen on board my ship, I am anxious to transfer them to one of their own nationality, and shall be glad if you are willing to receive them."

Captain Briggs pursed his lips.

"Well, sir," he said, "I have a full complement of hands and a few passengers, and if I took them I should have to put them ashore at the next port."

"I tell you frankly that two of them are lads, whom I believe to be honest and brave. But one, a man named Sternway, has laid himself open to the law by mutiny and murder, and whom you would of course hand over to the authorities."

"Of course, sir, if you force me to take him I must; but really I think his chances of getting his deserts would be greater by his remaining in your charge than by being placed in mine."

"So let him be, then," was the reply. "But will you receive the others?"

"Yes."

"Order the two lads who sought our protection in the Bay of Algiers to stand forward!" cried the captain, in a loud voice; "John Tempest and Joe Jilks."

No sooner had the name of Jack been called when cries of surprise came from the boat below.

Jack cast a glance downwards, and saw that two of the occupants had sprung to their feet and were glancing eagerly upwards.

"It is Hal—it is Charley!" cried Jack.

"Hurrah!" cried Hal, waving his hat. "It is Jack himself—our old friend Rough and Ready Jack!"

But Jack could not reply then, for they had to obey the order of the captain and stand forward.

A few questions, a few answers, and they were ordered to go over into the boat.

Jack's voice trembled with emotion as, on his own and Joe's behalf, he thanked the captain and his officers for the kindness they had shown them; and then, with a beating heart, he went over the side and slid down into the arms of his two long-lost friends.

CHAPTER XLVIII.

THE FRIENDS HAVE MUCH TO TELL—WAITING FOR THE CAPTAIN—OFF FOR THE ENGLISH VESSEL.

THE skipper of the "Betsy" accepted the captain's invitation to join him and a couple of his officers in the saloon to crack a bottle of wine.

The friends, therefore, had plenty of time to ask and answer each other's questions, and to tell each other some of his adventures.

"Dear old chums," said Jack, huskily, as he held a hand of Hal's and Charley's in his own, "I cannot tell you how happy I am to meet you both."

"And we to find you, dear boy," said Hal.

"I feel as if I could dance for very joy," cried Charley.

"And I almost weep like a girl for the same cause," said Jack, "for I tell you, dear old boys, that I had almost given up the hope of ever meeting you again."

"And the others, Will, Tom, and Sam," said Hal.

"All of you," replied Jack, "for my life has been more than once in danger, but those yarns will be too long to recount now. But know you anything of the other three?"

"Yes. They went to sea in the 'Mountain Flower,'" said Hal.

"What! that coffin ship?" cried Jack, in surprise.

"That was all a lying yarn of that crimp, who played a deep game to rob us. The 'Mountain Flower' really was commanded by Captain Henry Goodson, as fine a gentleman as ever sailed salt water."

"You surprise me," said Jack.

"Thought I should; and we would have gone with them if we could have got away," said Hal.

"What prevented you?"

"That sham Boatswain Bob," was the reply.

"And I'll wager he wishes now we had gone?" said Charley.

"Why?"

"Because he might not now be doing seven years."

"Who—Bob?"

"Yes. We managed to put him and a few of his disreputable companions away. The game he played us did not do so well for him as he expected. He was collared, and though he had a first-rate counsel, and somebody found plenty of money to help him, he was brought in guilty and sentenced to seven years."

"Serve him right," said Jack; "I am glad to hear it. That is one rascal who is justly served. And so Tom, Will, and Sam went out in the 'Mountain Flower,' after all?"

"Yes; but what's the name of your ship, Hal?"

"The 'Betsy'"

"What is she?"

"A trader, and carries passengers as well as cargo."

"And the captain's a good sort?"

"He's a perfect seaman, and we have an angel on board."

"An angel!" said Jack.

"Yes, with a wooden leg."

"A wooden leg?" laughed Jack.

"Yes, and a long one it is too, I can tell you. Chips has offered lots of times to cut the corns off its foot, but lor'! he only gets a prod with it."

Jack laughed and Joe listened with open mouth.

"Never know'd wooden legs had corns," he said.

"Bless you, you don't know everything," said Charley; "but who is this, Jack?"

"Don't you remember him?"

"No."

"I knows you, sir," said Joe.

"You do? Why, where and when?" he asked, looking fixedly at the lad.

"I used to sweep the crossing over agin the 'Grand Turk,'" replied Joe.

"Oh, I recognise him now," Charley said. "But there's something different about him."

"I should rather think there was," said Joe. "I didn't wear such clothes then; I've grown to be a swell."

And Joe looked admiringly at the

garments with which he had been furnished.

"I will only tell you this now, lads, that I have owed my life more than once to my poor friend Joe."

"Then tip us your fingers, Joe," cried Hal, "for whoever befriends Rough and Ready Jack I must claim as my friend, too."

"And mine also," said Charley.

Joe shook their hands, and seemed to grow several inches higher.

"Master Jack," he said, "I feels proud to know as how I'm getting into good company."

Up till now the others in the boat had listened in silence, but now one of them held out his hand to Jack, saying—

"As we are likely to be messmates for awhile, I'd like to shake hands with you."

Jack gave him his hand.

"Put it there," said the other, proffering his own. "I like the cut of your figure-head."

Jack, with a laugh, grasped the brown extended hand and pressed it warmly.

"I can tell a man by the pressure of his fist," said the sailor, "and I know we shall be friends."

"I hope so," replied Jack, "for heaven knows that I have too many enemies."

"You'll find none on board the 'Betsy,'" said Hal.

"Unless he offends the Angel, and then he must look out for squalls."

"And crushed toes," added Hal.

"I'll do my best not to aggravate this lady," laughed Jack. "What is she?"

"She's the stewardess, old Sam Slops's wife," said Hal.

"And is he the steward?"

"Yes."

"Has he got a wooden leg?"

"Bless you, Jack, no," said Charley; "and he don't want one either, for he gets too much of his wife's."

Captain Briggs now came over the side, and dropped into the boat.

The line was cast off, and in another minute the boat was heading for the "Betsy."

CHAPTER XLIX.

HAL AND THE SKIPPER OF THE "BETSY"—A STRANGE DUEL IN THE PANTRY.

THE captain of the trading ship spoke not a word to any in the boat, but sat, thoughtful and absorbed, in the stern-sheets.

It was evident to all in the boat that he did not like having the two lads given into his charge.

Still, he felt glad that the American captain had not forced him to take Ralph Sternway also on board the "Betsy."

Such a man on board, despite that he would be in irons, might succeed in corrupting some of his crew, and bring about a mutiny.

He clambered onto his own deck with his usually jolly expression of features overcast, and nearly sent the Angel flying as he ran down his cabin stairs.

"Well, whoever did see the likes of that?" said the Angel, staring after him as he slammed his cabin door to. "Wonder what's been and gone and up-

set him like that! I'll go and ask Sam, and if he don't tell me, let him look out for his toes."

And Mrs. Slops made her way back to the steward's pantry.

The sailors, with Jack and Joe, having scrambled on deck, the boat was hoisted up, by the order of the first mate, Mr. Williams, and then Hal repaired to the captain's cabin, while Charley proceeded to the steward's pantry.

Hal, finding the cabin door closed, knocked, and was bade enter.

Captain Briggs had taken so great a fancy to his young clerk that he had treated him as his equal, and made him acquainted with many incidents of his life.

Hal had informed him of his friends, and how they had all determined to go to sea together; of what had separated them, and of his fears that Rough and

Ready Jack had been done away with by his enemies.

"I sha'n't want you to-day," said the skipper. "I'm not in a humour for books now."

"I hope nothing occurred, sir, to cause you pain or offence," said Hal.

"Well, yes and no, my lad. We are some distance yet from the Bahamas, and contrary winds have kept us back for days. We have several passengers, and they have got to be fed, so I did not want a couple of youngsters put on board, when Slops tells me that we are running short of provisions."

"It was of them, sir, I wished to speak to you," said Hal.

Captain Briggs looked up in surprise.

"You remember, sir, of my telling you about my friend, Jack Tempest?" said Hal.

"Yes," replied the skipper.

"The tallest of the youths you took off the man-of-war, sir, is my old friend and companion, Rough and Ready Jack."

Briggs leaped to his feet.

"You don't say so?" he exclaimed.

"But I do, sir," replied Hal; "and you may judge of my joy and surprise, when he descended into the boat by my side."

"Truly, Providence does bring strange things about, lad," said Briggs. "I had begun to hate the fellow for coming here at such a time; but my dislike to him has gone in a moment, for if he is your friend, Hal, I know I shall be be bound to like him."

"He is a noble fellow, captain," said Hal, pleased at what the skipper had said; "and so I am sure, you will admit when you know more of him."

"The Yankee captain told me a little, and how he had defied the Algerines to take him and other Englishmen off his ship. But how the dickens came the lad to be in Algiers at all?"

"I have myself but learned little of what has happened to him since I last saw him in the 'Black Boatswain,' near the docks, sir; but since you will not require me any more to-day, with your permission I will invite him and Joe into my cabin, and learn from them their adventures since I lost sight of him."

Captain Briggs thought for a moment, and then he said, kindly—

"No, no, my lad; bring the young-sters here, and let me hear the yarn as well."

Hal was delighted.

"And tell the Angel to get us some tea as soon as she can, and send in enough for four of us. Well, this is a strange go; you lose him in London, and find him on the Atlantic. But there, bring the youngsters here and let's hear what they have got to say."

With a light heart Hal sped away in search of Jack and Joe, and also to order the Angel to make tea for the captain, himself, and friends.

Before he sought the long-lost but newly-found chum, he hurried to the steward's pantry, the door of which was open, as it generally was during the day.

The sight that met his gaze through the opening, was one that made him pause on the threshold and shriek with laughter.

Charley had screwed himself up into one corner of the small apartment, with his hands pressed to his sides, and laughing immoderately, while in the centre of the apartment one of the strangest of duels was taking place between the Angel and her husband.

What had brought about this peculiar duel Charley, of course, knew, though Hal did not.

True to her word, Mrs. Slops had entered the pantry, and demanded of her husband what was the reason of the captain looking so glum, and his manner being so perturbed.

Slops assured her that, not having the least idea himself, he was unable to give her the information she required, and told her also that, if she was so anxious to know, she had better go and ask him herself.

This reply to her question caused the Angel's wings to flutter—no, we mean her wooden leg to tremble violently.

Sam Slops saw the danger signal, and bounded off as far as he could.

Charley, who had now entered the pantry, also saw the warning of breakers ahead, and drew himself as far as possible out of reach of that wooden weapon Mrs. Slops so loved to wield.

Sam saw that his answer and advice had seriously ruffled the Angel's feathers, and tried to squeeze himself through the partition that separated the pantry from the adjoining cabin.

Mrs. Slops put her natural leg forward, and fixed its foot upon the floor; then she thrust her wooden leg forward, and put its foot down fiercely upon Sam's toes.

With a howl of pain Sam gave a thrust with both hands, and the Angel, with a scream, sat down heavily on the floor, then Sam took a leap over his wife's head and landed in the centre of the pantry, where he seized the injured foot in his hand, and hopped about on one leg, moaning aloud.

Mrs. Slops did not attempt to rise, but turning round in a sitting posture, she brought her wooden leg with such force against the straightened leg of her husband, that it doubled up beneath the blow, and he fell with a flop into his wife's lap.

Now Sam always went about his duties in a kind of skull cap, for Time had, with a ruthless hand, plucked out his hairs till it had left his head bald.

Mrs. Slops, unable to get a hold of his hair, fixed her fingers firmly in the cap, and having torn it from his head, proceeded to thrash his scalp with it with all her force.

Sam thought it best to get up as quickly as possible, which he did, but before he had got firmly on to his feet, the lady's wooden leg shot out like a piston-rod, and catching Sam fairly at the bottom of the back, sent him flying head-first against the shelves, from which hung nearly every article required in his business.

The manner in which these articles were slung from the shelves was such as to prevent their falling down with a clatter.

Only one thing was displaced, and this was a rolling-pin, often used in rolling out dough for cakes, which it was her duty to make and then consign to the cook.

In his pain and anger Sam seized this, and as the wooden leg shot towards him again, he used it as a weapon of defence to parry the thrust.

Mrs. Slops, however, did not attempt to rise from her sitting position (she was almost as tall as her husband), and with very little stooping Sam managed to cross weapons with her, but, be it to his honour said, he struck her only on her wooden leg.

Indeed, he stood only on the defensive.

As the leg shot out and upwards, to the right and to left, Sam parried the thrusts, though he found it hard work to do so.

The perspiration rolled down his fat cheeks as he turned his strange weapon first on one side and then on the other, and the pantry was filled with the sounds of the clashing timbers and the laughter of Hal and Charley, neither of whom could move a step to stop the strange combat.

At length the lady's thrusts became slower and weaker, till Mrs. Slops either went, or pretended to go, into hysterics.

Then Slops dropped the rolling-pin, Charley came from his corner, and Hal entered the pantry to give the captain's order.

Then he went on deck, where he found Jack and Joe, and told them that Captain Briggs had invited them to come to his cabin.

Hand-in-hand our hero and his friend descended to the cabin, where the skipper of the "Betsy" was introduced to Rough and Ready Jack.

CHAPTER L.

THE CAPTAIN'S TEA PARTY—JACK RELATES HIS ADVENTURES—MRS. SLOPS MAKES HER APPEARANCE IN SEARCH OF JOE.

CAPTAIN BRIGGS scrutinised Jack with a critical eye, and then turned his attention to Joe.

"A fine-looking fellow the tall one," he mentally muttered, "and brave and honest to boot, or I'm no judge of a fellow's phiz, but I don't exactly make out the other one. There's more play in him than work, I'm thinking; and more chaff than sound reasoning; and yet I don't dislike him, hang me if I do."

Jack, always at his ease, answered the skipper's questions firmly and respectfully; but Joe blurted out his answers, and ever and anon cast a look at Jack, which plainly said—"Tell him for me."

However, he gradually became more at his ease, and when Briggs said he dare say the boy would not mind partaking of a mug of tea, all Joe's diffidence vanished.

Presently Sam Slops came in with the tea, looking very hot and much flurried.

"Hallo, steward!" said the skipper. "So the Angel sent you with it, did she?"

"Yes, sir; she's a bit upset herself, as I suppose that young man has informed you," answered Sam, pointing to Hal.

Hal burst out laughing.

"He never told me anything," said Briggs. "What's the matter with her, Sam?"

Sam shrugged his shoulders.

"She's had one of her fits again, sir," said Sam.

The captain's face lit up with a smile.

"Poor thing," he said, "she suffers greatly. She must cause you a deal of anxiety and pain, Sam."

"You'd say so, sir, if you'd got my crushed toe," replied the steward.

"Is the poor lady violent when she is taken with a fit?" asked Jack, addressing Hal.

The captain overheard the question, and roared with laughter.

Sam arranged the table, and retired, putting his foot painfully to the ground.

"Violent!" said the captain, as the steward closed the door behind him, "I swear by Neptune and his trident, I'd slip my cable and drift into another world if I had such an Angel for a wife. So she's been fluttering her wing again, Hal?"

"Her wooden one, sir, and with a vengeance," replied Hal, as he took the seat motioned him by the captain, as did also the others; "but you would have laughed, sir, had you seen her."

"If I was Sam, hang me if I wouldn't hide away her wooden leg, and let her hop about on her natural pin," said the captain. "The poor fellow is getting as thin as a hurdle with her constant goings on."

"The steward is pretty stout for a thin one," laughed Hal.

"Aye, but I knew him when he was so stout he could not have stooped to pick up a guinea," replied the captain; "and it beats me whatever he could have seen in that woman to have married her."

"She's all right at times, sir," said Hal; "and extremely kind to the lady passengers."

"She is made up of equal quantities of good and bad, lad. But what riled her this time, I wonder?"

"I cannot say to a certainty; but you may be sure it was a mere nothing, for Sam gives way to her in everything, for the sake of peace and quietness. But I do wish you had seen the duel, sir."

"Duel! What do you mean?"

"The duel between the Angel and Sam," was the reply.

The captain's cup was stayed halfway between the table and his lips, and his eyes opened wide with surprise.

"Do you mean to say that Sam has struck her?" he cried. "By heaven, I will tie him up to the gratings, and give him a dozen with a rope's end. No, bad and vexatious as she is, I won't allow a man to strike a woman on board my ship."

"Do not misjudge the steward, sir," said Hal. "If you will permit me, I will tell you what I saw when I went to the pantry to order the tea. The actual cause of the scene I do not know, but Charley told me what I myself did not witness."

"Well, what is it, lad?" said Briggs.

Hal related the whole of the affair, and when he had finished, the skipper lay back in his chair and roared aloud with laughter.

"I'd give a year's pay to have seen it," he said, when at last he could speak. "Ha, ha, ha!"

And off he went into another fit of laughter, in which Hal, Jack, and Joe joined.

"And so poor Sam had the pluck to defend his shins," said the skipper, at last; "but I reckon that rolling-pin is so dented with the Angel's stump, that Chips will have to put his plane over it before it will be fit for use again. Well,

well, get your tea lads; and when it's over you shall tell me your adventures."

The tea was soon finished, and the captain rang the bell on the table for the steward to clear away.

Sam answered the summons.

"How is the Angel now, steward?" asked the captain, with a sly twinkle in his eye and a broad grin on his face.

"A little easier, sir. She says she'll have a cup of tea with a drop of rum in it, and then turn in," replied Sam.

"Well, it's pretty well time, since you have been having a nice turn out, I hear."

"It was none of my seeking, sir," said Sam, eagerly.

"I believe you, Sam. If the Angel turns in, who is going to wait on the passengers?"

"Myself and Charley, sir."

"Very well. But, Sam!"

"Yes, sir."

"Don't you think you could manage to get that confounded wooden leg out of the way for a time?" asked Briggs.

"Well, sir, I might; but then what's she to do without it?" asked the steward.

"Why, let her hop about on her natural one, of course, and when she asks for it, tell her she won't get it back till she promises not to use it so indiscriminately at every little thing that annoys her."

"Do you think that would cure her, sir?" asked the steward.

"Try it, Sam," was the reply.

"I will, sir."

And gathering up the tea-things, Sam left the cabin.

"Hal, just hand me my pipe, and give me a light," said the captain.

The youth complied, and as soon as Captain Briggs had got the strong cavendish well alight, he said, looking at his watch—

"Now, Master John Tempest—Rough and Ready Jack, I hear, you are usually called—in a short time I shall have to take my turn on deck and relieve my mate of his charge, and so I should like to hear of your adventures since you left London."

"As I have nothing to disguise, sir," replied Jack, "I shall only be too happy to comply with your request."

And Jack, without a moment's hesitation, began his story.

As our hero's adventures are already known, there is no need to repeat them here.

It will be sufficient to say that he kept back nothing, and that at the end, when he had finished, Captain Briggs felt for him that respect and admiration which Hal Houghten had long before won.

"Now," he said, as he rose to go on deck and take his turn, "if Slops can spare him, you can bring Charley here and spend the evening together."

The lads thanked him.

"But, mark me, I can have no skulkers on my ship, so you will have to work for your food. Yes, yes; I know what you would say, my lads, that you are only too willing. As to your duties, Jack, I will assign them to you in the morning, but Joe's I can decide now. He shall assist Slops in the pantry and Slush in the cuddy. As we are running short of provisions, we shall have to put into the Bahamas, and then I can decide what's to be done with you both."

And with these words the captain left the cabin.

When he had gone, Joe blew a long, low whistle.

"What's the matter, Joe?" asked Jack.

"The Angel, Master Jack. She's a warm one, ain't she?"

"So it would seem," replied Jack; "but you'll know all about her soon. You heard the captain say you would have to assist Charley to wait upon her and the steward."

"He's a funny-looking chap," said Joe. "And, oh, ain't he a fool."

"A fool! Why?" asked Hal.

"A soft one, I mean, sir," replied Joe. "Would you let your missus wallop you with her wooden leg?"

"I have not got a wife yet, Joe; and when I get one, I won't marry one with a wooden leg."

"Did Slops marry his with it, or did she have it after?" asked Joe.

"I think she had a wooden leg when they were married, but I am not certain," said Hal, "for it don't do to believe all the sailors tell you. But, Joe!"

"Yes, sir."

"You'll have to look out for that leg," said Hal.

"That's what I'm just going to do, Master Hal; once I get hold of it—"

"What then?" asked Jack, noticing the mischievous twinkle in Joe's eye.

"It'll depend upon circumstances," replied Joe; "but you'll see."

"Now, mind what you are about, Joe," said Jack, warningly.

"Oh, I'll take care of myself, you never fear," said Joe. "But, I say, Master Jack, who does the captain mean when he says I'll have to help Slush as well?"

"Slush is the cook; you saw his cuddy on deck, didn't you?" said Hal.

"Was that him who was cooking the wittles?" asked Joe.

"Yes; that's Slush."

"What a beastly name," said Joe. "It's worse than Slops."

"It's not his real name," said Hal, "but the nickname he gets from the sailors."

"Oh! is that it?"

"That's it. Most men have a nickname aboard ship. The carpenter's name is Sinclair, but he is always called Chips."

"Ah! I understand," said Joe. "I wonder what they will call me?"

"Joe—which is Joe?" cried a shrill voice, as the cabin-door was thrown open and Mrs. Slops came stumping into the cabin. "Are you Joe?"

"Yes, I am Joe; what do you want?"

"You get off to the pantry and wash up. We are short-handed, with Charley away. Move yourself or I'll move you."

Up went the wooden leg threateningly.

"No you don't," cried Joe, "or I'll move you."

And with a quick snatch he seized the stump and held it fast.

CHAPTER LI.

JOE GETS A TASTE OF THE ANGEL'S QUALITY—THE PURLOINED LEG—AN INHUMAN SACRIFICE.

MRS. SLOPS tried to drag her wooden member from Joe's grasp, but in vain.

Joe held on like grim death, and the irate stewardess made a clutch at Joe's hair.

But Joe jerked his head back and the leg forward, and the Angel was obliged to hop from side to side to prevent herself from falling.

"Leave go, you young varmint, leave go, or I'll make you!" she cried.

"Make away," said Joe. "Stand still, missus, or you'll be going over flop."

"I'll tear your eyes out, you impudent young rascal! Leave go, I say!" she shrieked.

And she gave her leg such a vicious thrust forward, that the end of it, striking Joe in the stomach, sent him over, chair and all, on to the floor.

In order to save himself, Joe released the imprisoned member.

"I'll teach you, I will!" cried the stewardess. "Take that, and that, and that!"

And down came the end of the stump three separate times on the boy's side and chest.

Neither Jack nor Hal could stop her for laughing.

"I'll dance a hornpipe on your body, you young viper," she cried.

But this time Joe was too quick for her.

As the leg descended for the fourth time, Joe again seized it, and giving it a sharp and sudden hoist, sent the Angel's tall form flying half over the table.

Before she could recover herself, Joe was on his feet.

"What do you think of her, Master Jack? Isn't she a caution?" said Joe.

"And you'd better take caution, Joe," said Jack, in a low voice.

"And let her larrup me with that thing? Not if I know it," said Joe.

"Now, out you go!" said the Angel, pointing to the door.

"Go out yourself," said Joe. "You ain't no right here."

"Oh, ain't I?" said Mrs. Slops. "We'll soon see about that. Now go!"

"Sha'n't for you," said Joe.

"Won't you—oh, won't you?" jerked out the Angel.

Down came the wooden leg, with a thud, on Joe's foot.

"You beast!" yelled Joe. "If you was a man I'd smash you, I would."

"I'd like to see the man as could do it. A few of them have tried it on in their time, but I've just given 'em something like this, and they soon knocked under to the Angel."

She swung round that terrible weapon of hers to give Joe a blow across the legs.

But, either by accident or design, Jack pushed the overturned chair between her and her would-be victim, and so great was the force of attraction, that the wooden leg of the lady came with a clash against the wooden leg of the chair.

The lady's leg stood the shock, but the chair leg did not.

It was snapped clean off, and went flying across the cabin, passing so close to Jack's head that it was a wonder it did not strike him.

Unheeding what she had done, she again made for Joe; but that youth had seized the back of the chair, and every time she made a prod at him, interposed the piece of furniture between his body and the Angel's wooden member.

Charley now entered the cabin.

"Hallo!" he said, "what's the row here?"

"Oh, it's only the Angel flapping her wing," replied Hal.

"Should have thought she'd have had enough of that for to-day," Charley said.

The Angel turned upon him.

"Oh, you do, do you?" she hissed. "Then that will just show you that I haven't, Mr. Cheeky!"

Charley drew back out of reach of that leg, and, holding out his hand and pointing at her, said, in a determined tone—

"Now, I give you warning, Mrs. Slops, if you force me to forget you are a woman, it will be your own fault if I knock you down."

"Charley, Charley!" cried Jack.

"I know what you would say, dear boy, and I know what you think; but I've felt blows from that stump more than once—blows as unmerited as they were cruel and uncalled for, and I will never submit to them again."

"Bravo!" said Joe. "I never hit a woman, or thrashed a cripple; but this here long, skinny-jibbed thing ain't no woman! It's a she-demon in disguise, and I wonder the captain don't have her thrown overboard."

The Angel literally foamed with rage at hearing this.

Her wooden leg played a tune on the floor, but she seemed powerless to raise it higher than half-an-inch.

"And so he would have done, no doubt, but for one thing," said Charley.

"Because she'd stir up the mermaids with that stump of hers?" asked Joe.

"No, not that," said Charley.

"What then?" asked Joe, still watching the angry woman, the scar on whose face had turned from livid white to blood-red.

"Because her nature is so sour, she'd give all the fishes pains in their insides, and any of them caught, if eaten, would spread the cholera throughout the ship," said Hal.

"Well done, Hal," said Jack, patting him on the shoulder. "Let them beat it who can."

And then all four of them burst out laughing.

"Oh, that I should live to see this day!" screamed Mrs. Slops.

"Why didn't you die before, then?" said Joe. "Nobody asked you to live, I'll bet twopence."

"A poor lone woman—for I haven't got a husband that's fit to call a man—to have to submit to the jeers and insults of a set of—of—"

"Gentlemen—right down slap-up swells, as knows how to behave themselves, and who would scorn to carry a wooden leg about with them to attack peaceable people. I'd have you put in a madhouse and fed on brimstone and treacle all the rest of your life," said Joe.

"Oh, save me from doing him some terrible injury," half screamed the stewardess. "I'll go to the captain, and tell him that if he don't send you adrift in a boat at once, I'll—I'll—"

"Go and hang yourself," said Joe; "and as I doesn't bear you any ill-will for what you've done to me, if you don't think that there bag of bones won't put enough strain on the rope, I'll come and hang on to that wooden leg of yours, so as to help you to break your neck. There now, that shows you what a forgiving nature I've got."

Mrs. Slops could stand no more.

She kicked the chair aside, scattered the lads right and left, and stumped furiously out of the cabin.

Thud, thud, thud, went her wooden leg.

When Sam heard that peculiar thud, he knew that he had to look out for squalls.

So he grabbed the rolling-pin and hid it quickly beneath his coat.

Forewarned was to be forearmed.

The stewardess stumped into the pantry and flung herself into a chair.

Sam did not know what to say, or whether it would be better not to say anything.

"Rum!" she gasped, "or I shall faint!"

"You said you would turn in; why don't you?" asked Sam.

"I asked for rum, didn't I?" cried the Angel.

"Yes, my dear, and you shall have it," replied her husband.

He gave her a glass, which she tipped down her throat in an instant.

"The lad is coming to wash up, I suppose?" said Sam, after a pause. "Strange, my dear, wasn't it, that friends parted in London should meet here at sea? And, of course, Captain Briggs, under such circumstances, could only request that Charley should be released from his duties, so that he could be with his newly-found friend."

"Samuel Slops," the Angel cried, severely.

"Yes, my dear."

"Don't talk to me."

And the wooden leg began to play a quick tattoo on the floor of the pantry.

"Mr. Slops," she cried, hoarsely.

"Well, my darling?"

"Didn't I tell you not to talk to me? You call yourself a man, and see the loving, tender-hearted wife of your bosom insulted by boys. Sam, Sam, I despise you, and that's my good night to such a thing as you."

And casting a look that was intended to be one of withering scorn and contempt upon him, she flung open the door that led out of the pantry into their sleeping apartment, and closed it with a bang behind her.

"Thank heaven!" sighed Sam.

And grasping the rum bottle in his hand, he thrust its neck between his lips, and only a gurgling sound for a time broke the silence of the pantry.

Meantime, Jack had to tell his adventures over again, as Charley had not been present when our hero had related them, both to his friend Hal and the captain.

He had been assisting to wait upon the passengers in the saloon, from which place the captain was for the first time absent at meal times.

Never did the Angel let her temper run riot before the passengers.

She was a woman who had an eye to business, and knew that the better her conduct the higher the tips would be, so she gave double vent to it in the pantry.

After about an hour, Jack and Hal strolled up on deck, acccompanied by Joe, and Charley sought the pantry, where he found Sam alone.

"Where's the Angel?" asked Charley.

"Turned in, thank heaven," said Sam, "and snoring like a pig. But, I say, I've got it."

"What, Sam?" asked the under steward.

"The prodder and basher. Here it is."

And Sam held up the Angel's wooden leg.

"Hurrah, Sam! where can you hide it?" asked Charley.

"Blest if I know," replied Sam, "because she's bound to look for it in every hole and corner here."

"Give it to me, Sam, and I'll hide it in the cuddy when Slush ain't there."

"Take it, lad. But, I say, Charley, the captain told the missus to fetch that young fellow he brought aboard to-day to wash up for you while you were with your friends. Won't he come?"

"Of course he will, but I tell you, Sam, he won't put up with too much of the Angel's temper. He's been a rough one himself in his time, and if she begins on him he'll cut up rough on her; otherwise he's a first-rate fellow, and I know you'll like him, Sam. I'll send him to you."

Charley wrapped his handkerchief over the wooden leg and went on deck.

Meantime Hal had introduced Jack and Joe to the carpenter, the sail-maker, the boatswain and the cook.

"And so this youngster's to bear a hand with me when I want him," said Slush. "Well, I'll be glad of his help, for work's heavy this voyage."

"I'll do my best," said Joe, "but, as I never had anything to cook, I ain't no hand at that sort of work."

"Oh, I'll do the cooking," returned Slush, "but you can look to the fire, fetch water, peel the potatoes, and so on."

"I can do all that, sir," said Joe, confidently.

"Well, come with me, my lad, and I'll show you where to get the wood for the fire and the water for cooking."

"Cut along with him, Joe," said Charley. "Go forward with you, lads, and I'll join you in a minute."

Jack and Hal strolled forward, and Charley darting into the cuddy, took his handkerchief from round the wooden leg and opening a cupboard under the cook's board slipped the timber limb into it and closed the door.

Then he hurried along to join his friends.

Shortly afterwards Slush and Joe entered the cuddy, and the cook pointed out the places where the articles of his trade were kept.

"You get what wood you can from Chips in the morning," he said, "and if he gives you more than you want, throw it into that cupboard there, for we often want some to set the pots a-boiling, I can tell you. Now you will know how to begin in the morning."

Joe thanked him and went after Jack and his companions.

Berths were found for Jack and Joe among the sailors in the forecastle, and when darkness rested on the sea they turned in.

At six o'clock next morning Joe tumbled out of his hammock and went on deck to commence his duties.

He opened the cupboard under the board and found a few handfuls of chips and, what surprised him beyond measure, a wooden leg.

Joe looked at it, turned it over and over, and wondered how it could have come there.

All of a sudden he remembered the captain's advice to Slops, and blew a low whistle.

"Blest if the steward hasn't been and taken his missus's leg," he said, "and hid it here so as she sha'n't find it. He's an artful one, and no mistake, is that Sam Slops."

He piled what chips he could find on the fire, and then went to the carpenter's shop for more; but Chips was not there, neither could he find him.

"I must do the best I can," said Joe, "till I can see him."

So he returned to the cuddy, set light to the fire, filled the huge kettle and set it over the blaze, but soon the fire went down, and he went again in search of the carpenter, but could not find him anywhere.

"What's to be done?" thought Joe.

"The water is to be boiling by seven, and I can't obtain a bit of wood to get it ready."

Then his face suddenly lighted up.

"Hal said that all the men say that that leg of the Angel's is too long and always getting in the way, and I had made up my mind, if I got a chance, I'd chop a lump off it. It's just the thing to keep the fire going till I can get some chips. So here goes, row or no row."

Joe went to the cupboard and brought out the Angel's leg, and going up to the stove thrust the lower half of it into the fire.

"Oh, won't the Angel rave and the men be jolly glad," said the lad, as he gave the leg another thrust to drive it further into the stove.

"BAXTER SECURED THE POOR FELLOW'S SHARE OF THE VALUABLES."

CHAPTER LII.

THE MARCH THROUGH THE DESERT—SUFFERINGS OF THE MUTINEERS—A CRUEL DEED—THE SAND STORM.

BAXTER SHARP and his companions had performed their cruel work effectually.

Not one of the party who had started to convey them to Morocco survived.

The wounded were ruthlessly slain, despite their appeals for mercy.

One by one they were butchered in cold blood by the desperate mutineers.

Then they were deprived of their arms and any valuables they possessed, for though slaves, many of them had trinkets of gold upon their persons in the shape of rings and armlets, as well as coins of gold and silver.

Baxter appropriated the slave-dealer's scimitar and gold inlaid pistols, which he found in his tent.

The turban which had been kicked from Kula Arabi's head contained several precious stones.

And these were torn from it, and divided amongst the white men.

A search of his tent by Baxter discovered a small bag of leather, which contained a large sum; and when nothing more was to be found, the men lay down on the sand to sleep, and Baxter Sharp took possession of the tent and couch of the deceased slave-dealer.

At sunrise next morning all were astir.

A breakfast was prepared and partaken of, and then Baxter, addressing the men, said—

"It would be as well, perhaps, were these bodies concealed in the sand; not that I imagine anyone is likely to come hither, but it is best to be on the safe side; and if hidden from sight, they can tell no tales."

The men set to work, and soon holes were scooped out in the sand, and the bodies of the slaves and the slave-dealer consigned to them.

Baxter tried to secure the horse, but the animal kicked out with its hind legs so viciously, that none durst approach it closely, and then it dashed away like the wind, in the direction from which they had come.

"Confound the beast!" said Baxter Sharp; "the brute will raise an alarm. We must get out of this as quickly as possible."

"Where do you intend to go?" asked one of the men.

"Not back to the bay, you may depend upon that," replied Baxter.

"Why not?"

"Because we should be putting our heads into the lion's mouth," was the reply. "We must get out of Algiers as quickly as possible."

"But where shall we go to?" asked another.

"To Morocco."

"But how can we find the way?" asked one.

"I have read when a boy that— But never mind. Let's get towards the mountains. I know it lies somewhere at their base."

"Yes, perhaps so; but what are we to do for food till we reach the place?" said another.

"We must live upon the fruits we can find," was the reply; "unless—"

"Unless what?" interrupted two or three of his companions.

"We can fall across a small encampment, or an isolated tent of the Arabs. In either case food is sure to be stored within."

"And purchase some of it?"

"If they will sell it," said Baxter; "but if they refuse, then we will take it from them."

"If they will let us," observed one.

"We are armed," said Baxter, tapping the hilt of the scimitar he had secured to his side. "As we possess both gold and jewels, we will try fair means first; but should they fail, then we must not hesitate to use foul."

No one rebuked his remark, for every man's hand among them was stained with blood.

"So now let us set out, while the day is young," said Baxter, rising. "I only wish we could have caught that horse, for travelling over these sands is heavy work."

One or two were for persuading him to retrace his steps to the bay, and run all risks of identification and capture, but Baxter would not listen to this.

" Better death than slavery," he said.

So the murderous band set forth, keeping the chain of mountains in front of them.

At midday the heat became so great that they had to rest.

Before them they could see groves of trees, but could not expect to reach them for some hours.

Beneath their shade might nestle an Arab village, and to approach it in so weak and exhausted a state would have been sheer madness; for though these wandering Arabs are, as a rule, generous, yet if aroused by suspicion, insult, or doubt, they become cruel and merciless.

The mutineers shared what provisions they had brought with them from the scene of the slaughter, and then lay down on the hot sands to sleep.

Despite the heat and want of shade, they soon sank off to slumber.

Baxter Sharp was the first to awake.

He sat up and looked around him, and then up at the sky, where the sun rode like a huge red ball in the cloudless heavens.

Baxter shuddered.

" It looks like a ball of blood," he said.

His lips were parched, his tongue was dry and hard, and his temples throbbed violently.

" Fools !" he muttered; " why did we not bring water with us? We might have guessed we should find none on the way."

As he gazed out into the far distance, he started with a glad cry.

There, not a mile away, was a huge lake, its waves dancing in the sunlight, and looking like a large mirror.

He sprang to his feet and shaded his eyes with his hands.

The lake vanished as if by magic, and with a groan Baxter Sharp knew that it was but a mirage.

Then he looked round upon his still sleeping companions, and a horrible thought flashed through his brain.

They had aided him to secure his liberty, but might they not lead him into danger ?

They were a rough, uncultivated, thoughtless body of men, to whom discretion was a thing unknown, and whose ignorance and impetuosity might rouse up foes where he hoped to find friends.

They slept, and the knife he had secured was long and sharp.

Twice did he half draw the weapon from his belt, and thrust it back again with a shudder.

" No," he said at last, " we must live or fall together."

Awaiting awhile to compose his feelings, he aroused his companions.

Like him, they awoke with parched lips and dried tongues and throats.

Like him, they saw the mirage, and shouted for glee.

But when, in obedience to his command, they shaded their eyes with their hands, they saw that it was only fancy, and that the silver lake had vanished into the burning sands.

But there before them was the oasis in the desert.

If amongst those trees they found an Arab village, a fountain would be sure to be near at hand.

So once more they set out, but this time more wearily than before.

Hours passed, and the sun was sinking in the heavens, yet they had not reached the hope-for goal.

Suddenly one of the men staggered and fell, and his companions raised him up, but he was too weak to proceed, and Baxter brutally said—

" Let him lie where he is ; we cannot wait for him. Go on, and I will follow you."

The others staggered on, leaving Baxter with the fainting man.

They believed that he would try to revive him.

But Baxter Sharp had no such thoughts.

A man who had evidently been seized with a long illness would be a burden to him, so when the others had proceeded some distance, he drew his knife and bent over the sufferer.

" Water," gasped the man. " Oh, in mercy give me water. My brain is on fire—fire consumes my throat. Water —oh, but for one drop ! "

" There is no water here," hissed Baxter Sharp, brutally. " I, too, suffer, but am silent. This then to make you the same."

The glittering blade shone in the red sunlight for a moment, and then was hidden in the breast of the man beneath him.

With one groan of agony the hapless wretch died.

Quickly Baxter secured the poor fellow's share of the valuables they had divided, and wiping his ensanguined blade on the man's jacket, he returned it to his belt, and rose to follow his companions.

"We cannot be hampered with a sick man," he muttered. "So it was better to put him out of his misery at once; better for him and us too."

But he found that his own weakness was growing upon him, so he called to his companions to stop, for he began to fear he would be unable to overtake them if they kept on.

But his parched tongue refused to utter his words above a whisper, and they heard him not.

The men were pressing on as fast as they could for the oasis, and not one turned his eyes from it to look back for Baxter Sharp.

Gradually the sun's disc became of a deeper hue.

Then a faint zephyr came sweeping over the sands.

It fanned the heated brow of the murderer pleasantly.

But darker and darker grew the sun.

Higher and higher rose the wind.

Then came a strange swishing sound through the air.

The sun hung like a small black-red ball in the heavens.

The whole scene became overcast. His companions gradually faded from his sight.

The darkness of night fell upon the earth—a sound like the mighty rushing of waters filled the air, and Baxter Sharp, with a cry of horror, threw himself face downwards on the sands.

Not a moment too soon, for the sandstorm was upon him, cutting and lacerating his flesh, and tearing his garments to shreds in its course; and then it swept on and away, leaving the murderous wretch buried beneath a huge heap of sand, bleeding, powerless, and despairing.

CHAPTER LIII.

THE COOK DETERMINES TO FINISH THE LIMB, AND GETS FINISHED HIMSELF—JOE EXPLAINS WHAT DID IT, AND THE CAPTAIN HOLDS HIMSELF TO BLAME.

WITH the aid of the wooden leg Joe soon set the kettle singing, and by this time Slush made his appearance in the cuddy.

"Ah, my lad, I see you have got the fire going," said the cook.

"Yes, sir, and the water is nearly boiling," replied Joe. "What shall I do now?"

"Scrub down the board and make things ship-shape, and then you can go and help in the pantry."

"Yes, sir."

"I see Chips has given you a good lump of wood to set the pot boiling."

"I can't find him, sir," replied Joe. "I had to make shift with what I found in the cupboard."

The cook looked hard at the boy.

"You didn't find that chunk there," he said, pointing to the piece of timber which Joe had stuffed into the fire. "I wanted such a clump as that last night, and there was nothing in the locker but a few small chips."

"I certainly found this thing there when I looked in about half-an-hour ago," said Joe, "and, as I could not find the carpenter, I thought I'd use it, sir."

"Strange that I didn't see it last night," said Slush, looking hard at the piece of timber. "Why, save us from floundering in a gale of wind, if it ain't a wooden leg!"

"I thought it looked like one, sir," said Joe, innocently.

"Why, pitch and perriwinkles, it must be the Angel's," cried Slush, as he pulled it from the fire.

"One of her left-off ones, sir, I suppose," said Joe, "and she put it in there to be burned, I reckon."

The cook looked scrutinisingly at the boy, but Joe's face still wore an expression of innocence.

"I never knew she had a couple," said Slush, "though we all on board know that the one she wears is long enough for two. I can't make it out at all."

"Can't you, sir?" said Joe.

"Dash me if I can," cried the cook, thrusting the smouldering leg into a bucket of water. "And here's full half of it gone. I wonder if anyone has been playing Mrs. Slops a trick and stole it from her?"

"Lor', sir, who'd do such a thing?" said Joe.

"Can't say; the steward would not, that's certain," said Slush. "I'll see old Slops about it as soon as I have got the breakfast ready."

"Hadn't you better see Mrs. Slops, sir?" asked Joe.

"Hang Mrs. Slops," cried the cook. "There, now you can go and see what you can do for the steward."

Joe kept his countenance till he got out of the cuddy, and then he sat down on a coil of rope behind it and indulged in a chuckle.

"Oh, my! won't there be a shine when the Angel misses her leg. But then, how should I know it wasn't put in the cupboard to burn? Oh, I ain't going to take any blame for it, not me."

And Joe chuckled again.

Thud—thud, came to his ears.

Joe looked round and over the top of the hatch-way door caught a sight of the stewardess.

Thump—thud—thump—thud!

"Oh, she's got another one," said Joe, "I can hear it playing a tune on the deck. I suppose she's a coming to see whether the coffee's ready. I'll slip off now and get to the pantry while she's away from it."

And Joe dodged along on the other side of the ship, and made his way to the steward's pantry without being observed by the stewardess.

Certainly the sound she made on her way along the deck to the cook's cuddy would have led anyone to imagine, who did not see her, that she still possessed her wooden member.

But such was not the case.

Unable to find her wooden leg, which she first accused her husband of purloining and then berated Charley soundly for doing the same thing, she made a virtue of necessity, and, using a broom as a crutch, set forth to inquire if the coffee was ready for the passengers' breakfast.

She walked awkwardly, if not painfully, for the crutch was too short, and the hairs on its head were stiff, and forced their way through her cotton garment at every step.

It may be well imagined that her temper just then was not particularly angelic.

The cook was not engaged at his duties in preparing the morning meal, but was seated on the bucket beside the stove, with the half-destroyed leg in his hand, and shaking his head over it, while he muttered—

"I'd like to know how it came here, I would. That boy couldn't have brought it, or he wouldn't have looked so innocent as he did. But who put it in the cupboard, and when was it put there, that's the puzzle? There can't be any mistake about its being the Angel's. Now, what's best to be done with it—let her have it back as it is, or put the rest of it into the fire and say nothing about it?"

He thought a moment and then added—

"It will prevent her rowing with me and the boy, so here goes. Let the thing burn."

He half rose to place it upon the fire, when a shrill voice shrieked out—

"No, you don't, you villain!"

And Mrs. Slops, by the aid of her peculiar crutch, swung herself through the doorway in the centre of the cuddy.

With a cry of surprise, the cook turned with the half-burned leg in his hand.

Like a flash, the broom handle hit him on the forepart of his head, and with a thousand stars flashing before his eyes, he sat quickly down upon the edge of the bucket.

Over went the pail, and over went the cook, while the remains of the wooden leg went spinning into the broad ash-pan of the fireplace.

"It was you, was it?" cried Mrs.

Slops, in shrieking tones. "It was you who stole my leg, you brute, you monster, you—you—"

Crack! crack! came the handle of the broom across the cook's arms and shoulders, and it is more than probable that in her rage she would have inflicted considerable injury upon the half-dazed man, had not Captain Briggs appeared at the door, and sternly demanded what was the meaning of such a scene.

Mrs. Slops replied by dropping the broom, leaning against the board, and bursting into tears.

The cook rose from the floor like a man in a dream.

His garments were dripping with water.

"Slush, what does all this mean?" asked the skipper, severely.

The cook drew his hand across his forehead, saying—

"I don't know, sir."

"Don't know!" cried the captain, angrily.

"I know I was just getting off that bucket when I received a terrific blow which felled me like an ox, and then a lot more blows before I could get up. But what for, sir, I do not know," said the cook.

"Oh, you wicked man!" sobbed Mrs. Slops. "Wasn't you burning my leg? There, sir—there it is in the ash-pan."

The skipper crossed the soaked floor of the cuddy, and looked into the ash-pan.

Then he turned to the cook.

"Slush," he said, "this is carrying a joke too far—it's really too bad. Though the stewardess does not always make a good use of it, yet her misfortune makes it a necessity to her. This is beyond a joke, and I am both annoyed and pained that you should have perpetrated it."

"What good is it to me?" sobbed Mrs. Slops. "It's half burned up already, and he was going to burn the rest. Do you think I could stand that, sir? No; if it had been Slops himself I'd have served him the same, I would."

"I am not surprised at your anger on this occasion," said the captain, "for this is a paltry and unmanly revenge to take upon you."

"Captain," said Slush, "do not be too hard upon me. I did not burn the thing myself, though I confess that, finding it half consumed, and, as I believed, useless, I was about to throw the remainder of the limb on the fire."

"Did not burn it!" cried Captain Briggs. "Then who did?"

"I found it in the fire when I entered the cuddy, and took it out and extinguished it in the bucket of water."

"Who made the fire?"

"The new boy Joe, and if you will have him summoned here, he may throw some light upon it."

"Pass the word to the steward's pantry, and tell Joe to come here," cried the captain to one of the crew.

In about half a minute Joe entered the cuddy, touching his cap.

"Joe, did you light this fire?" asked the skipper.

"Yes, sir."

"And you burned this woman's leg?"

"No, sir," replied Joe.

"Do you mean to tell me that you did not burn that thing lying there?" cried Briggs, pointing to the half-consumed piece of timber.

"The fire burned it, sir, not me," replied Joe. "I found it in the cupboard there with some chips, and thinking that it was an old one and put there to burn, I thrust it under the kettle to make the water boil quickly. I hope I ain't done wrong, sir, 'cos if I have, how was I to know it?"

"Humph!" said the captain, "you found it in the wood cupboard? Well, it was only natural you should imagine it was intended to be burned. Never mind, Mrs. Slops; it is not irretrievably ruined, and Chips shall splice a piece to it, and make it as good as ever for you. What's done can't be undone, so now see about breakfast."

As the captain walked away, he muttered—

"By Neptune! I'm the most to blame, for I told Slops to hide her wooden leg."

CHAPTER LIV.

THE SAVAGE FLOTILLA—BOARDED BY THE SAVAGES—A DESPERATE FIGHT.

It was a dull and rather cold morning when the 'Betsy' found herself off the Bahama Islands.

Jack had come upon deck to join the captain's watch, and his gaze was riveted upon the land, rising higher and plainer as the mists cleared away before the rising sun.

Several of these islands were wholly deserted, while others were but sparsely peopled.

As the 'Betsy' sailed in between two of the smaller islands, Jack noticed several black dots upon the shores, and was for a time puzzled to make out what they were.

But gradually these appeared to move from place to place, and finally, gathering in a body, came down to the surf.

The captain was pacing the quarter-deck in deep thought.

It was evident that he had not observed what Jack had seen.

Our hero continued to watch, and at last he saw several boats put off from the islands, and evidently being propelled towards the ship.

Each boat was loaded with men from stem to stern.

"I do not half like the look of that," muttered Jack. "I'll draw the captain's attention to them."

So thinking he strode aft, and touched his cap to the skipper.

"Ah, Jack Tempest," said Briggs, pausing in his walk; "what is it, lad?"

"I thought, sir, I would call your attention to those boats which have just put off from yonder island."

And Jack pointed out where the little vessels were.

Captain Briggs followed the direction of his finger.

"A fishing party, I fancy," said the captain. "They cannot be coming to barter provisions, for on these islands nothing will flourish, and those we seek lie farther on. But get me my glass off the binnacle, Jack, and we'll see what these fellows are up to."

Jack ran and fetched the captain's glass, and handed it to him.

The skipper fixed the glass to his eye, and looked for some time at the advancing boats.

"Canoes and proas," he said, "and each of them carries more than is necessary for the working of boats on an honest expedition, but I see no arms of any kind. Just get into the rigging, lad, and try what your younger eyes will make out."

Jack sprang into the rigging of the mizzen-mast, and Briggs handed him his spy-glass.

Putting his arm round the shrouds to steady himself, Jack took a long look through the glass.

"Well, my lad, what do you think?" asked Briggs.

"That they are neither engaged in fishing, sir, nor coming on a peaceful errand. They are evidently a war party, for I can make out hatchets and spears in the bottom of more than one of the canoes," replied Jack, descending to the deck.

The captain took the glass from his hand, and sprang himself into the rigging.

After a good look over the fleet of canoes and proas, which gradually drew together as they advanced, he sprang down, saying—

"It looks ugly, my lad; but whether for us or others, I cannot say. They may be on their way to one of the other islands, or they may be making for us. If it be the latter, I'm afraid we're in for a tough job, for my ship is scarcely prepared to resist an attack from any quarter."

"Still, it would be well to be prepared for the worst, sir, as far as in your power lies," said Jack.

"Aye, lad, think not that I shall fail to do my duty to those under my charge and the ship's owners. We shall not knock under without a struggle if the worst comes to the worst; but I fancy our fears of an assault will prove groundless. However, forewarned will be forearmed, lad. Keep your eye on their movements while I'm below."

The captain dived down the companion.

Jack watched the boats looming up larger every minute, and soon was able to count the number of men contained in advance of the rest.

A junction had now been made between the two parties, and the savages, using their paddles dexterously, kept their canoes up with the fast-sailing proas.

It was now certain that their object was the merchantman, and their business anything but of a friendly nature.

The mate, who had turned in, was aroused by the captain, for, despite his words to Jack, he felt that danger was brewing, and that ere long he would have to defend his ship against a desperate foe.

The arm chest was opened, and its contents were brought forth and carried on to the deck.

When the officers had armed themselves, each with a brace of pistols and a cutlass, the men who had gone below and turned in were aroused, and the rest of the arms distributed amongst them.

When all had assembled, Captain Briggs addressed his officers and crew.

"Men of the 'Betsy,'" he said, "stress of weather and want of provisions have forced me to run for the Bahamas, and by so doing it is evident that we have brought a trouble upon us quite unlooked for, but one, I am sure, you will all help me to meet and beat off."

"Aye, aye!" cried the men.

"If I am not mistaken, we shall be outnumbered five to one; but those who approach are savages, while you are Englishmen. Though the odds are great, I know you will not flinch from opposing them, and, with heaven's aid and the pluck of true British seamen, drive these men back to the barren islands from which they have come."

A true British cheer was the answer, in which none joined louder than Joe and Rough and Ready Jack.

The boats were but a short distance from the ship now.

Gradually they spread out, and the natives seized their arms, wi   had lain hitherto in the bottoms of their vessels.

"Down—down, every man of you!"

cried the captain, as he saw the savages fit the arrows to their bows.

Down dropped everyone behind the bulwarks as a flight of arrows sped through the air, burying themselves in the masts and spars, and went hurtling over the ship into the sea.

Then arose a yell that was almost blood-curdling, and on came the natives with a rush.

"Ready to repel boarders!" cried Briggs. "The fiends will try to board us fore and aft and in the waist. Go aft, half-a-dozen of you; Jack Tempest, remain with me. You, sir, to the bows," he said to his first mate; "and you take charge of the men aft," he cried to the second mate, "and strike—and strike hard!"

Joe had seized a hatchet, and Jack had been given a cutlass.

The men were at their posts in a moment.

Not a moment too soon; for, armed with short spears and hatchets, the savages came clambering up the sides and stern of the vessel.

As their heads appeared above the bulwarks or their hands seized the rails they were hurled back into the canoes or the sea.

The captain, Jack, Joe, the sail-maker, carpenter, and cook guarded the waist.

Here the rush was greatest.

With cutlass, hatchet and pistol they were repulsed time after time; but still the savages pressed forward, uttering the while the most discordant cries.

Fight as they would—and every man fought like a demon—the savages at length got a footing upon the deck.

Now they could use their spears as well as their hatchets, and a terrible hand-to-hand encounter ensued.

Side by side with Captain Briggs, Jack and Joe dealt fast and furious blows on every side, and so fierce was their resistance that they gradually forced the savages to fall back.

The gratings had been taken off the hold to get out the water-casks, and no one had thought to close them in the excitement, and Joe, who perceived the yawning opening in the deck, shouted as he struck down a huge savage—

"Drive them into the hold, Jack!"

Charley, Hal, and three of the passengers now joined the captain and Jack in their struggle amidships, where the fight raged most furiously, and, seeing the wisdom of Joe's advice, they rushed upon the savages with renewed vigour.

The assailants had not observed the yawning orifice in the deck, and, pressed backwards by the desperate blows and furious onslaught of the Britons, they went tumbling over the edge of the hole, and fell with loud thuds into the depths below.

"Down with them!" cried Captain Briggs. "Give no quarter to the wretches! Bravo, Jack!"

A burly savage made a stroke at the captain with a hatchet, but before the weapon reached the skipper's head a blow under the ear from the iron fist of Rough and Ready Jack laid him senseless on the deck.

Then Jack's cutlass clove another to the brain, and the savages who still had the power to fight fell back slowly to join their companions astern.

Here the sailors who had gone aft were having a desperate struggle with the enemy, and it seemed as if they must give way, so numerous were the foe who had gained the deck from that part of the ship.

Every pistol had been emptied, and there had been no time to re-load them, so both officers and men had to fight with cutlass, hatchet, and knife.

Nearly all the Englishmen had received wounds, more or less severe, but none as yet had been fatally injured, though several of the savages had been put out of the fight and lay in their blood upon the deck, or maimed and powerless in the hold.

Those remaining of the savages who had secured a footing from the waist now joined their comrades astern, and in their turn, Captain Briggs and his men were forced back.

At this moment came a shrill voice from the companion-way—

"Come on, Sam, to the rescue. Now you niggers, the Angel's on the rampage, and you'll have to look out for squalls."

CHAPTER LV.

MR. AND MRS. SLOPS JOIN IN THE FRAY, AND GREATLY ASSIST IN GAINING A VICTORY—DEFEAT AND FLIGHT OF THE SAVAGES—JACK FINDS A NEW FRIEND.

A MALEDICTION escaped the lips of Captain Briggs as he heard the voice of the Angel and the thud of her mended leg coming up the companion-way to the deck.

"Why can't she keep below?" he said. "We are hard pressed enough heaven knows, without having to look after her."

Jack and Joe both wished her at the bottom of the sea just then.

"You are wounded, Hal," cried Jack, as, with cutlass and fist, he struck right and left.

"Nothing, Jack," replied the other; "only a scratch."

But his pale face and blood-dripping arm denied his words.

"Fall back, Hal," cried Jack, "you are hurt severely."

"Not while I have power to fight by your side, Jack," was the reply."

Jack could say no more.

He required all his breath, for he was, indeed, hard pressed. .

But the next moment a cry escaped his lips.

Captain Briggs had been struck down with a hatchet.

The blow had fallen upon his head and shoulder, and he fell at the feet of his assailant.

Jack's cutlass swept like lightning round his head, and the savage who had struck down the skipper fell lifeless at his side.

Jack stood over the body of the captain to shield him from the wretches who, it was evident, were pressing on to victory, and only too eager to finish the work which their comrade had been unable to perfect by the terrific blow of Jack's cutlass.

But Jack, despite the fury of the

savages, still bestrode the body of the captain, his cutlass flashing hither and thither and inflicting terrible wounds wherever it struck.

Seeing their captain down, officers and men alike rushed to the spot, and, maddened at the skipper's fall, they plunged so fiercely into the fight that the natives were hurled back some distance.

Before the savages could recover from the fury of the onslaught, the steward and stewardess reached the deck and forced their way between the combatants.

There was no time for surprise or remark from anyone when they perceived that Mr. and Mrs. Slops were each armed with a pair of bellows.

"Let them have it, Sam," cried the stewardess. "You keep back, you men of the 'Betsy.' Here's the Angel to the rescue!"

Up went the two pairs of bellows, and furiously worked the hands of Sam and his wife upon their handles.

Out poured a stream of dust from each nozzle into the eyes, mouth, and faces of the startled savages.

"Give it them, Sam. Hurrah for Old England!"

With yells the savages fell back, and the men lifted the captain to his feet.

At any other time Jack and his friends would have roared with laughter.

Mrs. Slops had filled the bellows with ground pepper and snuff, and this they poured into the eyes of the savages, causing them to shriek with pain, and jump about as if they were mad.

Blinded by the smarting and burning dust, the savages could now neither advance nor retreat, and Jack, seeing the demoralisation into which they were thrown by the foresight and courage of the Angel and her husband, shouted in ringing tones—

"Now's our time, boys. Down with them, and the ship is saved!"

The English wanted no second bidding. With a rush they flung themselves upon the foe, and cut and struck them down on all sides.

In one of the rushes Jack dropped his cutlass, but he could not stop to secure it, so the brave youth struck out with his fists, and the demoralised savages went down like nine-pins before his sledge-hammer blows.

Nobly was he seconded by Joe, his friends, and the sailors, and at length the blinded and suffering natives were driven to the stern and knocked overboard or flung into the sea, where desperate efforts were made to save them by those left in charge of the proas and the canoes.

The Angel had given her bellows to Sam, and whispered something to him which sent him running off the deck and down the companion.

And now that she saw the fight had been won, she set her newly-spliced leg in motion, and beat a pæan of victory on the quarter-deck.

Soon not a savage remained on board the "Betsy" save those in the hold and the dead and seriously wounded who lay upon her deck.

Several of the crew had received cuts from hatchets or wounds from spears, but all save Captain Briggs were able to keep on their feet.

The work of rescue still went on around the ship, for those in the boats were noble enough not to leave their comrades to drown.

The captain recovered his senses, to find himself supported in the arms of his second mate and a passenger.

"How goes the fight?" was his first question.

"The savages have been forced overboard," replied the mate, "and the day is ours."

"Thank heaven!"

"Let me help you below, sir," said the mate.

"No, no," replied Briggs; "I shall be all right in a minute; that fellow's hatchet stunned me, that was all."

He put his hand to his brow, and brought it away covered with blood.

"If you will not leave the deck, sir, allow me to tie this handkerchief around your head," said the passenger, taking his silk handkerchief from his pocket. "I fear that you are more seriously hurt than you imagine, and thanks to that brave lad, Jack Tempest, you are still alive."

"Ah! do I owe my life to him, then?" said Briggs, faintly.

"You would certainly have been slain if he had not bestrode your body and fought for you as he did."

"Brave boy, I will not forget him,"

said the captain. "Thank you, my head feels easier already. But you are sure there is no further danger?"

"None, sir," said the mate. "There is not a savage on board who has the power to raise his hand."

"Lead me to a seat, then."

They led him to a coil of rope, and he sat down upon it.

"Well, well," he said, "we cannot foresee what is going to happen. I felt terribly annoyed at first at having that lad thrust upon me, and but for him I should now be a dead man."

"Come along, Sam," the stewardess cried, stamping her wooden leg on the deck, "move your stumps, man. Here's a splendid chance to let them have it, while they are hauling the niggers out of the water. Here, give me one pair, and we'll make them sneeze their heads off. Hi, hi! you in the canoes, look out!"

Her cry caused the savages in the canoes to look up, when puff, puff went the bellows in the hands of Sam and his wife, and a couple of streams of fine powder went flying downwards from their nozzles.

Though a great quantity of it reached the eyes of the savages, yet a greater quantity still was forced back upwards by the wind, and the Angel and her husband were treated with a dose of the physic they had prepared for their foes.

"Ah—ah—tiss-u!"

"Yah—oh—yah—tiss-u!"

"My eyes are full," cried the Angel.

"I—I—tissue!" cried Sam.

"You fool, you didn't put the pepper in right, and your carelessness has blinded me," cried Mrs. Slops.

"My dear, I'm—I'm—"

And Sam could say no more for sneezing.

Fortunately their cachinnations caused them to duck their heads every moment, or the spears and hatchets flung at them from the canoes might have caused them serious injury, if nothing worse.

"Now then, lads," cried the first mate, "we don't want this carrion here, throw the beasts into their canoes. Over with them. If their fellows like to save them they can, or let them sink if they like!"

The men raised the wounded and dead from the deck and bore them to the side.

"Look out, there," yelled the first mate. "If you want this carrion, take it and be off, or I'll put a few ounces of lead into your ugly carcases."

And he tapped the pistol he held in his hand.

The sailors tumbled the savages over the rail into the canoes, though not a few of them fell into the sea and had to be fished out.

But the dead sank like stones, and those that fell into the canoes were instantly thrown out again by the occupants.

"There are those in the hold sir," said one of the men.

"True, I had forgotten them."

He loaded his pistols and then said—

"Get lanterns, and follow me. But be on your guard, for some of them may be able to do mischief yet."

Lanterns were procured, and the first mate led the way down into the hold.

Several of the crew followed him, whilst a few remained at the opening on deck, while the rest watched the savages, ready to give an alarm or resist any further attempt to board the ship.

It was a sickening sight that met the gaze of those who descended into the hold, among whom were Jack, Joe and Charley.

The natives had fallen a depth of fully twenty feet, and struck in their fall the barrels that had been placed beneath ready for the men to take ashore and fill with fresh water.

The sharp iron-bound edges had caused them terrible injuries, for there lay one with his head cut in twain, another with a broken back, and all more or less maimed.

Two of them were dead.

These were sent up first. Jack shuddered as he helped in the work.

"Ugh!" said Jack "what a sickening sight."

"You may well say that," Charley said. "But we are not to blame; they brought their fate on themselves."

"And they wouldn't have felt any pity for us if they had taken the ship," said Joe. "I bet they'd have showed us little mercy."

"You may depend upon that, my boy," said the mate. "If they had beaten us in the fight, there's not one of us but would be as stiff as this fellow here."

And he touched the dead savage with his foot.

"Take him up and drop him into the sea, for his fellows will do so for a certainty."

The second corpse was sent up, and then, after a pause, the maimed and wounded were hauled up.

The party then left the hold, and proceeded on deck.

The wounded were thrown to their companions, and when the last had been laid in the boats, the canoes and proas sheered off.

"Good riddance to bad rubbish," cried Joe, as the vessels began to move away. "Won't try it on again, will you, you cry babies?"

Joe's words had reference to those who had received the pepper and snuff in their eyes, and who were frantically trying to remove the smarting dust from their optics, which ran water.

Whether Joe's words were understood cannot be known, but several of the savages rose in the canoes, and a flight of arrows and spears were sent at the speaker, and those near him.

The first mate's cap was carried off his head by an arrow, one of the crew received the point of a spear in his left shoulder, and Joe had his jacket pierced by an arrow, the barb just cutting the skin of his arm, and causing him to leap a foot in the air.

Quick as lightning the first mate levelled his pistols, and fired at those in the nearest canoe.

The savages, evidently expecting a volley, began to paddle quickly away.

The proas, having hurriedly shifted their sail, went skimming over the waves like things of life.

"Thank heaven!" said the mate, fervently, "that danger has been faced and frustrated."

"And not a little of our victory is due, sir, to Mr. and Mrs. Slops," said Jack.

"It certainly was a brilliant idea," said Charley.

"But they've had to take some of their own physic," said Joe.

"What do you mean?" asked Jack.

"Why, Master Jack, they didn't think it right to share all the pepper and snuff between them as was up here, so the steward fetched a dose for them in the boats, but the wind blew a lot of it back into their own eyes, and it was a regular case of the blind leading the blind after that."

"Oh, that's bad," said Charley. "I'll see if I can do anything for them."

"One good turn deserves another," said Joe, "so I'll go with you."

"That's right," said Jack; "for I should be sorry if any harm befell them."

Joe and Charley went away for the pantry, to which Mr. and Mrs. Slops had staggered by the aid of feeling rather than sight.

"Do you think the captain is much injured, sir?" asked Jack.

"I hope not, my lad. His head is cut, but I do not think deeply. The blow stunned him, and thanks to you, the next, which doubtless would have killed him, was stopped. I shall not fail to represent your gallant conduct to Captain Briggs."

"I beg, sir, that you will not notice what I have done. It was the least I could do in return for the kindness that both I and my friend have received at his hands."

"You are a noble-hearted fellow, Tempest," said the first mate. "I am glad I have met you, and am proud to shake the hand of so true and brave a lad as Rough and Ready Jack."

CHAPTER LVI.

ARRIVAL AT NEWFOUNDLAND—ON BOARD THE WHALER—JACK'S WISH AND BRIGGS'S COMMENDATION.

THE deck was washed down, the course of the vessel looked to, and the "Betsy" ploughed her way through the waves.

The captain and Hal were conducted below, the medicine chest overhauled, and their wounds dressed.

The captain's injury was not so severe as was anticipated.

The savage's hatchet had struck sideways, and the wound, though a bad one, was large and painful

Hal's arm was cut nearly to the bone, but the wound was bound up with a cooling and healing lotion, which gave him considerable ease.

The rest of the company, for one and all save Jack and Mr. and Mrs. Slops had received more or less injury, were attended to in a kind, if rough way, and the passengers, at least the male portion of them, offered, as far as their abilities would permit them, to assist the crew in their labours, an offer which was accepted with gratitude by the captain and his officers.

A good look-out was kept, but nothing further in the shape of danger presented itself, and in due course the anchors of the "Betsy" were dropped, and she rode at her moorings off the island of New Providence.

Here they lay for three days getting in water and provisions, and by the time they were ready to heave anchor and continue the voyage all were comparatively well again.

Joe's wound was thoroughly healed, and Hal was able to use his arm without much pain or exertion; the crew were also able to proceed with their duties, and Captain Briggs to take his turn in navigating the vessel.

With a cheer they once again set sail, and with fine weather and favouring gales sped on their way.

New Orleans was reached without any event occurring worth relating, unless it was that Mrs. Slops seemed to have grown good-tempered and affable, and treated both Charley and Joe with consideration and kindness.

Her wooden leg did not come into play so much as formerly, and Chips avowed that it was because in splicing the timber limb he had reduced its original length by several inches.

Here the "Betsy" got rid of her passengers, and unloaded.

Then she took in a cargo for New York, and several passengers.

The voyage was pleasant, and everybody appeared happy and contented.

The captain could not bear to part with Jack and Joe, who, by their bravery, had endeared themselves to him and his officers and crew, and so our hero agreed to remain with him till he finally set sail from the west on his return to England.

At New York the ship was again unloaded and her passengers went on shore, after presenting Captain Briggs with a flattering credential, and Mr. and Mrs. Slops with a few gold coins.

At the great western city the "Betsy" took in a cargo for Newfoundland, but no passengers, and once more set forth on her voyage.

At lenght they reached the great cod fisheries, and not only Jack and Joe but their two friends also were thunder-struck at the numerous craft they found there.

It had been Captain Briggs's intention to sail from here home, but a freight was offered him for New York, and studying the interest of his owners in preference to his own desire, he again loaded up his ship, promising the crew that after this voyage the "Betsy" should set sail across the Atlantic for the port of London.

Here the whaler, the "Pride of the Arctic Ocean," had put in for repairs, and was waiting the finish of these, and the filling up of her complement of men, since half-a-dozen of her crew had deserted her.

Captain Briggs seldom went on shore without a companion.

Sometimes Jack accompanied him, and sometimes Hal, or one of the "Betsy's" officers.

Jack and the skipper were standing on the wharf one morning, when the captain of the whaler, whom business had brought ashore, accosted them.

He was a man standing fully six feet, but with that invariable stoop in the shoulders so common to men who go down to the sea in ships.

His face was as brown as a berry, his features regular, and his eyes black and piercing.

Both having business at the same place, they entered the office together, and when the business had been transacted, the whaler's captain, whose name was Samuel Robbs, invited Captain Briggs and Jack to go on board his vessel and dine with him.

The invitation was accepted, and our hero, for the first time, made his acquaintance with a whaler.

There was a great deal to interest

Jack on board, though there was a great deal of dirt as well, for the smoke from the coppers in which the blubber had been boiled during her former voyage had begrimed everything around.

The decks were stained with oil, the rigging reeked with oil and soot, but this only represented to our hero evidences of hard work and a rough life at sea.

"I should like to take a voyage to the Arctic regions," thought Jack; "it would be something to talk about when I return home; besides, there is excitement and danger in such a life, and for these reasons I should enjoy it all the more."

And with these thoughts in his mind, Jack examined the boats, the lines, and windlasses, and the harpoons and hatchets, also the huge knives with which the captured leviathans of the sea were cut up, and their flesh prepared for the coppers and the casks.

While the two skippers smoked their pipes, drank their spirits and water, and told yarns, Jack roamed over the ship from stem to stern.

In fact, nothing escaped his notice, and though everything was so different to what it had been on board the "Betsy," a longing to join the whaling crew grew stronger and stronger upon him, till at last he made up his mind to speak to Briggs on the subject.

After some time the two captains came on deck.

"When do you expect to be ready to sail?" asked Briggs of the other.

"In a week or ten days," was the reply. "And you?"

"I expect all my cargo will be on board to-morrow night, and if so, we sail next day."

"For New York?"

"Yes; where I shall load up for home, and where I fancy I am not the only one who will be glad to arrive."

And he looked at Jack in a peculiar manner.

This gave Jack an opportunity of speaking.

"If you mean me, sir," he said, smiling, "I was just thinking of trying to go as far from it as possible."

"Not home-sick, lad?" asked Robbs.

"No, sir; though I confess I should like to see my dear mother, but with that exception, I would be only too glad to visit all quarters of the world, and the Arctic regions more especially."

"Ah, my lad," said Robbs, shaking his head, "you would soon wish yourself out of them."

"I do not think so, sir," replied Jack; "and were it not that I should have to part from my kind friend, Captain Briggs, and have to say good-bye to my chums on board the 'Betsy,' I would ask you to enrol me amongst your crew, for neither work nor danger was ever yet feared by Rough and Ready Jack."

The two captains looked at Jack, and then at each other.

Jack watched them narrowly.

"My boy, I know little of the whaling business," said Briggs, after a pause. "But this I do know, it is a life of danger and hardship."

"Neither work nor peril, sir, would deter me," said Jack.

"You are a good lad, and a willing one," replied Briggs, "that I'll vouch for; and a plucky one, too, in the bargain, as my presence on this ship attests."

Then turning to Robbs, he added—

"Captain, I owe my life to the courage and intrepidity of this lad."

"Indeed!" said the other.

"It's truth," said Briggs, "and I'll spin the yarn, and if, after I've said my say, you don't admire the lad as much as I do, you never smelt salt water."

The two men sat down on a greasy block amidships, and Briggs not only told the whaler of the fight with the natives of the Bahamas, but gave his friend an outline of Jack's career as far as he himself knew it.

Many an admiring glance did the whaler skipper cast towards Jack, who had drawn out of hearing, and leaning over the greasy rail watched the enormous fleet of fishing boats stretching away on either side of him.

"Would you part with him?" asked Robbs, at length rising from the block.

"It would be like sending my own son adrift," replied Briggs; "for I tell you, I have learned to love that boy."

"That's only natural, seeing what he did for you," was the reply. "But who could help admiring him after the character you have given him? If the lad would join my ship, I'd make him second mate—first he should be, only he wants experience."

"He must choose for himself," said Briggs. "But I tell you, when he gets back to his chums and begins to think the affair seriously over, I do not fancy he will then feel disposed to part with them."

"How many of his particular friends have you on board the 'Betsy?'"

"There's two as staid as himself, and another, a young rip that wants a firm hand to hold him in."

"Is he so bad as that?" asked the whaler.

"Bad; not a bit of it," said Briggs. "He's as full of animal spirits and mischief as an egg is full of meat; you can't be angry with him, though you may pretend to be. Up to all kinds of jokes and capers. Here, there, and everywhere. By Neptune, I never came near such a boy."

"He will work?" asked the whaler.

"Like a nigger. Nothing comes amiss to him, only you must not drive him."

"I expect I shall have to start short-handed, and I wish you could prevail on these lads to sign articles with me."

"No, no," said Briggs, "I won't persuade them at all. If they would like to take a whaling voyage instead of returning with me, they are welcome to do so. I shall miss them, I know, but then I won't stand in their way; they must choose for themselves. If I won't persuade, I won't say or do anything to deter them."

"Then it would cause you no feeling of annoyance, Captain Briggs, if I spoke to this lad about it?"

"None in the world," was the reply. "I should be the last to stand in the way of his following the bent of his own inclinations. I always think it best to let a high-spirited lad have his own way in some things."

"Then I will just have a few minutes' talk with this youngster," said Robbs. "What is his name?"

"John Tempest, but he is called by his friends and the crew of the 'Betsy,' Rough and Ready Jack."

"Why have they given him that name?"

"Because," replied Briggs, "he is always ready to stand foremost where danger or oppression is to be found; because he is strong and chivalrous, and ready to prove by word or blow that he is a true Englishman, and a brave and honourable lad."

CHAPTER LVII.

RALPH STERNWAY IN GAOL—THE RUFFIANS HE MEETS THERE—THE CONSPIRACY—
A HORRIBLE DEED—FREE ONCE MORE.

SOME time before the "Betsy" had reached New York, Ralph Sternway had been handed over by the captain of the "Pennsylvania" to the American authorities, who had communicated his crimes and arrest to the ambassador for Great Britain.

Pending the decision as to what was to be done with the assassin of Captain Hamed and his crew of Moors, the British ruffian had been placed in prison.

A close watch was kept on him for some days, but as he seemed thoroughly resigned to his present position, the watch was relaxed.

In the same part of the gaol in which Ralph was confined were three men whose desperate characters and wicked deeds had, after a long series of crimes, caused them to be hunted down and placed in durance vile.

One of these ruffians had been charged with more than one murder; another was a card-sharper and notorious horse-stealer, who, in endeavouring to avoid capture, had buried his knife in the heart of one of his pursuers; while the third was the chief of a gang of white men and Indians who had banded together to rob the mails and their passengers on the roads between city and city.

"BAXTER DREW A HEAVY BREATH, AND MURMURED SOME WORDS OF THANKS."

No. 11.

Such villains were not long in fraternising with each other, and only waited the first opportunity to murder their gaolers and escape.

They knew at a glance that Ralph was as desperate a ruffian as any of them, and that something which invariably brings rogues together soon enrolled him in the trio's plot.

As a rule, two gaolers appeared together in the cell where these men were confined, the one standing guard with his hand upon his weapon, while the other supplied the requirements of their prisoners.

Three days after Ralph's incarceration, only one gaoler appeared.

"Where's t'other one?" asked one of the ruffians. "Have you given him a holiday to go and see his missus?"

The gaoler unthinkingly, replied—

"Poor fellow, he slipped in the corridor a few hours ago, put out his knee-cap and injured his ankle, and the doctor says he must lay up for a few days."

"Sorry for him," said the horse-stealer, "for he seemed a good sort."

"He wasn't a bad one, by a long way," replied the prison official, as, his work for the time being ended, he passed out, locking the door behind him.

As soon as he was gone, the men looked at each other and grinned.

"They will be putting another in his place to-morrow," said one; "so if the thing's to be done, it ought to be done to-night when he brings our supper."

"It must," replied the mail robber, "we may never get another chance before our trial, and they will take care we don't get one afterwards."

"But how is the job to be done?" whispered Ralph, who well knew to what they alluded. "We have no weapons—not even a knife."

"No weapons!" cried another; "what then are these, Britisher?"

And he held up his hands, spread out, and worked his brown fingers.

"Once his neck is in these here pinchers, he'll choke quickly enough, I'll warrant you; and what's more, he won't be the first one what's had his life strangled out of him by them."

"Is that so?" asked Ralph.

"It is. It was just at the edge of a wood, bordering a road where I had put up many a job. I was lying in wait there for the mail coach, while my band were concealed deeper in the woods, waiting my signal that the coach was coming, when all of a sudden down the moonlit road came tearing a horse and rider."

"Yes?"

"I drew back deeper into the shadow to watch, and pulled out my pistol. The moon's rays streamed full upon the advancing horse and rider, and as he came on at a gallop I recognised Jem Blake, the guard of the Brinsville mail, and plainly saw that he carried the letter bag on the horse's back behind him."

"Go on, mate," said one, as the ruffian paused.

"I could see at a glance, also, that he had no saddle, only a piece of matting to sit upon, and I concluded that some accident had happened to the coach, and that the guard had been sent on one of the horses to carry the mail to Brinsville."

The fellow paused a moment, and then, leaning nearer to his companions, concluded—

"I kept well in the shadow of a large tree, and as the horse dashed up, I fired at its rider, but at that moment the animal took an upward bound, and I missed Jem Blake, but brought the horse to his knees.

"In a moment Jem had flung himself to the ground and grasped the pistol in his belt; but I did not give him time to draw it, for, with a bound, I sprang from the shadow into the moonlight, and with both hands grasped him by the throat, and hurled him to his knees.

"A few minutes later Jem's head fell forward, and his chin rested on my wrist. I had strangled the life out of him, brave and powerful as he was, and I flung the dead body aside, just in time to secure the wounded horse as it struggled to its feet."

Bad as they were, his listeners could scarcely repress a shudder.

"Then you think that luck might serve us to-night?" asked the card-sharper.

"I do."

"And will you try it?"

"Liberty is worth something," replied the ruffian, grimly.

" We will leave it to you to settle him, then," said Ralph; " but then we have got to get out of this place."

" True; the way will have to be found, I suppose. Where there's a will a man can generally find a way. But hist! I hear footsteps. Not a word ! "

The fellow held up his finger for silence.

The footsteps passed along the stone corridor, and grew fainter and fainter, and then were heard no longer.

" Going the rounds," said Ralph.

" Just so. Now let's arrange our plans. You, Britisher, ask him when he brings our supper if he has any reason to know when you are likely to be taken before the judge—anything you like, so as to draw his attention off me, and you two other fellows get between him and the door, and, if you can, secure his hanger, and leave the rest to me. There must be no noise—nothing to cause an alarm to be raised or a suspicion of foul play to reach the ears of either prisoners or gaolers, the thing must be done silently and quickly; do you understand? "

" We do," was the reply.

Gradually night came on, the daylight that entered the cell grew fainter, and then the lamps in the stone corridor were lit, their rays penetrating faintly through the iron bars over the door of the cell.

Again the footsteps of the patrol were heard, and then silence once more reigned.

" He'll be here with the food soon," said the ruffian, as he turned back the cuff of his coat. " You know your part? "

" Yes," replied Ralph.

" And you? " he said, looking at the others.

" We understand."

Nothing more was said.

Half-an-hour passed, and they heard doors opened and closed, and they knew that the moment for attempting their plan was approaching.

Presently the key turned in the lock, and the cell door was opened about eighteen inches, and an arm was thrust through the opening, the hand of which held a tin dish on which were hunks of bread and pieces of cheese.

" Here's your supper," said the gaoler. " Catch hold."

The ruffians looked at each other.

Did the gaoler suspect anything?

It was the first time that he had not boldly entered the cell.

" Well, can't you bring it in," cried the horse-thief. " You don't expect gentlemen like us to wait upon ourselves, do you? "

" Take it," said the gaoler, " unless you want me to carry it back."

And as he pushed his right arm further through the opening and grasped the edge of the door with his left hand, he thrust his head also through the orifice.

With a bound the ruffian who had agreed to strangle him, thrust forward both hands and closed the door sharply upon the gaoler's neck.

The tin dish fell to the floor, and the victim essayed to utter a cry, but ere it could escape his lips Ralph flung the weight of his body upon the door, and the sharp iron edge cut cruelly into the flesh of the choking man.

The others now assisted in the horrible work.

They, too, pressed against the door with all their might.

The eyeballs of the poor fellow bulged in his head.

His tongue protruded, black and swollen, from his mouth.

His nose, eyes, and ears began to stream with blood, his chin rested upon his chest, and the fearful deed was accomplished.

" Catch hold of him, so as to prevent him falling," whispered the ruffian who had closed the door upon the man's neck, " and drag him inside."

One of them grasped the dead gaoler's head, and then the door was opened sufficiently to allow of the passage of the body.

Softly he was lowered to the floor of the cell, and his keys and hanger were taken from him.

All this was done quickly and silently.

Then the body of the murdered man was drawn across the cell, and placed out of sight of anyone who might open the door.

" Follow me," said the ruffian; " I have been here before and know the prison well."

He looked up and down the corridor, and then stepped forth, the others followed him, and when all were outside the cell he turned the key in the lock, and with silent footfalls they made their way along the passage.

At the end of this was the gaoler's lodge, and opposite to it the outer door of the gaol.

The lodge was deserted, but over the fireplace hung a huge key.

To secure this was the work of a moment, to fit it into the lock of the door but another.

With a slight grating sound the key turned, the lock shot back, and the heavy door swung open.

Over its threshold bounded the four villains ; the door was then locked on the outside and the key flung far away.

"Now," cried the principal of that villainous crew, "each man for himself, for it is death to him who is captured."

CHAPTER LVIII.

THE RETURN TO CONSCIOUSNESS—THE TENT IN THE WOOD—AN ARAB'S FEARS AND DOUBTS.

THE fear of a horrible death lent to Baxter Sharp a fictitious strength, and exerting it to the utmost, he managed to push some of the sand away, so as to enable him to breathe more freely.

The task he then set himself was an arduous one.

It was with great difficulty that he could force up the sand so as to enable him to raise himself to his knees.

But he did so at last, and looked over the desert.

The flat surface had been piled up into hillocks, and had the appearance of the billows of the sea, for roll upon roll of sand met his gaze.

Nowhere were his companions to be seen, and from the changed nature of the ground, only the tops of the trees of the wood towards which they had been journeying could now be distinguished, and which gave it the appearance of being far more distant than before.

Above, the sun rode like a ball of gold in a sky of cerulean blue, and the hot, fierce rays poured down upon the bare head and bleeding body of Baxter Sharp.

With a groan of mingled pain and despair the villain suffered his lacerated face to fall into his sand-seared hands.

"Oh, this is horrible," he said; " powerless and alone—better, far better to have perished in the storm."

Then a shudder ran through his frame, and he muttered—

"No, no; I am not fit to die."

After awhile Baxter managed to draw himself on to the top of the sand, and, exhausted with his exertions, he laid his smarting body down and gradually sank into slumber.

But his mind was not at rest.

Fearful visions floated across his brain, horrible and mocking forms seemed to stand before him, and he groaned in his sleep.

When he awoke, night was upon the scene.

The moon and stars rode high above him, and the hillocks cast strange shadows across the sands.

A dull, heavy pain was at the back of his head, his body was sore and stiff, and he shivered with cold.

His eyes felt dull and heavy, and his lips were dry and swollen.

Through his parched and parted lips he breathed the words that he had last heard, the words of his last victim—

" Water ! Oh, but for one drop ! "

In reply to his inarticulated prayer seemed to come to his ears a sound of fiendish laughter.

He raised his aching head, and gazed around him.

Only the hillocks of sand, and the shadows they threw at their base met his gaze.

Then his head sank back, and he knew no more.

When Baxter Sharp awoke to consciousness, he was no longer lying beneath the midnight moon on his bed of drifted sand.

He lay upon a kind of couch at one side of a tent, the curtain of which was thrown back to admit of light and air.

Through this he gazed out upon trees, beneath which a magnificent black horse was tethered, and beyond these he saw two or three women and children grouped around a well, from which they were hoisting, by the aid of a bar of wood placed across another, the water that sparkled in its depths below.

All this Baxter Sharp took in before he could thoroughly realise he was not dreaming.

Then he turned his gaze around the tent.

With the exception of the bed on which he lay, it was absolutely without furniture, only a few vessels for holding water stood on the floor, and a gun and spear rested against one side of the tent.

"Where am I—how came I here?" he asked himself.

As he uttered these words a figure entered the tent.

It was that of a tall Arab, attired only in a loose white robe, girded in at the waist with a band of red cotton, and with slippers on his feet.

His coal-black beard was here and there streaked with grey.

As he strode up to the couch he fixed his dark, piercing eyes upon the face of Baxter Sharp, and gazed at him intently.

Then, muttering something, he turned to the opening, and called to those at the well.

A woman, whose features were as regular as those of a Grecian statue, and whose figure was perfection, and every motion graceful, looked up at the call, and then seizing her vessel which stood filled with water at her feet, she hurried towards the tent, at the threshold of which she paused.

The Arab pointed towards the couch.

The woman gazed towards it, a look of pity mingled with pleasure in her eyes.

Then, entering the tent, she dipped a small vessel into the larger one she had brought from the well, and carrying it to the couch, held it to the lips of Baxter.

The fevered lips felt the cooling liquid, and he drank eagerly.

Not till he had drained every drop the little vessel held did the woman draw it from his lips.

Then Baxter drew a heavy breath, and he murmured faintly some words of thanks.

She to whom they were addressed, though she did not understand the words, evidently guessed their import, for she laid her hand gently on his forehead and smiled upon him.

Then she turned to her husband—for the tall Arab, whose years could not have been less than fifty, was the husband of this young and peerless beauty.

"He will live," she said, in a language that Baxter was a stranger to.

"It is the will of Allah," replied the Arab.

Then looking fixedly at his wife, he added, in a lower tone—

"Would it were not so!"

"Why?" she asked. "Because he is a Christian?"

"Nay," he replied, drawing her from the tent; "but that I feel I have plucked a serpent from the jaws of death, who will, sooner or later, return my kindness by burying its poisoned sting in my heart."

The woman looked up in his face, and tears came into her eyes.

"Oh, Allah forbid!" she said. "Could I think the Christian would return our care and kindness with ingratitude my knife should end his life and your fears."

And the moist eyes flashed fiercely as from the folds of her short white dress she drew a long and narrow blade, set in an ivory handle.

But, as if ashamed of the action, she put back her dagger and smiled.

"You have watched too long by the Christian's couch," she said, "and the close air of the tent has weighed heavily upon your health and spirits. Day in and day out, at sunrise and sunset, you have watched and waited for the Christian's returning reason, instead of flying over the desert or on to the mountains astride your noble horse, who, from his late want of exercise, appears to have grown as melancholy as his master."

The Arab smiled, and strode up to the horse and patted its sleek neck and side.

The beautiful animal rubbed its head against his master's face and breast, and showed by its actions its delight at being caressed.

His wife joined in her husband's caresses, and the animal returned them.

"How long think you he will be ere he is well enough to leave our tent?" asked the woman.

"Allah alone can tell," replied her husband. "But I would he were strong enough to do so now."

"Up till now you have pitied him," she said.

"Till now I had never seen that expression on his face—the look in those eyes, as he gazed from his couch out through the opening of the tent towards you and the other women at the well."

Then seizing his wife's hand as it caressed the horse's mane, he said, in a hissing whisper—

"As you love me, as you revere Allah and his Prophet, trust not that man."

And he nodded his head towards the tent in which Baxter Sharp lay.

"What do you fear?" she asked.

"I know not," he replied. "But something whispers me that I had better served my happiness and yours had I trampled his insensible carcase beneath the hoofs of my steed than have stopped to succour him in the desert."

"Oh, my husband, anger not Allah by such thoughts," she said. "It was he who led you across the sands to where the Christian lay, exhausted, bleeding, dying; it was his will that your hand should pluck him from the grave and restore him to life and strength."

He drew her to him and kissed her forehead softly.

"You are right," he said. "You teach me my duty to man and to Allah. I but wrong the one and insult the other by my fears and suspicions. My path is clear, and I do wrong to swerve aside from it. That man is a charge confided into our hands by Allah, and I must act towards the Christian as I should towards a true believer."

The gloom vanished from his brow and a smile came into his face. The woman pressed his hand within her own, then raised it to her lips.

"Now you are indeed again your own true self," she said. "I must watch more often and for longer spells beside the sick man's couch. Such work is not fit for men, to whom air and exercise are as necessary as food and drink. Leave the Christain to my care, and follow your usual pursuits. It is man's duty to work, woman's to watch and pray."

"Light of my life," he said, in tender tones. "Oh, if aught befell thee, my peerless—"

She stopped his further utterance by playfully placing her hand upon his lips, and pealing forth a low and silvery laugh.

"Still a flatterer," she said, "and we have shared the same tent these ten long years."

"And I shall remain your lover even after death," he replied.

"Do not talk of death," she said, "Do not fear any ill will befall me. As well look for storm in sunshine or think of finding earth in Paradise."

The Arab replied only by a pressure of her hand.

Together they entered the tent, and together they stood beside the couch of the Englishman.

Baxter, during their absence, had tried to realise how he came there, and after a while the real facts had dawned upon his mind.

He had been found by the Arab in the desert, and brought by him to the wood in which his tent had been reared.

Here he had been nursed back to reason, if not to health and strength, by his saviour and the beautiful Arab woman who shared his love, home, and fortunes.

How would he reward their care and kindness, he mentally asked himself, with his eyes fixed upon that lovely woman's face, and the answer his black heart gave trembled in his bosom.

CHAPTER LIX.

JACK AND HIS FRIENDS RESOLVE TO SHIP ON BOARD THE WHALER—CAPTAIN
BRIGGS'S ADVICE.

THE result of the whaler's conversation with Jack was our hero's promise that if Captain Briggs was willing that he should join the " Pride of the Arctic Ocean," and one or more of his friends would agree to join him, he would sign articles for a voyage to Greenland and home.

Shortly after, the captain of the " Betsy" and his young companion returned to their vessel.

"And so, my lad, you have elected to sail to the Arctic regions," said Briggs, as they were rowed to the ship, which lay a little way off the wharf.

"If you have no objection, sir," replied Jack; "and one, at least, of my friends will join me."

"I can have none, my boy," replied the skipper. "My only fear is that you will find life too rough on board the whaler."

"If I objected to that, sir, I should ill deserve the title my friends have given me of Rough and Ready Jack."

"True," said Briggs; "but you may be away a long while. A whaler cannot always return when her captain or crew wishes. Sometimes vessels in those regions are frozen in for months at a time."

"I am aware of that, sir," replied Jack. "And also that I have no other reason to be on the sea at all but from a love of travel and adventure; for, thank heaven, my prospects are bright, if not brilliant."

"Lucky dog," said the skipper. "Wish I could say as much for myself, but I will have to work for my bread until the great Captain pipes me aloft. But have you no wish to see your mother?"

"Yes," replied Jack; "but since I know that she wants for nothing, I wish to take this voyage before I go south, and settle down in the companionship of the mother I love."

"Do you think that she would like your going?"

"She is one who believes that foreign travel is beneficial to youth, and improving to the mind; and I feel sure that when I write her that I am about to visit the northern latitudes ere I return to settle down in England, if heaven so wills it, she will approve of my wishes and my resolve."

By this time the ship was reached, and Jack and the skipper clambered on board. Hal was close at hand when Jack and the skipper came on board.

"Back again, Jack?" he said.

"Yes, old boy."

"See anything ashore to amuse you?" asked Charley.

"No," replied Jack; "but I have been greatly interested afloat."

"Eh?" asked Hal.

"I and the captain have been some hours on board a whaler. You can see her lying off there, just beyond that fleet of fishing boats."

"I see her," said Charley. "What sort of a craft is she?"

"Oh, like all engaged in the whale fishery, I suppose," said Jack. "Oily, smoke-begrimed, and full of nauseating smells."

"Shouldn't care, then, to sail in her," said Charley.

"Nor I," put in Hal.

"Why not?" asked Jack.

"Never could bear the smell cf oil," said Hal.

"Especially rank oil, as I fancy that got from the blubber of whales must be."

"No doubt a whaler has its evils," said Jack.

"And its dangers," said Charley, "for they cruise in waters that are far from easy of navigation."

"But danger, my boy, is an Englishman's pride to overcome," said Jack. "If it were not for danger, what would be the use of courage? Were there no difficulties, how could they be assailed and conquered? For my own part, I have decided to sign articles for a voyage to Greenland and back, if one of you fellows will join me in the trip."

"Master Jack, I'll join you if you'll only let me," said Joe.

"Thank you, Joe; I knew that you would."

"I'd like to see them big fields of ice as Slush was a-telling me of the other day, and them lights what he calls the roarerbariliuns, and the great floating mountains that glitter in the sun like the dress of a harlequin in a pantomime."

"I have read a good deal about the enchanting scenes to be witnessed in the Arctic seas," said Jack, "and I long to visit the cold and cheerless North; but I do wish that, since Captain Briggs would be willing to part with you, I could induce you to join me."

Hal and Charley were silent for a moment, and then the former held out his hand.

"Jack, I am with you," he said.

"And so am I," added Charley—"since Captain Briggs will not feel annoyed at our leaving him."

"Hurrah!" said Jack. "But, I tell you, boys, if heaven guides us safely back from those wild regions, I sail south and bid farewell to a life on the ocean wave."

"Do you mean it, Jack?"

"Yes, for then duty and affection will call me home to cheer and comfort the declining days of a dear mother's life."

"Ah, Jack, it is well to be you," said Charley.

Then he laughed, and held out his hand, saying—

"But I do not envy your good fortune, old chum, for well do you deserve it."

"Thank you," replied Jack, "and I hope that it will ever be my aim to do so."

"You ever will, Jack," said Hal, "for you're thoughtful as well as brave."

"And so you have determined to go with me," said Jack.

"If her captain will take us," replied Hal. "Of course, that as yet has got to be seen."

"And you mustn't forget that we are perfect greenhorns, and may be more annoyance than help," said Charley.

"I have the whaler captain's promise that he will ship any or all I may take on board with me."

"Yes, but he may fancy we know something of the work," said Hal.

"On the contrary, he is well aware that he or others will have to instruct us in our duties."

"And think you he would be willing to do so?" asked Charley.

"I am sure of it," replied Jack.

"What sort of man is he?" inquired Hal.

"Rough in appearance, but kind in tone and manner. He is tall and stalwart, and has an eye that seems to look you through and read you like a book."

"And his mates?" asked Charley.

"Were ashore. Indeed there was only a shipkeeper on board, as far as I could see, besides myself and the two captains."

"Do you think you will like him, Jack?"

"I'm sure I shall."

"Then so shall we," said Joe.

"That's a foregone conclusion," said Hal. "But when does she sail, Jack?"

"As soon as her repairs are effected—in a week or ten days," was the reply.

"Do you think there will be an Angel in the ship?" asked Joe.

"No, you may depend there will be no woman on board," replied Jack.

"That's all right," said Joe. "We've had enough of the one here."

"I am sure Mrs. Slops has wonderfully improved of late," said Jack.

"All put on, Master Jack. The time was coming round for the tips, don't you see," said Joe, "and so she put on her best behaviour."

"Joe, don't be uncharitable," said Jack.

"I ain't," replied Joe. "After the passengers had gone ashore you should have seen the change that came over her. She'd got used to the feel of that mended leg of hers, and I, Slops, and Charley knows it; don't we, sir?"

"Rather," said Charley. "She's getting about as bad as ever."

"And a lot worse," put in Joe.

"Well, she will not trouble any of us long," said Jack, "if you still keep in the same mind."

"I have made up my mind," said Hal. "I shall go."

"And I shall not draw back," said Charley.

"And I won't, unless Master Jack does," said Joe.

"All right, then, that's settled," said Jack. "Of course you will inform Captain Briggs of your decision."

"Certainly," replied both, "and at once, so that he may, if he desires, procure hands in our places."

"Well, cut along, all three of you," said Jack, "and get over the job at once."

"Ain't you coming, Jack?" said Hal.

"No, for I have arranged everything with him before."

The two sought the skipper in his state-room, where he was engaged with Slops in looking over the list of the articles procured by the steward for the voyage back to New York.

"All right, steward," said the skipper, handing him the list. "I think everything is down there that is necessary; I cannot see anything has been forgotten."

He was about to leave the cabin, when the three lads entered.

The captain guessed their errand.

"Don't run away, steward; wait a moment," said Briggs.

The steward drew back.

"Well, my lads," he said, "I suppose you have come to tell me that you have decided to ship with your friend Jack for a voyage to the Arctic seas?"

"Such sir," said Hal, "is our wish, unless you desire that we should return with you to England."

"I will not deny that I shall be sorry to part with you," said Briggs, "but I will not stand in opposition to your desires. Besides, young men should see as much of the world as possible, it tends to make them better Christians and more worthy citizens. Travel annihilates prejudices, and shows men and things in their true colours. So, I say go, and take with you all the good wishes of your true friend, Captain Briggs."

And rising, he shook hands with each.

"Now, lads," he said after a pause, "I have only this advice to give you—do your duty in whatever sphere you may be cast. Let truth be your bowsprit, honour your helm, and your hope and trust the sheet-anchor, and then you'll weather the gales and storms of life from whichever quarter they may blow."

"That's the sort of advice," said the steward, who had listened open-mouthed, and learned for the first time that the lads would not return with him in the "Betsy." "But lor'! lor'! what will Mrs. Slops say when she hears of this?"

"As I do," said Briggs, "I hope. May heaven bless and prosper them."

"Amen!" said Slops solemnly. "But, oh, what will the Angel say?"

"I'll tell you," said Charley, with a grin. "She'll say that, now those young rips are gone, I shall have nobody's shins but Slops's on which to ply my wooden leg."

CHAPTER LX.

SIGNING ARTICLES—A RUN ON SHORE—PREPARING FOR THE VOYAGE—THE MAN WITH THE BLACK BEARD.

THE "Betsy's" cargo was all shipped and stowed away in good time.

The men were ordered to be on board over night, and the anchors were heaved and secured to the cat-heads before eight o'clock in the morning.

Then Jack and his friends took a final farewell of all on board.

Both captain and officers parted with them with regret, and the Angel fairly sobbed over Joe and Charley, at which the men winked at each other, touched their lips, and by signs intimated that Mrs. Slops had, early as it was, been indulging in something stronger than tea.

A true British cheer followed the lads as they went over the side into the boat that was to take them ashore, and this was again and again repeated as the little vessel glided towards the wharf.

As soon as the boat returned, the "Betsy" was got under weigh, and as she glided away from the shore, Jack and his friends waved a farewell to those whose kindness had endeared them to their hearts for ever.

They watched the ship till she lay low down in the horizon, and then turned away to enjoy a short spell on shore.

Our hero and his friends during the day waited upon Captain Robbs on board the whaler, the "Pride of the Arctic Ocean."

Jack introduced Hal, Charley, and Joe to the bluff old whaler and his first mate, Seth Spinner, a man of about thirty years of age, standing five feet two inches, but with an enormous breadth of chest, and muscles that stood out like knots upon his brown arms and forehead.

"So you have made up your minds, lads," said Robbs, shaking Jack by the hand.

"Yes, sir," replied Hal; "we have come to sign articles if you are willing."

"Aye, aye," said the skipper. "You look smart lads, and won't be afraid of work, I can see. So come into the cabin, all of you, and Spinner, you come too."

The mate took a short, black pipe from between his lips, knocked the tobacco out of the bowl on the rail, and blew the burning weed into the water.

"I'm with you, captain," he said.

They all went below, and the articles were soon signed, and witnessed by Seth Spinner.

Jack could not repress a smile as he saw the laborious way in which the mate wrote his name.

"Avast, youngster," said the mate. "I didn't have as much schooling as you did, and I'm a sight more used to holding a harpoon than a slip of a thing like this you call a pen. It ain't my best, as the youngster says, for I'll swear I could do it a sight better with the tip of a marline-spike."

"No offence, I hope," said Jack.

"Offence be blowed," replied Spinner. "I don't feel offended when a whale knocks me overboard with his flukes, so 'tain't likely I'll be hurt at what you say or do."

"This young man will be my second mate, Spinner, and I hope you and he will get on well together," said the captain.

"No fear of that, captain," said Seth. "He's a fair sailing craft I can see by his figure-head."

"I am satisfied that we shall be good friends," said Jack.

"'Twon't be my fault if we ain't," was the reply. "But I reckon you'll be a bit green in our trade till I and the cap'n lick you into shape for the duties aboard a whaler."

"I shall only be too glad to learn," replied Jack, "and I am sure I may say as much for my friends. If we fail in any duty, it will not be for the want of trying to succeed."

"All right, lads. When can you come aboard?" said the skipper.

"At any time that you may be pleased to name, sir," replied Jack.

"Then say a week from to-day. I don't suppose we shall be quite ready to sail, though I hope to, and no doubt you'll be glad of a run ashore."

"Yes, sir," replied Jack.

"Well, since you have signed articles, you can have each of you a month's pay if you wish it," said the skipper.

Jack cast a glance round at his friends before he replied, and then he said—

"Sir, on behalf of myself and friends I thank you; but Captain Briggs paid us for our services on board the 'Betsy,' and, consequently, we have sufficient for our present wants."

"Well, I made the offer not knowing how you were placed, and, besides, it is one more often expected than not by the men when they sign."

"I know it is the custom, sir, for sailors to receive money when they engage to ship; but as we can do without it—"

"All right, my boys. If you don't take it you can't lose or spend it; but should you find that you run short, you can still apply to Captain Robbs."

The lads thanked him, and went on shore.

Here everything they came across was strange and interesting to them.

On all sides the smell of fish prevailed.

They visited the large curing and packing houses, and for the first time realised what a tremendous business was done in fish.

They went from place to place, always meeting with something to admire or instruct them, and as they had vowed never to touch intoxicating liquors, and keep out of rough company, and were always sober, they passed a week of great enjoyment.

Then they thought it was time to go on board the whaler.

Captain Briggs had been very generous to the lads, and, although Jack and Joe had no claim upon him whatever, he insisted on presenting them with a sum of money.

The greater portion of this they laid out in the purchase of clothing suitable to the climate into which they were to sail, and with their new though rough garments in their possession they went on board the whaler.

"Had your fling ashore, lads?" said Spinner, as he confronted them on the deck.

"Yes, sir," replied Hal, "and greatly enjoyed ourselves, as everything was to us so strange and novel."

"Aye, aye; I guess it was. There's not another fishing place in the world like Newfoundland."

"Is the captain aboard?" asked Jack.

"No; but he will be to-morrow."

"When do you expect to sail, sir?" asked Jack.

"Sir be hanged!" cried Spinner. "We're a rough sort here. Call me Seth or Spinner, and leave the sir for the 'old man.'"

"What old man?" asked Jack.

The mate roared with laughter.

"The skipper. We call the captain the 'old man,'" said Seth.

"Oh!" said Jack. "I was not aware of that."

"We're not so particular aboard a whaler as they are on a man-of-war or a first-class merchantman. As I told you afore, we're a roughish lot, and the oil and the smoke knocks all the gentility out of us. But then we're none the worse for that as I knows on."

Jack smiled.

"You asked when we expected to sail?" continued the mate.

"Yes."

"In three days. The crew will come aboard to-morrow night, and we shall get under weigh by the next night I reckon."

"Then they are getting on well with the repairs?"

"Better than I expected. They'll have all taut and trim in forty-eight hours."

Jack found that though he was an officer he would have to rough it pretty considerably; but he had made up his mind to take things as they came.

He would have to berth with his companions and a portion of the crew, but he did not mind that, while his friends were only too glad to be with him.

The captain came on board the next day.

The repairs were finished in good time, provisions were put on board and stowed, and then the crew came on board just as night was falling.

Several were known to the captain and his mate, but half-a-dozen fresh hands had been engaged in the place of those who had left the ship.

Amongst the new batch was a man that fixed Jack's attention.

He was rather above the middle height, walked with a slight limp, and had a habit of looking furtively out of the corners of his eyes.

His hair was black and curly, his whiskers and beard bushy, leaving little of his face to be seen besides his eyes, nose, and lips.

He appeared to be about forty years of age.

Jack looked long and scrutinisingly at him.

Why he did so, he could not have told.

He had never seen the man before, he assured himself. Yet he pondered in his mind who could he at any time have encountered, that the figure, if not the face of the sailor, reminded him of.

For some time he tried to think, and then, with an exclamation of vexation at what he considered ridiculous, he turned away.

Had he looked back instantly he might have seen a strange expression in the man's eyes, and noted the fiercely clenched teeth which the half-parted lips revealed.

When Jack returned to the waist of the vessel the man had gone below.

Joe, looking more like a sweep than anything else, came up to him.

"Why, Joe, what have you been doing?" asked Jack, smiling.

"Cleaning out a copper, Master Jack," was the reply.

"You are as black as a negro, Joe."

"And just about as greasy, sir," replied Joe. "But what's the odds as long as you are happy, Master Jack?"

"It is honest work," replied Jack.

"And slippery as well, sir. If I was to roll myself on the pavement you could have a slide in summer, free gratis for nothing, and break a leg into the bargain."

This jesting remark of Joe's caused Jack's mind to revert to the man with the limp.

"Joe," he said, softly.

"Yes, Master Jack."

"Did you see that fellow with the bushy whiskers and the limp come on board?"

"No, sir; but I see him down below just now with the others."

"Did you ever see him before?" asked Jack.

"If I had I should have recollected his ugly phiz," replied Joe. "Did you, sir?"

"No; and yet there is something about him that puzzles me," said Jack. "I may be wrong and unjust, but I have taken a dislike to the man, and for what reason I must confess I cannot explain."

"People have strange fancies at times," said Joe, as he passed on; "but there's generally something in them, after all. I'll keep my eye on Mr. Black Muzzle, and try and find out if he is sailing under false colours."

And Joe saw nothing yet to convince him of this; in fact, no better or more willing sailor assisted in getting the whaler under weigh on her voyage to the Arctic regions.

CHAPTER LXI.

THE SAILOR'S VISION—SUSPICIOUS MOVEMENTS—THE ICEBERG—THE CASTAWAY.

THE voyage to the frozen seas would have been an uneventful one, but for one reason, which occurred at night, just as the watch was changing.

Jack, who was officer of the watch, had occasion to hurry below just as the bell struck, and the men were robing themselves for their duties.

The hairy-faced sailor, who had given his name as Phil Harman, and who up till now had shown himself to be a practical seaman, and whose willingness and intrepidity had gained for him the respect and admiration of the officers and the crew, had only been partially aroused by the sound of the bell and the movements of his messmates.

He lay in his hammock, where the red light of the smoking oil-lamp fell upon his face.

A gasping cry that had issued from his lips had caused Jack to gaze towards him, as well as those who were hurriedly pulling on their clothes to relieve their comrades on deck.

The man's eyes were open, but staring and glassy.

His features were convulsed, and his fingers clutched fiercely at the blanket of his hammock.

"Off—off!" he gasped, "I did not shut the door on your neck. Turn those staring eyes from me, or I shall go mad. Away! Ah!"

He sprang up in his hammock and glared around him.

"Had a bad dream, mate?" said one of the men, questioningly.

Phil Harman passed his hand across his brow, on which great beads of perspiration stood, and drew a long, deep breath.

"Yes," he gasped, rather than spoke, "I have had a terrible nightmare."

And he sprang tremblingly from the hammock.

"Is it time to go on deck?" he said.

"Yes, mate," replied another; "but hang me to the yard-arm if you do not look and tremble as if you had committed a murder and felt the rope round your neck."

Phil started so violently, that his body collided with that of Jack's, and our hero instinctively threw up his hands, and unintentionally pushed up the massive rolls of black hair which covered the seaman's head.

With a cry, Harman thrust Jack's

hand aside, and clasped his head with both his hands.

So quickly was this done, that only Jack himself saw, or fancied he did, that those black locks were false, and that they covered a head of hair of a different colour and texture.

"I beg your pardon, Mr. Tempest," he said, hurriedly. "A sudden pain in my foot caused me to slip back and run against you."

"Do not let that annoy you," said Jack, "but tumble up on deck as quickly as possible, for Seth Spinner can't bear skulkers."

"Am I a skulker?" asked the man.

"Certainly you are not that," replied Jack, "whatever else you may be."

"What do you mean?" asked Phil, fiercely.

"Nothing," replied Jack.

"Do you know anything against me?" asked Phil.

"No."

The man muttered something under his breath, and mounted the ladder in rear of his companions.

Jack gazed after his retreating form till the off-coming watch commenced to descend the steps, and then he muttered to himself—

"I fancied that my early suspicions had entirely evaporated, but that stony glare, those muttered words, and above all, that false hair, brings them back to me with redoubled force. I know not why, but I seem to fancy that man has some ill-feeling towards me. And yet, why should he? I have never harmed him. But the feeling grows upon me, and I must watch him closely, and be upon my guard."

Joe, Hal, and Charley, who had also been in the captain's watch, came below with the others.

The relieved men sought their hammocks at once, but our hero and his friends remained for some time in conversation in whispers.

Jack related to them what had occurred.

"Evidently got something on his mind," said Hal.

"Do you think so?" asked Charley. "He goes about his work steadily and cheerfully enough, and the fact of his wearing a wig is nothing surprising."

"Perhaps not," said Jack, "but I had an instinctive dread of the man when first he came on board."

"I fancy he looks at me sometimes strangely," said Joe.

"What of that?" said Charley. "You are such a rum fellow I don't wonder at it."

"But it ain't a proper sort of look."

"What sort is it then?" asked Jack.

"It don't seem a straight and fair one, Master Jack. It's a round the corner sort of look."

The others laughed at Joe's description, and then Hal said—

"The fellow had a nightmare, that's all; so let's turn in."

The lads sought their hammocks and were soon fast asleep.

The forecastle resounded with the snores of the sleeping men, when a figure stole down the steps and entered the dimly-lighted place.

Like a ghost he glided on from hammock to hammock, listening to the heavy breathing of the occupants, and finally opened a sea-chest and rummaged among its contents.

"That boy half guesses who I am," he muttered to himself, "and Rough and Ready Jack is not the one to remain long in doubt. He will seek to turn suspicion into certainty, and I must be wary and prepared."

He drew forth a small dagger-knife, the blade of which for an instant glimmered in the lamp-light, then was hidden in the bosom of his jacket.

"Its point is sharp," he muttered, "and its wound, though small, is fearful. One prick with it, and the poison with which it is anointed will be swift in its action as the lightning's flash. But not to-night must the deed be done, or suspicion would fall upon me. I must bide my time and opportunity."

He silently closed the lid of the chest, cast a quick glance round the forecastle, and then strode silently up the steps to the deck.

He imagined that no eye had seen him.

But he was mistaken.

Joe had not slept; on perceiving Harman enter the forecastle, he had feigned sleep, but his eyes opened very wide indeed when he observed the man rummaging his sea-chest.

He also caught sight of the gleaming

blade, and noticed with what rapidity the man concealed the weapon in the breast-pocket of his sea-jacket.

But neither by word nor movement did Joe proclaim the fact that his senses were not steeped in slumber, but lay as if sleeping soundly as the man rose and left the forecastle.

When he heard his footfall overhead, Joe muttered—

"There's something wrong about that fellow, after all, and Master Jack, I fancy, has got reasons for suspecting him. But what can he need the knife for? If Jack don't like him, he is kind to him and civil. If he'd been that Baxter' Sharp or Ralph Sternway, I could have understood him wanting to pay Rough and Ready Jack out for old times, but he ain't either of them, not by a long shot."

So wondering and thinking, Joe gradually fell off to sleep.

When they tumbled out in the morning, the watch had come below.

Appearing on deck, they found the captain and his mate gazing ahead of the vessel.

Jack strolled towards them.

"Good morning, captain," said Jack, touching his cap respectfully.

"Ah, Tempest, good morning. Myself and Spinner were watching that berg yonder."

Jack looked in the direction, and saw a huge field of ice glistening in the rays of the rising sun.

Here and there layers of ice rose from its surface, and these were split into fantastic shapes, which fancy could easily make to appear the towers and spires of a floating city.

Jack continued looking for a time, and then he said—

"It is a large berg, sir."

"Fully a mile in length," replied the captain, "and nearly as wide as it is long."

"And as deep as it is high," Spinner said, taking his pipe from his lips to enable him to speak plainly.

"No doubt of that. We must give it a wide berth, Spinner."

"Aye, sir! for there's no telling how far the spurs under water may reach."

"Wear the ship, Spinner, for she is coming along at a good speed," said the captain. "Jack, hand me my glass."

Jack turned to the binnacle, and taking the glass off it, handed it to the captain.

For some time Robbs gazed at the berg.

Then he lowered the glass, saying—

"I have never seen a finer berg; the biggest ship that ever sailed would be but matchwood if she collided with it."

Spinner had moved away, and was issuing orders to change the ship's course.

Jack stood by the skipper's side, shading his eyes with his hand, and admiring the beautiful yet dangerous object ploughing its way through the water.

It was a long distance off, but ever and anon a sound like the crackling of musketry came to their ears.

"She is splitting up here and there," said the captain.

"I can hear she is," said Jack; "and do you notice that where one tower stood near its edge there are now three?"

"So there are, lad. Aye, and there goes the outer one over on its side."

As the captain spoke, a portion of the berg heeled over, and parted from the main body of the floe.

The captain handed the glass to Jack.

Our hero could not but admire the sight upon which he gazed.

It was like a fairy scene.

The spires and pinnacles glittered in the sunlight, whilst at their base lay deep black shadows, giving the appearance of dark caverns in the bed of ice.

Suddenly Jack uttered an exclamation of surprise, and took the glass from his eye.

"What is it, lad?" asked the skipper.

"Look—look there!" said Jack, pointing, "to the right of that second spire on which the sun shines so brilliantly. Do you see anything there?"

The captain took the glass and raised it.

"Where?" he said, at last.

"To the right of the second spire, and just where the shadows begin to fall," cried Jack, excitedly.

"I see nothing. Ah! wait a moment. Yes, there is something moving—a bear, perhaps, adrift on the berg."

"But the ice bear is white, and what I fancied I saw was black," said Jack.

"That's on account of the shadow,"

said the skipper, "but I have lost it now. No, there it is again, but higher up."

Jack strained his eyes, and as he gazed he saw something extend beyond the rugged side of the spire.

The captain also saw it through the glass, and blew a long whistle.

"What is it, sir?" asked Jack.

"There is someone afloat on that berg, and is signalling us. Order a boat to be launched, Jack, and though the risk is a dangerous one, we must take the poor wretch off, for heaven only knows but it may be our fate some day to be cast adrift in these dangerous seas."

Without a word Jack sped to superintend the launching of the boat.

CHAPTER LXII.

THE SEARCH ON THE ICEBERG—JACK'S DANGER—FACE TO FACE WITH RALPH STERNWAY.

UNDER the superintendence of Jack Tempest the boat was lowered, the calmness of the water allowing the vessel being got afloat easily.

When this was done, Jack reported the fact to the captain.

"You shall take command of her, Jack," said the skipper; "but I warn you the utmost care will be necessary to prevent her being stove in by the ice, for there will lay more danger under her keel than above her bulwarks."

"I will keep a good look-out, sir," replied Jack.

"There may be bears on the berg, so you had best take a few muskets and hatchets with you. In these seas it is best to be prepared for the unexpected."

"And the crew, sir?" asked Jack.

"Take your young friend, Joe, and Phil Harman with you, the others select for yourself," was the reply. "But stay," he added, "leave your other friends on board, there will be enough youngsters with you two."

Jack had intended that Hal and Charlie should accompany him, but he saw that the captain imagined it were better that older and more practical hands should take charge of the boat.

The ship had so tacked as to take her out of all danger of colliding with the ice, and the figure that Jack and the captain had believed they had seen was now shut out from view.

Jack ordered Joe and Harman into the boat, and then, selecting four others from amongst the most practical hands on board, secured three muskets, with powder and ball, and as many hatchets, then lowered himself into the stern-sheets and gave the order to pull away.

Joe and Phil sat forward in the bows on the same seat, and Jack took the tiller.

With a long, and a strong pull altogether, the boat was pulled clear of the ship and went skimming towards the berg.

The men on deck divided their attention between the boat and the iceberg.

Every now and then a loud cracking noise proved that some portion of the berg had broken away from the rest, either above or below the waves.

"That boy will have to be careful," said Spinner, who had approached the skipper, "or he'll find himself foul of the ice before he knows it."

"I have given him a warning, Seth," said the captain, "and he is as cool as he is courageous. So I have little fear of his coming to grief through his own folly."

"Can you see anything on the ice now?" asked the first mate.

"No; for altering our course a few points has shut out the side of the spire on which it appeared."

"These things, especially when they are breaking up, as this berg evidently is, take such strange shapes, that after all the ice may be as bare of life as a bald pate is of hair."

"That's true, Seth," said the captain, "the shadows take strange forms at times, but it's better to be deceived by the eye than steel the heart to a possible sufferer."

"JACK, WITH A POWERFUL TWIST OF THE ARM, FLUNG HIM TO HIS KNEES."

"Aye, captain, I wouldn't have kept the boat back if I could have done so; for better a fool's errand than that some poor coon should float into eternity on a field of ice."

"There's no chance of our striking now," said the skipper.

"I think we are well out of range," replied Spinner.

"Then have the sails laid back, and let's await the return of the boat."

The mate nodded, and going forward, ordered the ship's way to be stopped.

Soon the "Pride of the Arctic Ocean" rode almost motionless upon the waters.

The men and Joe pulled with a will, and Jack searched the depths below for any indication of danger that might lay lurking there.

Now and then he caught sight of a submerged spur, and issued his orders plainly and rapidly, while by the aid of the tiller he assisted the rowers to avoid the hidden danger.

Fully an hour passed before a spot on the huge berg presented itself on which a landing on the ice-floe could be made with any degree of success.

It was a kind of bay between two of the enormous spurs which shot out from the side of the ice-field some distance into the sea.

Here, for several yards, was a comparatively smooth surface, but beyond this hillocks of ice rose one above another, till they reached the height of a ship's mainmast.

But if a landing could be effected, Jack saw nothing beyond to daunt him.

Once he gained a footing on the berg, he knew that he would have a long distance and a rough path to travel to reach the spires between which he had first observed what he believed to be a human figure signalling the ship.

With a great deal of skill and no little perseverance the boat was steered up the bay, and by the aid of oars and boat-hooks drawn close to the floor of the berg.

Jack, taking two of the muskets in his hand, sprang on to the floor of ice.

"Joe," he said, "you come with me, and bring a hatchet along with you."

The lad did as he was requested, and sprang to Jack's side.

Jack handed him one of the muskets.

"Four of you remain here with the boat," said Jack, "and one of you come with us. Have a care you do not let the boat drift, but await our return to this spot."

"Aye, aye," cried the men.

"Now which of you goes with us?" asked Jack.

"I go," said Phil Harman, seizing the remaining musket and springing on to the ice.

Both Jack and Joe would have preferred a companion in their search from among the other four, and the former regretted that he had not named the one to accompany him.

But he said nothing.

Why should he object to the man?

He was ignorant of what Joe had seen in the forecastle, and the fellow had always been respectful to him and obeyed his orders with cheerfulness and alacrity.

Yet he felt he could not trust him as he could have trusted others.

Half ashamed of the feeling, he again ordered the boat to remain in the bay, and then turned and made his way up the berg.

For a short distance their course was comparatively easy, but when the hillocks had to be surmounted, their task became arduous in the extreme.

Requiring the use of hands as well as feet, Jack secured his musket to his back, and ordered his companions to do the same.

By this means they were able to cling to the ice, which in parts offered no roughness to aid their ascent, and down the side of which they more than once slid.

Jack led the way, Joe followed closely, and the rear was brought up by Harman.

As a false step might bring about a severe tumble, Jack did not look behind him.

Had he done so, he might have observed a strange gleam in the eyes of Harman, and seen again the clenched teeth gleam between the half-parted lips.

But neither Jack nor Joe saw this, and by the aid of hands, knees, or feet, surmounted hillock after hillock, their bodies one minute bathed in sunlight, the next steeped in shadow.

Beyond these hillocks was a comparatively smooth space, stretching away for some two hundred yards or more; then hills of ice rose one upon another, until they culminated in two huge spires, that towered up like church steeples, a hundred and fifty feet above the sea.

The scene now presented to the eyes of Jack and his companions was indeed a glorious one.

The morning sun shone full down upon the pinnacles, turning them into towers of gold and silver, which reflected all the colours of the rainbow.

The two paused to rest and gaze on the enchanting scene.

"It is indeed a glorious sight," said Jack.

"Beats a transformation scene hollow," said Joe. "Only wants a lot of fairies and the smell of oranges to make it natural, Master Jack."

"Natural!" said Jack. "Where could you find a more wonderful work of Nature that this? See, yonder it has all the appearance of a castle in ruins; there rises a church spire, and there is the gateway of some cathedral."

"Fancy can picture many things and places here, sir," said Harman. "As you say, yonder arch does look like the doorway of a cathedral, and, bringing the gaze lower down, you could almost fancy you looked upon its burial-ground, for those splashes of ice have greatly the resemblance of tombs."

"What a fine place to be buried in," said Joe.

Jack turned to the boy, as a shudder he could not suppress pervaded his frame.

"Come on, Joe," he said, almost sharply. "I fancy it must have been between those spires we saw, or fancied we saw, a human being making signals to us."

As Jack turned to Joe, Harman's eyes glittered vengefully.

He saw that Joe's words had struck a chill to Jack's heart.

"Does he dream of his fate?" he muttered to himself. "Do coming events really cast their shadows before?"

He fell back a pace and felt in the bosom of his jacket.

"It is there," he said, "but it shall not remain there long, if I can help it, without finding a sheath for its bright blade."

Somehow Joe's words, and those of Harman, had a depressing effect upon Jack, and the longer he gazed upon the scene upon which they were advancing the more plainly arose before his vision the gaping door, the tall spires, and the burial-ground of a cathedral.

The imagined tombs lay in deep shadow, thrown over them by the spires, while through the huge doorway columns of ice appeared to form a wide nave.

"Bah!" muttered Jack, at last, angry with himself, "instead of shuddering at such a sight, my heart should leap with joy and admiration."

The way once more became rough and toilsome, and a full hour passed before the three stood in front of the huge opening in the ice, and within the shadow thrown by the spires.

"Now our search begins in reality," said Jack, "for if we have not been deceived, and some person is indeed on the berg, it is near here we shall find him. You, Joe, go to the left and search round the spire on that side; and you, Harman, search the right, while I devote my attention to the centre, and whether successful or not, let us all meet again on this spot after the work is done."

"All right, Master Jack," said Joe. "Don't you go to lose yourself."

Harman bent his head and turned away to the right, and Joe, hesitating only a moment to press Jack's hand, went off in the opposite direction.

Jack passed under the deep archway of ice, the shadows gathering blacker round him, whilst at the other end the ice glowed like myriads of diamonds in the sunlight.

On he went, and had just got to the edge of the shadow, when a slight sound breaking the stillness caused him to turn and stand face to face with Phil Harman, whose upraised hand grasped a glittering dagger.

Jack recoiled with a cry of horror, but recovering himself in a moment, he sprang upon the ruffian, seized him by the wrist and throat, and with a powerful twist of the arm, flung him to his knees.

As he fell heavily, the wig, whiskers and beard dropped to the icy floor, and with a cry of surprise that echoed and re-echoed through the archway, Jack exclaimed—

"Ralph Sternway, by all that's wonderful!"

CHAPTER LXIII.

SAVED BY A BLOW—THE MUSKET SHOT—BREAKING OF THE ICE—DRIFTING APART.

In his surprise at seeing his enemy before him, Jack slightly loosened his grasp upon Ralph Sternway.

The villain in an instant took advantage of this, and with a desperate wrench, freed himself from Jack's hold.

With an oath he bounded to his feet.

"Yes!" he thundered, "it is Ralph Sternway, and you, Jack Tempest, are a dead man."

Jack had rested his gun against the side of the arch, and with a bound sprang towards it.

But ere he could reach it Ralph was upon him.

Only in time did Jack turn to see the gleaming dagger raised aloft.

Another moment and it would have been sheathed in his bosom.

In that instant Jack saw his danger and realised it.

His fist shot forth, and with a blow that would have felled an ox, Jack struck the dastard to the ground.

So heavy was the blow that the descending blade was hurled out of Ralph's grasp, and sent flying across the archway as Joe came rushing forward.

"Master Jack—Master—oh, what is this?"

And the boy recoiled as he saw the wigless head and uncovered face of Ralph Sternway.

"The viper!" he gasped. "I knowed he was a bad one, but I didn't think it was him. Oh, Master Jack, he ain't hurt you, has he?"

"No, Joe," said Jack, as he took his musket; "but never have I been nearer death than I was just now. I almost felt the thrust of that knife, so close was its point to my heart."

"Thank heaven it did not prick you, Master Jack, for you'd been a corpse if it had only scratched your skin."

"Why, Joe?"

"Because it's poisoned."

Jack looked at the boy questioningly.

Joe instantly and quickly told him what he had heard and seen when the villain imagined all were fast asleep in the forecastle.

"And you never told me," said Jack.

"I did not want to make you feel more uncomfortable than you were about the man," replied Joe; "and besides, I wasn't sure he meant it for you. But look to him, Master Jack, or he'll be up again in a moment."

Ralph showed signs of recovering.

Joe sprang for the knife and handed it to Jack.

"Take it," he said, "and if he tries to hurt you again, let him taste his own poison."

Jack thrust the thin blade into his belt.

"By heaven, I will!" he said; "for that man will, sooner or later, have my life if I show mercy to him."

"Say the word, Master Jack," cried Joe, "and I'll send a bullet through his skull."

And Joe pointed the musket he held at the head of the fast-reviving ruffian.

"No, no, Joe! I dare not kill an insensible man."

"Well, I ain't so particular," replied Joe. "I'd shoot him as soon as I'd tread on a beetle. Bah! the viper would be only too much honoured by having a good bullet and powder wasted upon him."

They were still in the shadow of the frowning arch, though not six feet from where they stood the sun lit up the ice, and threw prismatic hues around.

Ralph was far nearer consciousness than either Jack or Joe fancied.

Indeed, he had heard and understood nearly all that was said by the two youths.

He had been foiled in his attempt upon Jack's life, and his disappointment made him even more furious to take it, if possible.

He knew that if he tried to rise he would have both Jack and Joe upon him, and that if he fled for the boat, those who had charge of it would convey him a prisoner to the ship, and that, sooner or later, he would again be consigned to a prison, charged with murder and attempted assassination.

So, with closed eyes, he lay and thought deeply.

He had been foiled, and was now at the mercy of him he had thought so easily to destroy.

If he could but make them believe he was dead, that the blow he had received had proved fatal, then might they leave him, and give him a chance to escape, even if it was on the ice floe.

Then, as he felt something press hard into his back, he remembered the musket strapped to his shoulder.

He had some difficulty in repressing the cry of joy that rose to his lips.

Oh, that the two friends would move away and give him a chance to get at the weapon.

How quickly then would he spring to his feet, and battle for life and revenge.

As if fate played into his hands, Joe said—

"Master Jack, I was so flabbergasted at seeing who this fellow really is, that I forgot all about the other one."

"Who, Joe?"

"The man out there on the ice."

"Ah, you have found someone, then?" cried Jack.

"Yes; but he has hurt his leg jumping from the place where he hailed the ship, and he can't get up without help, and so I ran to tell you."

"Go to him, Joe; do what you can for him, and leave me here to watch this villain. If I had the means, I'd bind him, and carry him back a prisoner to the ship."

"He don't look as if he wants any binding," said Joe, bending over Ralph. "I reckon you've given him his deserts, Master Jack."

"Killed him!"

"Looks like it, and no mistake," said Joe.

"Impossible," said Jack; "I've only stunned him. But he is powerless for a time. So run, Joe, and see what you can do for the poor castaway, and help him here."

"You'll be careful of that viper, Master Jack," said the boy.

"Fear not for me, Joe. I have both gun and dagger, so am well prepared to meet and foil any treachery."

"I'm off, then, and if I can get a sight of the boat, I'll motion for one of the men to come here and help us."

"All right, Joe. But stay; take this flask of spirit, the poor fellow may need a pull at it."

Jack handed him a small flask which he had brought from the ship for the service of any poor fellow they might find on the ice.

"It will give him strength," said Joe. "Now, don't you let that fellow fool you if he's only playing artful, but I do think his artful games are over for good and all."

So saying, Joe, with his gun in one hand and the flask in the other, dashed out of the archway into the sunlight beyond.

Jack leaned upon his gun and surveyed the man at his feet.

"I hope I have not got the blood of that villain on my hands," he muttered; "though if I had killed him I was justified in doing so. But such a villain should hang, like the cur that he is, and perish by the rope of the executioner."

At this moment a loud crackling sound smote Jack's ears, and with it mingled a cry of human agony.

Jack started, and looked round.

"Good heavens!" he exclaimed. "Can that cry have come from Joe?"

He listened intently.

For a few moments all was still.

"I must have been mistaken," Jack thought.

But he was not mistaken.

The cry was repeated, and this time in shrill tones of agony.

Jack could remain passive no longer.

In his anxiety he dashed towards the opening of the arch, and as he peered eagerly without, Ralph Sternway sprang to his feet.

"Fool!" he hissed; "that cry was your death-knell, Rough and Ready Jack."

In an instant the musket was in the villain's hands and pointed to the form of Jack.

As the finger of Ralph pressed the trigger, Jack's foot slipped on the shelving ice, and he fell forward and rolled down the decline in front of the arch.

At the same moment, the roar, as of a whole field of artillery, shook the floe to its foundation.

The crashing as of a hundred peals of thunder reverberated around, and then the spires toppled over, crashing in the ice on which they had stood; the archway and columns collapsed, and fell in one mighty heap of ruins.

Cracking, roaring, swaying and heaving, the huge floe parted in fifty places, and the dissevered portions of the ice field drifted apart.

Crashing with and grinding against each other, the huge blocks splintered themselves into smaller bergs, and changed in form and size the whole surface of the floe, and drifting every moment farther and farther apart, bore on the bosom of separate bergs Jack, Joe, and the bruised, maimed, and bleeding form of the man who had caused the catastrophe—Ralph Sternway.

The concussion of air brought about by Ralph's musket had destroyed the field of ice, had separated friend and foe, and caused the boat to be ground to matchwood between the two spurs that, breaking away from the main body, had floated together.

One of the crew, with the life crushed out of him, had sunk to rise no more; and this was the blood of another human being upon the guilty soul of the smuggler.

The other three clambered on to one of the spurs, which soon drifted away over the ocean.

The breaking up of the ice was witnessed by those on board the whaler.

The crashing and grinding of the bergs together was held with bated breath and sinking hearts by those on board.

Horror and despair for a moment held them powerless, then came the thundering tones of Captain Robbs—

"Out with the boats!"

The men flew to their work.

The boats were down and manned with a speed that was surprising.

Into the first sprang Hal and Charley, their faces as white as the sea foam, their forms trembling as an aspen in the wind.

In their horror and anxiety for those who had gone to the ice-field, neither captain nor crew could give utterance to words. Gestures bid the men to do their utmost, though one and all feared their labours would be in vain.

Where one solid field of ice had lain, a hundred bergs now floated, one moment crashing together and splintering each other, and then, rebounding, went swirling away over the waste of waters.

To guide the boats amid the ice was, indeed, an arduous and a dangerous task. Death confronted the crew on every side; destruction loomed above, below, around them, but the brave men, with clenched teeth and bated breath, kept to their dangerous work, and only gave up the search when coming night warned them to return to the ship.

It was, indeed, an anxious and despairing night that passed on board the whaler—a night that seemed as though it would never end, and day once more dawn upon the world.

When light again visited the sea, few bergs were to be seen.

The others had dispersed, gone beyond the sight of those who so eagerly scanned the waters around.

Again the boats were manned and the bergs approached, and as the last of the half-dozen—that was all that was to be seen now—was being examined, a human form was discovered lying upon it.

Hal and Charley, hoping that it might be Jack, gained a footing on the berg, and reaching the place where the man lay, discovered that it was a stranger, and that he was dead.

With sorrowful hearts they returned to the boat, and the berg drifted away with its cold, dead burden.

But where was Jack, Joe, and the rest?

Were they living or dead?

Heaven and themselves alone could answer, as they drifted farther and farther apart at the mercy of the wind and waves.

CHAPTER LXIV.

ALONE ON THE ICE—THE SUDDEN AWAKENING—'TWIXT LIFE AND DEATH—
A TIMELY SHOT.

It was some time before either of those who had been on the ice when the shot of Ralph Sternway caused it to shiver in pieces recovered sufficiently to realise what had happened.

But gradually the truth dawned upon them.

Around them rose and fell, and tossing and rolling hither and thither, huge blocks, at times separated by wide streams, at others clashing together with deafening sounds.

Jack was first to raise himself to his feet.

"Great heavens!" he cried, "the floe has split up into fragments and we are lost."

Then he looked eagerly around, and his heart sank within him.

"Joe—Joe!" he cried. "Where is poor Joe?"

But only the rolling ice met his gaze.

He looked for the spires, the arch— but they had disappeared.

The whole scene had become changed as by magic.

Jack strained his gaze on every side.

With his hand-shaded eyes he scanned berg after berg, but not a human being could he see.

He could make out the ship, with her sails aback, some five miles from him, that was all, besides the sea and the huge bergs tossing hither and thither on the bosom of the waves.

Jack's heart sank within him, and with a long deep sigh he sat down on a mound of ice and buried his face in his hands.

He remembered that, as he fell and slid down the incline before the arch, he fancied he had heard the firing of a gun close to him, but now he believed it was the noise of the parting ice that had struck upon his ears.

He awoke to life as it were on the edge of the berg, which, as far as he could judge by the survey he had taken, was not more than a hundred yards long and something like half as wide. The height was several feet above the sea.

Ever and anon the berg plunged, as if to bury itself in the waves, and then shivered, creaked, and crackled as if in mortal agony.

Now it came with a crash against another berg, then it would spin around with the concussion, or bury itself half under the water.

But gradually the bergs grew wider and wider apart, tossing this way and that way, as wind or current swept them along.

Fainter and fainter grew the whaler, and then she seemed to sink into the sea.

Her hull disappeared, then her masts; and Jack felt he could hope no longer for succour from her.

Gloomy indeed became his thoughts now.

As far as he could discover he was alone upon the sea, with only two bergs now within range of his vision, and these evidently bare of all human life.

Jack's gun had gone in his fall; but of what avail would it have been to him had he still possessed it?

"And is it thus I am doomed to perish?" he muttered, "after all the dangers through which I have passed— to die of starvation or madness on this berg of ice? Heaven have mercy on me, and send me succour or death."

He now felt the cold intensely.

A numbness began to assail his limbs, and he again sprang to his feet.

He buffeted his arms, he stamped his feet to set his blood in circulation, and then walked as briskly as possible along the ice.

Towards the other end of the berg the ice rose in ledges and hillocks, but Jack did not attempt to clamber over the one or climb the other.

He could still see the two bergs he had observed before, and which, though some distance apart, appeared to be taking the same course as the one on which he stood. But, as yet, neither seemed to approach the other, but floated on parallel lines.

Jack watched them till his eyes grew dim and watery, and then he turned his gaze over the sea.

The red sun was sinking slowly into the ocean, and soon darkness would be upon the waters.

Jack shuddered as he thought of the coming night, for when the sun had sunk beneath the waves then would the cold become intense, and he had nothing wherewith to shield him from its piercing chill.

"Perhaps morning may bring me help," he said, "if I perish not to-night. Oh, heaven be praised that neither Hal nor Charley left the ship!"

He continued to walk the ice, and then, as the sun sank lower and lower into the waves, he paused beside the mounds, and said—

"These will at least break the force of the wind, and shield me somewhat from its icy breath. Here will I rest, though to sink to sleep may be to sink to death."

Crouching beneath one of them, he watched the sun sink beneath the waves and darkness sweep with sable wings across the sea.

He was fairly tired out with his day's work, and despite all he could do to keep his eyes open, they gradually closed, and he sank into an uneasy slumber.

The wind rose and the waves rolled high, gaining in force and power every minute; still our hero slept on.

The roaring of the wind, and the lashing of the waves against the now heavily rolling berg, were powerless to arouse him to his misery and his cheerless surroundings.

On through the darkness sped that island of ice, and on through cold and danger slept Rough and Ready Jack.

Hours passed, and then a fearful crash, followed by a grinding sound, woke Jack Tempest.

It was still dark, save where the heavily rolling waves were lighted with a phosphorescent glow.

It was some moments before Jack could realise where he was, and his terrible and lonely position.

But gradually all came back to him, and he staggered to his feet like a drunken man.

He could scarcely stand, so benumbed were his feet and legs.

He leaned against the mound, at the base of which he had slept, and muttered—

"How heavily the wind blows. It must have been a storm, and the thunder roused me. How cold it is! it seems to pierce my very bones. Oh, that day would come!"

He shivered with cold, and his teeth chattered in his head.

He tried to move, but it was some time before he could do so, and then only slowly and tremblingly.

But at length he somewhat recovered from the numbness, and he stamped his feet on the ice to get some warmth into them.

He felt faint and hungry.

But he had nothing with which to satisfy his craving for food.

"If help come not soon," he muttered, "it will be too late."

Was it fancy, or did someone seem to echo his words.

"Too late—too late!" he fancied he heard.

"'Twas but the echo of my own words," he said to himself, "though I knew not I had spoken aloud."

The wind carried the salt spray into his face, and he again sought the shelter of the hillock of ice.

Oh, the loneliness of his position, how terrible it seemed to him then!

It struck as cold a chill to his heart as did the icy wind to his frame.

Again he sank down at the base of the mound, and again the cold drew him to sleep.

But his slumber, though heavy, was less peaceful than before.

Terrible visions floated through his brain.

He was encompassed by enemies; danger and death assailed him on every side.

The hands of Baxter Sharp were at his throat, and the knife of Ralph Sternway at his bosom.

Hal, Charley, Joe, all were powerless to help him.

He tried to struggle, but in vain; for the fingers of Baxter sank deeper into his neck, and the blade of the ruffian, Sternway, was raised for the death blow.

One more desperate effort he made to release himself, then with a cry he woke.

But, oh! what an awakening.

Day had come, but between his gaze and the rising sun knelt Ralph Sternway, his face seared with wounds and blood.

In his right hand he held the dagger which he had taken from Jack's belt, his left grasped the neck of his victim.

Jack thought he was still dreaming, but that fancy was dispelled in an instant.

"Ha, ha!" came in a faint hissing laugh from the villain's lips. "Thrice—thrice have I been baulked in my revenge, but now my vengeance is sure."

"Villain, and here on this berg!" gasped Jack, struggling to rise, but his limbs were powerless.

"Here—here!" hissed Ralph. "Yes, the fiend of evil guided me to this berg on which you lay, that I might kill you ere I die. To you I owe all my misfortunes—all my sufferings. I swore to be revenged, and thus, Rough and Ready Jack, I keep my oath of vengeance!"

Weak as was Ralph Sternway, for his wounds were many, yet so powerless had the cold rendered Jack, that he could not wrest himself from the feeble grasp of his remorseless foe.

With a hurried prayer to heaven, Jack closed his eyes and awaited the blow.

Ralph raised the poisoned blade, but held it suspended while he gloated, fiend-like, over his once powerful but now powerless victim.

"You thought you were rid of me for ever, Jack Tempest; that you were safe from the vengeance of the man you taunted, struck, and despised. Ha, ha! what a fool's paradise is that in which you have been living. I broke prison, helped to murder my gaoler, that I might track you down and kill you. Ralph the smuggler never forgets and never forgives. The hour I have longed for—panted for, has come at last; and even while the hand of death is probably upon me, I hold my enemy in my grasp and strike for vengeance!"

"And so do I; and hard, too," cried a voice.

Ralph Sternway looked up sharp.

The cry that rose to his lips was drowned in the crack of a musket, and he fell forward across the breast of Jack, the blood spurting over the ice from a wound in his neck.

"Just in time. Hurrah!"

"Joe!" gasped Jack.

"Joe it is, Master Jack. Ain't you glad to see me?"

"Oh, Joe, you have saved my life."

"That's what I meant to do," replied Joe. "Thank heaven I did it, too, and took that fellow's as well."

And Joe, throwing down his musket, stooped and dragged Ralph off the body of his friend.

Then he bent over Jack and held the brandy flask to his lips.

Jack took a draught of the liquor, and, pressing Joe's hand, murmured—

"Heaven bless you, Joe, my saviour!"

Then his overstrung nerves gave way, and Jack lay insensible in Joe's arms.

CHAPTER LXV.

REPENTANCE OF RALPH—DEATH INTERRUPTS RALPH'S STORY—EXIT STERNWAY—A SAIL IN SIGHT.

THE bullet which Joe had fired at Ralph Sternway was fast doing its fatal work.

The ruffian had but a short time to live. His life's breath was fast ebbing with the blood that poured from his wound.

Joe could not be deceived as to the man's fate.

Crushed and maimed by the falling ice, he was doubly weakened by his sufferings on the floe, so that he had not his usual strength to aid him now.

He presented a horrible sight as he lay there, with the poisoned dagger grasped in a death clutch.

As Joe gazed down upon him a feeling of pity took possession of his heart.

He bent down and placed the flask to the dying man's lips, and poured a few drops of its contents down his throat.

The spirit seemed to revive him somewhat.

He fixed his glaring eyes upon the boy's face, and whisperingly gasped—

"I am dying!"

"I reckon you are," said Joe; "but you have brought it on yourself."

"Jack Tempest?" asked Ralph.

"Oh, he's all right, or soon will be, and no thanks to you either," said Joe.

"He is not dead?"

"Not by a long way," said Joe.

"Thank heaven!" gasped Ralph.

Joe looked at the writhing wretch in surprise.

Could he have heard aright?

"Thank heaven!" again gasped Ralph, faintly.

"Do you mean that?" asked Joe.

"I do."

"And you tried to kill him?"

"More than once," said Ralph, speaking with difficulty.

"And now you are glad that Jack is not dead?" said the boy.

"Lift me up," gasped Ralph. "You cannot fear me now."

"I never did," said Joe. "But there, do you feel easier now?"

Joe raised Ralph's head, and supported it on his knee.

"Yes, I can breathe easier."

"Take another pull at this," said Joe, holding the flask again to his lips. "If it hadn't been for that brandy, I believe I should have been a goner before now."

Ralph let some of the liquor pour down his throat, though the burning sensation it caused him made him writhe and gasp with pain.

Still, it seemed to give him strength, and, after a time, he said—

"Boy, I have been a bad and cruel man."

"Don't I know it?" said Joe. "And so does a good many others as well."

"I have committed crimes at which my heart now stands appalled—crimes for which heaven now makes me suffer, and for which soon I must answer there!"

He raised his hand for a moment and pointed to the sky, then, with a sigh, he let it fall heavily to his side.

For the first time Joe observed that his hand still clutched the poisoned dagger.

Laying Ralph's head back upon the ice, he tore the weapon from his grasp, and threw it beyond the reach of his hand. Then he said, sternly—

"Was that for Jack's heart? Would you commit murder when death hovers over you?"

"I swear by Him in whose presence I must soon stand, I never thought of such a deed."

"I won't call a dying man a liar," said Joe, "but I won't believe you, even with that oath."

A look of pain passed over Ralph's blood-stained features.

"And why should you?" he said. "I have been treacherous, and do not blame you, boy, for distrusting me now. But before my last breath is drawn I must speak with Jack."

"I'll see if he can talk to you," said Joe.

Jack had recovered, and was sitting up, collecting his thoughts.

"Are you better, Master Jack?" Joe asked.

"Yes. What a fool I must have been to let myself be so overcome," said Jack.

"Here's a drop left," said Joe, handing Jack the flask. "It will help pull you together."

"You are ever thoughtful, Joe."

Jack drank, and feeling stronger, staggered to his feet.

"And Ralph Sternway?" he asked, huskily.

"Has taken his ticket for the other world," replied Joe.

"Dead?" said Jack.

"Not quite," replied Joe; "and he says he don't want to die, neither, till he's said something to you."

"The villain!" cried Jack, "what can such a ruffian have to say to me?"

"Didn't ask him, Master Jack."

"I will hold no communion with such a monster. Even in his dying agonies I despise him."

"Master Jack," said Joe, "he cannot harm you more, and you are too good to deny even a dying murderer's last request."

Jack replied not for a time, then he said—

"Yes, I will hear what he has to say."

Ralph heard these words, and a look of joy passed over his face.

"What would you with me?" asked Jack, kneeling by Ralph's side as Joe again raised the dying man's head onto his knee.

"Do an act of justice," gasped Ralph.

A sneering smile crossed Jack's lips.

Joe tied his neckerchief round the bleeding neck of Ralph.

"Justice!" laughed Jack. "When and where, Ralph Sternway, smuggler and assassin, did you ever learn that word?"

"Here—now," replied Ralph. "What I never felt or knew in my health and strength I know and feel in dying."

The sneer died off Jack's lips.

"Do you then repent your crimes?" he asked.

"I do."

"Would you, had you have slain me —had I lain dead there, murdered by your hand?"

"No, for then the fear of death, the feeling that soon I must meet Him whose laws I have outraged, whose power and punishment I have so long defied, I should not have experienced. No, Jack Tempest, I should have triumphed in your death and gloried in my revenge."

His voice grew fainter, and his breathing shorter.

Joe held the flask to Ralph's lips, and poured between them the few drops left in the little vessel.

Again the glazing eyes brightened, and motioning to Joe to raise him higher, he said—

"Jack Tempest, hear my dying words, and heed them well."

I will listen," said Jack.

"With my death you will be rid of one enemy," said Ralph, "but another remains to work your ruin."

"I know, Baxter Sharp," said Jack.

"He, I believe, is as powerless now to harm you as I am," said Ralph. "A slave has no power. I would warn you of another—the worst, the most unprincipled of all."

"Of whom do you speak?" asked Jack.

"Of him who tempted me and Baxter Sharp to kidnap and destroy you—of him who offered us a large reward to bring to him the proofs of your death!"

"Who is he who should do this, and for what purpose?"

"His name is Hugh Wentworth, and his motive that he might secure your fortune—the money and estates that come to you untrammelled at your mother's death."

"What wild story is this?" asked Jack. "I know no one of the name of Hugh Wentworth."

"Hugh Wentworth," mused Joe. "Why, that was the name my mother gave the man who brought about her ruin, her misery, and her death. The name of the monster whom she bade me beware and punish if ever I had the power to do so. But what a fool I am —there are hundreds of Wentworths in the world."

Weaker and weaker grew Ralph, and his eyes were again fast glazing.

"Jack Tempest," he said, "that is not the real name of your foe, which I learned from Baxter in his cups, his real name is—"

"Is what?" interrupted Jack, grasping Ralph's shoulder in his anxiety to learn the name.

"Is—is—oh! heaven have mercy— mer—"

Blood belched from Ralph's mouth, his frame shivered, and, with a gurgling sigh, his head rolled heavily on Joe's arm.

Ralph Sternway was dead.

Jack and Joe gazed upon the wretched man for some moments before they could realise that his last breath had fled, and his guilty soul gone forth to meet its Maker.

For some minutes neither Jack nor Joe spoke a word.

Then the latter looked up at his friend, and said—

"A bad one to the last, Master Jack. I don't believe he ever meant to tell you straight."

"Say nothing hard of him, Joe," said Jack. "It is for another and a higher One than us to judge him now."

"But that won't tell you who the fellow is, Master Jack," said Joe, as he laid Ralph back on the ice and rose to his feet.

"Wentworth—Hugh Wentworth!" muttered Jack. "Where can I have heard that name, for I remember now that I have heard it somewhere?"

"It was the name of the villain who destroyed my poor mother," said Joe.

"Oh! yes, I remember," cried Jack. "The name of your father, Joe."

"Don't call him that, Master Jack!"

cried Joe; "though I know from my mother's dying words that he is so. But father or no father, let him beware the hour we meet."

"You may never do so, Joe."

"It were better we do not!" cried Joe, "for then I should remember my mother's dying words, and see before me the white, dead face in the moonbeams; and then I should fly at his throat and strangle the life out of him. Oh! Master Jack, heaven grant that we may never stand face to face and I know him for my mother's destroyer."

Jack could tell by the boy's flashing eyes, hissing tones, and clenched hands that he would have no mercy upon the man who had blighted his own and his mother's existence.

Though anxious for a time to change the subject, yet Jack felt just then too upset to think.

"Joe, his sight is hateful to us. Let us consign his body to the waves, and hide him for ever from mortal ken."

"Yes," said Joe. "I've seen enough of his ugly face, and we'll drag him to the edge of the berg and roll him over into the sea, though I reckon the fishes even will flee from contact with the body of such a villain."

Together Jack and Joe dragged Ralph across the ice and to the verge of the berg.

"I wish we could serve Baxter Sharp the same way," said Joe, as with his foot he pushed the body over the edge into the sea.

They watched it sink beneath the waves, and as they turned away their gaze and looked up a glad cry escaped their lips, for there, not three miles from the berg, a ship under full sail was bearing down upon them.

CHAPTER LXVI.

ANXIETY OF THE CASTAWAYS—A DANGEROUS SLEEP—A SUDDEN AWAKENING—IN THE NICK OF TIME.

A CRY of joy burst from the lips of Jack and Joe as the white sails of the vessel broke upon their vision.

Larger and larger she loomed up before them.

Then suddenly a mist arose between the berg and the ship, and finally shut out the rays of the sun.

A dark cloud had descended upon the sea, and a blacker cloud still upon the heart of Jack and his youthful companion.

Had they been seen by those on board?

If not, what hope was there now of making their presence known on that rolling sheet of ice?

"Now isn't that a shame?" said Joe,

"Indeed it is disheartening," replied Jack. "But perhaps we have been seen, Joe."

"I hope so," replied Joe; "but I've been so used to disappointments all my life, that I'm afraid this is only another of them."

"Let us hope for the best," said Jack.

But his tones were rather those of despair.

"I can't fire my gun to let 'em know where we are, for I've got no powder," said Joe.

"Nor I; that was lost when the ice was shattered," said Jack. "But, Joe, were you on that berg there with Ralph?"

And he pointed to the berg that still hugged the side of the floe on which he had drifted along.

"No, Master Jack," was the reply. "The piece I was on just touched the tail end of this, and then swung off yonder. I had just time to leap when the bergs parted. I was higher than you or Ralph were, and when I made out you two I was so upset that it's a wonder I didn't fall into the sea."

"I am glad you did not, Joe; but for you, I had now been lying where the smuggler does."

"That's certain," replied Joe. "Lor, Master Jack, how my fingers did tremble when I pulled the trigger!"

"It was a good aim though, Joe."

"Yes, thank heaven!" said Joe, fervently, "but it was the hand of Providence that guided that bullet, Master Jack."

"It saved me!"

"There is no denying that. Another moment, and that poisoned dagger had done its awful work."

And Joe crossed the ice to where the dagger lay, and brought it to Jack.

"He must have taken it from my belt while I slept," said Jack.

"No doubt."

Jack returned the weapon to his belt, and then tried to pierce the misty curtain.

"Can you see anything of the ship, Joe?" he asked at length.

"Not the shade of a shadow," replied Joe.

"Oh, that the sun would disperse the vapour," said Jack. "Hark! what was that?"

Jack lifted his hand, and, together with Joe, listened.

"I can hear only the swish of the waves as the ice plunges into the sea," said Joe. "What did you think it was?"

"It sounded like a cheer," said Jack. "There it is again!"

Joe strained every nerve.

"I hear it now," he said; "but it is a long way off, sir."

"It must come from the ship we saw."

"Yes; but if we can't see them, do you think they can see us?" asked Joe.

"I hope so. But listen, Joe."

They listened for some time, but only the splash of the waters met their ears.

"Let's shout, Joe. Perhaps our voices may reach the vessel."

They shouted together as loud as they were able, but though they listened intently for some indication eir voices had been heard, they ⸱   ⸱ in vain.

It was fully a couple of hours before the mist lifted.

In vain they searched the sea for the ship. It was nowhere to be seen.

The berg which had joined the ice on which they stood had broken away, and was seen rising and falling a long distance to the westward.

Jack and Joe felt their hearts sink within them.

They were alone on the waste of waters, hungry, athirst, and benumbed with cold.

Each knew and felt how poignant was the other's thoughts and feelings, and they sat down side by side and prayed for succour, or for death.

And so the day passed.

They had grown too wretched for words to comfort each other, and, at length, when the sun sank out of sight and the stars peeped from the clouds upon the wretched castaways, the two lads sank to slumber.

Hours and hours passed, and still they slept.

They saw not the ship that bore down upon them; heard not the shouts of the sailors as they lowered a boat; heeded not the flashing oars as they cleaved a passage through the waters for the little vessel that one moment rose high on the waves, and the next was buried in the trough of the sea.

Neither did they hear the loud, joyous shouts, or heed the wild gesticulations of the two youths who had sprung from the boat on to the berg but a few feet from where they lay sleeping what appeared to be the sleep of death.

"Hurrah, hurrah! It's Jack—it's Joe! Hurrah!"

And the voices of Hal and Charley fell upon ears deaf now to the beloved tones of their friends.

The cries of Hal and Charley brought others from the boat.

One of these was Seth Spinner.

"It's Jack and Joe," cried Hal.

"Muffins and marline-spikes!" exclaimed Seth, bending over Jack. "It's no mistake that we have found them at last, but—"

He paused, and his brown face paled.

"Oh, do not say that it is too late," cried Charley clutching the mate's arm.

"Don't be too sure, lad," replied Seth. "He may still breathe."

The mate took a bottle from his pocket, and bent over Jack.

For a moment he felt his wrist, and then he thrust the neck of the bottle into the lad's mouth.

The other man turned his attention to Joe, and when Seth withdrew the vessel from Jack's lips, he stretched out his hand for it.

Seth resigned it to him, and the bottle was placed to Joe's lips.

That youth gave a gasp, and then a cough.

"He's alive, at any rate," said the man. "Here, take this, one of you, and I'll set him on his feet."

He dragged Joe up and gave him a shake.

"Come, lad," he cried; "rouse yourself."

"Who are you shaking on?" said Joe, dreamily.

"He'll do," said the man. "Leave him to me."

Charley, who had taken the bottle, turned to Hal and Seth, who were chafing Jack's hands with their own.

"Jack, dear Jack," cried Hal.

"Wake up, Jack; you are safe, and with friends," said Charley.

"Don't you know me, old chum?" asked Hal.

"Here, let him take another pull at the brandy," said Seth.

The neck of the bottle was again applied to Jack's lips.

This time he showed signs of awakening.

"That's it," said Seth. "There, lads, he's as good as a dozen dead ones yet."

The sailor who had helped Joe to his feet, walked him along the ice, till at last Joe glanced into his face, saying—

"Is it my watch?"

"Yes, youngster; hurry up," was the reply.

Joe passed his hand across his brow, then looking around, as if in search of something, he began to realise where he was, but not what had happened while he slept that sleep which promised no awakening in this world.

Like one in a dream he continued to gaze around him, and then he cried—

"Master Jack!"

"He's all right, lad," said the man. "Don't you know me, I'm Bill Atkins, the harpooner?"

"Yes; but—"

"Don't talk yet awhile, but pull yourself together. You are safe now, and we'll soon have you and Tempest aboard again."

Joe again pressed his hand over his forehead, and then his gaze wandering around lighted upon Jack, supported on his feet by Seth and Hal.

"Thank heaven!" gasped Joe. "We are saved."

"Yes, my boy, and only just in time," said Atkins. "But better late than never."

"And Jack?" cried Joe, trying to get to his friend.

"He'll be all right in a minute," said Hal. "Jack, old boy, you are with friends."

Jack could not reply in words.

He held out his hand, and his friend grasped it.

"You have had a hard time of it, lad," said Seth. "But you'll be all right as soon as we get you aboard and between blankets. Here, try and take another pull at this, it will help to thaw you."

Jack suffered the neck of the bottle to be again placed between his lips.

He recovered quickly now, but he would have fallen had Seth released his hold of him, so benumbed and powerless had his legs and feet become with lying throughout the night on the ice.

"We'll carry him to the boat," said Hal.

"And you go and help Atkins to bear Joe," said Seth, "for the sooner we are all of us clear off this berg the better."

An ominous cracking sound had fallen upon their ears.

"Look sharp there," cried Seth, calling to Atkins. "The sun has melted the ice, and I fancy it is breaking up."

As he and Hal lifted Jack in their arms, a louder detonation fell upon their ears.

"Quick!" cried Atkins. "A moment's delay may hurl us all to destruction!"

He flung Joe to his shoulder.

"Look out," thundered Seth to those in the boat; "take these poor fellows in. Quick! the ice is bursting asunder."

Willing hands aided them to get Jack and Joe off the ice and lay them in the bottom of the boat, into which the others scrambled as quickly as possible.

"Give way," cried Seth, "or we'll be swamped."

"Quick, lads, or we are lost!" cried Atkins. "Heaven help us!"

The boat shot away from the ice, and not a moment too soon, for with a crash the berg parted, and the portion on which the men had stood toppled over onto the very spot where the boat had ridden a few moments before.

CHAPTER LXVII.

CREEPING TOWARDS HEALTH AND STRENGTH—THE CAPTAIN LEARNS OF THE FATE
OF RALPH—THE SHADOWY FOE.

DURING the previous day the " Pride of the Arctic Ocean" had fallen in with the spur on which the three sailors had saved themselves when their boat was crushed to atoms by the grinding ice, and these men were now in the sick bay, to which Jack and Joe were immediately conveyed upon their arrival at the ship.

Captain Robbs was delighted at the lads' recovery.

So, indeed, were all on board the vessel.

In his joy the captain ordered extra grog to be served out, after which the sails were trimmed, and the vessel headed for the coast of Greenland.

A weight of anxiety had been taken from the men's hearts, though more than one felt sorry for the loss of their messmates, Phil Harman and the poor fellow who had been crushed to death by the colliding spurs, between which the boat had awaited the return of Jack and his party.

There was no mistake as to the actual fate of the boatman, but at present that of Phil Harman, or rather Ralph Sternway, remained a mystery even to Hal and Charley.

Jack and Joe, however, speedily recovered both health and strength.

Everything that could be done for them was done, and the crew vied with each other in their attentions to the two young men.

In three days Jack and Joe could leave their hammocks, and on the fourth both came on deck.

Captain Robbs shook them by the hand, and asked them how they felt.

" I'm getting all right, captain," said Jack, " thanks to the kindness and attention of all on board."

" I'll be able to stand on my head as well as ever soon," said Joe; " but I ain't quite got back the proper feel in my legs and feet."

" It's a mercy you were not frozen to death," said Robbs.

" I dare say such would have been our fate, sir, but for the timely coming of the boat to our rescue," responded Jack.

" And still one of our brave fellows is missing," said Robbs.

Jack and Joe glanced at each other, but said nothing.

" Tom Lammel has been accounted for. He, poor fellow, was soon out of his misery."

And then, in answer to Jack's inquiring look, the captain related what he had heard from the three men taken from the berg.

This was the first Jack and Joe learned of the unfortunate man's fate, for those on board had studiously avoided mentioning anything of an unpleasant nature to the still suffering lads.

" I am inclined to think that Phil Harman was crushed to death on the ice, or we might have found him as we did the poor fellow who attracted us to the floe."

" Joe discovered him, sir."

" Yes; he had broken his leg," put in Joe.

" Is he on board the ship, sir?" asked Jack.

" No, my lad. When your friends discovered him, he was dead, and so they left his body where they found it."

" Who was he?" asked Jack.

The captain shook his head.

" No one knows, evidently some poor castaway, on whom there was nothing to establish his identity. If we could have found Harman, even though dead, it would have set our minds at rest."

Again Jack and Joe exchanged glances.

" Captain Robbs, we can tell you his fate," said Jack.

" Eh? You can?"

" Yes."

The captain looked anxious, and Seth, who overheard the words, joined them.

" Was he killed by the falling ice?" asked the captain.

" No, sir. But if you will permit me and Joe to sit down, I will explain to you how Phil Harman, as you call him, came by his death."

"HE LEANT FORWARD AND LAID HIS HAND ON BAXTER'S SHOULDER."

No 13.

Seth rolled a bucket towards Jack with his foot, and turned it bottom upwards.

On this Jack sank, for his legs were still weak and painful.

A coil of rope was dragged forward and formed a seat for Joe.

"Phil Harman, as we call him," said the captain. "Wasn't that the man's name?"

"It was not," replied Jack.

"Well, perhaps not; a good many ship under false names, more's the pity, for then, if anything happens to them, their friends get no information. Here, come forward, lads," he added to Hal and Charley, who stood a little way off, and appeared anxious to join their friends.

The lads were not slow to take advantage of the invitation.

They sprang to the side of Jack and Joe.

Jack quickly put the captain and Seth into the secret of who and what the supposed Phil Harman was; his previous doings before he had signed articles to sail in the whaler, and the incidents which had happened on the ice.

Neither Jack nor Joe kept anything back, and when the story was concluded, the poisoned dagger was produced as evidence of the intention of Ralph Sternway to assail the life of Jack Tempest, and gratify his revenge where his crime would be almost certain to save him from punishment.

For some few moments after the recital, no one spoke.

But at length Seth took a quid of tobacco from his mouth, then flinging it vengefully on the deck, said—

"That, for such a shark! I would have liked to have had the blowing of his brains out myself. Tip us your fin, Joe. From this moment I shall love you like a brother."

"Proud of the relationship," said Joe, as the sailor pressed his hand.

"It's a strange story," said Robbs.

"But a true one, I assure you," said Jack.

"I do not doubt it, my lad," replied the captain, quickly.

"I am sure you do not, sir," said Hal; "for Jack Tempest is the soul of truth."

"Still, though true, it is strange," said Robbs; "and I for one am only too glad now that I have learned the villain's true character that it is impossible for him to ever again set foot on this deck."

"And he wouldn't have trod its planks as long as he did if I'd known the varmint he was," said Seth, breaking off an inch of pigtail and slipping it into his mouth. "I'd have dropped him overboard with as little compunction as I'd put a harpoon in the hump of a whale."

"I should have been tempted to have sent him adrift on the ice-floe," said Robbs. "But, lads, don't stop too long on deck. I want you to get well and strong before we reach the whaling grounds."

"Funny to call them whaling grounds," said Joe.

"Why?" asked Seth.

"'Cos it sounds as if whales went on shore to be caught," replied Joe, with a grin.

"Youngster, you've got sharp since your spree on the ice, ain't you?" said Seth.

"We were sharp set, sir."

"There's no mistake about that," laughed Robbs, "and it was a blessing that you had that brandy with you, my lad, or things would have been different from what they are now."

"A nip wouldn't come amiss now, captain," said Seth.

"Get some."

Seth went to the cabin and brought up a pannikin of brandy.

"I thought I'd bring a nip for all, Captain Robbs," he said.

The captain smiled, and motioned him to give the liquor to the boys.

Jack, however, declined it.

"It will do you good, lad," said Seth.

"I firmly believe I owe my life to the liquor; but I have made a vow never to indulge in it again as a drink. As a medicine, I welcome it; but as a beverage I despise it. Thank heaven, I am going on all right, and can now respect my promise to drink intoxicating liquors no more."

"You'll take some, boy?" said Seth, handing the pannikin to Joe.

"I ain't made a vow like Master Jack, so I'll just smell it," said Joe.

He raised the pannikin.

"Well, it's the first time I ever knew a fellow to smell with his mouth," said

Seth, as Joe lowered the vessel from his lips.

"That's because my arm is weak and they set my mouth under my nose," said Joe.

Seth offered the brandy to Hal and Charley.

Both declined it with thanks, explaining that they, too, had forsworn its use, save in the direst necessity.

"And you are wise lads," said Robbs, as he, too, motioned back the vessel. "Not just now, Spinner."

"It's a pity to waste good liquor," said the mate, "and it's a sin to throw it overboard, so —"

The pannikin stopped his further utterance.

When he withdrew it from his lips he drew a long breath, and turned the vessel bottom upwards.

"No fear of the cold after that," he said.

"But there might be worse," said the captain, as he turned away.

Seth, too, set about his duties.

The vessel, with every sail bellying to the breeze, ploughed the waves like a thing of life.

The air was sharp and invigorating, and everyone seemed to be happy and contented on board.

Hal and Charley remained with their friends.

"Only think, Jack, that none of us suspected that fellow with the black muzzle to be your enemy, Ralph the smuggler."

"Ralph the murderer," said Joe.

"I am not surprised that you did not, dear boy," said Jack, "for you had seen so little of him, and that ashore; but why I did not penetrate his disguise is a wonder, seeing the dislike I took to the fellow the moment he came aboard."

"He's powerless to harm you now, Jack," said Charley.

"That's certain," said Jack; "but there are yet two living whom I must still beware of."

"Baxter Sharp?" said Hal.

"Yes, if he ever escapes from slavery," said Jack.

"But who is the other, old man?" asked Charley.

"At present to me a stranger," Jack replied.

"A stranger?" said Charley.

"Yes."

Then Jack related the confession of the dying Ralph to his chums.

"Wentworth?" mused Charley.

"Never heard of him before," said Hal.

"I fancy I have," said Charley, "and yet for the life of me I can't make out where."

"I've heard it," said Joe, "and I'll never forget it. But it ain't the same fellow, that's pretty certain."

"Perhaps, after all, it was a lie of Ralph's," said Hal.

"I don't think so," said Charley. "Baxter and Sternway wouldn't have kidnapped Jack only out of revenge for the thrashing he gave them. There was somebody or something behind that, and I'd advise Jack to be on his guard."

"I, too, think so," said Jack. "There is a greater villain still in the background, whom time may bring into view, and if ever it does, let him beware, for he will find no child to play with in Rough and Ready Jack."

CHAPTER LXVIII.

THE TEMPTER AND HIS VICTIM—A CHANGE OF TACTICS—A MYSTERIOUS ERRAND.

FEW men in the world are more high-spirited, brave, generous, and hospitable to the stranger than the Arab.

But he also has his faults.

He is revengeful and avaricious.

Claim his hospitality, and he is your friend.

Excite his cupidity or his revenge, and he at once becomes your deadly foe.

Baba Ali and his wife, Mona, did all in their power to nurse back Baxter Sharp to health and strength.

Day after day saw a great improvement in the villain's health, till at length he was able to leave his couch and sit at the tent opening, to enjoy more fully the breeze that played among the trees.

The village was a small one.

It contained not more than a dozen tents, the inhabitants of which always had a kind word or a gift for the Christian whom Allah had sent amongst them.

The women, as they passed to and from the well, offered him a drink of the cold water from their jars.

The men, as they noted his restoration to health, murmured, "Allah be praised!" and the children brought him dates, and gambolled about him.

With kindness on all sides, Baxter ought to have felt both grateful and happy.

But he did not.

His evil soul panted for more than he received, and he vowed to secure that which he more dearly prized now than aught else.

And that was the love of Mona, his nurse, the wife of the man who had saved his life.

As he grew stronger and required less care, Baba Ali's absences from his tent grew longer.

His former fears and presentiments had been dispelled, and he saw no dishonour hovering about himself, or danger assailing the woman he loved.

But for all that the serpent had stolen into Eden.

The brave and generous Arab had warmed and nourished the viper that would, at the first opportunity, turn and sting him.

Baxter had not been idle during his sojourn in the Arab village.

He had picked up a good deal of the language of the people, and could fairly make himself understood, and also understand what was said to him.

Mona's heart was a sympathetic and a pitying one.

It was also free from all suspicion.

The looks, gestures, and words of Baxter fell upon flattered, but unsuspecting ears.

When she gave him food and drink, he pressed his lips to her hand.

But she saw no harm in this; might it not be the custom of his countrymen to thus express gratitude for favours conferred?

Therefore she never mentioned to her husband how the Christian acknowledged her kindness to him.

But, as the absences of Baba Ali grew longer, the fervour of Baxter became stronger, and one evening as the red sun tinged the sands with its sinking rays, he flung his arms around her and strained her passionately to his bosom.

"Mona, Mona," he cried, huskily, "I love you!"

The young woman's surprise held her powerless.

Again and again he pressed his lips to hers.

"Mona, sweet Mona," he cried, in passionate accents, "you are young, you are beautiful. Why then waste your life in toil and poverty, when you may be rich and envied—when every desire of your heart can be gratified; where slaves shall do your bidding, garments of silk and golden thread take the place of the cotton robes; where trinkets of gold and precious stones shall adorn your head and arms, and wealth, luxury, and happiness encompass you?"

She struggled to free herself from his embrace.

But his gaze seemed to fascinate her.

It held her spellbound.

She could not speak, and finally became passive.

Only the words came from her half-parted lips—

"Oh, Allah! guide—oh, Allah! protect me."

And yet in her heart she acknowledged that she had almost learned to love the stranger given into her charge.

Baxter, villain though he was, was an adept at divining character and reading thought.

He saw in an instant that he was not hateful to her—that with his specious words and false promises he might win her to him.

"Hear me, Mona," he said. "Be not frightened of one who loves you even as man loves the angels. It was fate working out the will of Allah that sent me here to take you from a life of bondage—from a life of slavery, and bear you to a home your beauty and your graces too well deserve."

"My husband!" the woman gasped. "Christian, I am a wife."

"Say, rather, a slave," said Baxter.

"Think, Mona, you are young, and you sold your youth and beauty to one old enough to be your father."

"He has ever been kind and loving to me," she said, as she again strove to wrest herself from his encircling arm.

"True, but his love is cold, and his kindness is but the kindness he bestows upon his horse. His steed serves him, so do you; his steed is beautiful, you are lovely; but it is not love that burns within his bosom for either—it is, that he must be kind to those who serve him; but love is a passion which few, if any, of his countrymen ever knew or experienced."

"Let me go," she cried. "You insult my husband, and me through him."

"Nay, I am sent hither by Allah to save you," he said.

"Save me?" she gasped.

"Yes, from poverty, from toil, from the curse of having to work for one whom age will soon prevent toiling for himself. Have you no desire to save and keep your youth, your beauty? Will you refuse to leave behind you the misery and toils of a wandering life—refuse to share the adoration, the comforts and joys I can open up to you? Ah, Mona, I can shower all the blessings a woman can ask or dream of upon you, if you but consent to bestow upon me in return your love."

"And shut my soul for ever out of paradise!" she said. "Oh, Allah, be this a man, or a demon?"

And, with a stronger effort than before, she flung off Baxter's hold.

He attempted to take her again in his arms, but she repulsed him.

"Touch me not," she said. "I have pitied and I have succoured you, but love you—oh, Allah, never!"

"And why am I so hateful in your eyes?" asked Baxter. "I too have pitied— pitied you till my heart has grown sad to see you toil from morn till eve in poverty, when I knew that a brighter existence was far more worthy of one so lovely, so peerless. My heart has sickened with the thought that one who would grace a palace is content to share a wretched Arab tent, that one whose nature proclaims her born to govern should grovel as a slave at the feet of a master."

"Baba Ali is my husband," she said.

"Say, rather, your master."

"Still he is my husband," she replied.

"The women of my clime are free, be they wives or maidens," said Baxter; "free as the air that blows over the desert and ruffles the leaves of the trees —free to come, to go, to do this or that; for their husbands are lovers, not masters; and women are honoured, not condemned to a life of slavery."

Mona buried her face in her hands.

Baxter felt emboldened.

He saw that he had set her thinking, that the picture he had painted had taken hold of her imagination, if not her heart.

But one thing that blocked his way to success he felt now was her husband.

He did not attempt to place his arm around her.

He laid his hand on her smoothly-rounded arm, and said—

"Mona, would you not change this life if you could—would you have entered it had you met me before you allied yourself to your aged husband?"

She did not reply.

But Baxter heard her sigh, and knew that she was weeping.

Gradually his arm stole around her shoulders.

"Mona," he said, huskily, "the hour fast approaches when I must leave the tent of your husband—when I shall sail across the seas to my magnificent home in England, where all that wealth can procure will be placed before me at my bidding, where every hope, every desire will be gratified. Will you, then, toiling in rags and poverty, think of one who would have rescued you from a life of misery, and made you the sharer of his love, his wealth, his happiness?"

Her sobs grew deeper and louder.

"Leave me! Oh, Allah, take him from my path!" she cried, "lest, in a moment of madness, I forget my duty to my husband and to thee."

The smile of a fiend was on Baxter's face now.

"But that you are a wife, would you love and fly with me?" he whispered.

"Man—fiend! tempt me no more," she cried.

"Mona," he said, "disguise is useless, for your words have told me you love me."

"I dare not!" she cried.

"Wherefore?" he asked.

"Because I am a wife, and my love and obedience is my husband's," she said.

"Then he alone stands between us?" said Baxter.

"And ever will," she said. "Speak no more, I have sinned in listening so long."

"Is it a sin to love where that love is returned a hundredfold?" Baxter Sharp asked.

"It is a sin to perjure your soul and plunge it into everlasting misery," she replied. "It is a sin—nay, a crime to blight the heart and dishonour the name of him who made me his wife."

"But were you free," he said; "would you then drive me from you, spurn the love I offer, the wealth I could lay at your feet?"

"I am not free," she replied, "therefore my love and duty is my husband's, and my home where he shall pitch his tent."

"Bravely said," cried Baxter, laughingly. "Well done, thou true and noble woman."

She looked at him in unfeigned surprise.

"Ah, Mona," he said, seizing her hand and pressing it, "I did but try you—I did but jest. I know how brave, how true are the women of my own clime, and I wanted to prove that the wife of a nomad could be as pure and noble as the daughters of the South, and you have shown me they are, and though as the wife of another I am forbidden to love, yet will you ever remain enshrined in my heart as a proof of a kind, noble, and loving Arabian woman."

Her tearful eyes brightened up with smiles, and a feeling of joy usurped the place where a moment before doubts and anxieties had reigned supreme, and with a muttered blessing to Allah, she pressed his hand.

Alas! she knew not the hypocritical soul of Baxter Sharp—dreamed not of what was passing in the villain's mind, or of the object on which he set forth, when he stole like a thief from the tent in the dead of the night.

CHAPTER LXIX.

THE DOUBLE MURDER ON THE MOUNTAIN PATH—BAXTER ALTERS HIS PLANS—THE ANIMAL AVENGER.

LITTLE dreamed the villain, Baxter Sharp, as he stole forth upon as unholy an errand as ever man set out with, that other eyes and other ears had seen and heard all besides their own.

The wife's prayer to Allah had been answered, for there had stood one without the tent ready to guard and protect her should the hypocritical villain further pursue his suit.

Accident had brought a friend of her husband's to her tent door, and hearing voices at that unusual hour, something induced him to listen.

And as he listened, his disgust grew deeper and stronger.

He leaned forward with bated breath, and his fingers entwined round the haft of the long knife he wore in his girdle.

Baxter Sharp little dreamed then how near he was to death.

But his change of tone, the hypocrisy of his last words, deceived not only Mona, but the watcher, and as if ashamed of the part of eavesdropper, he released his weapon and stole silently away to his own tent.

But when he flung himself down to rest he could not sleep.

A voice seemed to whisper in his ear—

"Be wakeful, be watchful!"

So persistently did this still voice ring in his ears, that he arose and seated himself at the door of his tent.

But all was silent. Not a breath of air rustled the leaves of the palms.

The silence of the grave reigned throughout the encampment.

The shadows of the trees lengthened as the moon sank behind them, and the night growing cold the Arab was about to arise and again seek his couch, when another shadow fell across the sand in front of his tent.

He drew back into the darkness of his dwelling, as, with silent footfalls, Baxter Sharp passed through the encampment.

"Mona is safe, but whither goes the Christian at this hour?" he muttered. "Baba Ali, my friend, is absent—can he mean ill to him? Ah, my heart whispers me it is so. Ali will return from the mountains at daybreak, and thither do the feet of the Christian wander. Allah be my guide, and forgive me if I wrong the stranger in our tents."

He drew his bournous closely around him, took his spear from the wall, and strode out into the night, letting fall the curtain of the tent behind him.

A moment only he hesitated, and then with quick step, but silent strides, he followed in the footsteps of Baxter.

The moon had sunk out of sight, the stars grew less brilliant in the blue ether, and darkness stole over the scene.

Still the Arab kept Baxter in sight, flinging himself prone on the earth when the villain turned to gaze back upon the encampment.

Then, as he pursued his journey towards the mountains, like a phantom the Arab stole on his track.

"But one thing, and one only, stands between Mona and me," muttered Baxter, "and that, her husband. How small an obstruction to a desperate man! What matters one more crime when its reward is a beautiful woman, and a sure passport to escape to the sea coast, where I shall need neither her love nor her services more?"

And the villain chuckled in his cold-blooded infamy.

"Ali said he would descend from the mountains at daybreak, and join his wife before the encampment arose for the labours of the day; but he dreams not of the hand that will stay him, nor does Mona of the means I take to win her to my arms."

Again the villain uttered a low laugh, and looked around. In the darkness he saw nothing to alarm him.

"Who will ever suspect the truth?" he muttered. "Not Mona, not those in the camp, for the deed will be done and I back in the tent ere any are about, and the crime will be set down to other hands than mine. It will be easy, in his surprise at our meeting and his horror at the story I will tell him, to account for my presence there. I will stab him to the heart. Then my way will be clear, and my task easy. Ha, ha!"

Still on he kept, never once now deeming it necessary to look behind him.

He reached the foot of the mountains and the rough road that ran up them from the plains, and here awaited the coming of the man who had saved and succoured him—awaited to reward all his kindness with death.

From the tent pole where Ali hung his saddle and bridle and his weapons of war and the chase, Baxter had taken the hunting-knife, for which Ali had no use on his present journey.

His own weapons had been lost in the sand storm, or in his struggles to escape after it had passed by where he lay.

Arrows of light pierced the black clouds in the east, and throwing himself down by the roadside Baxter waited, with his gaze fixed upon the ascending path.

So intently did he watch, while he nervously fingered the haft of the knife in his bosom, that he saw not the crouching figure advancing behind him—the form that flung itself down behind a boulder that skirted the path some ten feet away from where the villain lay.

Time passed, and then down the steep and rugged road came Baba Ali, holding his noble Arab steed well in hand as he made his way slowly along the difficult and dangerous incline.

Baxter watched him as he approached, making sure the while that his knife could be drawn in an instant.

"There must be no need for a second blow," he muttered. "No time allowed to put him on his guard. The stroke must be swift and sure!"

The unsuspecting man approached the spot where Baxter lay, his whole attention riveted upon his horse, as it trod its dangerous path to the plain.

When within a dozen feet, Baxter

sprang up and into the centre of the path.

The horse saw him before its rider, and reared up.

It was not till then that Baba Ali looked up with a start.

Seeing Baxter, he recognised him in an instant.

Surprise, however, at meeting him there, and at such an hour, held him dumb.

He reined his horse in till it reared back on its haunches.

"Ah, my kind friend," cried Baxter, springing forward. "How I have prayed for your coming!"

"You, Christian, here?" gasped the Arab.

"Well may you wonder, kind saviour of my life," cried Baxter. "But weak as I still am, though I had fainted by the way, still had I come to hurry your return to the encampment, to bid you hasten to your sick wife, that angel of kindness to whom I owe such a debt of gratitude that man can never repay."

And, as if in mental agony, Baxter clutched at the saddle and sighed heavily.

"Allah! what do your words portend?" cried Baba Ali, in quivering tones.

He leant forward, and laid his trembling hand on Baxter's shoulder.

"My wife sick, whom I left in health! Oh, say not so, Christian."

"Alas, Ali, I fear she is sick unto death—*even as art thou!*"

Swift as a flash Baxter's hand went from his own bosom to that of the Arab's.

A shriek of agony burst from the Arab's lips, as Baxter withdrew the blade, and he fell forward upon his horse's neck.

"True to the heart," cried Baxter, as with the hand that held the ensanguined knife he caught the steed's bridle, and with the other hurled Baba Ali over the horse's side into the roadway. "The work is done, and its payment is—Mona."

"Vile Christian, you lie!" thundered a voice. "The reward of your infamy is death!"

But for the spring aside that Baxter gave at this unlooked-for voice, that moment had been his last, for the spear thrust full at his chest passed between him and the horse, and the fury of the unmet thrust precipitated the Arab forward.

Before he could recover himself Baxter's knife was again raised, and the blade thrust deep in the back of the man's neck.

The blow proved as fatal as that he had struck at Baba Ali.

The spear fell from the man's hand, and he sank down at the feet of his murderer.

For a few moments Baxter gazed upon his victims, then he muttered—

"So, my footsteps have been dogged from the encampment. Confusion! to return there now would be to ensure certain death, for I have been suspected, watched, and tracked, and others, even now, may be upon my trail."

He looked eagerly around him.

So far as he could see, he was alone.

"This must alter all my plans," he said. "I must give up all thoughts now of Mona, and fly. I may, however, delay pursuit, if such is intended, and once across the mountains I may baffle it altogether. Confound the luck, it always plays against me."

He flung the ensanguined knife down by the side of his last victim.

Then picking up the spear that had so nearly ended his own career, he bathed its blade in the blood of Baba Ali, and laid it beside him.

"After all," he muttered, "they may think these two have met, quarrelled, and fought. Still, since my coming here was known to him, evidently it may be known to others, and to return to the encampment would be to rush to my own doom."

He hesitated for a moment whether or not to possess himself of any money or valuables the bodies might have about them.

Knowing that robbery would proclaim aloud the presence of a third party on that terrible scene, he decided not to rifle his victims.

"Once in sight of a town across the mountains," he muttered, "and I will abandon the horse lest the animal get me into trouble, for who that knows Baba Ali would fail to recognise his steed? But I delay, I must be away. Farewell, Mona; though I must leave you, yet I gain my liberty if I lose your love."

He patted the horse's neck and sprang into the saddle.

The steed reared, and it was with some difficulty that Baxter turned his head up the mountain path and urged him forward.

But at length taking the bit well in his mouth, the animal dashed forward at a terrific pace, and, despite the steepness of the ascent, soon carried him beyond his victims, who lay cold in death far below him.

On, on, he rode, till the brow of the mountain was reached, and below him, deep down in the morning's sunlight, glittered the domes and minarets of a large city.

Here he paused to survey the scene below him, and suffer the panting steed to gain breath.

Away to the right he could see a huge mass of water, and in that direction he urged the horse.

The sun was high in the heavens when he reached the outskirts of the city, and he knew that he was near the shore of the sea, or the mouth of a large river.

"Now," he said, "to start the horse back; I dare take him no farther."

He turned the animal's head, and leapt from the saddle.

"Carry my love to your mistress," he said, brutally, as he struck the horse's flank with his clenched hand. "Go, for you, too, have served my purpose, and I want you no longer."

He gave the animal another and a heavier blow, and, goaded to fury by such treatment, the Arab steed reared, launched out its hoofs, and with them struck Baxter, maimed and insensible, to the earth.

Then, with a whinny of triumph, the horse flung up its head, and galloped madly up the mountain path.

CHAPTER LXX.

IN THE POLAR SEAS—THE START FOR SHORE.

In due time the "Pride of the Arctic Ocean" found herself off the coast of Greenland.

The whaling ground had been reached at last.

Jack and Joe were strong and well again, and with Hal and Charley looked forward eagerly for their first pursuit of the whale.

Everything had been got in readiness for the hunt.

A good look-out was kept, and all on board were eager to hear the cry—

"There she blows!"

Winches were examined, harpoons burnished and sharpened, and everything got ready in order to start when the boats should be ordered away.

The principal harpooners were Captain Robbs, Seth, and Bill Atkins.

It was seldom that either missed the mark when he launched the spear from his hand.

"Now, boys," said the first mate, addressing Jack and Joe, "you'll be in my boat, and Hal and Charley will go in the captain's. And I tell you that you will have to keep your eyes peeled and your nerves steady if you don't want to come to grief."

"You need have no fear of us," said Jack. "We are not in the habit of losing our heads in the moment of danger."

"Yes; that may be so; but tackling a whale is risky work, I can tell you; and if you get in the way of the lines when she dives, muffins and marline-spikes! but it's two to one you get cut in half, or carried over the side of the boat, and if the varmint tries, as it will sometimes, to wipe the paint off the bulwarks with its tail, it is strike out for your lives, my lads, and no mistake about it!"

"We know it will be no child's play, sir," said Joe. "But what's them things over there, Mr. Spinner?"

"What, on the edge of the ice, yonder?"

"Yes."

"Them's penguins."

"They are birds, Joe," said Jack.

"Birds and penguins?" said Joe. "Are they what they make quill pens of?"

"Oh, don't you want to appear simple!" laughed Jack.

"But ain't they, really?" asked Joe.

"Get out!" said Seth. "None of your poking your fun here, Master Joe, or I'll put a rope's-end over that woolly jacket of yours."

Joe grinned.

"You'll have to catch me first," he said.

"I wouldn't be long doing that, nimble as you are, my joker," replied Seth.

"They are a comical-looking lot of fellows," said Jack, gazing at the birds that sat in hundreds on the icy shore. "They look like a lot of parsons gone to sleep."

"Just fire a gun amongst them, and they are lively enough then," said Seth.

"Do you ever have any sport with them?" asked Jack.

"Oh, yes. The lads will knock them over when they go ashore, for they will let you get close to them without moving; but the sport's too tame. But for right down sport in these parts there's nothing like hunting a polar bear."

"They are tough customers I have heard," said Jack.

"You may say that, lad. They are tough customers to tackle."

"More dangerous than the brown bear?" asked Jack.

"So I'm told," replied Seth. "But I never met a bear ashore in other parts except where they peeps from behind iron bars, so can't say which is the worst of the two. But I do know something of the jokers as sails in the polar seas."

"Did you ever have a fight with one, Mr. Spinner?" asked Joe.

"Yes, my lad."

"And beat him?"

"No, it was all the other way, lad," said the mate.

"You had to give him best," said Joe.

"And he'd have given me worst, I can tell you, if it hadn't been for Captain Robbs. The brute got me down on the ice, and was just going to make a meal on me, when the skipper sent a ball crashing through his head, and the varmint lost his dinner. I tell you it don't do to be too familiar with a polar bear."

"I should like to make the acquaintance of one," said Jack.

"And shake hands with him," said Joe.

"He'd precious soon shake you, youngster," said Seth. "But you may have an opportunity of meeting one, Tempest, before we fill up our casks."

"Then we may go ashore?"

"Yes. The men often go ashore."

"I'm glad of that," said Jack, "for I should like to try a shot at a bear and carry home his skin as a trophy."

"More likely he'd have yours to make a meal on!" laughed Seth.

Several days passed, but no sight of a whale was observed; and the captain and crew grew impatient.

As yet they had not fallen in with other whalers, and Captain Robbs determined to shift his ground, as he called altering the position of his ship.

The lads, one and all, longed for a turn on shore.

This wish was gratified sooner than they expected.

After rounding an icy peak and sailing into a wider expanse of water, they saw a column of smoke ascending on the shore.

Captain Robbs looked towards it, and then turning to Seth, said—

"An encampment over yonder."

"That's so," said Seth. "That smoke means Esquimaux."

"We'll sail in closer," said the skipper, "and then I'll go off in a boat and pay them a visit."

Jack, who stood by, touched his furry cap.

"What is it, lad?" asked Robbs.

"I heard you telling the mate you were going ashore, sir."

"Well, what then?" said the skipper. "You have no objection, have you, Tempest?"

Jack coloured to the roots of his hair.

"It would be presumption on my part to do so, sir," he said.

"Why, lad, you blush like a school miss. Pshaw! I had no meaning in what I said. Now what is it you would say?"

"I was going to ask a favour of you, sir," said Jack.

"Then ask it," said the skipper.

"I was intending to ask your permission to allow me to go with you in the boat."

"I intended to take you, Jack."

"I am glad of that, sir," replied our hero.

"Yes, you and your mates can go, as none of you have ever been ashore in these parts before."

"All four of us?" asked Jack, delightedly.

"Yes."

"Thank you, captain," said Jack, turning on his heel.

Hal, Charley, and Joe received the information with delight.

"You'll have to look out, Joe," said Charley, "for the natives of these parts are cannibals."

Joe opened his eyes wide.

"Are they, Master Jack?" he asked.

"Yes, Joe; and of the very worst sort," replied Jack.

"You don't say so?"

"But I do, Joe. They actually live on whale's blubber."

"What!" said Joe.

"Eat the blubber of whales, Joe; and if they can tackle anything so beastly as that, they would naturally look upon you as a rare delicacy."

"I'd like to catch them trying it on," said Joe.

"Then I shouldn't," said Hal. "I've no wish for an Esquimaux to put himself outside of me."

"Don't care much about going on shore now, do you, Joe?" asked Charley.

"If Master Jack goes, you don't find me hanging back," replied Joe. "If he runs any risk, I reckon I won't be far away from him."

"Joe, you are a noble-hearted fellow," said Jack.

"If I am, who made me so but you?" said Joe.

"Set your mind at rest. We were only chaffing."

"What, about the cannibals and the whales' blubber?" said Joe.

"About the cannibals — yes; but about the other thing — no."

"And do they really eat it?" asked Joe.

"They revel in it, so I have heard. Perhaps we may have a chance of satisfying ourselves as to the truth or falsehood of the assertion."

"I fancy it is only one of the mate's yarns," said Joe.

"He never mentioned such a thing to me," replied Jack. "I have read so."

"Then they are dirty beasts," said Joe.

"And they drink oil instead of water, Joe," said Charley.

"I ain't such a fool as to believe that," said Joe.

"But I tell you they do," said Charley; "and when it's night for months together, they put a ball of spun yarn in their mouths, and set fire to the end of it, and it serves as a candle to light them about in the darkness, or how do you think they would be able to see what they were doing of?"

"You'll do," said Joe, "and I'll wind up the slack of your yarns. You forget that, if I doesn't know everything, I was brought up in the Dials."

"Then you don't believe it, Joe?" said Charley.

"That yarn is too greasy for me to lay tight-hold of," replied Joe.

The lads laughed and went about their duties.

In about an hour's time Captain Robbs ordered a boat to be got ready for him to go ashore.

"We will each take a gun with us," he said, addressing Jack. "Not that we have anything to fear from the Esquimaux, but it is always best to be prepared for what might happen."

The boat was soon ready, and Robbs, with our friends and two of the crew, pulled away for the shore, leaving Seth to take charge of the ship till their return.

CHAPTER LXXI.

ON THE FROZEN SHORE—A LITTLE SPORT AND CONSIDERABLE DANGER—JACK TO THE RESCUE.

IT was no easy matter to steer the boat through the ice which the summer sun had melted and caused to break away from the huge sheets which had to be crosssd before the actual land was reached.

But Captain Robbs had guided a boat in these intricate channels many a time before, and was almost as dexterous as a Greenlander in the management of the little vessel.

Bidding the two men whom he had brought with him secure the boat and follow them, the skipper, with the lads shouldering their guns, made his way in the direction of the smoke.

But, some time before he reached the spot where he believed it had ascended, the vapour had disappeared, and reach-a higher ledge and looking down upon a sort of valley, they saw a party of Esquimaux fast disappearing in their sledges in the distance.

"A hunting party bivouacked for a meal, I expect," said Robbs. "They have harnessed up their dogs and deer, and there they go."

"I don't see any dogs, do you, Master Jack?" asked Joe.

"They are drawing the sledges, Joe."

"What, the dogs?"

"Yes."

"Why don't they have horses, or donkeys?" asked Joe.

"Because they could not find food here for such animals, even if they could stand the climate."

"Ah, I see," said Joe. "Only donkeys will eat anything."

"Except ice," said Charley. "They only would like it then when they partook of a sherry cobbler.".

"A sherry cobbler?"

"Yes, Joe."

"What's that?"

"Something snobbish, you may be sure," said Jack.

"Of course, I know a cobbler's a snob, but I never heard of a sherry one."

"Or a shabby one, eh?" said Hal.

"Rather, a few of them; there was heaps of 'em where I was brought up," said Joe.

"Tell him what a sherry cobbler is, Charley."

"You see, Joe, sherry cobbler is a sort of drink. Wine freezes here in winter till you can break it with a hatchet, or a mallet and chisel, so they are obliged to thaw it with a lump of ice."

"Thaw it with ice?" said Joe.

"Fact, my dear boy," said Charley.

"Yes, you can pitch the hatchet that won't break the frozen sherry," said Joe. "Didn't I tell you before that I wasn't born yesterday, and that if you want to catch a weasel asleep you mustn't expect to find him in the Dials?"

"Hist! lads," cried the captain, bringing his gun to his shoulder.

"What is it, sir?" asked Jack.

"Foxes—there—see?"

"There's quite a bunch of them, sir."

"They are well within range, I take it, so let them have it sharp."

The lads had thrown their guns to their shoulders, and the next moment the report of the discharged weapons echoed along the icy shore.

Three of the polar foxes fell with bullets in their heads and bodies, and the rest went scurrying away at a wonderful pace.

"What is that?" cried Jack, lowering his gun and looking up.

Myriads of birds rose from the ice, startled by the noise of the guns, and with discordant cries and a loud flapping of wings, circled above their heads or went flying out to sea.

"Load up, quick," said Robbs, " and we'll take a few of these fellows back to the ship for supper. Hey, you two, just go and drag those foxes here; their skins may be useful if their carcases ain't."

The guns were quickly loaded, and their contents emptied into the birds which circled in large flocks around them.

Some twenty fell at their feet.

"A good shot, sir," said Jack.

"It was so, Tempest; but, then, we could scarcely fail to hit them, so close were they together," said the captain. "Besides, many of these Arctic birds are bad flyers, and there is not much sport in shooting them."

"I'll have another pop," said Joe, raising his gun.

"Hold!" said Robbs. "Not so fast, youngster."

Joe lowered his weapon and turned to the skipper.

"Look there, lad," said Robbs, pointing to the birds which the men were gathering up and piling alongside the three dead foxes; "there's enough food there for every man aboard to have a meal off, ain't there?"

"Yes, sir," said Joe.

"Then enough is sufficient for the present. I always set my face, lads, against wanton destruction of life—at least, of that life which is necessary to our existence. Wanton and needless destruction has brought misery upon thousands. And now, lads, since my object in coming ashore is defeated by the departure of the Esquimaux, we'll get our game on board and return to the ship."

Then seeing a look of disappointment on the boys' faces, he added, quickly—

"But we shall return and penetrate a deal farther than this, my lads. You'll have enough of Greenland, I take it, before we leave it."

The birds and foxes were carried over the ice to the boat by the sailors, Hal, Joe, and Charley, who left their guns with Jack and the captain to bring on with them.

"It is indeed a wild and desolate place," remarked Jack.

"You may well say that, lad," replied the skipper; "but if it appears so now in summer, what think you it must be in winter, when there are months of darkness, and the cold so intense that a gun-stock clings to the hand and burns it like fire?"

"It must be dreadful, sir, and none but a native could of course exist through such a time," said Jack, with an involuntary shiver.

"And yet, Tempest," the captain said, "I live, do I not?"

Jack started back, and opened his eyes wide in surprise.

"Have you passed a winter in this heaven forsaken land, sir?" he asked.

"Yes."

"On board your ship, of course? I suppose you got frozen in the ice?" said Jack.

"No, my lad. I got left behind. The ship sailed away without me," replied Robbs. "I'll tell you all about it one of these days, and you'll confess that I and my three companions have experienced to the full misery, desolation, and despair."

"Thank heaven you struggled through it all, sir," said Jack.

The captain shrugged his shoulders.

"They say all is for the best, lad, and perhaps it is; but I can tell you that during those months of darkness I more than once felt inclined to destroy my own life."

"I am glad you did not, sir," said Jack, "for then I should not have met you."

The captain smiled at this remark, and gave his hand to Jack.

Then he picked up two of the guns that lay at his feet, saying—

"We'll get to the boat now, Tempest. We shall have many a hunt ashore yet. I expected I might learn from the Esquimaux the whereabouts of the whaling fleet, for the ships should have reached Greenland before me, seeing how we were delayed for repairs."

"Then you expect to find other ships here, sir?" said Jack.

"Yes; fleets of them come out every summer."

"I know, sir, that many engage in the fishery, but I was not aware that you were within sight of each other."

"Ah, my boy, you've got a lot to learn yet," said the skipper; "and so have I too, for the matter of that; for the longer we live the more we learn. But pick up that gun, lad, and heave ahead."

Jack picked up the other gun, and each with a weapon across either shoulder took their course for the boat.

They had passed some half way over the ice towards where the boat was moored, and were skirting a huge ledgy hill of ice, when a sound caused them to look around.

The skipper took a step back, and

Jack's heart seemed for a moment to stand still.

There, within ten yards of them, crouching on a ledge of ice, were a large she-bear and her well-grown cub.

"Heavens!" gasped the skipper; "and all the guns but mine are loaded with small shot."

Even as he spoke Robbs let one of the guns fall at his feet, and levelling the other full at the head of the crouching bear fired.

A roar of pain came from the animal as it sprang to its feet and then sank back again.

Jack, letting go one of his guns, fired the other at the cub.

But, though the aim was good, the small shot had no effect upon the wool-covered hide of the cub, which turned to its mother and began licking the side of her head, from which blood was flowing.

Jack seized the other gun and sent its contents into the bodies of the animals.

But the thick hair turned such small shot aside, though it again roused the bears to energy and rage.

Once more they crouched for the spring.

The captain quickly emptied the contents of the remaining gun into the face of the old bear, hoping, at least, to blind her.

This done, he reversed the gun in his hand, and, clubbing it, rushed forward just as the huge animal rose in the air.

The next moment the skipper lay upon the ground with the enraged and wounded bear's claws fastened upon his shoulders.

Jack turned with his gun clubbed to aid the captain.

At that moment the cub made its spring, and Jack swinging his gun round met the animal with a blow that hurled it to the earth.

He could tell by the crashing sound that he had crushed in the skull of the cub, and then he turned all his attention to succouring the skipper.

The bear's paws were fastened in the shoulders of the recumbent man, whilst in its huge jaws it crushed the gun Robbs had instinctively thrust towards it.

"Quick! Jack, quick, before he drops the gun for my throat," gasped Robbs, who was powerless.

Jack needed no second bidding.

He sprang forward with his gun, cut a circle through the air, and with a blow that shattered its stock to fragments, he laid the bear, crushed and dead, across the captain's chest.

CHAPTER LXXII.

JACK AND HIS FRIENDS HAVE THEIR FIRST EXPERIENCE IN WHALE HUNTING—A NARROW ESCAPE—LASHED TO A WHALE.

CAPTAIN ROBBS's wounds, though painful, were by no means dangerous.

In a day or two he was as strong as ever.

By this time they had fallen in with the fleet.

It was about mid-day when the look-out raised the cry so welcome to the ears of the whaling crew—

"There she blows! There she blows!"

All eyes followed his outstretched hand across the sound.

Joe and his friends for the first time saw the huge fountains of water that proclaimed the presence of a whale.

Looking intently they perceived smaller fountains rising beside the larger ones.

"There's two of them, Joe, I fancy," said Jack, turning to his friend.

"Aye, lad," said Seth. "That's a female whale and her cub."

"A young whale?" said Joe.

"Yes, you can tell that by the spouts; but there's no time for talk now."

In an instant all was bustle on board the whaler.

Boats were got ready and manned.

Jack and Joe followed Seth Spinner into one of the boats.

Hal and Charley, as before arranged, formed a portion of the crew of the captain's boat.

The third boat was manned by Bill Atkins and half-a-dozen of the crew.

In a very short time they were pulling towards the whales.

But they were not alone in the huut.

The presence of the huge animals had been descried by the look-outs on other ships.

Boats were pulling off from the vessels of the fleet.

"Boys we must have those whales," said Captain Robbs. "If we can capture the cub the mother is bound to become our prize."

Hal and Charley thought differently, but, of course, said nothing.

"Pull with a will, lads!" cried Robbs; "we are the nearest to them, but Seth will have his boat in for the first throw if he can."

"It don't matter whether you, sir, or the mate gets the first stroke, seeing as he is one of us," said Hal; "though I should be mad if one of those boats yonder got the whale."

. "It's the honour, lad," said Robbs, "that's it. The one who throws the harpoon first has the honour d'ye see?"

"Yes, sir; and you shall have it, if possible," said Charley.

They strained every nerve, but Seth's boat pulled ahead of the captain's.

"You lubber!" cried Robbs, "you'll get the first throw, after all."

Though Seth did not hear the words, he shook his head at those in the captain's boat, and stood up with the harpoon in his hand.

"We'll have the first throw, boys," he said to his crew.

Jack and Joe now entered into the excitement of the hunt.

At length the boat was near enough to the whales.

"Stand by with the bucket and the hatchet!" cried Seth.

Then he poised the harpoon.

For a moment he stood like a statue.

Then he hurled the fatal dart.

It went whizzing through the air, and buried itself fair in the hump of the young whale.

With a roar the wounded animal dived, leaving a tinge of blood on the water, and after it dived the mother, uttering a roar like a bull in agony.

Away went the line, and round flew the windlass with a velocity that proclaimed the need of both hatchet and bucket, for the rope fairly smoked as it uncoiled itself from the drum.

Should the diving whale cause the whole of the line to pay out, the ready axe was there to sever it, and prevent the boat being dragged down by it.

But the line did not pay out; there was yet some fathoms round the drum when the whales arose to the surface.

"I'll have a throw for the big one," said Jack.

"Wait, lad," said Seth. "The old whale is certain if we secure the cub."

"I'm not so sure of that," whispered Jack to Joe.

"Nor I neither. Lor', Master Jack, ain't it a whopper!"

Again Seth drove a harpoon into the young whale.

It dived again, but came up immediately.

"Hurrah!" cried Seth. "Haul her in, boys!"

Then occurred an incident that could not fail to touch a sensitive heart.

The old whale, oblivious to all danger to itself, turned to save her offspring from falling into the hands of the sailors.

She took the cub in her fins, and strove to tear it away from the harpoon.

Now Jack and Joe saw how easy the capture of the old whale would become.

Barbed harpoon after harpoon was thrust into its back.

Its struggles became fearful.

The whale lashed the waters with its tremendous tail, sending high showers around and causing the rowers to pull this way and that for their lives.

Then, at last, finding itself at their mercy, with a roar that reverberated around for a long distance, the mother released its cub, and instead of diving, dashed for the boat.

Seizing the gunwale in its huge mouth, it shattered the boat as easily as a lucifer matchbox could be crushed in a man's hand.

Not a moment too soon came the cry from Seth Spinner—

"Leap, leap for your lives!"

"JACK'S STRONG ARMS CLEFT A PASSAGE TOWARDS THE WHALE."

The crew sprang from the boat into the sea.

Joe leaped with the rest, but sprang in the direction of the whale.

Alighting on the animal's head, he seized hold of a harpoon whose barbed end was buried deep in the back of the huge whale.

For the present he was comparatively safe.

Having crushed the boat, the whale lashed its tail with greater fury, enveloping itself and its rider in a perfect deluge, which, but for the frantic grasp of Joe on the harpoon, must have washed him from his feet.

Then the suffering whale dived.

Joe's feelings at that moment may be better imagined than described.

He let go his hold of the harpoon, so that he might rise to the surface of the sea.

But horror! the rope had kinked around his legs, and he was powerless.

A lifetime of misery passed over him.

Frantically he struggled to release his legs.

But in vain.

His breathing was stifled, strange noises rang in his ears, and a heavy weight lay upon his head and heart.

Suddenly the whale rose, and Joe shot up into the light again.

But now he was powerless to help himself.

Confused noises assailed his ears for an instant, and then all was still.

When Joe opened his eyes he was in Jack's arms.

He saw that he was still on the back of the whale, which now lay like a log on the bosom of the ocean, and then his head lay heavily on Jack's chest—he had fainted.

When the boat was crushed in by the huge jaws of the whale, the other boats were close at hand.

Captain Robbs and Bill Atkins had both raised their harpoons for the throw, but the danger of their messmates diverted their attention from the whale to those struggling for life in the boiling waters, churned to foam by the furious lashing of the animal's tail.

Efforts were instantly made to save the struggling swimmers.

One by one they were dragged into the boats.

More than one was bruised and bleeding, but none had lost their lives.

Jack was the last to be hauled into the captain's boat.

A shout from the others caused him to turn and see the whale just disappearing with Joe on its back.

"Heaven help him!" he cried.

"Grant it may," said Captain Robbs; "but—"

He paused.

Jack felt his heart sink within him.

"But?" he echoed. Then he added quickly, "He will soon come up, and then we will save him."

The others, who had not observed what the skipper had, thought the same, and eager eyes were fixed on the frothy sea.

"That rope will keep him down till it is too late, I fear," said Robbs.

"Rope—what rope?" asked Jack.

"The line has twisted about him. I could see that plainly," he said.

"Then if he can't kick out of it he's done for," said one.

"Oh, heaven forbid!" cried Jack, standing up and drawing the knife at his belt. "Hal, Charley, we'll save him or—"

"Hold!" cried Robbs, laying his hand on Jack's arm. "Would you too rush to certain destruction?"

"Oh! what is to be done?" asked Jack.

"Wait," was the reply. "The whale must rise soon. See, there she comes. Stand ready!"

Up through the waves rose the huge carcase of the whale.

As it did so three harpoons were buried in its hump.

One was launched by Robbs, and another by Will Atkins, whilst the third was hurled by Hal and went true to its aim.

A cry of horror escaped Jack's lips.

There, lying across the shoulder of the whale, was the form of poor Joe.

The animal did not dive again.

It lashed the sea to foam, while the white froth became deeply tinged with its blood.

Again the harpooners sent their barbed spears into the carcase of the whale.

Every dart caused Jack's heart to throb with terror, lest the cruel barb might find a sheath in Joe's recumbent body.

Jack could stand it no longer.

With a bound he sprang from the boat into the sea.

His strong arms cleft a passage towards the whale, whose lashings and bellowings grew fainter and weaker, and reaching the huge animal, and just escaping a blow from its fin, Rough and Ready Jack clambered on to the whale's carcase.

By grasping at the harpoons, Jack made his way to where Joe lay.

With a fear that the worst had befallen his true but humble friend, Jack flung himself on his knees beside him.

" Joe, dear Joe ! " he cried, as with his knife he severed the line that held him.

Then he raised Joe in his arms.

Joe opened his eyes, a deep sigh escaped him, and then he fainted again.

The dead whales now lay like huge logs upon the bosom of the sea, and Jack and Joe were taken into the captain's boat.

Joe was saved, but never would he forget his first experience in hunting the whale.

CHAPTER LXXIII.

DEPARTURE FROM GREENLAND—JACK MEETS WITH OLD FRIENDS—FOR ENGLAND, HO !

THE capture of one whale is very much like that of another, and it is only when some accident occurs that the monotony of the pursuit is broken.

Whales were plentiful, and the fleet had what was termed a good season.

Now and then a visit was paid to the shore.

Roaming bands of natives were occasionally met with, and Jack and his friends learned much of their life, manners, and pursuits.

The season was drawing to a close, and the fleet was making preparations for bidding farewell to Greenland, ere the darkness and excessive cold set in.

A final visit was paid to the shore by the captain, Jack, and his friends. A few Arctic foxes were shot, but no bears were seen, so that little excitement was met with.

In a few days the signal was given to sail for home.

And neither Jack nor any member of the crew regretted their departure.

All were anxious to get out of those dangerous and inhospitable seas before the frost set in severely.

The utmost care was required in navigating the ship, but everyone performed his duty willingly and cheerfully, and in due time, with favouring gales, were sailing merrily for port.

As on board the " Betsy," Jack and his friends had become great favourites with the officers and men, and when at last the vessel anchored in port, not a few but regretted that our hero and his companions would sail with them no more.

On the last night of their stay on board the " Pride of the Arctic Ocean," the lads, together with Seth Skinner, were invited into the captain's cabin, and then he told them of the sufferings he and his three companions had experienced in passing a winter in Greenland.

" I hope no such experience may ever be yours, lads," he said. " Months of darkness, with the breath freezing on your lips, and cold iron burning the flesh as though it were red-hot. Ugh ! three years have passed, and even now I shudder when I think of that winter I passed beneath the frozen mountains of Greenland."

The next day Jack and his friends took leave of Captain Robbs and his ship, and engaged a passage in a coasting vessel for New York, from whence they intended to start for England.

New York was reached in safety, and after a few days' run ashore, Jack sought out a ship bound for Great Britain.

There were three that would sail within a week, and as our young friends had the wherewithal to pay for their passages, it mattered little which they chose.

It was resolved to go in the first, which, on their visit to the shipping office, they found to be named the "Mountain Flower."

No sooner did Jack learn the name of the vessel than he wondered if it could be the ship in which himself and companions had hoped to find berths, in England.

"If it is the same, we may find our old chums, Will, Sam, and Tom on board," said Jack.

"I hope we may," said Charley.

The next morning early they paid a visit to the ship.

They found the second officer, the steward, and a few of the crew, but the captain, who was indeed none other than Harry Goodson, and the rest of the crew were ashore.

But, on enquiry, they learned that their old friends were still enrolled on the ship's books.

They explained to the first mate that they had taken a passage for home, and he in return promised that their berths should be got ready for them.

The vessel would sail in two days, and if they desired to go in her they were requested to be on board in good time.

On leaving the ship they passed three young men on the wharf, but in the stout figures and bronzed features of the sailors they recognised no one whom they had met before.

They would have continued on their way but that a remark of Jack's caused the others to look round quickly, and one of them remarked—

"It can't be, and yet I never heard Jack Tempest speak if those tones don't belong to him."

The words caught the ears of Jack, and he swung round upon his heel.

"Bill Forsyth!" he cried. "Is it possible?"

"What, Jack, old friend!"

And Bill clutched at Jack's shoulder and looked eagerly into his face.

"Yes, it is Jack, your old friend and companion, and here is Hal and Charley."

"And here Sam and Tom," cried the others, holding out their hands.

"Hurrah!" shouted Hal.

"After many roving years—months, I

mean," cried Charley, "how sweet it is to feel your flipper, old boys."

A general handshaking and congratulations took place, and then Joe, who had stood aside, was introduced to the newly found friends, who soon recognised in the bright, healthy, young seaman the once poor waif of the Seven Dials.

The whole party returned to the temperance hotel where Jack and his companions had put up, and the rest of the day and the evening was passed in asking questions and answering them, and in a recital of the adventures through which all had passed since they left Old England's shores.

It was indeed a joyous and a happy reunion.

At a late hour their newly found friends left for their ship.

The next day, however, they met again, and on this occasion Jack introduced himself to the captain.

Goodson, who had known Jack's father, took great interest in his friend's son.

He was a genial-hearted and strictly honourable gentleman, and when he learned a good deal of our hero's history, which he did in the many conversations he had with him, he resolved, as far as in his power lay, to assist Jack in discovering his unknown enemy.

"Depend upon it, my lad," he said on one occasion, "that those two ruffians, Sharp and Sternway, were egged on by a greater and more artful villain than themselves."

"Such, sir, is now my opinion," returned Jack, "and but for the death of Sternway I might have learned who he really is."

"The clue was indeed a slight one; but one spot of blood has sometimes betrayed a murder; and besides, time works wonders, you know, Jack."

Jack smiled and shook his head.

"Could I have learned his real name it might have assisted me," he said; "but Ralph died ere he could breathe it. All that I could learn was that his Christian name was Hugh, and his assumed surname was Wentworth."

"Hugh, Hugh," muttered the captain, thoughtfully. "Don't think that that's much of a clue; but the motives—if we could guess the motives of the rascal, we might then spot the man."

"What motives could he have, sir?" asked Jack.

"Ah, what? That's what we want to find out."

"I have never injured anyone that I can remember," said Jack.

"Not intentionally, I'll swear," said Goodson; "but you may have done so unintentionally, my boy."

"I do not think so, sir."

"Not with words or actions, perhaps; but still you may have injured him, or rather you may stand in his way."

"How, sir?"

"To position—to wealth, perhaps."

Jack opened his eyes wide.

"In whose way can I stand?" he said. "I have no brother, therefore—"

"But have you no other relative, Mr. Tempest?" asked the captain.

"None, sir; my father never spoke of any, at least. I always believed he was an only son."

"Humph!" said Goodson, "then that idea is exploded, and I can think of no one who could desire your death so that he might secure the fortune left to you by your father."

Jack shrugged his shoulders.

"Nor I, sir," he said.

"Still, keep your eyes and ears open, lad," said Goodson. "The unexpected is generally that which occurs. However, you know that one of your enemies is powerless to harm you now, and probably the other."

"Yes, Sternway is rendered powerless by death, and Sharp, I think, I have little fear of, for he is a coward at heart, and would scarcely dare to act alone."

With this the subject dropped.

But it was not wholly forgotten by Captain Goodson.

He thought long and seriously over it, but could come to no conclusion.

Only of one thing he felt certain, and that was that Jack had a foe other than the smuggler and Baxter Sharp.

Who he was time might reveal.

The voyage was a favourable one.

In three weeks the white cliffs of Albion were sighted, and the friends got a sight of their native land after their long and adventurous wanderings.

It was not long before the "Mountain Flower" sailed into port, and dropped anchor at her old moorings in the docks.

There, nothing seemed to have altered, though those who now gazed upon their surroundings had.

"Home again," said Jack; "and yet how short a time it seems since we left it."

"Yes," replied Hal; "and everything looks just the same as it did then."

"Nothing different. There's that villainous den the 'Black Bo'sun,' yonder; there the gates; and round there, I'll wager, we could find the old chandler and his favourite public-house, the 'Midshipman.'"

"No doubt," said Charley. "But I'll tell you who you won't find, Jack."

"Who?"

"Ben the Bo'sun."

"If I did, I'd knock him down," said Jack; "the villain!"

"And I fancy I'd try to douse his top-lights," said Hal.

"The law keeps him from our vengeance," said Jack.

"And a good thing, too," put in Charley.

"We'll give such as him a wide berth in future," said Jack.

"Rather," remarked Hal; "and a very wide one, too."

When the ship was fairly settled at her moorings, Jack, Hal, Charley, and Joe prepared to leave her.

The steward had looked up their luggage and piled it on the deck.

The custom-house officer had examined it, and given them an order for passing it ashore.

Jack placed a piece of gold in the steward's hand, which the old man accepted, with a smile and several good wishes for its generous donor.

"You'll come and see me, old chums," he said, "as soon as you have seen your friends—you won't fail now, will you?"

Of course Bill, Sam, and Tom promised.

"Joe, you will come to my house with me?" said Jack.

"No, Master Jack," replied Joe.

"No! and why not?" asked Jack.

"Master Jack, I'm only a poor fellow, and I ain't fit to—"

"Here, shut up that talk!" said Jack, almost angrily. "You are good enough to be my friend; that's enough for me, and so it is for those who have any care for me."

"Well, Master Jack, you know—"

"I know this, Joe—that as you have befriended me, so will I befriend you. I owe to you a deep and lasting debt of gratitude, and those who love me must help me to pay it: and they will, too, Joe."

Joe drew the back of his hand across his eyes.

"Really, Master Jack, you are too generous to the poor waif of the Dials."

"I value not my friend by his worth in worldly goods, but by the nobleness of his soul," said Jack. "You have over and over again proved your worth, Joe, and while life is spared me you shall find no truer friend than Rough and Ready Jack!"

CHAPTER LXXIV.

THE LAST STRUGGLE—VILLAINY FOILED AND HONESTY TRIUMPHANT—CONCLUSION.

"My master declines to see you, my good man," said the servant, looking suspiciously round the hall and very attentively at the hat and coat rack.

"Not see me?" cried the other fiercely, and banging his crutch down with a thump that made the servant leap back as though he had been shot.

"Indeed, my poor man, my master is so importuned by beggars, that he has made up his mind not to see or listen to any of them again."

"Oh, he has, has he?" and the blear-eyed cripple sat down on the hall chair. "Now, flunkey, you can go and tell your master that he will have to see me, either in his own house or at some other place where it won't be to his interest to be forced to go."

"If you don't go away I'll send for a policeman."

"If I do go I'll send a couple here for your master, so you had better go and inform him at once."

"John!" cried a voice from above.

"Yes sir," replied the servant.

"If that fellow, whoever he is, down there does not instantly go out, kick him into the street."

"Hadn't you better come and do it yourself, Mr. Hugh Tempest?" cried the cripple, rising.

"Hugh Tempest!" cried the servant. "My master's name is Wentworth."

"Is it? Well, I came to see Mr. Wentworth, then, and I must see him."

The servant hesitated, then advanced a step as if to perform his master's orders.

"Keep back!" said the cripple, "or I may brain you with my crutch."

"John!" cried the voice of a tall, white-haired man, as he came down the richly carpeted stairs, "do not harm him. I remember the poor fellow now, and promised to assist him, and—"

"You will keep your promise," said the cripple, meaningly. "Here, flunkey, I desire no witness to your master's kindness to me, so you can go."

John looked at his master.

"Yes, go, John," said Wentworth; "the poor fellow is half demented and needs humouring."

The man bowed and departed, and Wentworth placed his hand on the knob of the library door, which opened into the hall.

"Come in here!" he hissed.

The cripple hobbled in on his crutch, and Wentworth closed the door.

"So it is you, Baxter Sharp, is it?" he cried, fiercely.

"It is the remains of your tool, Mr. Hugh Tempest—Wentworth, I mean," said Baxter leaning on his crutch and boldly staring in the other's face.

"I thought you were dead long since!" hissed Wentworth.

"You hoped so, you mean," returned Baxter.

"Insolent. You were somewhat less offensive in your tone and manner when last we met, you scoundrel."

"Scoundrel," sneered Baxter. "Well, that does come well from such a villain as you."

Wentworth raised his hand.

"Say such a word to me, and I will knock it down your throat!" he hissed.

"When did you learn to insult and defy me, you miserable dog?"

"When I had got you securely in my power," was the reply.

"When I learned your real name, and your true motive for inducing myself and Ralph Sternway to murder your nephew, Jack Tempest."

"It is a lie! The boy is not my nephew, and I never incited you or others to murder him. He was an upstart who dared to insult me, and I engaged you ruffians to punish him by carrying him off to sea, nothing more; and instead you confess you have murdered the youth."

"I did not murder him, though he more than once nearly killed me," said Baxter. "But look here, Mr. Wentworth, you may fancy that it is worth your while, now that your purpose has been served, to assume that you have me at your mercy, but I tell you this, and I swear it, that *I have you at mine.*"

Whatever Wentworth's intention may have been it is certain that after one look at Baxter Sharp's face his manner changed.

"Bah!" he said, "you are a fool, but I have no wish to harm you."

"You cannot—*you dare not.*"

Appearing not to hear this, Wentworth said—

"Why did you not send me word who you were?"

"Because I had no desire to reveal my name to your servant."

"It would have saved a scene had you done so."

"Perhaps."

"And now why have you come to me?"

"First to fulfil my promise; and secondly to claim my reward," said Baxter.

"And now, where is your smuggler friend? Does he await his share outside?" sneered Wentworth.

Baxter gave a start.

Ralph, then, had not escaped and returned to England, for if he had he would have waited on Wentworth for payment.

"Why did you start? Have you murdered him as well as poor John Tempest?" asked Wentworth.

"No," said Baxter, "nor have I slain Rough and Ready Jack. But we waste time and words. I came to tell you all

that has passed since we parted at the 'Black Bo'sun,' near the docks, and ask of you that payment which you promised to us for obtaining for you the two hundred thousand pounds—Jack Tempest's fortune—which you, as his disgraced and degraded uncle, but for Jack's removal, would never have possessed the power to claim."

Wentworth stamped his foot.

"Nay," cried Baxter, "denial or equivocation is useless, and once more I warn you that you are in my power, and that a word of mine, even now that Jack Tempest is no more, would rob you of the wealth for which you toiled and lived, and consign *you to a felon's doom.*"

Cold drops of perspiration broke out over Wentworth's face.

"We cannot talk here," he said. "Where can I meet you to-night?"

"At the old house in the Dials, and in the same room where we plotted Jack Tempest's doom," replied Sharp. "But I warn you, though I shall be alone—for I, too, want no listeners—that I shall be prepared for any treachery.

"You may contemplate removing me from this world, but by such an act, committed even in secret and in silence, you would draw tight the noose *around your own neck.*"

"At ten, then. Now go. I will be there."

"And bring the money—ten thousand pounds—with you. *Fail at your peril.*"

Then, throwing open the door, he stumped out into the hall, saying, in loud, grateful tones—

"I'll never forget your kindness, sir. The thanks and blessing of poor cripples be yours, good sir. Good day, sir. I'm so sorry I forgot myself, but I was driven mad with poverty. Heaven bless you, sir!"

Then he threw open the hall door, turned a look upon Wentworth that meant "fail at your peril," and hobbled down the steps into the street.

Wentworth closed the door himself, and, like a man in a dream, staggered up the stairs to his apartment.

The church clock had scarcely finished striking the hour of ten, when a tall, cloaked figure entered a dark passage of a gloomy house in Seven Dials, and stumbled up a dark staircase, as it had once done before, and tapped softly at the door of a back room on the first floor.

The door opened, and Baxter Sharp, leaning on his crutch, stood in the door-way.

"You have come," he said, "and I knew you would. Enter!"

He drew back, revealing a candle in a bottle on the table, with a jug beside it.

The cloaked man entered, and Baxter closed and locked the door.

"Sorry my accommodations are so mean and small," said Baxter. "But as we will neither of us desire the other's company long, we will get business over as quickly as possible. We are alone, and we can speak without fear."

"Begin, then," replied Wentworth, throwing himself into a chair.

"It will be necessary to give an account of all that has happened since the night of the drugging of Jack Tempest at the 'Black Bo'sun.' Of course you would not be such a fool as to have imagined for a moment that myself or Ralph did not thoroughly understand that Jack Tempest was to be put out of this world."

"I expressly said he was *not* to be murdered!" said Wentworth.

"Then, without proof of his death, could you ever expect to obtain the fortune your brother left to his own son?"

"Stay; before you interrupt me, let me tell you a short story."

Baxter fixed his eyes upon his companion's face, and said—

"A gentleman who had amassed a large fortune in commercial pursuits in the City of London had two sons, Hugh and John. One was a spendthrift and a rake; the other, plodding and perse-vering. Both, when old enough, assisted in the business of their father. Well, to make a long story short, Hugh robbed his father, and, finally, to pay his gambling debts and pursue the disreput-able life he was leading, forged not only his father's, but others' names to large amounts. His villainies were traced and discovered. To save himself he con-fessed his crime, and implored his father, on his knees, to save him from a felon's dock."

The face of Wentworth was as pale as death, and his lips quivered.

"On these conditions his father forgave him—that Hugh Tempest should never more pass under his name; that he would take a thousand pounds, leave the country, and never return to it, or ever claim, at his parent's death, a single coin that his father had amassed; that he sign the confession of his own guilt and all other conditions made."

Wentworth sat like a statue, and Baxter continued—

"Hugh Tempest did sign, and then he went forth into the wide world, and enlisted in the East India service, and that evidence which was to be brought up and used against him if ever he re-turned to England while a single heir of his father's lived, no matter how far de-scended, and those signed documents, were placed in the hands of old John Tempest's solicitors, never to be brought into the light of day while their condi-tions were fulfilled."

For the first time the features of Wentworth relaxed.

"A very pretty romance; but how comes it, then, Mr. Baxter Sharp, that you should have ever heard of those papers, if ever such did exist?"

"I will tell you," answered Baxter. "Twenty years ago I entered the office of those solicitors as an office boy. The life soon grew irksome to me, and I determined to rob my employers. A chance offered itself, and amongst the other things that I purloined were those papers. I fancied, when destroying some others, that the day might come when I could make money out of them, and so I hid them away and waited. No matter how I recognised the man at first who had signed them; but his actions and villainies afterwards established, without doubt, his identity, and that man is *yourself*—Hugh Tempest, falsely calling yourself Hugh Wentworth!"

"Ha, ha, ha!" laughed Wentworth, rising. "You have played a clever game, Baxter Sharp, but *you are foiled!*"

"Foiled! How foiled?" cried Baxter.

"The last heir—Jack Tempest—is dead—*murdered* by you!" Wentworth cried. "And those documents are not worth the ink that signed them. Further, my nephew being dead, I am at liberty to claim his fortune, and none dare deny me its possession. Baxter Sharp, you have outwitted yourself!"

"We shall see. Jack Tempest is *not*

dead. We were taken captives by Algerian pirates, and myself, Jack, and Ralph sold into slavery. I alone escaped, at the sacrifice of limb if not of life. He is a slave of the Bey of Algiers, and *here is the proof!*"

Baxter took a paper from his pocket, and pointed out a paragraph to his companion.

"Malediction! He lives!" cried Wentworth.

"He does; but only you and I know where. Now, Hugh Tempest, shall I sell, for ten thousand pounds, my secret to the authorities, or those fatal documents and my silence to you?"

"Baxter Sharp, you are a cunning and a clever scoundrel, and I am at your mercy. Give me the papers, then, and swear you will never divulge that John Tempest lives in slavery."

"And the money—the ten thousand pounds?"

"Are here!"

And Wentworth drew a roll of notes from his bosom.

Baxter's eyes glistened.

"You swear there is the sum agreed upon?"

"I swear it."

"Enough," said Baxter. "Then I will fetch the papers."

He hobbled to the door and threw it open.

"Where are you going?"

"To where they are hidden."

Wentworth listened to the crutch as it thumped on the floor, and then he hastily drew forth a small pistol, which he thrust into the roll of notes he had laid on the table.

"I shall have much to do yet before I ever secure that boy's fortune, but I'll find a means to prove that he perished at sea. But first to remove this Sharp from my path."

In a few moments Baxter returned.

"The money," he said, "and these are yours."

And he held up a packet.

"How know I what they are unless I see them?"

"Look at them, then, if you doubt me," said Baxter; "but if you attempt to rob me of them, or turn your hand to grasp a weapon, I will brain you with my crutch."

And giving the packet into Went-worth's hand, he swung up his crutch like a mallet.

Wentworth examined them for a few moments, and then said—

"I am satisfied. Here are the notes."

He held out the roll, and Baxter let fall the crutch, saying—

"And I am silent!"

As his fingers touched the roll, there was a flash, a report, a loud shriek, and Baxter fell to the floor, shot through the heart.

"Aye, whelp!" hissed Wentworth, "*you are silent*, and I am free!"

"Don't make too sure of that, messmate," cried a voice.

With a cry of surprise, Wentworth turned to see a tall, powerful-looking youth standing in the open doorway.

"The deuce!"

"No," replied the young fellow, stepping forward; "only poor Joe."

"Stand back!" cried Wentworth, "or I'll send your soul to Hades."

"I rather think you've sent your own there, though you have only killed a shark. Look here, you'll stay here till the police come. Polly's gone for them, and we won't keep you long."

For a moment Wentworth glared upon the young sailor; then, with the howl of a maddened tiger, he sprang upon him.

Joe—for he indeed it was—was borne backwards into the passage.

Recovering from the suddenness of the shock, Joe in turn gripped Wentworth by the shoulder, and the two rolled struggling over onto the floor.

"You swab, you don't give me leg bail!" cried Joe. "Hi, Jack, bear a hand here! Hi, Jack—Jack Tempest—steer this way!"

"Jack Tempest!" exclaimed Hugh, ceasing to struggle.

"That's him, and you're the villain, are you, as Ralph Sternway said was his enemy? Oh, me and Polly's heard all your goings on, and I swear, now I've got my grapnels on you, you won't cast them off."

"Joe! Joe! where are you, lad?" cried the voice of Jack.

"Here, Master Jack, here! He is the fellow, and I've got him pinned to the deck."

"Was it Baxter Sharp?"

"Yes; but come here."

"Confound the darkness! I can hear

your voice, Joe, but can't tell where you are."

"Up the stairs, Jack—up here!" cried Joe.

Wentworth heard stumbling footsteps below, and redoubled his exertions to rise.

"I'm coming!" cried Jack.

"Come quick. He's got the strength of a giant," yelled Joe.

"Yes, you cur, and the fury of a fiend," cried Wentworth, as, getting one hand free, he struck Joe a blow on the neck that hurled the youth off him.

In an instant he was on his feet, and before Joe could recover himself, the villain dealt him a fierce kick in the side.

"Furies seize you!" he cried. "Had I time, I'd kill you as I've killed him."

Then he turned to dash down the stairs, and run full butt against Jack, who was groping his way up to the landing.

The shock was a heavy one.

Jack turned a complete somersault, and lay stunned in the passage below.

Wentworth lost his balance, but, clutching at the balustrades, saved himself from falling.

At this moment there arose beneath him the cries—

"The police! The police!"

A fearful oath escaped from Wentworth's lips.

"Foiled again!" he cried.

Then, as a stream of light flashed up the dirty stairs, he turned and sprang for the landing.

As he leaped past Joe, that young man shouted—

"Quick—quick! or he will escape!"

Joe bounded after him, but the ruffian re-entered the room where Baxter lay, and flinging the door to ere the lad could prevent it, locked it in Joe's face.

"If I am taken, I am lost!" gasped Wentworth. "Ah, the window!"

Joe was thundering at the door, and calling upon those below to hurry up.

Wentworth sprang to the window, and tore aside the filthy blind.

All was black as the grave without.

He tried to force up the window, but it was nailed down.

Curses loud and deep escaped him.

"Ah, the crutch!" he cried, as, seeing it, he picked it up from the floor.

"This shall smash for me a path to liberty."

As, with its heavy arm-rest, he dashed in the glass and frame, a terrible crash came upon the door, which, flying open, precipitated a couple of police officers across the body of Baxter Sharp.

Behind them into the room sprang Jack and Joe.

"Keep back!" thundered Wentworth. "The first who moves a step towards me dies!"

The cruel, strange weapon of which he had possessed himself he whirled above his head.

Its length of reach and its terrible swing caused both lads to pause, brave as they were.

"Surrender!" cried one of the policemen, springing up. "In the name of the law I call upon you to surrender!"

"Stand back, or you rush upon your death!" hissed Wentworth.

But the policeman, finding his comrade by his side, sprang forward, crying—

"Seize him—he is ours!"

There was a fearful crash as the head of the crutch descended, and the officer lay with a shattered skull upon the floor.

Then hurling the weapon from him, with a bound Wentworth sprang through the shattered casement.

"By heaven! he shall not escape!" cried Joe, as there was a crash below. "Follow me, I know this place well."

He bounded from the room, and Jack, aided by the officer's lantern, sped down the steps after his friend into the yard.

A figure was seen climbing the low wall.

"There he is!" shouted all three in a breath, as they sprang towards it.

Finding it impossible to escape, Wentworth turned at bay.

"I'll never be taken alive!" he cried. "This to your heart!"

They saw the flash of a glittering blade, and Jack with a cry of pain sank to the earth.

"Monster, I'll kill you!" shrieked Joe.

And with a spring of fury, and all heedless of the steel that had injured his friend, he seized Wentworth by the throat.

Wentworth's arm was free.

Once more the gleaming blade was raised, when there was a flash mingled with a scream and a report, and the knife fell from Wentworth's hand, and his body dropped against the low wall.

"Joe — dear Joe!" cried a girl's voice. "Oh, say it was not too late!"

"Polly, you have saved me," cried Joe, as he let go his hold of Wentworth, who sank down at the foot of the wall.

"Played out, struck down, and by a woman!" gasped Wentworth. "May the blight of— Oh—oh!"

He half rose, then fell back on the earth insensible.

*   *   *   *

But little is to be added to our story, and that only by way of explanation.

Baxter Sharp, after the kick he had received from the Arab's horse, had been found by a party of English sailors, carried on board their ship, and proclaiming himself an escaped slave, had obtained its captain's sympathy and a voyage to England.

Being almost without means, he had betaken himself to his old haunts in the Dials, and set himself to find Wentworth, who had changed his residence.

At length he found where he resided, and our readers know what transpired.

Of neither Jack's fate nor that of Ralph's, had he any knowledge, and he had resolved that, as soon as he obtained a large sum from his employer, to go to America, in order to escape the vengeance of either, should they still exist.

How he fared we know.

Joe, who was always anxious to find Polly, made several visits to the Dials, and at length discovered that she still carried on her business as orange seller, and resided in the same locality.

Jack had accompanied him in his search on the night when he met her; she informed him that Baxter Sharp was a cripple, and in the neighbourhood, and that she had seen the man she had before observed enter the house in which she believed Baxter still lived.

"Then if so there's villainy afloat, and we may still learn something," said Joe. "Let us try and spy upon them."

"I will be at hand if I am wanted," Jack had replied, who thought Joe's only object was to get a *tête-à-tête* with Polly.

Knowing the houses well, they had stolen into the one where Baxter and Wentworth were engaged, as we have seen them, and listened in the darkness to all that transpired.

Crouched back in the shadow of the landing, they had seen the crime committed through the partially-opened door.

Then Polly had fled for the police, and Joe confronted the murderer.

Wentworth—or rather, Hugh Tempest —was conveyed to the hospital; and learning that he had but a few hours to live, and knowing that his secrets and papers were now in the possession of others, he confessed who he really was, his former crimes, and his desire to secure the death of his nephew, so that he might inherit his wealth.

Also did he confess that he had betrayed a poor, but trusting girl, and that he also knew that the offspring she had been forced to desert in her misery and poverty, had obtained a precarious existence in the streets of the great Metropolis.

His end was a warning to all who sin from selfish motives.

Baxter Sharp was buried in a pauper's grave on the same day that his tempter was laid in the grave of the Tempests.

Jack's mother took Polly into her service, and after another voyage, Joe settled down, and they were married.

Jack, having plenty of means, only became a sleeping partner in a firm in the City, and married, on his mother's death, the daughter of a corn merchant.

Amongst their most welcomed and honoured guests were Joe and Polly, Hal, Charley, Will, Sam, and Tom, who never failed to pay, at every opportunity, a visit to their old and valued friend, ROUGH AND READY JACK.

Printed by ALFRED BRADLEY, at the London and County Printing Works, Drury Lane, London, W.C.

www.ingramcontent.com/pod-product-compliance
Lightning Source LLC
Chambersburg PA
CBHW08083925062 6
47161CB00009B/3120